CP
54

Twenty-Eight
and a Half
WISHES

Center Point
Large Print

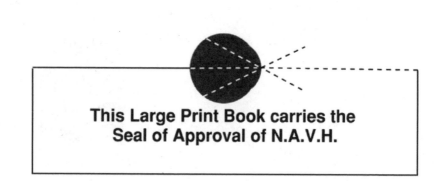

**This Large Print Book carries the
Seal of Approval of N.A.V.H.**

Twenty-Eight
and a Half
WISHES

A Rose Gardner Mystery

Denise
Grover Swank

CENTER POINT LARGE PRINT
THORNDIKE, MAINE

This Center Point Large Print edition is published in the year 2016 by arrangement with Crooked Lane Books, an imprint of The Quick Brown Fox and Company, LLC.

The text of this Large Print edition is unabridged. In other aspects, this book may vary from the original edition. Printed in the United States of America on permanent paper. Set in 16-point Times New Roman type.

ISBN: 978-1-62899-826-9

Library of Congress Cataloging-in-Publication Data

Names: Swank, Denise Grover.
Title: Twenty-eight and a half wishes : a Rose Gardner mystery / Denise Grover Swank.
Description: Center Point Large Print edition. | Thorndike, Maine : Center Point Large Print, 2016. | ©2011
Identifiers: LCCN 2015042086 | ISBN 9781628998269 (hardcover : alk. paper)
Subjects: LCSH: Large type books. | GSAFD: Mystery fiction.
Classification: LCC PS3619.W355 T877 2016 | DDC 813/.6—dc23
LC record available at http://lccn.loc.gov/2015042086

In memory of Mrs. Connie Davis
my high school English teacher
who always expected more from me.

And to
Trace, Ross, Julia, Jenna, Ryan and Emma
—you were always my wishes

Chapter One

It all started when I saw myself dead.

Rain hung heavy in the air that Friday afternoon. The air conditioning of the old municipal building didn't know how to handle it, making the office especially chilly. I'd just returned from lunch and grabbed my worn red sweater out of my drawer as I sat down at my workstation. The fluorescent lights flickered overhead, casting a sick gray pallor over the room.

I sucked in a breath to prepare myself for the next few hours. All that rain was bound to ruin a lot of Memorial Day Weekend plans, making the DMV customers even crabbier than their usual.

"Number fifty-three," I called out over the counter as I turned on my computer screen.

A scruffy man in his mid-thirties approached and plopped his paperwork on the chest-high counter in a huff.

"I need to renew my plates," he said. Irritation made his voice scratchy.

I looked him over as I tugged the paperwork down. Gray-tinged stubble covered his face, a sharp contrast to his shaggy dark brown hair. His light brown eyes held a menacing glare. I chided myself for my foolishness. Everyone has menacing eyes at the DMV on a Friday afternoon, even the sweetest of grandmas.

"Let's have a look at your paperwork," I said as I glanced at the neatly stacked forms. "Mr. Crocker."

I pulled the clip off the stack and examined the documents. He had all his required papers: the license renewal form and his personal property tax receipt, but his proof of insurance was expired. I glanced up with great reluctance. Mr. Crocker had to have been in the reception area at least thirty minutes and he had the look of a man tired of waiting. He gripped his keys in his hand, like he could squeeze a glass of juice right out of them. His eyes jumped around the room as he studied all the DMV employees behind the counter, landing on one person and moving onto the next.

Just as I was about to explain the situation, I felt the all-too-familiar tingle of a vision coming on.

Oh, crappy doodles.

Like a photograph in my mind, I saw me. Deader than a doornail.

I stared at Mr. Crocker and gasped, my eyes so big I felt them drying out. My jaw dropped so far I was amazed it didn't hit the counter. Just as the words "You're going to kill me" began tumbling out, a black fuzziness flooded my brain.

The next thing I knew, a buzz swept through the DMV and it wasn't from a swarm of bees. The

DMV staff and customers had crowded around me.

I opened my eyes. My forehead throbbed where it must have smacked the Formica.

"Rose Gardner, what in heaven's name happened to you?" The voice of Betty, my boss, boomed in my ear. I knew I must have fainted because one minute I sat gawking at the man who was planning to murder me and the next I was practically making out with my workspace. Not that I ever made out. I was a good girl, after all—twenty-four years old and I'd never even been kissed.

Sitting up, I raised my hand to my head and lightly probed the growing knot with my fingertips. "I don't know . . ." I mumbled, squinting from the light. Fear slithered in my gut as I peered over the counter to see if Mr. Crocker was still there. He stood to the side, pushed out of the way by a couple of elderly women eager for what had to be the best gossip in Henryetta all week. He eyed me warily, and my heart raced as I wondered how much I said before I passed out.

Now, I'd had a multitude of visions all my life. I was gifted, or cursed—depending on who you asked—with *the sight*. My grandma on my father's side had it. People respected her and considered her the Oracle of Lafayette County, Arkansas.

But me? I was just a freak.

Most of the time I paid it no mind. I kept to myself and everyone in my town of Henryetta liked it that way. While my grandma saw helpful information such as droughts and locust infestations, I was cursed with seeing useless and mundane things like Mrs. White's toilet overflow or the ear infection in Jenny Baxter's baby. None of that would be so bad if I kept what I saw to myself, but my visions didn't work that way. Without any volition of my own, whatever I saw just blurted right out of my mouth. Most of the people who knew me thought I was a snoop or a gossip, the only rational explanation to reason away my knowledge. But Momma had another opinion. She declared me demon-possessed.

But in my twenty-four years, I'd never had a vision about me, so seeing myself dead was quite the shock. I scrunched my eyes, trying to remember what I'd seen. I was leaning back on Momma's sofa. Blood spread out behind my head, blending with the pink cabbage roses and seeping into the ivory background. My open eyes had a dull, glazed stare. All I could think was how angry Momma was going to be about all that blood on her favorite sofa. I didn't think there was enough hydrogen peroxide in the entire state of Arkansas to get out that stain.

"Rose!"

My eyes flew open. A crowd of people had gathered around, watching to see if I'd pass out again. After I considered Momma's impending outrage, it was a definite possibility.

"I'm . . . I'm sorry. I don't know what happened." I said between gasps of air. My eyes glanced to Mr. Crocker, who crept backward with a look of annoyance.

"I'll tell you what happened," said Suzanne, who worked at the counter next to mine. "She was processing that license renewal and the next thing I know she mumbled 'You're' and then her head fell forward and whacked the counter." Suzanne's favorite obsession was herself so it amazed me that she had caught that much. But then again, she didn't much like me so my guess was that she welcomed the opportunity to gather more ammunition. She leaned back in her chair, arms crossed in front of the cleavage bursting out of her low-cut blouse. She tilted her head and her mouth lifted into a mocking half-smile.

"I just felt a little dizzy, that's all. I'll be fine." I tucked a stray strand of hair behind my ear with a shaky hand.

"Oh, no. No way. You might think you'll be fine, but you just fainted. You sit there for a minute and then you're goin' home." Betty's voice was as large as her oversized body. Every person in the room heard her proclamation.

"Seriously?" Suzanne asked, sounding like a toddler on the verge of a fit. "I asked you four times already if I could leave early to get a head start on my weekend and you said no. All Freaky Rose has to do is beat her head on her desk and she gets to go? That hardly seems fair."

Betty put her hand on her hip and narrowed her eyes. "Suzanne," she drew her name out slowly as if she were talking to a small child. "Rose never calls in sick and hardly ever takes a day off. You, on the other hand, call in all the time and have used all your vacation days. But next time you wanna leave early, I'll let you go. As long as you beat your head on your desk first."

"Yeah, well, the only reason she never takes time off is because she doesn't have a life." Suzanne eyed me as if I were a cockroach about to scurry across the floor.

Betty scowled then surveyed the room, taking in the gawkers lined up against the counter. "All right, show's over, folks. Y'all get back in your seat unless your number's been called."

The crowd broke up, people grumbling and whispering. No sane person balked at Betty's orders, not even the fuming Suzanne. Her eyes shot flaming arrows of hate toward me as she fluffed her bleached blonde hair.

Suzanne leaned toward me and hissed. "Don't think I'm not on to you, Miss Goody-Two-Shoes."

I turned toward her in surprise. I had no idea what she meant. But then again, I suspected she didn't either. My clammy palm rested on Mr. Crocker's paperwork, reminding me I hadn't finished processing it. But as my head swiveled around and searched the room, I saw he was gone.

I couldn't understand that. Why would he just abandon his personal papers?

I sat at my desk trying to slow my galloping heart and glanced down at the paperwork. His first name was Daniel and he lived on Highway 82. I tried to memorize the address, knowing that if I wrote it down, Suzanne would catch me and make a big deal about it. I told myself I was crazy, or paranoid. Or both. My demon possession had branched out into new areas.

I grabbed my purse and headed out. I pushed open the heavy metal door, searching for Mr. Crocker before I entered the humid parking lot. Nothing. I shook my head at my overactive imagination. *Seriously, Rose.* My visions didn't always come true and this one seemed too preposterous to consider. The logical explanation to his leaving was that I freaked him out. Just like I freaked out everyone else in Henryetta.

Nevertheless, when I reached my car, I looked around for signs of someone preparing to jump out and grab me. Where should I go? If I went home, Momma would ask questions. I'd rather give Suzanne's hammer-toed feet a pedicure than face that. I turned left, toward the edge of town. A visit to my sister sounded like a good idea.

Violet lived in a new neighborhood on the outskirts of town, still in the city limits but hanging on the edge like it couldn't make up its mind. She lived in a new house, my older sister's dream come true. She hated the one we grew up in, the old and worn-out home I still shared with our Momma. It only needed a little tender loving care, but Momma insisted it was a waste of time and money to paint and add fresh curtains. Not to mention that in her eyes, it was greedy. Momma tried to avoid the seven deadly sins like they were Satan himself.

Violet lived in a cookie-cutter replica of every other home on her street. The houses were only a couple of years old, each one in various pastel shades. Most of the yards were bare of land-scaping, with just an occasional tiny tree here and there. But Violet took great pride in her home, and flowerbeds full of red begonias lined the walk from the driveway to the front door and the backyard was bursting with more. Violet loved flowers.

I parked my old Chevy Nova in the driveway. It was Daddy's old car. It became mine after he died during my freshman year in college, when Momma made me drop out of school to take care of her. The car was old, but well maintained. Not that it mattered. I didn't drive it much. I had nowhere to go. Or, more accurately, Momma said I had nowhere to go.

My knuckles rapped the metal door. I didn't want to ring the doorbell for fear I'd wake up my niece and nephew from their naps. The door swung open, and the shock of my unexpected visit was written on Violet's face.

"Rose! What on earth are you doing here at this time of day?" She gripped the edge of the door with one hand and held a dishtowel in the other. She looked like one of those greeting cards of women from the fifties, only those were spoofs and Violet was the real thing.

Not that I was making fun of her. Violet was everything I longed to be. Pretty. Married. A mother. *Free*.

"I'm sorry to barge in on you, Violet," I said with a sigh, "but I wasn't sure where else to go."

Violet's eyes widened with concern and she moved out of the entrance. "Of course. Come on in." She led the way to the small kitchen where the mouth-watering smell of chocolate chip cookies greeted me. A mixing bowl sat on her tiny kitchen island, along with a cooling rack covered in a fresh batch of cookies.

I perched on a bar stool in front of the island and snatched a cookie so fresh that it folded over as I lifted it from the rack.

"Want some sweet tea?"

"Mmmhmm." I mumbled through a mouth full of cookie.

Violet poured us both a glass and sat on a stool. She sipped her tea as she watched me over the top of her cup, waiting. I loved that about Violet.

15

While Momma was always quick to snap and drag every piece of information out of me, Violet was content to wait.

I set my tea on the counter, careful not to let the sweat-covered glass slip through my fingers.

"Violet, do you remember me ever having visions of anything *bad?*"

Violet scrunched her nose. "Bad? You mean like the time you told Miss Fannie her husband was sleeping with her best friend?"

"Well . . ."

"Or the time you told Bud Fenton his business partner was cheating on the books?"

"No. . . ."

"Or . . ." Her eyes widened in terror, "when you told Momma that Ima Jean was going to win first place in the pie contest at the Fenton County Fair?" Violet shook her head at the memory. Then she nodded, raising her eyebrows. *"That* was a bad one."

I shuddered. Up until that year, Momma had always won the pie contest at the Fenton County Fair. She never forgave me for it. "No," I hesitated and sipped my tea. "Worse."

Violet appeared stumped as she tried to reason what could be worse than taking away Momma's blue ribbon. She waited.

I cleared my throat. "Um, today I saw a vision about me." I paused, letting the full weight of it settle in the room.

"You? But that's impossible. You've never seen yourself in a vision before." Violet cocked her head. "*Have* you?"

I pursed my lips and shook my head. "No, I'm sure I saw someone else's vision. It just happened to be about me."

Violet grabbed a cookie and took a nibble. "Who was it? What did you see?"

For some reason, I didn't think I should tell her. The seriousness of the vision, and the fact I knew the name of the man who killed me scared the bejiggers out me. To speak it would make it real. To remain silent left it in the realm of the nebulous otherworld. I shrugged. "Just a customer at the DMV. Nothing special."

I worried Violet would push harder, but mentioning the DMV jogged her memory. "That reminds me. What are you doing here eating my cookies when you're supposed to be at work?"

I shrugged again then grabbed another cookie. "Dunno, it was a slow day."

Violet squinted her disbelief. "On a Friday? At the end of the month?"

Henryetta was a small town, and word was bound to get out about Freaky Rose fainting at the DMV. Violet would be upset if she heard it from someone else. "Well, I don't know what happened. I was sitting there at my desk, trying to work and suddenly I just fainted and whacked my head on the counter."

Violet leaned forward and examined my forehead. "Oh, I see it. Do you want some ice for that?"

"No, I'm fine."

"Why did you faint? You've never fainted before."

"No, but I was really cold."

"Do people faint from cold? I can see hot . . ." Violet bit her lip and looked out her kitchen window as she considered it.

"I dunno, Violet. I just fainted." I regretted the harshness of my words. "I'm sorry, Vi. I'm tired."

Violet's eyes got as big as the hubcaps on her husband Mike's four-wheel drive pickup truck. "You don't think you're pregnant, do you?"

Her question shocked me more than seeing my own lifeless body in my vision. "Good heavens, no. NO!" To be pregnant meant I had to . . . with a man. Fire flooded my face and I placed my glass against my cheek. "How could you ask such a thing, Violet Mae Beauregard?"

"Well . . ." Violet said slowly and searched for the right words.

"Do you think so little of me? How could I be pregnant? You know I've never . . . ever . . ."

Violet plastered an indignant look on her face and lifted her chin in defiance. "Well, maybe you should. Have you ever considered that, Rose? It's the twenty-first century, for heaven's sake. People have sex."

I shrank away from her in horror. "How can

you say such a thing? Momma would have a conniption."

"And maybe that's why you should, Rose. Momma needs a few conniptions. You need to stand up to her. You're fritterin' your life away. You're gonna regret it one day, mark my words."

We sat in silence while I digested Violet's pronouncement. There was no denying I'd thought everything Violet just said, but they were just thoughts. Ugly and hideous thoughts. I couldn't *act* on them.

"Momma needs me, Violet. You know that. I'm all she's got left."

"And why is that, Rose?"

I stared at her like she'd asked me to explain how to assemble a nuclear bomb.

"I'll tell you why. She's an abusive old woman who's run everyone else away. Why, even poor Daddy had to die to escape from her."

"Violet Mae!"

Violet squirmed in her seat and leaned closer, lowering her voice. "You know it's true, Rose. Everyone says so. The question is why do you put up with it? You're a grown woman."

I would have loved to stand up to Momma. I couldn't do a blessed thing right in that woman's eyes, but somehow, every time I tried, I froze up like the power lines in a raging ice storm. I looked down at my glass of tea, running my finger around the rim. "It's not that easy."

"Well, of course it won't be *easy*. You've let her ramrod you for twenty-four years. But Rose, it's time. You can't let her control you for the rest of your life."

I sighed, a deep and heavy sigh. If only sighs could carry all my troubles away. But after a big exhale, they were still there, as large as ever. "I know. But not today, okay? Can I just hang out with you and the babies for a while? I can't go home and deal with her right now."

Violet reached over and gave my shoulder a big squeeze. "Of course! Ashley will be so happy to see you and you won't believe little Mikey. He's almost walking." Violet beamed with pride.

I envied Violet. Always the pretty one, she was blessed with blonde hair and blue eyes while I inherited boring brown hair and murky hazel eyes. Violet had experienced so much more of life even though she was only two years older. She married her high school sweetheart right after graduation and started having babies several years later. She and Mike, her husband, seemed happy. I couldn't help but wonder if that was because Violet had very little to do with Momma.

A little later, four-year-old Ashley woke up from her nap. We played tea party until thirteen-month-old Mikey got up and showed me his tottery walk. I glanced up at the clock and realized it was after five.

"Oh, I have to go," I said.

"Do you have to, Aunt Rose?" Ashley asked, her big blue eyes begging in an earnest plea. She looked so much like a younger Violet that my breath caught in my throat.

"I'm sorry Ashley, but I do. Grandma needs me."

Violet made an ugly face, but to her credit, she didn't say a word. I gave her a big hug after I picked up my purse. "Tell Mike I said hey."

I left her house and cute little neighborhood, working my way past the DMV and to the older part of town where Momma and I lived. Traffic wasn't bad in our town of eleven thousand, but a little after five o'clock on a Friday and a holiday weekend to boot, I had to stop at the lights longer than usual.

When I pulled onto our street of older bungalows, I knew I was late. The rustle of curtains in the front window as I parked in the gravel driveway confirmed it. Momma had been watching for me.

The over-grown landscape encroached on the broken concrete sidewalk. I had to sidestep the bushes to walk to the side of the house. Daddy had taken great pride in his house and would be upset to see the state of things. He'd always kept the hedges neatly trimmed, the yard meticulously cut, and a multitude of flowers blooming along the edge of the walk. Daddy had loved his flowers. I

21

often wondered if that was how Violet and I had gotten our names. Momma would never say. I did the best I could with the yard, but it was a big lot and Momma refused to hire anyone to help maintain it. I was lucky to get the lawn mowed and tend to my rose garden in the back.

I walked in the side door and set my purse on the kitchen table. The sounds of the television filtered in from the living room. I knew Momma would be watching the national news on the Shreveport channels we used to get with our giant antenna outside. Now the news came through a little black box that sat on top of the TV. Momma resisted the box and pronounced it a government attempt to spy on us, but the alternative meant no television since Momma refused to get cable. Momma declared cable full of pornography, though what I'd seen at Violet and Mike's house looked perfectly respectable. Even if I could have convinced her otherwise, she would never have stood for *paying* to watch television.

"Hello, Momma. Did you have a good day?"

I heard her harrumph. "I most certainly did not. Ya left the air conditioning on. It cooled off so I had to go through the entire house and open all them winders."

"I'm sorry, Momma. They said it might rain so I worried you would have to close the windows if I left them open."

"I ain't made of money, Rose Anne."

"Yes, Momma." I let the detail that I paid the electric bill slide right on by.

I opened the refrigerator and pulled out the meatloaf I'd made in the morning before work. I would've asked Momma to put it in the oven so it would be ready when I came home, but she claimed she couldn't bend over anymore. She was only sixty-two years old, but you couldn't tell by the way she behaved. Our eighty-two year old neighbor, Mildred, often acted younger than Momma did.

"Why're you so late?" she called from the other room.

I ignored the *so late* comment. I was only ten minutes later than usual. "It's the Friday before Memorial Day, Momma. Everybody's trying to get out of town and head to the lake. The intersections downtown were plum crazy."

There was a moment of silence as I pulled a bag of potatoes from the cupboard.

"I heard about your faintin' spell."

I sighed and grabbed the peeler from the drawer. It didn't surprise me she'd heard already. Gossip in Henryetta spread faster than a smallpox plague in an internment camp.

"I heard ya had a fit right there at your desk, thrashin' and foamin' at the mouth and flingin' your arms everywhere. I must say it didn't surprise me one bit, what with your demon and all."

"That's not what happened, Momma. I just got a bit dizzy after lunch is all. I lost my balance and hit my head on my desk."

"Hmm . . . that's not what I heard from Mildred."

"Momma, Mildred wasn't even there. I promise you, it was nothing."

"Hmm . . ."

Her voice faded into the national news anchor's monologue. Momma loved the nightly news. Nothing made her happier than watching carnage and pestilence sweeping through the world so she could mutter, "I told you so" to the television. Momma said the world was the devil's playground and the people in it weren't nothing but the devil's Barbie dolls, dressed up in floozy clothes and lettin' loose in fancy cars, God bless their souls. The fact that a good portion of the world lived in poverty remained lost on her.

I finished peeling the potatoes and started them boiling on the stove. Cleaning the scraps out of the sink, I peered out the little window. A soft breeze fluttered the gauzy curtain while I studied my next-door neighbor pulling a lawn mower out of the dilapidated, rusted shed behind his house.

He wasn't from around here which made him an outsider, kind of like me. I'd never talked to him. I was too shy to approach a man, especially an attractive man close to my own age. He had moved into the old Williams house a couple of

24

months earlier. The neighbors suspected he was single since they never saw a woman come and go. Trust me, if a woman had shown up, it would have been caught by the eyes of the Busybody Club. The elderly women of the Neighborhood Watch loved to snoop under the guise of being vigilant.

My neighbor wore a T-shirt and jeans. He leaned over to check the gas in the mower, giving me a perfect view of his posterior. A blush rushed to my face when I realized I'd been staring at it. I turned away and wiped stray potato peels from the kitchen counter with a dishrag as I heard the mower start.

"That infernal Yankee is interruptin' my news!" Momma shouted from the other room. While the mower could be easily heard with all the windows open, it wasn't even close to drowning out the news anchor's voice.

"Momma, he is *not* a Yankee." In Henryetta, being a Yankee was a serious offense, the term synonymous with liars, thieves, and murderers. And not necessarily in that order.

"Mildred said she heard he was from Missoura. *That* right there makes him a Yankee. Besides, it don't matter where's he's from, he ain't from around *here*."

There lay the actual problem. He wasn't from around here, which meant no one knew anything about his family. In this neck of the woods, the deeper the roots of your family tree, the higher your social esteem. My neighbor was a sapling transplanted into a prehistoric forest. It amazed me that he lasted this long.

"People move around nowadays, Momma."

She harrumphed again. "Not in Henryetta they don't."

The sound of the television rose, competing with the buzz of the mower. I tried my best to ignore both while I finished making dinner. My mind wandered to my vision earlier. Violet and her children had been a great distraction but with the company of just myself, my thoughts presented themselves like unwelcome house-guests. I'd never seen something really bad before, and the fact that it was about me scared the stuffing out of me. But I also realized my visions didn't always come true. I'd never met Daniel Crocker before today. Why on earth would he want to murder *me?* People ignored me, mocked me, and even gossiped about me, but murder me?

The best thing I could do was just forget about it.

Chapter Two

The annoying beep of my alarm broke the early morning silence. In a rare act of defiance, I didn't turn it off. I lay on my back, one arm draped over my head, and gazed at the water-stained ceiling. Dreams of bloody furniture, scruffy men, and an angry Momma had plagued my sleep, causing me to toss and turn so much the sheets knotted into a tangled mess. I would have loved nothing more than to sleep in, but Momma would have none of that. She considered sleeping past eight in the morning slothfulness, another one of the seven deadly sins. No excuses were acceptable, not even illness.

I was twenty-four years old and I let my Momma tell me what time to get up every day. I felt hopelessly pathetic.

Momma shuffled down the hall. *Let me have five minutes of peace, you old biddy.* As soon as the words formed in my brain, I was contrite. What had gotten into me? Momma pounded on my bedroom door. "Rose Anne! Turn off that confounded alarm!"

It surprised me she didn't fling the door wide open. I learned years ago there was no such thing as privacy in this house. Momma made it her business to know everything about everything.

I blindly threw my arm in the general direction of the alarm clock. Even after the shrilling stopped, I continued to lie on the bed and tried to summon the energy to face yet another day with Momma.

"Rose! Whatcha still doin' in there? Get yourself outta bed."

The morning soon filled with household chores, which really meant that I dusted, vacuumed, and scrubbed the bathroom while Momma bossed me around. As the minutes ticked on, my anger brewed and grew acrid, like a pot of coffee that sat too long. I worked all week while Momma watched television and gossiped with the neighbors. On my day off, I was nothing but her slave. I decided I would clean until lunchtime, then run off to the library. When I announced my plans to Momma, she protested with a vengeance.

"Rose, you have to make two apple pies for the Memorial Day church picnic tomorrow."

"Momma," I said, drawing out her name, worried my raging volcano of anger would burst out through the words. After a lifetime of keeping my anger stuffed like money under a mattress, I wasn't ready to let it out now. "I can make them when I get back from the library." I pulled out the leftover meatloaf to make sandwiches for lunch.

"The Henryetta Southern Baptist Church is countin' on me to bring them pies tomorrow. I made a commitment and I intend to honor it. You're making them pies before you go."

Momma sat in a chair at the kitchen table and waited for me to serve her lunch, as if I was her personal servant and she was the Queen of Sheba. Suddenly, just like a light switch turned from off to on, I'd had enough. I slammed my palm down, causing the dishes on the counter to rattle. Her head jerked up as I turned to face her. Anger made black spots dance before my eyes. "Well, Momma, if *you* made a commitment, then perhaps *you* should honor it and make the pies." I practically shouted the last part, which from the look on Momma's face, surprised her as much as it amazed me.

"Don't you raise your voice to me!" Momma shouted back. "I will not tolerate you breakin' the Ten Commandments in my house."

I fumed while I finished making her sandwich then slammed the plate on the table in front of her. Turning back to the counter, I gathered the flour and butter to start the piecrust.

"You come sit here right now. You can make them pies after lunch."

I turned to her, with my hand on my hip. "Which is it, Momma? You just told me I had to make the pies before I go. Now you're telling me not to make them. What about your commitment? I'm making crust for the pies that you said *you* would make and then I'm leaving."

Momma looked aghast. I later wondered if she was stymied by what I said or the fact I finally stood up to her. No matter the reason, she obviously didn't like it. Her mouth puckered up like she'd just sucked on a lemon and her face turned a mottled red. I about fell over when I realized I had stunned her into speechlessness. That was a first.

It didn't take long to make the piecrust. Normally, I would have put the dough in the refrigerator to harden then roll it out several hours later, but I didn't want to commit to being home by then. I threw an abundance of flour on the counter. The sticky mess clung to the rolling pin, no matter how much flour I added. I knew the crust would be a disaster, but I didn't care. If anything, it filled me with self-righteousness. That's what she got for bullying me to do this instead of doing it herself. To add the *piece de resistance*, instead of peeling fresh apples, I pulled two cans of apple pie filling out of the cupboard. I opened them and simultaneously turned the cans upside down over the piecrust shells. The contents of the cans slurped and glooped out into the pie plates, the silence of the room filling with the sickening sound. I grabbed a spatula to spread the goo around then threw a crust on top of each.

A quick glance at Momma confirmed the intended effect; she was horrified by the sight of the cans. I knew I should feel contrite about the smugness that filled me, but I told myself I could feel guilt later. Right now, I was gonna revel in the glory of it.

The heat of the oven blasted my face when I tossed them in, but the fire inside me burned even hotter. I dumped all of the dirty bowls and utensils into the sink.

"I've set a timer; you can take the pies out when it goes off." I left the kitchen to get my purse and library books.

Momma found her tongue when I returned. I was surprised it took her so long. "I ain't got no idea what's gotten into you, Rose Anne Gardner. Don't you take that uppity tone with me. Your daddy must be rolling over in his grave."

"Don't you dare bring Daddy into this!" I yelled, not caring anymore. Shouting at Momma was like uncorking an oil well. Once it started spewing, it would take a whole lot of effort to make it stop. "Poor Daddy had to live with your evil tongue for years, decades even. I can't believe Daddy stayed with you! He was the sweetest, gentlest man and you just wore the life right out of him, Momma. I bet Daddy's doing a tap dance right now, rejoicing with the angels that I finally stood up to you!"

Momma rose from her chair, grabbing the table to lift herself up. "I'm not gettin' them pies outta the oven! I can't bend over. You know that."

"I don't give a cotton picking damn if you get them out or not! Get Mildred to do it or let 'em burn for all I care! I've done my part. I made your insufferable pies! Now I'm leaving!"

"Don't you curse in my house, you evil, demon-possessed child!"

"I am *not* a child, Momma! You treat me like one and up to now I've let you, but I'm an adult and I'm not tolerating this anymore!"

I threw the door open and walked out into the humid heat. Angry thunderheads brewed on the horizon, practically causing the air to boil. Everything in the cosmos raged in unison with me, validating the rightness of my tirade. The new neighbor stood in his front yard, talking to Mildred. Eyes wide in surprise, both turned to watch me walk to my car. Momma followed behind me. The windows of the house were still wide open and our shouting match had entertained anyone within a quarter mile. *Good, let them hear it.* I wanted witnesses to this historic occasion.

"You get yourself back in this house right now, Rose Anne Gardner! You come back and finish them pies!"

I dug through the contents of my purse, searching for my keys. Panic rose like the rising floodwaters of Blackberry Creek after a heavy rainfall, my sanity bobbing precariously on the surface. I could *not* have just told my Momma off, stormed out of the house and forgot my keys inside the house. Yet, I did. Obviously, my dramatic exits needed better planning.

Screw it. I gasped at my own crassness.

"Get your own damn pies out of the oven!" I shouted over my shoulder, adding to the neighborhood entertainment. The library was only a half-mile away. It would give me time to stomp off my anger.

"Rose, you get yourself back here *right now!* Don't you walk away from me!"

Her words clung to the air behind me as I continued down the crumpled concrete path, neighbors staring as if I were a three-headed cow. I lifted my chin and marched. *Go ahead! Get a good look!* I wanted to shout, but then I decided I'd made enough of a spectacle of myself for one day. I needed to pace myself; it was barely past noon.

By the time I pushed through the library doors, my anger had cooled. The smell of books dampened the rest. The library was my refuge, the one place I could go and escape from Momma's wrath. Every Saturday afternoon I spent several hours there, going on the Internet since we didn't have a computer at home or reading. Today I just wanted to read.

When five o'clock rolled around, the library's closing time, I wasn't anywhere close to being ready to go home yet. Instead, I walked several blocks to a cafe. Momma would expect me to come home and fix her something for dinner, but she wasn't an invalid. She could make her own meal.

After ordering my food, I finally dwelled on our fight. I knew I should feel remorse. At the very least, I should feel guilty. Yet I didn't. What I said had been a long time coming. If I had a cell phone I would call Violet with the news, but I didn't own one. Momma said cell phones were just a way for the government to record all your calls and at the very least a waste of money. As part of my stand of newfound independence, I decided tomorrow I would go to the cell phone store and get one. Momma be damned.

That made me contrite. Three curse words in one day and a crass phrase to boot. Maybe I *did* have a demon.

There would be a moment of reckoning when I finally showed up, but I wasn't ready to face it yet. I knew I was acting like a petulant child putting it off, but Rome wasn't built in a day and a sourdough starter took a week to create. I was gaining my independence after twenty-four years. I didn't need to rush into it all at once.

After I paid the bill, I stood on the sidewalk in indecision. I wasn't ready to go home yet. My other option was to find a pay phone and call Violet. I knew she or Mike would come and take me to their place for the night, and I found myself sorely tempted. But if I called Violet, she would be rescuing me and part of my new independence meant rescuing myself. I needed to stand on my own two feet and be a grown up. Loitering in the sweltering heat at the corner of Ivy Road and Madison Avenue, the cold, harsh reality slammed into me hard. Yes, I could blame Momma for my dependence, but I had to take some of the responsibility, too. I was a grown woman. I *let* her treat me that way.

I picked option three and walked to the nearby city park to stall longer. I passed between the concrete monoliths flanking the entrance, feeling prickly and a little trapped by the wrought iron fence that skirted the edge. I had to admit my vision made me a bit skittish, but I shook it off. In the vision, I was dead on Momma's sofa and presently, I was nowhere near Momma's sofa. Technically, it meant I was safe so I wandered to the small pond in of the middle the park. Azalea bushes surrounded the path, the blooms now faded and scattered amongst the gravel. A half dozen benches lined the trail, but walking helped my restlessness. I followed the path around the periphery, surprised there weren't more people milling around.

The crunch under my feet soothed my growing paranoia, but the image of my vision popped into my mind again. I shook my head and tried to chase it away. I hoped it wasn't true, but what if it was? But I couldn't just sit around and wait for Daniel Crocker to kill me. The only course of action I could come up with at the moment was to never sit on Momma's sofa again.

All the thoughts of my impending murder made me face the undeniable proof of my mortality. There were so many things I'd dreamed of doing. If I died, I'd never get a chance to try any of them. Violet was right. I was frittering my life away.

An epiphany burst into my mind, nearly knocking me over with the enormity of it. I would create a list, a list of things I wanted to do before I died.

I found a bench and dug through my purse, grabbing a pen and a Walmart receipt. I stared at the paper. There were lots of things I wanted to do.

Number one was a decision I'd already made. *Get a cell phone.* I dug out a library book, placed the receipt on top and wrote my first item. Then I smiled, a smug smile full of pride. Another of the Seven Deadly Sins. How many could I commit in one day? I briefly considered adding them, but I wasn't sure I could go through with lust. Besides, the desire to act out all the sins in a twenty-four hour period just seemed wrong. I needed to space them out more. Maybe a week. Number two: *Commit all Seven Deadly Sins in one week.*

I felt very wicked. This was how the road to ruin started. One minute you're exasperating your

Momma by not turning off your alarm, the next you're plotting the damnation of your soul. But then again, according to Momma, my soul was already damned. Number two stayed.

New rule: once the item got on the list, the only way it could be marked off was if I'd done it.

After number two, the list poured out. *Get cable TV. Get my own place. Buy some makeup. Visit a beauty salon. Get a pedicure. Ride in a convertible. Drink a glass of wine. Drink a beer. Go to a bar. Dance. Get a boyfriend. Kiss a man. Do more with a man.* (That was all I could bring myself to say.) *Get a dog. Dress like a princess.*

I continued to write, my words getting smaller as I got closer to the bottom of the receipt. *Wear high heels. Wear a lacy bra and panties. Eat Chinese food. Go to Italy. Learn to knit. Ride a motorcycle. Fly in an airplane. Jump on a trampoline. Fly a kite. Have a picnic in the park. Play in the rain.*

I had twenty-eight items when I realized there was room for only one more at the bottom. I stared at it, unsure what to put, yet afraid to fill in the spot. What if there was something I hadn't thought of yet? In the end, I wrote the number twenty-nine and left it empty. There too many possibilities to limit myself to only one more.

I read the list with a mixture of pride and embarrassment. Proud of myself for finally deciding to embrace life. Embarrassed I wrote it. How many other people needed a list to make them do the things they set out to do?

The sun lowered in the trees and even though I didn't want to go home, I also didn't want to walk in the dark. Henryetta was a fairly safe town, and while I was trying to shed my conservative past, I wasn't quite ready to risk my life just yet, especially with my new list. I carefully folded the receipt, tucked it into my wallet, and walked to the entrance of the park.

Streetlights blinked on in the dusk, pools of light dotting the street. My gait alternated between a brisk pace and a reluctant stroll as I made my way home. Soon Momma's house wouldn't be home. Like a can of ice cold Coke just poured in a glass, giddiness bubbled up and filled my heart with fizzy joy. I had to stop myself from skipping. Maybe I should search for my own place tomorrow, too.

Our house came into view and I found the porch light off, the windows dark. Momma was frugal, but she would have turned on the living room lamp by nine o'clock and she wouldn't have gone to bed already.

I walked up to the side of the house, preparing for a verbal barrage, but stopped short when I found the door slightly ajar. It creaked as I pushed it open in slow motion.

"Momma?" I called into the dark kitchen. The

ticking of the Dollar General rooster clock bounced around the blackness and filled me with a heavy dread. My eyes adjusted to the dark and I made out the outlines of the furniture. The kitchen table and chairs, all in their places. The old children's song with the line *all in their places with bright shiny faces* started to play in my head, an odd thought to have when you knew deep in your gut something bad was about to reveal itself.

I stepped through the door, unsure how to proceed. I decided to just move forward. "Momma?"

I reached for the light switch, but nothing happened. My heart thumped wildly as though it were a rabbit trying to escape from my chest. "Momma?" my voice grew more insistent and frantic. I shuffled to the doorway of the living room. The streetlight poured in through the open window and I saw her upright on the sofa.

"Momma?" I gasped, somehow knowing she wouldn't answer.

I inched closer and wrapped my arms around myself as I tried to keep my wits about me. The outside light illuminated the side of Momma's face, casting long shadows from her sharp profile. Her eyes were open, as well as her mouth, which sagged as though she was getting ready to utter another complaint. Perhaps she was, before she acquired the three-inch hole in the side of her head.

I stood in horror, unable to move, mesmerized and terrorized by the sight. Time stood still, the tick of the clock in the kitchen couldn't keep up with the metronome of my racing heart. Finally, I turned my head from her gaze, realizing fully for the first time that it was the stare of a dead woman.

I walked into the kitchen and picked up the phone in a daze. It shouldn't have surprised me to hear no dial tone, but I stared at the receiver, puzzled. *Huh? Maybe I should have got that cell phone before I came home.*

Later I would think these strange thoughts to run through my mind, but in the moment they didn't seem so odd. I replaced the phone in its cradle, unsure what to do next. I needed to call someone. *Who? Oh, the police.*

I stumbled out the door and walked to the new neighbor's front door, as if I were a zombie, wide-eyed and emotionless. I rapped on the door and he opened it moments later, shirtless and wearing a pair of jeans, eyes widened at the sight of me on his doorstep. His hair was tousled and he smelled of sweat and man. We had never even exchanged a word until that moment, although I found myself thinking how rude I'd been not to make him a pie welcoming him to the neighborhood. My mind tripped on the pie thought. I wondered if Momma had gotten the pies out of the oven, or if they were still in there smoldering to a crisp. But then again if they were burnt, I would have smelled them.

His eyes narrowed as he stared at me, unsure what I wanted, confused by my appearance at a time that wasn't appropriate to be calling. He placed a hand on one side of the doorway and leaned his weight into it, waiting.

"Uh . . ." I began, unsure what to say, forgetting why I was there. Why was I there? Oh, Momma. "Uh . . . I just got home and . . ." How did one delicately put that her Momma's head had been bashed in? "My lights and phone are out . . . and . . ."

"Do you need to call the electric company?" He eyed me warily.

"No . . ." I shook my head, confused. "Uh, yeah, maybe. But I think I need to call the police first."

His eyes widened.

"I think my Momma's dead." I scrunched the corner of my mouth as I tried to decide if she was really dead or not. Yeah, she was probably dead.

He left the doorway, but reappeared in a flash a cordless phone in his hand, already punching numbers.

"What happened?" he asked over the top of the handset.

"I'm not really sure." My voice trailed off as the air became murky and the ground beneath me started falling away. "I think I need to sit down."

Two wicker chairs sat on his porch. He grasped

my arm and led me a few steps toward one. I sat and rested my elbows on my legs, leaning forward. I felt his hand on the back of my head as he pushed it between my knees and began talking to the 911 dispatcher.

I barely heard it, because it didn't matter. Momma was dead and it was supposed to be me.

Chapter Three

Henryetta is a pretty safe town, so, any time there's a murder, word spreads fast. Especially if it's the murder of an upstanding citizen in the community, meaning anyone who wasn't a derelict, habitual drunk, or criminal. While some would argue Momma's qualifications as an "upstanding citizen," there was no denying she didn't fall into the other three categories.

The police showed up about five minutes after my neighbor called. They blazed down the street, lights flashing and sirens blaring. The people soon followed. Kids might run out of their houses giddy with excitement at the first strains of music from an ice cream truck, but for the adults of Henryetta it was sirens. Fire truck sirens would do, but nothing piqued their excitement like the wail of a police car.

In all the ruckus, my neighbor acquired a shirt and someone brought me an afghan and threw it over my legs. Why someone thought my legs should be covered on a sticky, hot evening was a good question. It must have been a way to feel useful, like boiling water in a medical emergency. Nevertheless, I sat in the old wicker chair with a crocheted afghan across my legs, in too much shock to think about removing it, even as the perspiration pooled under the woolen threads.

When the police got out of their patrol cars, my neighbor met them at the curb. Flashlight beams bobbing wildly, they ran for the open side door of Momma's house. An ambulance pulled up, followed by two more police cruisers. I didn't know how many police cars the city of Henryetta owned, but I was willing to bet money all of them were currently parked in front of my house.

The crowd in the street continued to grow and my neighbor made his way back to his porch, clearly uncomfortable. I suspected he hadn't been in this type of situation before, which I supposed was a positive character trait. He stood about three feet away and crossed his arms over his chest, shifting his weight from side to side. He snuck glances at me like he wanted to say something until he cleared his throat.

"So . . . can I get you anything?"

His question stumped me. I had no idea if I needed anything. My mind felt detached from my body, like I was watching a movie playing in front of me instead of real life. Maybe I should ask for popcorn. I looked up at him with an expression of bewilderment.

He took pity on me. "I'll get you a glass of water."

He disappeared and left his front door open. A shaft of light made an abstract geometric shape on the front porch. The light attracted moths and June bugs, which flittered around and ricocheted off the columns that held up the porch roof. He emerged from the doorway and swatted the bugs away with one hand, a glass of ice water in the other.

"Thank you," I said as he handed the glass to me. "I'm sorry, I don't know your name."

"Joe McAllister."

I nodded my response, wondering why he didn't ask mine. "I'm Rose." I was sitting on his porch while the coroner put my Momma in a body bag. This seemed like a first-name-basis situation.

He nodded curtly. "Yeah, I know."

Unsure what to make of that, I realized I was in no shape to reason anything out.

Another car pulled up and Violet burst out like a ball from a cannon. "Rose!" She scanned the crowd searching for me in the madness.

I was about to call out to her when Joe shouted instead. "She's over here."

Violet jerked her head toward Joe and ran, leaping onto the porch. She collapsed on her knees at my feet. "Is it true? Is Momma dead?"

Tears welled up in my eyes, but didn't fall. I nodded my head.

Violet buried her face into my knees, the afghan now a hot, sweaty mess. "Oh, thank God it wasn't you! I was so scared."

I looked down at her head as she began to weep. I thought it odd I had the opposite reaction. It was supposed to be me, not Momma. The guilt that went along with that fact sat in the periphery of my mind, waiting patiently for the shock to wear off so it could rush in to take its place.

She looked up at me, her tears like streams of silver in the glow of the streetlights. "Why didn't you call me?"

I hesitated. "I don't know, Vi. Joe called the police. I didn't call anyone. Who called you?"

"Mildred."

Of course, Mildred would be the one to call. "What did she tell you?"

"That a motorcycle gang broke in and viciously attacked you both. Momma tried to fight them off and you were lucky to escape alive."

My mouth dropped open, aghast. How did these crazy rumors start? And then I started to laugh.

"It's not funny, Rose. I was scared to death!"

My laughter continued, turning into belly-busting giggles. Joe, who stood a few feet away, turned and watched me with a look of horror, as did the crowd lining the sidewalk and street.

"Rose!" Violet said, her words harsh. "This is not funny."

"No, no it's not." I choked out in my laughter. "But you have to admit, the image of a gang bursting in our house and Momma taking them on is hilarious. Can't you see Momma whipping out some Kung Fu moves?" Tears of laughter streamed down my face.

Violet's mouth lifted into a lopsided grin. "Well, when you put it that way . . ."

I felt the laughter shifting and before I knew it, I sobbed. My fear, the horror of what I'd witnessed, and the fact that Momma was dead all escaped through my tears. "Oh Violet, it was so awful. I found her on the sofa, and she had a huge hole in the side of her head. It was supposed to be me."

Joe's head whipped around to stare at me.

"Don't say that, Rose, of course it wasn't supposed to be you," Violet admonished. "It was just one of those random acts of violence. Thank God you weren't hurt."

I shook my head. "No, Violet, you know yesterday afternoon? When I asked you if you remembered me seeing anything bad before? This was it, this was what I saw, but it was me."

Violet looked around to see if anyone was listening. Joe's gaze had returned to the crowd. He pretended to not be eavesdropping, but I knew better. Violet lowered her voice. "Don't be tellin' anyone about your vision."

"I'm not stupid, Violet."

"I didn't say you were, sweetheart. But in case you start to feel guilty, don't tell anyone it should have been you. Just keep it to yourself. When all this settles down, we'll sort it out."

I nodded, grateful I had Violet there to help me.

The crowd murmured and we turned our attention to the side door. A body bag on a gurney came through the door, rolled by several men. Someone had strung yellow crime scene tape around the yard. A policeman lifted the tape so the coroner's parade could push through, the crowd parting like the Red Sea as they made their way through to the ambulance.

"I'm really tired, Violet. Could I stay with you tonight?"

"Of course, you can stay as long as you want. Why don't we get out of here?"

"You probably can't leave yet," Joe said, still facing the crowd. "I'm sure the police will want to get a statement from you about what happened. I'll go ask them when they can get to it."

His long legs easily stepped off the porch and he walked over to one of the officers, his hands tucked in his front jeans pockets. They exchanged words and Joe gestured in my direction with his shoulder. After another minute of discussion, he came back.

"Someone will be over in a minute."

Violet got up off the porch floor and moved to the other wicker chair, dragging it closer to mine. She reached out her hand and we laced our fingers, holding tight. Memories of our youth rushed back, our fingers wound together, linking us. We were each other's lifeboats in the storm of our mother's disturbances. It struck me that this was just one more in a long line of others before it, albeit this was her last. I laid my head on Violet's shoulder, like I'd done a million times before, closing my eyes. I took a deep breath, Violet's familiar comfort radiating through me, and I told myself I could rest for just a moment. Violet was there to watch over me, just like always.

"Ms. Gardner?"

I opened my eyes, realizing I had dozed off. "Yes?" I rubbed a hand across my forehead.

A stocky middle-aged man in dress pants and a button down shirt stood in front of me. "I'm Detective Taylor. We'd like to get a statement from you now."

Joe turned on the porch light so that Detective Taylor could see the contents of the notebook he flipped open. I told him everything from the moment I came home.

He looked up at me. "Ms. Gardner, your neighbors say you had an argument with your mother this afternoon."

I nodded. "Yes, I did."

Violet head snapped to me. "You did? You stood up to Momma?"

The detective raised his eyebrows. "I take it that it was unusual for Rose and your mother to argue?" He directed the question at Violet.

"They never fought, not even in high school.

Rose took Momma's verbal abuse and never said a word." Violet turned to me and wrapped an arm around my shoulder. "I'm so proud of you!"

Detective Taylor turned to me. "So why did you have your first fight today?"

I shrugged. "I dunno, nothing in particular. I guess I just finally had enough."

He nodded, a soft look in his eyes. "I can understand that. Years of dealing with your difficult mother, it's surprising you lasted this long. You must have carried around a lot of repressed anger. Maybe once you let that anger loose you couldn't control it and before you knew it, you were beatin' your mother in the head with a rolling pin."

"What?"

"Ms. Gardner, you have to admit it's a mighty strange coincidence that the day you finally tell your mother off is the day she ends up dead."

"Someone beat Momma in the head with a rolling pin?" Violet asked.

"Violet," I tried to shush her.

"The wooden one or the marble one?"

"Violet!"

Violet turned to me. "Well, I always wanted that marble one, but I don't think I want it anymore if someone bashed Momma in the head with it."

"Violet!"

The officer cleared his throat. "Um, it was a

wooden one and it was covered with dried pie dough."

The blood drained away from my face and my chest tightened. I made a gasping-gagging noise as I tried to catch my breath.

"I made a pie this afternoon." I choked out. "I put the rolling pin in the sink before I left."

"So it's safe to say your fingerprints will be on it when we check?"

"Well, yeah. I rolled out the piecrust. I didn't do the dishes before I left and I'm sure Momma didn't do them." I almost snorted. Momma would drop dead before doing the dishes. Oops, wrong choice of euphemisms.

"I think maybe we should have you come down to the station to answer some questions."

My mouth dropped open.

"You honestly don't think Rose killed our Momma, do you?" Violet asked. She said it like it was the most ridiculous thing he could have uttered.

"That's not for me to decide, but it does look suspicious ma'am."

I'd been suspected of many things but never murder. I knew I should be more worried, yet it seemed so preposterous.

Detective Taylor looked like he was about to walk away. But he turned back to me, almost as if it were an afterthought. "What time did you come home, Ms. Gardner?"

"Just a little bit before Joe called the police. I found Momma, then came over to Joe's."

"Did anyone see your car pull up?"

I shook my head. "I didn't take my car. I walked."

"And did anyone see you?"

My heart sank. "I have no idea."

And at that moment, the most inopportune time, I felt a vision coming on.

Crappy doodles.

This one was a snippet of a vision, I saw a footprint in the dirt, behind my house. When the image faded, I looked up at Detective Taylor. "You'll find a footprint behind the house, where someone cut the telephone line."

"*What?* How do you know that?" The detective bent over, getting closer, staring into my face.

Double crap.

Joe glanced my direction before he turned back toward the crowd.

"Lucky guess," I mumbled, looking down at my hands in my lap.

The detective flipped his notebook closed. "I'm really goin' to need you to come down to the station. If you wait here, we'll take you in a few minutes."

"I have to ride in a police car?"

"Yes, ma'am." He stepped off the porch and walked over to another officer.

Panic gripped me. "Violet, they think I did it!"

"I know, sweetheart, we'll get you out of this." She took my hands, looking over my shoulder, deep in thought. Then she turned to me, a strange expression on her face. "You didn't do this, *did* you?"

I jerked my hands back. "No! Of course not! How could you think that?"

She grabbed my hands again, stroking the back of one with her thumb. "I'm sorry, I knew you couldn't, but I had to ask."

I pursed my lips together in a pout. I knew this looked bad, but it hurt that she thought I could hit Momma hard enough to give her a hole in her head the size of a grapefruit.

"Rose," an insistent voice whispered in my ear.

I jumped. Joe kneeled next to my chair. I hadn't realized he'd come back.

"Listen to me, don't say anything to them without a lawyer. The police in this town aren't the most professional and they're bound to pin this on you just to save themselves a lot of work."

"What?" I wondered if somehow, without my knowing it, I had been cast in a Lifetime channel movie.

The detective and another officer were walking to the porch.

"Listen to me." Joe's voice was harsh. "Do *not* talk to them. Get a lawyer."

"But I don't know any lawyers . . ." I protested, fear squeezing my chest.

Joe turned to Violet.

She nodded, her eyes wide with fright. "I'll call Mike. I'm sure he knows someone."

"Good." Joe stood up. "Don't tell them I told you any of this. I'm just the neighbor who called the police."

The detective stopped to talk to a neighbor while the officer walked over. I stood up, confused. I thought Joe *was* just the neighbor who called the police. The policeman pulled a pair of handcuffs off his belt.

Hysteria bubbled up in my throat and I backed up, nearly tripping over the chair leg. "Violet, he's going to handcuff me!"

Joe threw me a look of irritation before he turned to the man, leaning against a column. "Officer," Joe said in a nonchalant tone. "I'm sure those aren't really necessary." His voice took on a lilting tone of old Southern money. "You're not arrestin' her. You're only taking her in for questioning. Besides, think how it looks, cuffing her makes it look like y'all can't handle a tiny little thing like that."

Detective Taylor stopped his conversation and walked over, rolling his eyes. "Ernie, how many times do I have to tell you? You can't just go cuffing people anytime you feel like it."

Ernie studied his feet, but returned his cuffs to

his belt. A scowl crossed his face. "Ms. Gardner, we'll be goin' now." He gripped my arm and walked over to the steps. I glanced at Joe, unsure what I just witnessed, but Joe had already walked in his front door. It closed without him giving me a second glance.

We approached the crowd, Violet trailing behind. "Don't you worry, sweetheart. I'm calling Mike right now. I'll get you out of this." She had her cell phone in her hand.

The crowd murmured as we reached the edge. They parted to let us pass. The looks on their faces told me they thought I was guilty. They knew nothing about what happened, but they knew I was Momma's weird daughter, and that alone carried enough weight to convict me.

The officer opened the back door of the patrol car and I slid across the seat, the vinyl sticking to the dampness on the back of my legs. He shut the door and a wave of claustrophobia choked me. What if they arrested me? What if I went into the police station and I never saw the light of day again?

I searched the crowd for Violet, desperate to see her face. I found her several rows back, her cell phone against her cheek and her worried eyes on me. My heart broke for her. Not only did she lose Momma, but now she was stuck worrying about me.

Ernie got in the car. We remained silent the short

drive to the police station. He helped me out and escorted me to a small room with a table, telling me someone would be in soon. A short time later, Detective Taylor entered the room and sat down across from me.

"It's been a busy night, Ms. Gardner, hasn't it?"

My mouth dried up and I swallowed, my heart pounding fast and furious. I looked down at my hands, which I twisted in my lap. "I refuse to answer any questions without an attorney present."

He leaned back in his chair and crossed his legs. "Now, Ms. Gardner," he said, emphasizing *Ms.* in a condescending, a no-nonsense tone that let me know he wouldn't put up with any foolishness. "There's no need for that. I just want to ask a few questions. We can all go home and go to bed if you'll just cooperate and answer a few more questions."

I squirmed in my seat. I had nothing to hide, but Joe seemed so insistent I remain silent, not to mention I could see the truth about the potential laziness of the Henryetta law enforcement. I lifted my chin and looked him in the eye, surprised at my backbone. "I'll wait for my attorney."

He grumbled under his breath and left the room. Exhausted, I laid my head on the table and wondered how long I would have to wait for my lawyer, whoever that might be. I wanted nothing more than to close my eyes, go to sleep, and wake up to find this was all a God-awful nightmare.

An hour later, the door opened and a woman entered and shut the door behind her. She wore jeans and a T-shirt, her auburn hair pulled back in a ponytail. "I'm Deanna Crawfield, your attorney. The police have agreed to let you go for now, but you have been warned not to leave Fenton County."

She was not what I expected for my lawyer. I presumed she would actually be a *he,* a middle-aged man in a three-piece suit to be specific. It took me a moment for her words to sink in. "But I didn't do anything."

"It doesn't matter whether you did or not at this point. What matters is the police department of Henryetta, Arkansas think you did. We'll meet first thing Tuesday morning after the holiday so I can get your side of the story, but if they come to talk to you between now and then, you call me." Deanna handed me her business card. "I highly suggest you don't forget and go cross the county line. Trust me, they'll be looking for a reason to arrest you."

I took the card and shook my head. "I rarely leave the county anyway."

Deanna held the door open. "Let's get you out of here so you can get some sleep. Your sister's worried sick about you."

I followed her down the hall to the front of the police station. Violet and Mike sat in plastic chairs, and Violet was wringing her hands like she was trying to squeeze the water out of a dish rag. They both looked up and Violet ran to me, wrapping her arms around my back in a tight embrace. She began to cry into my hair. I glanced helplessly over her shoulder at Mike. He gave me a half smile, then patted Violet on the back.

"Come on, honey. Let the girl breathe."

Violet pulled away and smoothed the hair out of my face. "Let's get you home, sweetie."

I nodded, holding back my own tears. The sooner I got out of there, the better.

We walked out the front doors, with Deanna reminding Violet that I needed to call her office first thing Tuesday morning.

At Violet's house, Mike put Ashley in their room so I could sleep in hers. Violet gave me a nightgown to sleep in. I changed and collapsed under the covers, too exhausted to turn off the pink princess lamp on the table. A few minutes later, Violet rapped on the door, pushing it open before I said anything. She came in, wearing a nightgown, and sat at the edge of the mattress.

"Are you okay, Rose?"

Momma was dead. I discovered her disfigured body. The police thought I murdered her. "Yeah, I'm fine."

"Do you need anything?"

"No."

Violet lay next to me and I scooted over, making room for the two of us on the twin-sized bed. She took my hand in hers, slowly and deliberately threading our fingers together, like she used to do when we were little girls. And just like that, I felt six years old again, with my eight-year-old sister next to me, shaking in fear as we listened to one of Momma's tirades outside our bedroom. My eyes flooded with tears while I gripped her hand, hanging on for dear life. Violet softly hummed the old lullaby she made up years ago, the one she used to sing to me when I was scared or sad. I drifted off to sleep, lulled into a false sense of security.

Yet again.

Chapter Four

When I woke up the next morning, I couldn't believe it was after nine. I wondered what the Henryetta Southern Baptist Church would do since Momma didn't meet her pie commitment. Then, I reminded myself it didn't matter. Momma was dead.

I sat up in Ashley's frighteningly pink princess room feeling like a little girl, but finding myself a suspect in Momma's murder seemed like a very grown-up thing. I couldn't let myself act like a child anymore. After twenty-four years, it was high time I grew up.

I walked out of the bedroom and leaned against the wall in the hallway, watching Violet and her family in the kitchen. Mikey sat in his high chair and Ashley played with a small pony at the table. Violet stood in front of her stove, a spatula in hand. Mike walked behind her and wrapped his arms around her waist before kissing her on the cheek. My heart ached for this, this sense of belonging. Violet would let me live here the rest of my life, and Mike, God love him, would too. But this was their family, not mine.

"Good morning," I said as I sat down at the table next to Ashley.

Violet twisted around, a bright smile etched into her face, but worry lines wrinkled the corners of her eyes. "Good morning! Did you sleep well?"

I yawned. "Yes, actually I did. I can't believe I slept so long."

A frown crossed her face. "It was a long night." She turned to the skillet and flipped pancakes. "We need to go to the funeral home today."

I hadn't considered that, but it didn't surprise me. I picked up one of Ashley's ponies and fingered the pink mane. "Okay."

"I thought I could send Mike over to get some of your stuff," she said with a forced brightness. "You just make a list and he'll get whatever you need."

It would have been an easy habit to slip into, letting Violet take care of me, but I felt a rebellion brewing deep inside. "Thanks Vi, but I think I'd like to go home."

Violet and Mike, who had been reading the Sunday paper, both gawked at me as if I had announced I was becoming a Tibetan monk.

"Rose, don't be silly. It's not like you're putting us out. We want you here. Isn't that right, Mike?" Violet turned back to the stove and dismissed the silly thought.

Mike smiled. "Rose, you're welcome here as long as you need to stay."

"I know, Mike, and I appreciate that so much,

but I don't want to stay here. I really need to go home."

Violet spun and faced me again, frowning like I was a misbehaving child. I worried she was gonna get whiplash with all the twisting around. "Rose, you cannot go back there! Momma was," she lowered her voice, "*murdered* there."

"I am well aware of that fact, Violet, considering I was the one to discover her."

"I'm not puttin' up with this foolishness. You're staying here, and that's that."

I looked at Mike. Our eyes locked and I could see he read the seriousness of my decision. He patted my hand and winked. "Violet, Rose is a grown woman and is capable of making up her own mind. If she wants to go home, then I'll take her home. When do you want to go?"

I smiled a thank-you. "Right after breakfast, if it's not too much trouble."

"No trouble at all."

"Rose! You can't go right after breakfast! We have to go to the funeral home at three o'clock."

"Then I'll meet you there."

Violet fumed all through breakfast. When we finished, I put on my clothes from the previous day, not bothering to take a shower. No sense getting clean, just to put my stinky clothes back on.

Mike waited in the living room. I stopped to kiss Ashley and Mikey goodbye, but Violet was noticeably absent. But as we walked out to Mike's truck, Violet ran out and pulled me into a hug so tight I suspected she was trying to graft me onto her own body, ensuring I could never get away again. I leaned back and smiled into her tear-filled eyes.

"I'm fine, Violet. I'll be fine."

"I just worry about you."

"I know you do, and I love you so much for it." My voice cracked and the floodgate of tears opened up. "But I have to do this. I know you don't understand, but trust me, okay?"

Violet bit her quivering lip and tears rolled down her cheeks. She slowly nodded her head.

I kissed her on the cheek. "Thanks. I love you."

"I love you, too."

I got in the truck and Mike pulled away from the house. Violet stood in the driveway, watching me go.

"You sure you're really gonna be okay?" he asked. "You know you're not putting us out staying with us."

"I know, thanks."

He parked his truck in front of my house. "Do you want me to come in with you?"

I hesitated. I really did want him to come in but couldn't think of what he would accomplish, other than allowing me to escape responsibility for myself. "No, I'm fine." I got out of the truck. "Thanks, Mike."

"Call if you need anything, Rose. I'll come straight over."

"I know. See you this afternoon." I walked toward the house as he drove away. Stopping next to my car, I scanned the yard, still in denial about the events of the previous evening. The scraps of crime scene tape lying in the bushes proved otherwise.

The side door stood slightly ajar. Whoever broke in had busted the doorjamb and now the latch no longer worked. I entered the kitchen, surprised to see my purse and library bag still on the table. After a little digging, I found my wallet, amazed it hadn't gone missing in all the excitement. The sink full of dirty dishes caught my eye. I'd get to those later.

When I stepped into the living room, I gasped at the sight of the bloodstained sofa, a square cut out from the fabric in the center of the stain. The surrounding curtains and walls were blood-splattered as well. I couldn't face cleaning the mess at the moment so I walked down the hall to the linen closet to grab a sheet. Covering the sofa seemed like a good idea until I could figure out what else to do with it. The dark hall made it difficult to see in the closet. I flipped on the switch, but the light didn't come on. The electricity hadn't been turned back on yet.

I knew the utilities connected at the back of the house and I decided to go check it out. I had no idea how to turn the electricity on, but I leaned over and parted the shrubs anyway, looking for the broken connection.

"I already called the utility companies for you."

I screamed and jumped up, clutching a hand to my chest. Joe stood a few feet away.

"Sorry. I didn't mean to scare you."

The now-familiar lightheaded feeling returned, but I shook my head to clear it. "That's okay. Thanks for calling."

"They said they'd be out early this afternoon, the electricity anyway. The phone will have to wait until Wednesday." He moved closer. "What are you looking for?"

I laughed. "I don't really know, I've never dealt with something like this before."

"How'd you know about the footprint?"

I tucked my hair behind my ear, suddenly nervous. How much had he heard the night before? "I'm sorry. What footprint?"

He raised his eyebrows. Joe gave me the impression he was a no-nonsense kind of guy.

We stared at each other, clearly at an impasse. I wasn't giving any information away and for him to press the situation further would be admitting he'd eavesdropped.

He threaded a thumb through a belt loop on his jeans. "So, what are you doing here?"

I suspected he meant snooping behind the house, but I decided to evade the question. "I live here."

"You're staying here?" His tone matched the shock on his face.

"Why does everyone keep saying that? I live here. Why wouldn't I stay here?" I started walking to the side of the house.

"Rose, do you think that's really a good idea? What if the people who did this come back?"

I stopped and studied him. The sun shone behind his head, the copper tones in his brown hair glinting in the sunlight. I squinted and tried to read his face. He was serious.

"You're not like everyone else in this town, are you?" I asked, amazement in my voice.

His face went blank. "What does that mean?"

I placed a hand on my hip, staring up at him like he was an angel dropped to earth. "First of all, most of the town thinks I killed my Momma, so other than you and my sister and her husband, no one and I mean *no one* is concerned I'm in danger. Second, why do you think they'll come back?"

He peered down at the ground, shifted his weight from side to side then shrugged. "I didn't say I did, but it makes sense that a single woman would be frightened to stay in the house her mother was just murdered in." He looked up into my face. "You have to admit, it looks a little suspicious, you coming back here to stay all alone the morning after she was killed."

My rebellion and fear twisted together into a

smoldering rage. "What are you saying, Joe McAllister? Either you think I killed my mother, or you don't. Which is it?"

His eyes locked with mine. "Well, it's not for me to decide, is it? It's for the great state of Arkansas and possibly a jury of your peers to decide that one."

I glared at him. I had never been so angry at anyone in all my life, not even Momma. I started to say something then stopped, not trusting the words that might come out of my mouth. Pinching my lips tight, I whirled around and left Joe standing in my yard as I stomped into the kitchen, slamming the door behind me. The door bounced off the frame and popped wide open. Joe was frozen in his spot, watching me with his expressionless face, his thumbs hanging in his belt loops. I shoved the door closed and leaned my back against it.

You shouldn't be so surprised. He's no different than everyone else. I was disappointed with myself for thinking he could be.

It wasn't until later, while I stood in the shower, thankful for gas water heaters, that I realized how miraculous our encounter had been. My entire life I had avoided conflict at all costs. When kids at school made fun of me, I ignored and avoided them. And when Momma berated me, I let her beat me down, sucking in all the pain and anger and hiding in my shell. So for me to stand up to

Joe was inconceivable, yet I did it without even giving it a second thought. How on earth did *that* happen?

After I got dressed, I stood at the sink and started to wash the dishes. Watching Joe's house, I frowned as I tried to figure him out then shook my head. There was nothing to figure out. Chances were I'd never see him again. We'd never talked before Momma's murder. No reason to think we'd converse after.

I finished just in time to leave for the funeral home. I shut the side door and stood outside staring at it, wishing I could cast a magic spell to keep bad people out. I laughed. Momma would have a conniption if she knew I thought such a thing. Right then, I'd settle for a lock.

Thirty minutes later, I sat at a table with Violet and Mike in the funeral home discussing all the details of Momma's funeral, surprised that there were so many. Truth was, I didn't care about any of it. Most of the town couldn't stand Momma, yet would show up because it was the proper thing to do then proceed to judge us on the pageantry of her burial. No one would admit such a thing happened, but all one had to do was stand in the back of the funeral home to hear it. Violet felt a need to save appearances, considering the circumstances that got us here. She also felt a need to try to redeem the Gardner family name. I thought it was too late for that, given my newfound status as Henryetta's most dangerous criminal. But I let Violet entertain her delusions.

We toured the casket room, assigned the macabre task of picking out the box Momma would be buried in. Wood or metal. Themed or not. Extra cushioning inside. Did Momma really need extra cushioning? She was *dead*. I wanted to point this fact out, but everyone acted so serious.

I shuddered. I didn't want to think about Momma buried in the ground.

"What do you think, Rose?" Violet asked.

I realized I hadn't been paying attention but didn't want to admit it. "Whatever you think, Violet."

She gave me a look that said *I need more help from you*. I vowed to be more supportive with future decisions. And I quickly regretted that pledge when it came time to pick out the vault.

"I had no idea people were buried in a vault," I whispered in Violet's ear as we stared at the models hanging on the wall.

Violet sighed. "That's because you weren't involved in this part when we planned Daddy's funeral."

I realized she was right. I stayed home when she and Momma came. It never occurred to me she had to do so much. I put my arm around her shoulder. "I'm sorry, Vi. Really, I'll help more."

She leaned her head against mine. "Thanks,

I'm taking you up on it. You're in charge of the flowers."

I started to say something, then stopped. I could pick out flowers. How hard could that be?

We decided the funeral would be on Wednesday. That gave the coroner time to perform the autopsy and ship Momma's body back from Little Rock. In the parking lot, Violet tried to convince me to go home with her. "Rose, you went back to the house already. You proved you could do it. Now come spend the night with us."

I was frightened, but I just couldn't let myself go with her. Sometime over the last day and a half, a revolt had sprung up inside me and there was no beating it down into submission. I needed to do this even if it killed me, which it very well might. I slowly shook my head and opened my car door.

"Rose, this is ridiculous. Do you even have electricity yet?"

"No, but Joe called the electric company and they said they'd be out today."

Violet grabbed my door as I got into the car. "But . . ."

"Violet, you need to get back to the kids. I'll talk to you later."

Mike dragged her away and I drove home eager to be alone. As I pulled into the gravel driveway, I discovered Joe crouched down at the side door of the house.

"What are you doing?" I asked when I got out, wondering if I had just caught him in the middle of being up to something.

"Putting a new lock on your door." He didn't look at me, just kept fiddling at the doorknob with a screwdriver.

"Why are you doing that?"

"To make it harder for someone to break in."

The unspoken *to kill you* hung in the air like a jumbo jet waiting to land. "Why would you do that? Especially if you think I murdered my own mother."

He turned his head and raised his eyebrows. "I never said I thought you murdered your mother. I said it wasn't for me to decide. And I'm doin' it in case you didn't and the person who *did* comes back, especially since you think it was supposed to be you in the first place."

I sucked in my breath. How much *had* he heard? "Well, thank you. I'll pay you for the lock and for your time, too."

"No need for the time, and the lock wasn't much." He gave the knob a jiggle then stood up. "I have a little sister. I only hope someone would do the same for her." He handed me a set of keys on a ring but didn't let go, his fingers and the keys in the palm of my hand. "I fixed the doorjamb too, so it'll hold better. But, Rose," he paused and looked into my eyes, "if someone wants in, they'll get in."

71

I suddenly questioned the sensibility of my plan.

"Is there anything you want to tell me?" he asked.

I blinked, trying to look confused. "Tell you what?"

He sighed and removed his hand, leaving the keys behind. "I'm next door if you need me, just give me a call. I left my number on your kitchen counter."

"You were in my kitchen?"

"Yeah, the door was broken. I had to go inside to remove the old lock."

"Oh." I felt like an idiot.

"Okay, I'm heading home now. If you have trouble sleeping drink a glass of wine or something to help, but not too much. You need to be somewhat alert if someone tries to break in."

I hadn't thought about terror-induced insomnia. "I don't drink."

He looked surprised. "You mean usually?"

"No, I mean at all. I've never had alcohol."

"Oh," he said, twisting his lips as he pondered the fact I was a teetotaler. "Well, if you need anything let me know." He folded up a towel on the ground, covered with a few tools and parts, and walked to his house.

When I turned to the door, I realized not only had he replaced the doorknob but installed a deadbolt too. *Why would he do such a thing?* I glanced over my shoulder at his front porch, but he was already out of sight. Sighing, I went inside and locked the door behind me. Joe was definitely a conundrum.

I slept fitfully, sitting up with every creak in the house. I got up multiple times and peeked out the windows for lurkers in the bushes. I checked the locks at least five times. When I got up at nine o'clock the next morning, I was tired but eager to busy myself with the day.

Momma's curtains seemed like a good place to start. I stood on the arm of the sofa to take them down. The old, tattered fabric fell, dust flying everywhere as it pooled on top of the sofa back. I needed new curtains; these would never survive the washing machine.

But first, I needed to get all the blood off the wall.

After getting a big bowl of hot soapy water, I scrubbed the dried splatters, which proved difficult to remove. I scrubbed harder and paint came off on the sponge, leaving bare spots on the wall. I sat on the arm of the chair and surveyed the damage. There was no way around it; I had to repaint. Suddenly, I had a new plan for the day, something to take my mind off my worries. I would repaint the living room and buy new curtains. And get a cell phone too.

I wanted to stand out in the yard and shout to the world. *Look at me! I'm making my own decisions!*

Instead I grabbed my purse and locked the side door with my new keys, glancing over at Joe's house as I got into my car. His car sat parked in his driveway and I reprimanded myself for even looking. What did I care if Joe McAllister was home?

I went to the cell phone store first, overwhelmed with all my choices. I felt very grown up when I picked out a phone and signed a contract. A legally binding contract. Something deep inside prickled at my joy, saying I was twenty-four years old, this was not that amazing, but I shushed it. I was gonna let myself enjoy it.

Next stop was the hardware store. I studied the paint colors, overwhelmed again. I told myself it was to be expected. For a woman not used to making decisions, I was forcing myself to face plenty of them recently.

My fingers slid down cards as though they were jewels, just waiting for me to pluck them out. I finally settled on a soft, pale yellow. The man in the paint department was helpful since I'd never painted before, assisting me with rollers and tape. He even disregarded my vision that his cat had clawed the side of his dining room table.

Walmart was next. I forgot to measure the windows, but there weren't many choices in lengths. Overwhelmed anew, I finally decided on plain off-white panels that would be soft and breezy with the pale yellow walls.

On my way to the checkout, something soft and shiny caught my eye. I was passing the edge of the lingerie department, if you could really call the underwear/pajama section at Walmart *lingerie*. My gaze had found a nightgown, a kind I had never worn before. It looked more like a slip than a nightgown, only it was a soft lavender and covered in tiny deep purple flowers. My fingers reached out to touch the fabric before my mind could tell them to be reasonable. Once they touched, there was no dissuading them. My fingers were ensnared by a nightie. As they slid over the silky cloth, my mind wondered what it would feel like to *wear* such a thing.

My face burned with shame. When had I turned so wicked? But the nightie was planted in my mind and sprouting like a fast-growing weed, spreading and choking out every thought until there was nothing left but the want of it. To shut up my evil thoughts, I pulled the hanger off the rack and stuffed it under the curtain packages. Then I looked around to see if anyone saw me.

When I checked out, my nervousness made me jittery. I half expected the girl at the register to give me a look of reproach, but she scanned the curtains and stuffed the nightie in the shopping bag without even flinching, as though she did that sort of thing every day. Then again, I guess she did.

I hurried home, eager to start my new project. But first, the blood-stained sofa had to go.

After shoving the kitchen table against the wall,

I scooted the sofa to the door and promptly wedged it in the doorway.

Crappy doodles.

I went out the seldom-used front door and tried pulling from the outside, with little success. Lodging my shoulder underneath, I tried to stand, hoping that might unwedge it.

"What on earth are you doing?" Joe asked behind me.

Startled, I screamed and fell on my butt. "Why do you keep sneaking up on me like that?"

He laughed. "I didn't 'sneak up on you,' I merely walked over to see what you were doing. What *are* you doing?"

I started to get up, surprised when he reached down to help me. "What does it *look* like I'm doing?"

"It looks like you're trying to injure yourself removing that sofa from your house."

I scowled at him. "It's covered in blood and I can't look at it one more minute. I had to get it out."

"Well, why didn't you come and ask me for help?"

I raised my eyebrows, stumped. "Honestly, it never occurred to me."

He grimaced and shook his head. "You need to angle it more, then it should come right out. Go in the house and take the back side. I'll take this end."

Once we got it outside Joe asked, "Now where?" Joe asked.

"I dunno. I hadn't thought that far. My entire goal centered around getting it outside."

Joe shook his head, muttering under his breath. "Let's put it behind the house for now. The neighbors are riled up enough without having to look at your bloody sofa."

His plan sounded reasonable but something about the way he said it got under my skin. We set it down in the backyard, away from the telephone line.

"If you like, I can have someone come and remove it tomorrow," Joe said.

"Thanks," I said, unsure what to do next.

"I'm going to check the door jamb and make sure you didn't bang it up too much."

My irritation returned, but he was right. I went in the kitchen and left the door open so he could examine the frame.

"You painting?" he asked, nodding to the paint cans.

"The living room. I tried to get the blood off the wall but mostly I just ended up taking off the paint."

"Have you ever painted before?"

I rolled my eyes. "I ain't building a rocket. How hard could it be?"

"I'm sure a professional painter might take offense to that."

"Well, I'm not hiring a professional painter."

"I'm not suggesting you do, but I can make sure you know what to do before you get paint everywhere."

"Why?" I asked. "Why would you help me?"

He raised his eyebrows. "I didn't say I was gonna paint the room for you. It's only a few pointers."

I appreciated his offer to help, but his attitude rankled me. Why did that man irritate me so?

Chapter Five

Joe ended up helping me move all the furniture into the dining room, then helped me tape. We didn't talk much while we worked, and after my initial nervousness of being near him in such tight quarters, I got used to his presence.

When we finished taping, he looked me up and down and raised an eyebrow. "You gonna paint in those clothes? Since you're new to this, you're bound to get paint on 'em."

I hadn't considered that, along with most everything else in my life, it seemed. I went to my bedroom and dug through the drawers for an old T-shirt and pair of shorts, self-conscious about changing with Joe in the next room. I assured myself it was unlikely he had X-ray vision. If he had it in his head to attack me, he would have done it already.

When I returned, he had drop cloths spread all over the floor.

"I don't remember buying that many," I said, puzzled.

"You didn't. A couple are mine. You could have made do with the two you bought, but you would have to keep moving them around. It'll be easier this way."

My mouth dropped.

He saw my hesitation. "If I overstepped my . . ."

"No," I shook my head. "I'm sorry. I'm marveling at how nice you're being and trying to figure out why."

His eyebrows raised. "I'm not sure what you're talking about. People can be nice without an underlying motive."

"Not to me they don't."

"Why not?"

Our eyes locked and he studied me, trying to figure out what I meant. He obviously didn't know me yet. *This friendship won't last.* I warned myself. *Don't get used to him.*

"Never mind," I mumbled and went out into the kitchen. My heart stopped at the sight of the shopping bags. He had to have gone through them to get out the drop clothes. *Did he see the nightie?* But the Walmart sack looked undisturbed. Feeling lightheaded, I took out the curtains and set them on the table, wadded up the bag with the nightie still inside, and stuffed it into the dishtowel drawer. I took a deep breath to calm my nerves and went back into the living room.

Before I knew it, we were both painting. I wanted to remind Joe that he claimed he wasn't going to help, but I knew better than push my luck. He was better and faster at it than me.

When Joe finished a wall, I stepped back and

took a good look, clasping my hands to my chest. "I love it!" I exclaimed, giddy with happiness. "It looks like early morning sunshine!"

He turned to me, a slow smile spreading across his face. "Yeah, I suppose it does."

We were almost done with the first coat when Violet burst through the side door. "Oh, thank God you're all right! I've been tryin' to call you all day! Why won't you answer the phone? I thought something happened to you! What on *earth* are you doing?"

Her rapid-fire questions made me I feel like I'd just been pelted with a BB gun. "I'm painting the living room." I glance over my shoulder. "Well, *we're* painting the room."

Violet was livid. "Why would you be redecorating when Momma's not even buried in the ground? It's bad enough that you're accused of killin' our mother, now you're *redecorating?* What are people gonna say, Rose?"

If Violet had slapped me in the face, it couldn't have hurt worse.

Joe cleared his throat. "I know this is none of my business, but Rose isn't redecorating. She's covering up the blood that was spread all over the wall. I offered to help her since she'd never painted before."

Violet's face told me that she never thought about the aftereffects of a violent crime on home furnishings.

"And her phone is out until Wednesday," Joe added.

Violet wasn't about to let her anger go so easily. "See? All the more reason not to stay here! You have no phone if you get into trouble or if something happens!"

Defiance riled up and I put a hand on my hip. "I got a cell phone this morning. I can use it if I need to."

"You *what?*"

"It's the twenty-first century. Everybody has a cell phone."

"Rose, honey, why do you need a cell phone? Honestly, who are you gonna call?"

I bit my lip to keep the tears from falling and looking even more like a fool in front of Joe. "I'm not leaving with you, Violet. I'm stayin' here."

We glared at each other, both of us sure we were right and the other was wrong. I knew I'd thrown her for a loop. Right there in my half-painted living room, I realized the truth of it. I had always done what I was told, whether Momma, who did it out of spitefulness, or Violet, who loved me dearly and thought she knew what was best. No matter the reason, I'd always done what I was told. Standing up to Violet threw her world off its axis.

"Goodbye, Violet," I said in an icy tone. I loved the stuffing out of her, but I was so angry I could spit.

"Rose . . ." Realizing that her bulldozing had backfired, she softened her outrage.

"Goodbye, Violet." If I backed down on this, I'd never be able to stand up to her again.

Violet looked torn as she turned to the door.

Joe took a step toward her. "I'm right next door if Rose needs me."

She let her anger loose on him. "You were right next door when our Momma was killed, too. A lot of good that did *her*." And with that she whipped around and walked out the door.

My mouth dropped open in shock. I'd never seen Violet be so rude.

Joe shut the door behind her and paused.

"Joe, I apologize for my sister's behavior."

He turned around to face me. "She's right, you know."

"What?"

"I *was* next door when your mother was killed and I didn't hear a thing. You'd be safer if you went with Violet."

It took me a moment to recover from my shock. "Go home, Joe."

His eyes widened. "What?"

"Go. Home." I enunciated each word slowly so there was no misinterpreting my meaning.

"Rose, wait a minute."

I walked toward him and opened the door. "I appreciate everything you've done to help me, but I'm done bein' told what to do. Thanks for all your help painting and thanks for installing the locks. Let me know how much I owe you."

Joe stood in the doorway. "Rose, I'm sorry. I wasn't trying to boss you around."

"I know, but you weren't even supposed to help me paint anyway, remember? You were just going to give me some pointers. You did, now you can go home."

Joe went outside, looking over his shoulder as he climbed down the steps.

Ah, crap. I felt a vision coming. *Go away, Joe. Go away.* "The dog's gonna get out the hole in your back fence." That one confused me. Joe didn't have dog.

"What?"

"See you around," I said, shutting the door and locking it.

I started to paint again, feeling lonely. Part of me was sorry I sent him away, but I knew I'd done the right thing. Besides, he would have figured out soon enough that I was a freak.

Several hours later, I finished the last coat. The sun had set, making it difficult to see the true color. Still, I could see it was bright and cheerful, yet not overly yellow. It should have made me happy but the fight with Violet ate at me, stealing my joy. Violet and I never argued and it made me question everything.

Was I being selfish? Was I stupid staying in the house? I couldn't imagine why anyone would want to kill me. I decided Violet had been right the night of the murder; Momma's murder was just a random crime and it would have been me if I hadn't fought with her earlier that day.

Nevertheless, I was still uneasy going to sleep that night.

The next morning I called Betty at the DMV and told her I wouldn't be into work until Thursday. She insisted I take off the entire week, and I could only imagine Suzanne's reaction to that. I wouldn't be surprised if she thought I killed Momma just to get out of a four-day work week. Seriously, I'm smarter than that. If I was going to go to that much trouble, surely I would have picked a five-day week instead.

Next, I called Deanna Crawfield's office to make an appointment but her receptionist said she had a family emergency and couldn't see me until Thursday afternoon.

The floral shop confounded what little decision-making skills I had left. I only hoped my choices would meet Violet's approval. While *I* couldn't care less what the town thought about Momma's funeral, Violet did. My newfound independence may have disappointed her, but I hoped I could make it up with this.

On the way home, I stopped by a local dress shop. I walked through the door and a wave of disbelief washed over me. I was shopping for Momma's funeral. I shook it off, determined not to let Violet down in this either since part of the funeral judgment included the attire of the surviving family members.

Normally, I would go in the store and hide behind the racks, hoping to go unnoticed. I didn't really want to be noticed today, but I decided it was time to be more assertive.

"Excuse me," I choked out to a saleswoman, ignoring my rising anxiety. "I need to buy a dress for a funeral."

The middle-aged woman motioned me to the back. "Are you goin' to the funeral of that poor woman who was murdered the other night?"

Her question didn't surprise me. Murder and mayhem were big news in Henryetta. I nodded.

She leaned close, half-whispering. "They say her daughter did it. Just bashed her head right in." She *tsked* after this.

My stomach churned. I suspected that was what the entire town was saying.

"Are you friend or family?"

I didn't want to lie but it seemed the best course of action. "Friend."

The saleswoman eyed me up and down, tilting her head and squinting her eyes.

My cheeks began to flush. *She knows who I am.*

"You look like you're a size six, am I right?"

I suppressed a sigh of relief. "Yes."

"I have several things that would work for a cute little thing like you."

I looked around to see who she was talking to. I was the only one in the store.

Handing me several hangers, she led me to a dressing room. I tried on a simple black dress first.

The saleswoman knocked on the door. "How are you doing in there?"

Watching myself turn from side to side in the mirror, I was surprised how much older I looked. Surely, Violet would approve. "I think this dress will work. But, uh, do you have something that would be good for the visitation tonight?"

My request excited the clerk and she returned with several skirts and blouses. With her help, I settled on a pale green skirt and a white sleeveless blouse.

"Do you have shoes to match?" she asked.

I paused and that was all the encouragement she needed. She returned with several pairs for me to try on. The first were black pumps with two-inch heels. I hoped I could figure out how to walk in them before the funeral the next day. The other was a pair of white sandals. As I slipped them on, I felt a vision coming.

"Your daughter is sneakin' out of the house to see her boyfriend at night."

The woman appeared startled. "What? How did you know I had a daughter?"

I shrugged. "Lucky guess." Thank goodness I was done shopping because she gave me a wary look.

I paid for my things and drove home, overcome with exhaustion. I wasn't used to shopping and wondered how people did it all day. I barely lasted a half an hour.

When I opened the kitchen door, the soft glow of the living room caught my eye. The warmth made me eager to put up the curtains and move the furniture back in. I briefly entertained the idea of asking Joe for help, but his car wasn't in his driveway. It was for the best. I needed to learn to do things on my own.

It was early afternoon, and I didn't have to meet Violet at the funeral home until six o'clock. I had plenty of time to work on the living room. I hung the new curtains and moved the chair and the television back in, trying to figure out how to arrange them. The lone chair looked ridiculous so I decided to bring out a slipper chair tucked in Momma's room.

I pushed open the door, the smell of dust and Estee Lauder perfume wafting out. Tears stung my eyes. Momma would never be in her room again.

I took a deep breath and let my eyes adjust to the darkness. The curtains were pulled shut, her bed made. I hadn't been in Momma's room in years and it felt like walking into a museum. I knew at some point I'd have to clean it out, but not now. I couldn't bear to think about it. Right now I only planned to take her chair. The upholstery of ivory with red flowers and green leaves would go perfect in the living room. I scooted it down the hall and placed it next to the other chair. It would work for now, but there was no denying I needed a new sofa.

I wondered how I could even be considering furniture when Momma lay in a box several miles away.

Since I stirred up a lot of dust, I took a bath before I dressed in my new clothes. A glimpse of myself in the mirror told me my scraggly hair wouldn't work with my new outfit. After finding some bobby pins in a drawer, I put my hair in a French roll, something I'd seen Violet do. I wasn't used to working with my hair though and it took me multiple tries until I finally got it to where it looked passable. Surveying the results, I decided Violet would approve. I ate a quick sandwich and headed to the funeral home.

Violet and Mike were already there. Violet took one look at me as I walked in, clearly not expecting what she saw.

"Rose, you look . . . different." She gave me a hug and a peck on the cheek.

"Good different?"

She pulled away and studied me. "Good . . . I think. Older. Just different."

Mike kissed me on the cheek. "You look beautiful, Rose. Violet just prefers that you look seventeen years old is all."

That wasn't the reaction I hoped for, but I'd take it. Mike was probably right.

Daddy's younger sister, Aunt Bessie, had already arrived along with her husband, Uncle Earl. They lived in Lafayette County, the next county over, but I'd only seen them a few times since Daddy's funeral. Momma made it no secret she wasn't partial to them. I always suspected it had something to do with Aunt Bessie being younger and more stylish. Uncle Earl rarely spoke but that made him guilty by association.

They both gave me warm hugs.

"Look at you, Rose, all grown up. You're beautiful, child." Aunt Bessie gushed.

"Thanks, Aunt Bessie." I shrugged off her comment. "It's good to see you." I meant it. She was one of the few people in the world who understood me.

She put an arm around my shoulder. "I'm sorry about your momma."

I thanked her, wondering why I didn't feel more grief. Mostly I felt freedom.

A man in a suit told us it was time. The five of us walked down a hall and he opened a door to the Magnolia Room, revealing an open casket against the far wall flanked by sprays of flowers. They made me feel like we were hosting a garden party and Momma was the hostess everyone came to see.

Laid in her coffin, Momma looked different.

Kind of like a new and improved Momma, only she was dead and couldn't enjoy it. They had fixed her hair and put a small hat over the spot where her head had been smashed in. She actually had on makeup, though it was kind of pancakey. But even so, she looked good, better than I'd ever seen her.

I stood in front of the coffin unsure of what was expected of me. Daddy's funeral was a hazy memory. Overcome with grief, I never wondered what to do. As I stared at Momma, I dug deep inside, finding my sorrow buried under all the pain she'd inflicted on me for so many years. Maybe Momma was right after all. Maybe I did have a demon.

Violet stood next to the casket and patted Momma's hand, tears falling down her cheeks. I couldn't help but wonder what she shed her tears for: the loss of the Momma we had or the loss of the Momma we always wanted.

Soon, the funeral home director returned. "People are beginning to arrive."

I remembered from Daddy's funeral that it was the family's duty to stand at the casket and greet the guests. Momma and Violet had done it before. I knew I couldn't get out of it this time.

Momma didn't have very many real friends, but everybody and their brother showed up, hoping to get a glimpse of the hole in her head. An elderly member of the Henryetta Southern

91

Baptist Church limped over and patted Violet's hand. "Your mother was a dear woman who will be greatly missed."

I raised my eyebrows in surprise. "Are you talking about Agnes Gardner?" I had a sneaking suspicion she was at the wrong visitation.

Violet dug her elbow into my side. "Thank you, Mrs. Stringer. It helps so much to hear that."

"She looks good, so good I almost didn't recognize her."

I almost laughed, but my side was already sore. I didn't need any more bruises.

As the evening went on, I discovered that visitations are all about lying. Momma never looked so good, both physically and in personality, as she did dead. We heard how wonderful, kind, clever, and generous she was, adjectives no one in their right mind would have used a week ago. People patted our arms, our hands, and one old coot actually tried to pat my behind. We got hugs, advice and offers of food. I say we, but it was really Violet. Most people talked to Violet, either outright ignoring me or staring at me, fearful. I suspected a good number of them thought I hid a rolling pin in the folds of my skirt, ready to whip it out at any moment and start bashing heads in.

While Violet greeted our guests, playing the perfect hostess, I listened to the people who stood in front of the casket.

"They must have some amazing morticians here. I heard her whole face was smashed in, but you can't even tell."

"She got what was comin' to her. She was a mean old witch."

"That youngest girl of Agnes' has never been right in the head. I ain't surprised one bit. I just hope the police have the sense to lock her up before she starts murdering the whole town."

In a room full of people, I never felt so alone. Tears burned my eyes and I wondered how much longer this would last but knew it was nowhere close to being over. Half of Henryetta showed up to see what they thought I'd done. Just when I was about to bolt, I saw Joe, standing two people back in line, wearing a pair of khaki pants and a short-sleeved button-down shirt. While everyone else's eyes were focused on the casket, his gaze was on me. His mouth lifted into a small smile.

I thought he would never reach us. The woman in front of him went on and on about the wonderful pies Momma had made the last few years. I bit my lower lip to keep from telling her those were *my* pies, but it wouldn't accomplish anything. Let Momma go out in a pie-blazing glory.

Joe shook Violet's hand. "I am sorry for your loss."

Violet gave him a curt thank-you, obviously still blaming him for something, the act itself a mystery.

Joe moved in front of me and allowed the person behind him to approach Violet. Grasping my hand, he said, "I'm sorry for your loss, Rose." He took a deep breath. "And I'm equally sorry for the other night. Still friends?"

He was serious. He thought we were friends. Although I knew I shouldn't, I smiled. "I'd like that."

"How are you holding up?"

Tears filled my eyes. "I'm okay." It was then I realized he was still holding my hand.

"Are you sure?"

I turned to the side and put my back to Violet and the person with her. Lowering my voice to a whisper, I glanced to the line of people next to the casket. "They all think I did this, Joe. The whole town thinks I murdered my own Momma. No one will talk to me, they just ignore me. They're all afraid I'm gonna start running around the room killing everyone." Tears fell down my cheeks and I wiped them off with the back of my free hand.

"I'm sure they're not thinking that."

"Joe, I *heard* 'em."

Joe rubbed my arm and to my dismay, I started to cry harder. He leaned over to Violet. "I'm going to take her out to get some air. I'll bring her right back."

Violet didn't look pleased, but even she had to admit my presence wouldn't be missed.

Aunt Bessie watched Joe lead me out of the room, her eyes lighting up. The visitors cast sneers in my direction. If lynchings were still legal in Fenton County, I knew there'd be a big public execution tonight, bonfire included.

Joe led me down a hall and out a back door. The sun had begun to set, hanging close to the horizon, the sky lit up in a pink splendor. We stood in silence, side by side against the brick wall, while I had a good cry. My tears unlocking the dam to my sadness over Momma's death. When my tears slowed, Joe held up a box of tissues.

I laughed. "Where did you get those?" I pulled several out and patted my face.

"I swiped them off a table. Figured you might need some."

I blew my nose, the noise interrupting the chirping crickets and slamming car doors. "Momma hated parties."

"I guess visitations are kind of like parties."

"Momma hated most everything. I know I shouldn't say it, but it's true."

Joe dug the toe of his loafer into the crack of the sidewalk. "Some people think they need to make the newly deceased look like a saint and ignore all the bad parts of them. But I always thought the bad parts were just as much part of them as the good. Nobody's perfect. We shouldn't try to remember them that way."

We stood in silence until Joe said, "I'm sure she

didn't hate everything. She loved you and your sister."

I twisted my mouth into a sad smile and turned my face toward him. "And there you would be wrong. My Momma hated me."

"I'm sure you *thought* so at times."

I faced the sunset, the sun dipping lower, almost touching the earth. I wished I could disappear with it.

"No, Joe. She did." Of course, he would want to know why. What mother could possibly hate her child without a reason? But I'd finally found a friend. He said we were friends. I wasn't willing to lose him just yet.

He waited for an explanation. I sighed and wiped the tears that started to fall again. "I'm not like everyone else. Momma always said I was evil and demon-possessed."

"Why on earth would she say that?"

My breath caught in my throat. The way he studied me made me nervous. I couldn't tell him. After seeing his compassion, I couldn't bear to see it replaced with the fear and disgust I saw in everyone else's eyes. "Sometimes I wonder if she was right," I said. "If you stick around me long enough, you'll figure it out too. Just like everyone else does sooner or later." I grabbed a tissue out of the box and wiped my face.

Joe's brow furrowed, like what I said went against the law of gravity. Impossible.

"Thanks for talking to me," I told him. "I better go back inside before Violet sends out a search party."

"I'll walk you in."

I put my hand on his arm. "Thanks, but you know what? You've got enough strikes against you, being new in this town. No reason to hurt your social standing any more by being seen with me. Good night, Joe."

I opened the door and took one last glance at him. He looked like he'd been blindsided. I supposed he had.

Chapter Six

I went back to the visitation room and plastered on a smile that said *thank you for coming but my heart is breaking*. And while the *thank you for coming* part wasn't true, the *my heart is breaking* part was.

A couple of hours later, my feet ached from standing and my cheeks hurt from smiling but a few stragglers remained. They munched on cookies while trying to determine the size and location of the hole in Momma's head from the placement of her hat. Aunt Bessie and Uncle Earl stayed the entire time. They brought bottles of water to Violet because she did so much talking over the course of three and a half hours that she had become hoarse. And me, too, because Aunt Bessie worried that I'd become dehydrated from the slow flow of tears that I couldn't stop.

Aunt Bessie and Uncle Earl were supposed to spend the night with Violet. But Aunt Bessie suggested they stay with me instead.

"Rose has grown an independent streak," Violet said in a snippy tone. "She might not let you."

I gasped. "Of course, they can stay with me. They can take Momma's room."

We said goodbye in the parking lot, Violet and I

giving each other awkward hugs. Aunt Bessie and Uncle Earl followed me to the house. I pulled into the driveway and gave Joe's house a mournful glance as I waited for them to get their suitcase from the car.

"I heard Mr. Williams died a few months ago. Who lives there now?" Aunt Bessie asked, the softness of her voice telling me she knew my look meant something.

"Joe McAllister."

"The young man from tonight?"

"Yeah, but don't be thinkin' anything about it, Aunt Bessie. We're just friends." My tongue tripped over the word *friends* and to my chagrin, I felt tears building again. "I never met him before the night Momma was killed."

She watched me unlock the door. "Isn't that deadbolt new? I don't remember seeing it before."

I'd forgotten she had the memory of an elephant. "Joe put it in for me when he fixed the broken lock."

"Oh?"

I ignored the question in her voice and flipped on the light. She oohed and awed over the new paint color, finding it perfectly reasonable and logical to paint two days after Momma died, given the circumstances.

Uncle Earl took their suitcase to the room. I offered to help change the sheets on Momma's bed, but Aunt Bessie suggested I put on pajamas and make us hot tea instead. I sat at the kitchen table with two cups ready when she entered the kitchen.

Even though I dressed for bed, I hadn't taken my hair down. Aunt Bessie stood behind me, taking out the pins, running her fingers through the strands. I closed my eyes, relaxing at the feel of it.

"Tonight was a long night, wasn't it?" she asked.

"Yes," I murmured softly, leaning my head back into her hands.

"Did Joe say something to upset you tonight?"

Tears burned my eyes again. "No, if anything he helped me."

"Then what made you so upset?"

"You mean other than the town folk of Henryetta rallying to grab their pitchforks?"

"Yes, I knew there was something else." Aunt Bessie was a hairdresser and knew how to massage someone's head and make them so relaxed they'd give up their deepest darkest secrets. After only a few minutes in her hands, I was too soothed to care.

"He said we were friends. He thinks we're friends, Aunt Bessie." I said it as if it were declared the eighth wonder of the world.

"So? Why can't you be friends?"

"Because I'm different. You know that."

"Your grandmother, my mother, had the gift of sight. She had lots of friends."

"But she wasn't like me. I'm different."

"Not so different. Besides, what's wrong with being different? Sometimes it's good to stand apart from everyone else."

"Momma didn't think so."

Aunt Bessie continued rubbing my head for a bit then finally spoke. "Rose, your momma had a hard life. There's things about her you don't know."

"That still doesn't excuse the way she treated me."

"No, but sometimes if we understand why someone does what they do it helps take the sting of the hurt away."

"What about the way she treated Daddy? That wasn't right either."

Aunt Bessie sighed and sat down in the chair next to me. "Your daddy wasn't a perfect man. No one is perfect."

"That's what Joe said tonight."

She patted my hand. "Then your Joe is a smart man." She took a sip of her now cooled tea. "Your daddy did some things that hurt your momma deeply. In fact, I think it's fair to say they broke her. Someday, you might want to know what happened, but now isn't the right time. When you're ready, come to me and I'll tell you everything I know."

I wasn't sure I'd ever want to know, but I nodded and drank my tea.

The next morning I padded around the kitchen, making breakfast and brewing coffee when Aunt Bessie came in.

"That living room looks so bright and cheerful in the morning light."

I smiled as I turned my head to look at the glow. "It's lovely, isn't it?"

"Have you thought about where you'll live now that your momma is gone?"

My heart skipped. "Why, I thought I'd stay here."

"I'm sure that's fine, but more than likely, Violet will own half of it. You two will have to work out some type of arrangement."

One more thing I hadn't considered.

Aunt Bessie patted my arm. "No need to worry, Rose. Violet has her own house, she won't want this one. You'll probably just buy out her half."

I stewed about it as I poured our cups of coffee.

"When was the last time you had your hair cut?" she asked.

I couldn't remember, so Aunt Bessie insisted on giving me a trim. She set me in a chair in the middle of the kitchen and snipped away with the scissors she said she always traveled with. I suspected she brought them with the sole purpose of cutting my hair, which had always annoyed the tarnation out of her. At one point during the cut, I had a vision and told her one of the hairdressers in her shop was going to leave and try to steal some of her clients. Aunt Bessie took it in stride, thanked me for my useful information, and continued trimming.

The amount of hair that fell to the floor alarmed me, but Aunt Bessie said to trust her. Which I did. It wasn't like my hair had a particular style anyway. When she finished cutting, she pulled out a fat curling iron and flipped out the ends.

"Okay, go check it out."

I went to the bathroom, Aunt Bessie on my heels, and we stared at my reflection in the mirror. I was speechless.

"It should be a lot lighter now. I razor-cut the edges and thinned it out a bit, you can take a big curling rod to the ends and flip them out or just wear it straight."

Aunt Bessie could have been speaking Greek for all I understand, but I didn't pay much attention anyway. I was too busy gawking at my hair.

"I can't believe it's me." I turned my head from side to side, watching my hair sway against my shoulders. It now sported layers and framed my face with long bangs, a far cry from the dry, lifeless hair I had before. I shook my head and it bounced.

"You've been hidin' too long, Rose Anne Gardner," Bessie said from behind me. "It's time to shed that cocoon and become the beautiful butterfly you're meant to be."

"Aw, Aunt Bessie." I gave her a big hug. "Thank you. I love it."

We dressed for the funeral. I felt very sophisticated in my dress and new hair. I tottered down the hall in my heels, wishing I had thought to practice in them sooner. Aunt Bessie approved and insisted on putting a little bit of makeup on me, telling me cosmetics were not the devil's oil paints, contrary to what Momma always said.

I rode in their car to the church. We arrived early, which meant I had time to practice walking before Violet and Mike showed up. I was finally getting the hang of it when they entered through the opposite end of the foyer. As I approached, Violet was asking Aunt Bessie where I was.

"Here she comes now." The pride in Aunt Bessie's voice was unmistakable, making me love her even more.

Violet's mouth dropped open. "What have you *done?*"

"Violet . . ." Aunt Bessie cautioned.

"What have you done?"

"Violet!" Mike voice was sharp with warning.

She turned to Mike, flinging her arm in my direction. "Mike, she went and got her hair *styled!* The day of Momma's funeral! Who does that? What is she thinking?"

"Violet, this is my doing," Aunt Bessie said. "I insisted on cutting her hair this morning."

"She could have stopped you!"

104

"Why?" Aunt Bessie asked. "Why would she stop me? For one thing, her whole life has been run by you and your mother, so what was one more woman telling her what to do? And second, there is nothing wrong with her looking beautiful. It's not like she showed up to your mother's funeral looking like a hooker."

Violet gasped, the sound echoing off the tiled entrance.

Aunt Bessie pressed on. "Rose looks very tasteful, very conservative. You should be happy for her."

Violet put her hands on her hips. "What are people gonna *say?*"

"And right there is the bottom line, isn't it, Violet? What are people gonna *say?*"

I couldn't believe the two women I loved most in the world were arguing. Over me no less. "Stop! Stop it the both of you!"

They turned to face me. Violet looked like she was about to give me a good throttling, then move on to Aunt Bessie.

"Violet, I'm sorry if you are unhappy with my new haircut, but I honestly had no idea what Aunt Bessie was going to do to it. I thought she was giving me a trim. But that being said," I smiled at Aunt Bessie, "I'm not sorry she did it. I love it and I'm sorry if you don't. And perhaps the timing was bad, but you and I both know that the people in this town are going to talk about me one way or the other. They always have."

Violet looked like she was about to start spitting out carpet tacks. Mike grabbed her arm and dragged her away from our group, their heads bent together in a heated discussion.

"Rose, if I had known Violet would react this way, I never would have cut your hair."

"Don't be sorry, Aunt Bessie, for heaven's sake, it's only *hair*." But the truth was that the problem lay much deeper. I was changing and Violet didn't like it.

Violet calmed down a little before it was time to go into a private room to wait while the mourners were seated in the sanctuary. Violet looked like she would burst out the door to escape my presence at any minute.

A few minutes after eleven o'clock, we walked to the front of the church. I offered a prayer of thanks that I didn't fall over in my two-inch heels.

Violet remained chilly at the graveside service, but I reached over and grabbed her hand, overcome with a wave of grief. I took it as a good sign when she didn't snatch it away, instead hanging on tight. We sat next to the open grave and clung to each other as we buried our last remaining parent. We were orphans. I choked back a sob of despair. Even if Momma hadn't been the best mother, she was still our Momma. And now we were alone.

We rode in an uncomfortable silence to the

church for the traditional funeral dinner. Any good Southern Baptist knows there's nothing that can't be fixed with a casserole potluck, death included. I told myself if I could just make it through the dinner, then I could return to my solitude, or at least my own inner demon.

We'd made it through the funeral and graveside service without mishap; I knew it was too much to expect to make it through the dinner, as well. Two older women watched me while I stood to the side of the buffet table. I recognized them as Momma's friends, if you could call backstabbing, busy-bodies friends.

Violet and Aunt Bessie made their hostess rounds while I did my best to stay out of the way. One of the women pointed to me, shaking her finger in outrage, then buried her face in their huddle. I did my best to ignore them, but they soon worked themselves into a chattering tizzy. A few moments later, they moved toward me and didn't waste any time getting to the point.

"You have some nerve showin' up at your mother's funeral looking like that." The ringleader pointed to my dress with a gnarly finger covered in gaudy rings. Ethel Murdock, self-appointed morality czar of Henryetta. I had no doubt that Momma and Miss Ethel spent many an hour judging the actions of the First Baptist Church members. Then they'd move on to the remaining citizens of Henryetta for good measure.

The blood rushed to my face and the all-too-familiar response to hide took over. I shook it off. It was time to stand up for myself.

"What exactly are you talking about? What's wrong with the way I look?" I asked in a shaky voice.

Miss Ethel's eyebrows knit together and her mouth puckered as if she were about to give me a kiss. I knew there was little chance of that happening. "You're dressed up all high and mighty. We know you never dressed like that before. You killed your own mother to get her money and you haven't wasted any time spending it, have you?" Her face turned red and splotchy. I worried Miss Ethel would have a stroke right there. I'd probably be blamed for that too.

Adrenaline surged through my blood. My chest constricted, cutting off my air supply. "How I spend my money is no concern of yours," I choked out.

Miss Ethel picked up her cane and waved it in front of my face. "You're not gonna get away with this! It's a travesty that you're walkin' around free to murder some other unsuspecting victim!" Her words echoed throughout the fellowship hall.

Beulah Godfrey stood behind Miss Ethel, her arms crossed and lips pursed. She nodded her head in agreement.

Anger riled up in me. I had no idea where this seemly bottomless pool of rage came from, but it just kept flowing out. "Well, I'm sorry you feel that way," I said through gritted teeth, "but this is neither the time nor place to discuss it."

My words enraged Miss Ethel more and she puffed up like a bantam rooster, thrusting out her chest and bobbing her head. She lifted her cane higher, swinging it around. "Don't you talk to *me* about time and place, you *murderess!*"

Miss Ethel lost her precarious balance and swung her cane as she flailed, catching Miss Beulah on the chin. Miss Beulah shrieked and fell sideways, landing smack dab in the big pan of mashed potatoes on the buffet line. She jumped off the table as if it bit her, her face and chest covered in the creamy mixture. In her haste, she bumped a bowl of red Jell-O salad, sending it sideways off the table toward Miss Ethel. Miss Ethel screamed as she saw it coming toward her, accidently falling on her bottom as she tried to get out of the way, the bowl landing on top of her head. Red gelatin dripped down her hair and into her startled face. Miniature marshmallows clung to her tight blue-gray curls like dandelion puffs caught in a spider web.

An eerie silence descended upon the fellowship hall and everyone froze, forks halfway to their mouths. The room looked like a scene out of "Sleeping Beauty." Nothing this good had happened at a Henryetta funeral since Elmer Wainwright fell out of his casket five years earlier.

I threw back my shoulders and lifted my chin, knowing I'd be blamed for this somehow.

Violet gave me a livid glare of *How could you?*

I turned and carefully walked out of the hall, praying I didn't fall in my heels. About one hundred pairs of eyes watched me leave. I could have crawled under a rock and died right there and it still wouldn't have been enough to escape.

Aunt Bessie followed me out as the room finally broke its spell with a roar of chaos. Violet remained behind. I was torn about that. I wanted my big sister to hug me and tell me it would be okay, but was fearful she'd come out and accuse me of ruining Momma's funeral. I suddenly realized how very alone I was now. Was my independence really worth the price I was paying?

We agreed that Uncle Earl would drive me home. Aunt Bessie could stay behind and help Violet, even though I suspected Violet didn't want her there.

We were almost home when Uncle Earl cleared his throat. "What that woman said, it wasn't right. Just remember that she doesn't know you. You can't change the opinions of small-minded people." He reached over and patted my arm.

My chin quivered and I bit my lower lip. Those were the most words I'd heard Uncle Earl say in years.

Uncle Earl dropped me off at home and went back to the church. Aunt Bessie and Uncle Earl came back later and spent the night again. I tried to call Violet before I went to bed, but she didn't answer. I left a rambling message on her machine, apologizing for upsetting her and begging for her forgiveness. I hung up, afraid I lost her forever even though Aunt Bessie assured me that all she needed was time to get used to things.

The next morning when Aunt Bessie and Uncle Earl left for home, Aunt Bessie asked me to come home with her. I would have gone in a heartbeat if I hadn't been ordered to stay in Fenton County. Besides, I had an appointment with my attorney that afternoon.

Deanna Crawfield looked much more professional on a Thursday afternoon than at two o'clock on a Sunday morning, but then again I think most people would. We sat at a conference table while she took notes on a legal pad. Deanna said the evidence was circumstantial. The cut utility lines and the busted side door were in my favor, but the fact nothing was stolen and my argument with Momma in the afternoon were not. She was surprised the police hadn't called me in for more questioning, which she saw as a bad sign. They were collecting more evidence first.

An hour later, I left feeling less than confident about my freedom. If anything, I wondered how long it would take for the Henryetta police department to show up at my door to arrest me.

On the way home, I stopped at a convenience

store to buy milk. While I dug cash out of my wallet, a Walmart receipt fell out onto the counter. I almost wadded it up before noticing the writing on the back.

My list.

I picked it up, staring in disbelief. In all the confusion, I'd forgotten about it.

"Do you want me to throw that away?" the clerk asked.

"No, that's okay . . ." I mumbled and carefully tucked it into my wallet. I'd figure out what to do with it later.

After I got home, I decided to search for Momma's will. I knew she had one made after Daddy died and I suspected it was in the lockbox in her bedroom closet. I couldn't believe Violet hadn't thought of it, but she probably figured she'd have to deal with me to read it. She never returned my phone call from the night before and she hadn't called to check on my attorney appointment.

The dusty box was on the floor in the closet, hidden behind a stack of empty shoe boxes. Inside, I found a stack of papers and pulled them out one by one. Momma and Daddy's marriage license. Daddy's death certificate. The deed to the house. At the bottom was a large envelope labeled "Last Will and Testament of Agnes Gardner." I opened the flap and pulled out a bundle of papers, all stapled together. I read the legalese, wondering if anyone really understood any of it, until I got several pages in and found Violet's name. Bequeathed to Violet Mae Gardner Beauregard was all Momma's money, her house and all its furnishings.

Everything.

The room became fuzzy and I worried I'd pass out and hit my head again. I put my head between my knees, gasping for air. Had she hated me so much that she left me nothing?

When the threat of fainting faded, I sat up and reexamined the page, sure I'd misread it. But I hadn't. Violet got everything.

I turned the page looking for my name. I found it the next page over. Rose Anne Gardner received a carved wooden box located in Momma's closet. A wood box?

I found it in the top shelf of her closet, a small wooden trunk about fifteen inches long and eight inches wide. It reminded me of a miniature pirate's chest with a tiny padlock holding it closed. I searched Momma's drawers for a key, coming up with nothing. It was fairly light so I knew it couldn't be packed with money. In fact, if I hadn't heard a small clunking sound, I would have wondered if it held anything at all.

I stared at the grimy chest, my inheritance, and realized in the matter of only a few days I had lost everything.

Chapter Seven

After the initial shock wore off, I got up to fix myself dinner only to discover I'd left the milk out on the counter. I slid the container on the top shelf and noticed a six-pack of beer, two of the bottles gone. I bent over, hanging on the door as I peeked in and tried to figure out how they got there. Momma never allowed The Devil's Brew in the house. Uncle Earl must have brought them and forgotten them.

I set the carton on the counter, staring at it like it was an alien pod dropped off in my fridge, about to pop out a gremlin at any moment. Because I knew something like that was bound to happen; Momma said nothing good ever came from a bottle of beer.

At the thought of Momma, my rebellion broke loose and burst out, filling me with thoughts of evilness. I pulled a beer out of the box and turned it in my hands. How could one little brown bottle be a fount of wickedness? In that moment, I decided if it was wicked, I was going to drink it. It took me nearly a full minute to figure out how to get the metal cap off and once I did, I held it in front of me. *This was it.* The moment I embraced evil. I took a big swig, then coughed and gagged, spewing out liquid like the cherub fountain in Mildred's backyard. Thank goodness I was standing in front of the sink.

So maybe a big gulp wasn't such a good idea.

I placed the bottle to my lips and took a tiny sip, my tongue protesting. The cold beer slid down my throat and warmed my stomach. How was that possible? Maybe it was Devil's Brew, especially since the only explanation I could come up with was magic.

Carrying the carton in one hand and my bottle of the Fount of Wickedness in the other, I went out the front door and plopped in one of the rarely used rocking chairs on the front porch. I briefly considered what the neighbors would think. Then I decided it didn't matter. I probably wouldn't live here much longer anyway.

After several more tiny sips, I marveled at the magical warmness spreading through my gut. My arms and legs became tingly and I thought my head was gonna float right off my body. The cares of the world suddenly didn't seem so bad. As I got used to the taste of it, my sips got bigger and the next thing I knew, it was empty.

I felt happy and carefree. If one bottle of beer could do that, I could only imagine how wonderful I would feel with two.

With some effort, I twisted the top off the second bottle and took a big swig. I sat watching the leaves of the trees in the front yard blow in the breeze.

"Rose?" Joe asked, sounding stunned. "What are you doing?"

I turned my head. He stood at the edge of the porch with my purse in his hand. I lifted the bottle up to show him. "I'm drinkin' a beer." I giggled then took another sip.

He climbed the steps and sat in the rocker next to me, setting my purse on the floor between us. "Yeah, I can see that. I thought you didn't drink."

I giggled again. "I don't, well, I didn't. But that was the old me; this is the new me and the new me drinks beer." I leaned over to him and whispered loudly. "And guess what? I *like* it."

Joe chuckled. "So I see." He looked down at the box, alarmed. "How many have you *had?*"

I waved the drink at him. "This is just my second but look how many there's left!"

"Mind sharing?"

I hated to lose one, but it seemed the neighborly thing to do. "Okay."

Joe picked up a bottle. He twisted the cap off a whole lot easier than I did and took a big swig. "Bad day?" he asked.

For some reason I found his question funny and my laughter spilled out until I laughed so hard I was crying. Joe rocked in his chair, sipping his beer. He watched patiently, waiting for me to settle down.

"It sucked." Then I started giggling again because Momma had considered *sucked* a bad word and tonight I was breaking all the rules. I settled down in a minute and took another drink. "Hey, what are you doin' with my purse?" I asked, noticing it on the floor between us.

"I saw it outside the side of the house, thought I'd bring it to you before someone took off with it."

"Huh," I said, contemplating how it could have gotten there. I must have set it down when I unlocked the door earlier. Thinking of the door reminded me of the locks. "Oh!" I exclaimed in a mini-shout, fairly certain Joe actually jumped in his seat. "I plum forgot I owe you money." I reached down for my purse, but had trouble grabbing hold of it. I thought that was funny and snickered.

"Rose, it can wait. You can just pay me later."

I finally got a good grasp and pulled it up into my lap. "No, I *insist*." I chuckled more because the *s* sound in the word *insist* sounded funny. I pulled the wallet out and shoved the bag off my lap. It landed on the floor with a loud thud. "Oops."

I opened my wallet. "How much do I owe you?"

"I don't remember. Just pay me later." He looked like he thought something was really funny.

"No, no, no." I wondered why it sounded like my words were slurred. "I might forget."

"Okay, pay me twenty dollars and you can cook me dinner sometime to make up the difference."

I dug through my cash, carefully picking through the bills. I found a twenty, taking great care as I pulled it out. The Walmart receipt fell out onto my lap. I reached over to hand Joe the money. He took it from me, his fingers brushing mine. I felt a strange tingling in my gut.

"Oh . . . ," I said, my eyes opening wide in surprise. I turned to Joe in fascination.

He looked confused at my reaction.

I thought about touching him again, but decided to take another drink of my beer instead.

"How long have you been out here?" he asked.

"I dunno . . . ," my voice trailed off. "Hmm . . ." I tried to think.

"When did you start drinking?"

"I dunno, not that long ago." I finished off my bottle and reached down for another.

Joe grabbed my hand in his, stopping me while I lifted it out of the box. "Hold on there, Party Girl. When was the last time you ate some-thing?"

Our heads were bent close together, both of us reaching down. I turned slightly to look at him. "I dunno . . ."

His face was inches from mine, his eyes full of mischief, but they quickly clouded over and turned dark and serious. He sat up, looking stiff and uncomfortable. "I'm gonna go get us something to eat. You wait here and *don't drink anything else.*"

"But there's another beer in there!" I protested in earnest.

He grabbed the bottle and stood up.

"That's mine! Give that back!"

"I will, after you eat something. Since you're new to drinking I'll teach you all about it."

That got my attention. "You will?"

"Yeah, when I get back. Just wait right there."

I watched my last bottle of beer leave with him. My hands settled in my lap and the receipt poked my palm. I unfolded the strip, smoothing it out. How long ago had I written my list? It felt like a lifetime.

I started reading, surprised at the number of items I could already mark off. I'd been more wicked than I thought. I'd completed three of them: numbers one, ten and eighteen—*get a cell phone, drink a beer* and *wear high heels.* Three items of twenty eight. I still had a ways to go, but those were three things I'd never done in twenty-four years. I'd made pretty good progress.

"What are you looking at?"

My head jerked up at the sound of Joe's voice. "Huh?"

"What's that?"

I loved beer. Normally, I would have been shy and hid my list, but beer gave me confidence I'd never had before. "It's my Wish List."

Joe handed me a bottle of water and a paper plate with a sandwich and some chips. He sat down with his own plate and water.

"Where's my beer?" I asked, panicked that he might have lost it.

He laughed. "Don't worry, I put it in your fridge. Rule number one of drinking: Beer is better cold."

I picked up the sandwich and took a bite. "Oh . . ."

Joe leaned over toward me. "That one is very important."

I nodded, seeing the seriousness of it. "What else?"

"Beer before liquor, you'll never be sicker."

I scrunched my nose. "What does that mean?"

"It means don't drink beer and move onto harder stuff; you'll get a pretty nasty hangover."

"Okay." I took another bite of my turkey sandwich. "Why did you bring me a sandwich? Why're you being so nice to me?"

He shrugged and grinned. "You gave me a beer, I repaid you with a sandwich. Good trade. Besides, that brings me to the next rule: don't drink on an empty stomach. Bad idea."

"Wow, I had no idea drinkin' had so many rules."

"You have no idea. Next rule: drink plenty of water so you don't get dehydrated."

"Really?"

"Yeah, take another drink. It will keep you from getting a headache tomorrow."

"I'm gonna get a headache?"

"If you drink too much and don't eat or drink water. We're gonna try to stop that from happening."

I took another sip.

Joe finished his sandwich and set his plate on the floor. "So what's on your list?"

"Wishes."

"Wishes? What kind of wishes?"

I handed him the list.

He took it and raised his eyebrows. "A Walmart receipt?"

I shrugged and nibbled on a chip. "I didn't have any paper."

"Number one, *get a cell phone*. Two, *commit all seven deadly sins in one week*." He jerked his head up, smiling. "What *is* this?"

The fuzzy feeling in my head was going away and I didn't want it to. "Can I have my beer now?"

Joe gave me a weird look as he went in the front door with the receipt still in his hand. He must have run because it felt like he'd just gone in when he came back, handing me an open bottle. He had one too.

"So about this list . . ."

I took a drink. Joe was right; beer *was* better cold. "I told ya already, it's my Wish List. It's all the things I wanna do."

"Looks like you took care of number ten tonight, *drink beer*."

"Yeah, lucky for me Uncle Earl left it behind." I giggled.

Joe continued reading. "Number fourteen, *kiss a man*." He looked up. "Rose, are you telling me you've never done anything on this list?" He sounded like he'd just been told there was no Santa Claus after believing his whole life.

"Oh, no . . ."

"Good, I didn't see how . . ."

"I hadn't done any of those things before *last week*. I've done three of them now." I held up three fingers to show him. "I bought a cell phone. I wore heels to Momma's funeral and I didn't fall over. And tonight I'm drinking beer." I lowered a finger as I ticked off the items, leaving my middle finger for the last. A second later I realized what I did and broke out into a fit of laughter.

When I stopped, Joe stared at me, his face very serious. "Rose, why did you write this list?"

I took another drink of my beer. "Cause I was tired of not living, you know?"

"No, what do you mean?"

I sighed for all I was worth. "I wanted to live my life instead of having my Momma tellin' me what I could and couldn't do and tellin' me how *evil* I was."

Joe took a drink of his beer, quiet for a moment.

"Rose, when did you write this list? Number four is *Get my own place*."

"I wrote it Saturday, before I came home and found Momma."

Joe reached over and took my hand in his. "Rose, did you kill your mother?" His voice was so quiet the cicadas almost drowned out his words.

I tried to snatch my hand away. "No! What do you care, anyway? You said it wasn't for you to decide, remember?"

His grip held tight. "You're right, I don't care. I'm just curious."

"What? Are you afraid I'll beat your head in with a rolling pin?"

Joe laughed and let go of my hand. "No, I'm not afraid of you, not how you're thinking anyway. If you came at me with a blunt object, I could fend you off with one hand tied behind my back."

I thought about arguing with him but decided maybe I'd prove him wrong later. I'd bide my time.

"Number twelve, *dance*. You've never danced?"

"Nope."

"Not even in your living room?"

"Nope."

"Now that's a damn shame. Everyone has danced in their living room."

"Not me."

"Number fifteen."

I turned to face him. "Which one is that?"

He glanced up. The teasing expression on his face looked forced. *"Do more with a man."*

For the first time since he started reading, I felt embarrassed. "I didn't say what I wanted. I just said *do more.*"

"Why do you want to commit all Seven Deadly Sins in one week? Why one week? Why commit them at all?"

I took a drink, suddenly tired of all his questions. "Look, there's rules with that list. I can only mark them off when I do them. If I don't do them, they can't come off. I wrote that one without thinkin'. I thought about how Momma always said I was committing deadly sins and I thought I was gonna commit them all and *enjoy it.* But one day just didn't seem right, you know?" I stopped to make sure he did.

He nodded with a smirk.

"So I decided one week would be more respectable. But what I hadn't thought about was keepin' track of them all. I think I'll have to write them down or I'll forget which ones I did and didn't do." I stood up. "I gotta pee."

Joe laughed. "All right. Do you need help getting to the bathroom?"

My snort told him what I thought of his ridiculous question. I turned to go inside the door, teetering because the porch began to wobble. I giggled again.

Joe got up and held onto my elbow. "Be careful."

I tripped over my foot and started to fall. Joe wrapped his arm around my waist and steadied me, pulling my body to his in the process.

We stood chest to chest, his arm holding me to him. My heart sped up and my breathing became shallow. The warm feeling down below returned with a tingling I hadn't expected but wasn't ready to lose just yet.

"Can you list the Seven Deadly Sins?" Joe asked, his voice barely a whisper.

I stared up into his eyes, mesmerized. "Envy, slothfulness, gluttony."

"Have you ever done any of those, Rose?"

I nodded slowly.

"That's only three. Do you know the other four?"

"Wrath, pride, greed . . . lust."

His face moved closer to mine. My heart beat even faster, trying to flip-flop out of my chest.

"Ever felt greed?"

"I don't know."

"Lust?" His mouth was inches from mine.

Overcome with a yearning I'd never felt before, I didn't answer, just studied his face.

"Have you really never been kissed? I find that so hard to believe." His free hand caressed my cheek.

I felt his breath on my face and something in me ached with a need I couldn't name.

His mouth lowered so close to mine, our lips almost touched. "I can help you with an item on your list."

"Which one?" I whispered, searching his eyes and trying not to go cross-eyed.

"Number fourteen, a kiss."

My heart thumped so hard I wondered if I was about to have a heart attack. But I decided if I was gonna die, then kissing Joe was probably a good way to go. "Can you make it a really good one?"

Joe laughed, tilting his head back, to my utter disappointment.

"So you can't make it a good one or you don't want to kiss me?" I asked, peeved.

He stopped laughing. "Neither." The hand around my waist inched up my back, pulling me even closer to him, which I hadn't thought possible. He did it slow and deliberate, like I was a mouse and he was a cat, playing with his prey. His eyes bore into mine, his mouth inching closer. My heart rate sped up again, the ache inside growing with every second.

"Are you sure, Rose?" he asked, a small grin lifting the corners of his mouth and making his eyes twinkle.

"Yes," I sighed and closed my eyes.

His lips touched mine, soft and gentle, pulling my lower lip between his. I felt his tongue dart out and tickle my upper lip. I gasped and he pulled me even closer, his mouth working magic on mine, igniting a bonfire in my gut that threatened to consume me. My legs felt weak and I wrapped my arms around his neck to steady myself. His response was to open his lips even more and do things with his tongue that I had never considered before. I clung to him for dear life, certain I would never survive the onslaught of fire raging through my body.

When he pulled his mouth away, we both panted, our faces inches apart. His hand cupped my face and his thumb stroked my cheek. "How was that?"

I thought about it, unsure how to respond. "It's hard to say, since I have nothing else to compare it to, but I think it was probably pretty good."

"Pretty good?" he asked with a mischievous look in his eye. "Why, if I didn't know better Rose Gardner, I would suspect you were a tease. Are you telling me that you need something to compare it to?"

I nodded, licking my lower lip where he had nipped.

His eyes followed my tongue. The playfulness fell away and his lips found mine, much more insistent this time, much more demanding. I never thought it possible to lose oneself in someone else, but I lost myself in him. When he stopped, I had no idea if I stood on my own. Turns out I didn't. Joe held me up with the arm around my back.

"Was that one better?" Huskiness filled his words.

"Does it get even better than that?" I asked, trying to catch my breath.

"Yes," he said, his breath tickling my face. "But it involves more than just kissing. You would have to move to number fifteen."

"Do more . . . ?"

"Yes."

"Can you help me with that one too?" I asked, eager.

Joe groaned, pulled my face to his chest and murmured into my ear. "You have no idea how much I want to help you with that, but I can't. You're drunk and it wouldn't be right."

I pulled back in protest. "I'm not drunk!"

"You most certainly are. Try to walk a straight line."

I had serious doubts about my ability to do that.

"There you go," Joe said, smiling. But he looked a little sad too. "Do you still have to go to the bathroom?"

I nodded.

"Can you make it by yourself?"

"I think so . . ."

Joe decided it would be better if he escorted me inside. I shut the bathroom door behind me, looking at my reflection in the mirror. My cheeks were flushed and my eyes sparkled. I'd never seen myself look that way.

When I walked out, Joe waited outside the door.

"Now what?" I asked. "Are you going to go home?"

"Not if you don't want me to. We could watch TV."

I smiled. "That sounds nice. But I don't have cable."

"Yeah, I know, because of number three. *Get cable TV.*"

"Why do I think I'll regret showin' you my list?"

He laughed. "Because you probably will."

"We can go to your house if you want, you probably have cable *and* a sofa."

"I think we can both squeeze in that chair over there." He gestured to the oversized one in the living room.

I blushed a little. For both of us to sit in that chair meant we had to sit very close together.

Joe took my hand in his. He sat in the chair and had me sit on his lap, my legs over the arm of the chair. I laid my head in the crook of his neck.

"Comfy?" he asked, turning on the television with the remote.

"Mmmhmm . . ." I had never felt so comfortable in all my life.

Between the beer, the coziness of being held and the murmur of the television, my eyes got heavy and I decided I'd rest them for a minute.

"Rose?"

"Hmm?" I hovered on the edge of wake and sleep, when you're straddling both but belong to neither.

"I *really* like your hair."

I fell asleep, lying against his chest listening to the soft beat of his heart in my ear, my own full of joy.

Chapter Eight

The next morning, beer and I mutually decided our relationship wasn't going to work out. I wondered why it decided to turn on me as I clung to the toilet, waiting to puke my guts out. Everything had been going so well the night before. I lifted my head, trying to remember what happened, and groaned when it all rushed back. I dropped my head in dismay, whacking my forehead on the porcelain. Just what I needed to help my already aching head.

What did I do? What did I do? What did I do? ran through my head like a Buddhist chant. What did I do? I drank a beer. And then another. Joe showed up. And he brought me a sandwich. I drank another beer. And he read my list.

I groaned again. He read my *list*. How could I have let that happen? Then I remembered our kiss. If my stomach hadn't been rallying the rest of my intestinal track into a march of protest, I might have enjoyed the rush of heat and anticipation that accompanied the memory. I remembered asking him to help me with the *do more* wish and I groaned again. What had I done? But I remembered both kisses and I couldn't find enough shame to muster any guilt. I felt like a fool and Joe surely thought I was a complete idiot, but I wasn't sorry I kissed him.

And there you had it; I was paving the highway to hell in beer bottles and kisses.

But I checked off another wish on my list. That brought a smile to my lips, right before I puked.

When I made my way to the kitchen, I found a note on the table, written on the back of a Stop-N-Go receipt. Next to it was my Wish List, which now had tiny check marks next to the numbers one, ten, fourteen and eighteen.

I picked up the gas pump receipt, the print small enough to fit on the three-inch long paper.

Rose,

I hope you feel okay today. Be sure to drink lots of water and I'll check on you later.

Joe

PS. In case you missed it last night, I really like your hair.

I clutched the receipt to my chest. My first note from a boy. Well, a man. Joe definitely wasn't a boy. Giddiness washed through me, in spite of my overall ickiness. I really wanted to share this with Violet, but I wondered if she was still mad.

The wooden box on the kitchen table caught

my eye. I had to tell Violet about the will and I needed to figure out where I would live. The thought of moving away from Joe filled me with sadness. *You're getting ahead of yourself. There's nothing between you and Joe.* But I hoped there was anyway.

I picked up the phone, took a deep breath and called Violet. She answered, her tone cool but not as chilly as before. Of course, she knew it was me from her caller ID.

"I miss you, Violet. I don't want to fight anymore."

"I miss you too. I'm sorry. Do you forgive me?"

I started to cry. "Of course! You're my sister, I *have* to forgive you."

We laughed, still awkward in our reconciliation.

"Look, Violet, we need to talk about Momma's will."

"Oh! How could I forget all about that? I'm sure it won't be that big a deal."

I forced cheerfulness into my voice. "I wondered if I could run over later and we could look over it?"

"Sure, want to come over for lunch? Then we can chat while Ashley and Mikey nap."

Lunch sounded like a terrible idea. The March of Protest began rumbling in my gut at the thought of it. "How about I skip lunch and come at naptime. My stomach hasn't been the best."

"Oh sure, darlin'. It's probably nerves."

I wanted to say, *No, I'm sure it's the beer,* but didn't trust Violet's reaction, so I said nothing.

"Why don't you come around two?"

I hoped that gave me enough time to get myself together. "Yeah, see you then."

I got a glass of water and lay down in my bed. I had woken up there that morning, but for the life of me couldn't remember how I got there. The last thing I remembered was falling asleep on Joe's lap, which brought a combination of embarrassment and joy. The logical explanation was that Joe helped me get here. A moment of panic filled me at the thought of being so out of it that I didn't remember going to bed. But I woke up fully clothed, minus my shoes. If Joe wanted to take advantage of me, he would have done it when I flung myself at him.

I napped, and felt a little better when I got up. Crackers and a hot shower also helped. When I arrived at Violet's house, my stomach had settled, but my head still ached a bit, nothing I couldn't manage.

I placed the trunk in a large paper shopping bag. I figured it was part of the will so I should bring it to show Violet. But anxiety ate at me as I knocked on Violet's door. I told myself I had nothing to be nervous about. It couldn't get any worse.

When Violet opened the door, she pulled me into a hug, the bag banging against the door.

"What's that?" she asked.

"I'll tell you in a minute. Are the kids down for their nap?"

"Yeah, let's go into the kitchen."

Violet poured glasses of tea for both of us, which I had trouble choking down. I hadn't decided if I would admit to the getting-drunk part, but I knew I couldn't leave until I told her about the kissing part of the previous night.

I set the envelope on the table and slid it to her. "Read this."

I sat back, gnawing on my lower lip. Violet sensed my anxiety and narrowed her eyes as she picked up the envelope and pulled out the papers.

I watched her face as she read, her expression changing from concentration to surprise, then horror. She looked up with huge eyes, the color drained from her face. "Oh, my goodness! I had no idea! I swear to you, Rose. I had no idea."

"I know, Vi. I know you didn't."

"What are we gonna do?" Her question sounded like a wail.

"I don't know. I guess you need to decide what you're going to do with the house."

"But that's not right, Rose. It's not fair."

We sat in pain filled silence. Finally, I patted her hand. "It is what it is."

"But I don't want it all! I want you to have half."

I twisted my mouth into a lopsided smile. "I got something, too."

"What?"

I pulled the box out of the paper bag and set it on the table. "This."

"What in tarnation is *that?*"

"I believe it is the wooden box bequeathed to me in Momma's will. You'll see it on the next page."

Violet flipped the page, running her finger down the print until she found my name. After reading it, she looked up, fire burning in her eyes. "What the hell?"

"Violet Mae!"

"What kind of nonsense is this? *A wooden box?* What's in there?"

I scooted it toward her. "I have no idea. It's locked."

She fumbled with the padlock. "We have to figure out how to get this off."

"I know, but I have no idea how. I couldn't find the key." Part of me didn't care what was in there. Anything from Momma couldn't be good.

Violet grabbed a dishtowel and scrubbed the dust off the top of the box. "There's writing under all this dust!" She bent over the box again, invigorated by her discovery, and traced the etching with her fingers. "It says Dora."

"Who's Dora?" I couldn't remember Momma or Daddy ever mentioning a Dora.

"I don't know . . ." her voice trailed off as she turned the box around, looking for more clues. "It's kinda like our very own mystery."

My laugh was only slightly bitter. "Yeah, I

suppose it is. We could have our very own *Let's Make a Deal*. Violet Beauregard, do you want to trade your inheritance for the mysterious contents of a small wooden box?"

Violet's eyes grew misty. "Rose, I'm so sorry. Really, I am. I'll make this right. I promise."

"Maybe you should wait to see what's in the box before you go offerin' me anything. There might be a pirate's booty in there." I tried to sound light-hearted. None of this was Violet's fault. There was no sense making her feel bad.

"How can you tease like that? Momma cut you out of her will!"

"No, she didn't. She gave me a box. Besides, it was no secret Momma didn't like me. I'll admit to being pretty upset when I found out, but I've had time to get over it."

Mostly.

"I should have been there for you," she said, "but I was being stubborn and spiteful. I'm sorry."

"It's okay, water under the bridge and all that. But I have other news to tell you." My face lit up into a big smile, eager to change the subject.

Violet's eyes twinkled in anticipation. It wasn't like me to get so excited. "What?"

"I got my first kiss last night!"

Her face froze in horror. "You *what?*"

I pinched my lips together in disappointment. That was not the reaction I expected. I lifted my chin in defiance. "I said I got my first kiss. And it was *wonderful,* thank you very much for asking."

She raised her hands in surrender. "Okay, back up. When? Where? Who?"

"Last night. On my front porch. Joe." I felt like I was playing a game of Clue.

She looked confused. "Joe? Joe who?"

I rolled my eyes. "Joe McAllister, my next door neighbor. Joe."

Indignation filled her eyes. "Did he take advantage of you?"

"No! It was nothing like that. We were sittin' on the front porch, drinking Uncle Earl's beer . . ."

"You were drinkin' *beer?*" Her voice raised several decibels.

"Sure, why not? Uncle Earl does."

"And you were drinkin' it on the front porch? In front of all the neighbors? The ones who think you murdered our mother less than a week ago? *And you kissed him? On the front porch?*"

I sighed in disappointment. "I thought you would be happy for me. Why just a week ago you told me I should have sex."

"With a respectable man! And not less than week after our Momma was murdered!" My words must have sunk in because she gasped and clutched her hands to her chest. "Oh, my dear Lord. You didn't have sex with him, did you?"

"Yes, Violet," I said in a haughty tone. "I did. I had sex with him right there on the front porch, next to the pots of geraniums. I had to move 'em though so Mildred could get a better view." I had to wonder what the neighbors might have seen if Joe hadn't turned me down.

"*Rose!*"

"And why would you think Joe isn't respectable? You don't know anything about him."

"Exactly my point, Rose. We don't know anything about him. Where does he work? What does he do? We don't know about his family."

Anger rose up and my hands balled up into fists in my lap. "There you go, to the heart of the matter. You don't know anything about his *family,* so that makes him suspect."

"That's not it, at all. He's takin' advantage of you at a vulnerable time. I don't trust him."

We sat in silence, my heart breaking that we were fighting again. What had happened to us?

Violet cleared her throat. "If you would like to go out on a date, I am sure Mike knows someone we could fix you up with."

"What?"

"You need to go out with a respectable man, from a good family. We can help you with that." The way she squared her shoulders told me she had made up her mind and wouldn't back down.

"So let me get this straight, if I want a boyfriend, you're gonna *get me one,* one from a respectable family?" I waited for her to deny it. She didn't. "Oh my stars! You are! That's exactly what you're sayin'! You think I'm incapable of getting a boyfriend on my own?"

"Rose, be sensible. You are completely inexperienced. You are twenty-four years old and never had a boyfriend."

"There are multiple reasons why . . ."

"Rose, reasons be damned, you are naive. Men will take advantage of you, honey. We have to make sure that you date men who will appreciate your . . . lack of dating history."

I stood up. "I can *not* believe you are doin' this." I grabbed the box and put it in the bag.

"Rose!" Violet protested. "Just think about it, sweetie. I love you. I don't want you to get hurt."

"Violet, I am not a child." I picked up my purse and the bag. "You have got to stop treating me like one."

"What has gotten into you, Rose?" she asked, following me to the door.

"I'm growing up, Violet. Deal with it."

I got in my car and drove out of her neighborhood, not ready to go home yet. She hadn't told me what she wanted to do with the house. Everything was a mess.

I drove past the dress shop and stopped on a whim. I felt good about how I looked at the visitation and funeral, and I was tired of wearing baggy, shapeless clothes. Besides, I could hear Violet in my head whining, "What will people say?" That settled it. I was shopping.

The saleswoman from the other day stood by the clearance rack when I entered the store. She saw me and did a double take. "You cut your hair."

I couldn't get over everyone's fascination with my hair. I half-smiled in response.

She seemed to forget the awkwardness of the vision I had of her daughter and helped me pick out several outfits. If I was gonna change, I was gonna change everything, ugly clothes included.

I left with multiple bags and lots of dollars poorer, but eager to get home. And hopefully see Joe.

I didn't see his car in the driveway when I pulled up, but I expected him to be at work. I went inside and boxed up most of my old clothes. I tried on one of my new outfits, a pair of capris and a sleeveless blouse. When I stared at myself in the mirror, I looked and felt like a different person. How was that possible?

I went out into the kitchen for a glass of water and noticed a message on the machine, realizing I'd forgotten to check it when I came home since I rarely got calls.

"Rose, hi. It's Joe. I just wanted to check on you and see how you're feeling. Umm . . . hey, if you're not busy, uh . . . I wondered if you might want to have dinner with me tonight. I should be home around six and we can figure something out. Bye." When the machine beeped, my smile rivaled the width of the Grand Canyon.

He wanted to eat dinner with me. I wondered if this counted as a date, then practically danced in the kitchen. Yes, it was a date. My first date.

I was really glad I went shopping.

I'd be a nervous wreck thinking about it until he got home so I needed something to occupy me. I could take my old clothes to the thrift store. I briefly considered starting to pack up Momma's stuff but didn't feel right doing it alone. Maybe I'd call Violet later and see if she wanted to help.

I loaded up my car and drove to the charity. I dropped off the clothes and returned home around five-thirty, surprised that Joe's car was in his driveway. When I got out of the car, he burst out the front door, his eagerness catching me by surprise. I met him in my driveway, my face beaming with happiness.

Joe looked serious when he reached me and he took my hands in his. "Rose." He stopped and smiled a sad smile. "How do you get more beautiful every time I see you?"

The heat rose to my face in spite of my attempt to stop it, but my heart was beaming with sunshine. He kissed me right there in my driveway, in broad daylight. But seconds later, he pulled back abruptly.

"Rose, I have to cancel tonight. I'm sorry to do it last-minute."

If we hadn't just kissed, I would have considered that he changed his mind about me, but his lips said otherwise. "That's okay." I wanted to ask why, but stopped, worried I might not want to know.

A car pulled up in front of his house.

"Oh, you havin' company?" I asked. The Busybody Club said he hadn't had anyone visit since he moved in.

"Yeah, a guest for the weekend. It was very last-minute." He sounded so nervous. And sorry.

"Okay . . ." my voice trailed off as a young woman got out of the car then opened the back door. A German shepherd jumped out. The woman looked over at us, the dog prancing beside her. She smiled as she approached, holding the dog's leash. I wondered if she was Joe's sister, although I didn't see much resemblance. She had red hair and was fair-complected while Joe had brown hair and was tanned.

Normally, I would have just stood there. Truth be told, normally I wouldn't have been there in the first place. The Old Rose didn't talk to people if she could help it. I decided the New Rose needed to act like a grown-up. It seemed strange Joe hadn't introduced us, so I plastered a smile on my face and forced brightness into my voice. "Hi, I'm Rose. I live next door."

She came closer and put her hand on Joe's shoulder. The way she claimed his shoulder, her fingers curling around his arm, I knew before she even said the words. "Hi, I'm Joe's girlfriend, Hilary."

My first instinct was to burst into tears and run away, but instead, I kept the fake smile frozen on my face. "How lovely to meet you." I was proud of myself. It sounded like something Violet would say. "I'm sure Joe is very excited you're here to visit." I cocked my head to grace him with my cheesy smile.

Joe looked like he wanted to hit someone.

"We should go inside, Joe," Hilary said, tugging his arm. "We have a lot of catching up to do."

He stumbled backwards, his face making a strange choking expression. Then he turned around and marched into the house with Hilary.

My feet rooted themselves to the driveway while my mind tried to figure out what happened. Joe's front door had hardly slammed shut before angry voices drifted out. I hoped she reamed him. I knew I wanted to, but instead I was stuck, unintentionally eavesdropping on their argument, although I only caught snippets of phrases.

Finally, my feet magically freed themselves. I turned around and walked into my house, feeling like an idiot. Violet was right. I had no idea how to date. What just transpired proved that. I picked up the phone and dialed her number.

"Hey, Violet, I was wondering if you wanted to help me clean out Momma's room this weekend."

"I'm sure I can get Mike to watch the kids for a

few hours tomorrow afternoon. How does that sound?"

"Great." I said in my forced happy tone. It scared me how easy it had become to use. "Say, Vi, I was thinkin' after I left." I paused. No chickening out now. "I think you might have been right. I'm really new to all this dating stuff and maybe it would be a good idea if you found someone for me to go out with." Better to let her think that than for her to know this was a rebound date. Leave it to me to have my first date be a rebound.

"Really?" She squealed.

I cringed. "Yeah, do you think you can arrange it?"

"I know I can. I'll call you back in a bit, okay?" She sounded so happy I wished I had agreed to this years ago. Not for me, but for her. All those years wasted looking for the perfect Christmas gift. Who knew I only had to let her play match-maker?

About fifteen minutes later the phone rang.

"Tomorrow night," Violet said, so excited she choked out the words. "You have a date tomorrow night!" Then she squealed again.

I held the phone a few inches away from my ear until she stopped. "Yay," I said with forced enthusiasm, although Violet didn't seem to notice.

"His name is Steve and he's an electrician. He works for Mike and his dad's construction business. He's twenty-six and never been married. His family has been around forever. His parents live on Maple Street. His dad works at the paper plant and his mother is a bookkeeper. Steve is so excited to meet you."

I almost asked Violet if I could see his pedigree papers, but thought better of it.

"He'll pick you up tomorrow at seven. Oh!" she gushed. "I can help you get ready and pick out your clothes. It will be like it should have been in high school."

Pretending we were in high school was a sobering thought, but it made me happy to hear Violet so excited. "That will be so fun!" I hoped my words didn't sound as fake as I felt.

Violet didn't notice. "I'll come over at two. We'll have time to work on Momma's room and then you can get ready."

"Sounds great."

I hung up, hoping I made the right decision. I told myself it was just a date. It wasn't like I was going to marry him.

But I couldn't stop myself from wondering what Joe would think.

Chapter Nine

The next afternoon Violet showed up at my door, her arms loaded with clothes.

"We're supposed to be taking clothes *out,* not in," I said as I held the door open for her.

She took one look at me and raised her eyebrows. "What are you wearing? Where did you get that?"

I had on a pair of jeans that Momma never would have approved of and a cute T-shirt that actually clung to the curves of my body. "I bought it yesterday and some other clothes too. I decided to embrace the new me."

I expected to embrace Violet's wrath with my proclamation, but she surprised me by eyeing me from head to toe, her arms still full. "I approve. Very cute. You might not need these after all."

"What is all that?" I asked as she dumped them on the kitchen table.

"Some of my clothes, for you to wear on your date tonight. But we'll check out what you got later."

We headed back to Momma's room. Violet threw open the heavy drapes to let the sunlight in and dust flew in all directions.

"You would think the woman was a vampire the

way she kept this room so cave-like." Violet said, looking outside. "Hey, who's the woman in Joe's backyard?"

I moved to the window. "Don't ask." I noticed her dog bounding around the yard. It occurred to me her dog had been the dog in my vision about Joe and his fence.

Violet turned to me and put her hand on her hip. "But didn't you and Joe—"

"I said don't ask." I turned my back to her as I began to tape one of the multitude of boxes I bought earlier that morning.

We spent the afternoon going through Momma's drawers and closet, pulling out clothes and putting them in boxes. I had considered using garbage bags, but it seemed so irreverent. It was distressing enough to dispose of the contents of a person's life. In the end, trash bag or cardboard box, it didn't matter. A lifetime of possessions were just gone.

When I voiced my thoughts to Violet, she snorted. "Please. Momma got everything she deserved and not enough if you ask me. Her will is livin' proof of that."

"But Aunt Bessie said that we didn't know everything. She said Daddy did something that nearly broke Momma."

Violet stopped folding the pants in her hands. "Daddy never hurt a soul. How could his own sister say that?"

I shrugged. "I pretty much told her the same thing, but Aunt Bessie said I'd want answers some day and she would tell me what she knew. She said Momma had a reason for being the way she was."

Violet scowled. "I cannot believe you are defendin' her, especially after what she did to you." She took the pants and spiked them into the box next to her to prove her point. "I'm still going to make this right, by the way."

"But Violet, what if it's true. What if Momma had an excuse for doing what she did."

Anger burned in Violet's eyes. "I don't care what happened to her. There is no reason that could excuse the way she treated us, most of all you."

Her tone told me she refused to discuss it any further. I was fine with that. I didn't like to think of Daddy doing anything so bad he could break someone.

Boxing up Momma's possessions was an easy job since we never considered keeping anything, not even for a memento. At five o'clock, Violet announced we were done for the day even though we hadn't finished everything.

"Time to go through your clothes and get ready for your date." She sat on my bed, clutching a pillow to her chest as I pulled my new clothing out of my closet and drawers to show her. "Bravo!" she said and clapped when I finished. "I love them."

"Really?" Her reaction at the funeral made me wary of her acceptance, but I had to admit I had caught her off-guard then.

"Yes, very tasteful and much more age-appropriate. You always looked like a Mini-Me of Momma before." She shuddered as she said the words.

I considered protesting, but she was right. "So, what do you think?" I asked. "What should I wear?"

Violet picked out a skirt and blouse and told me to take a shower and wash my hair. She would wait for me.

When I got out and dressed, Violet brought in my Walmart receipt. "What's this?"

"It's my Wish List," I said, brushing my damp hair.

"What kind of Wish List?"

"I don't know, things I want to accomplish before I die. Or more specifically, before I get arrested."

"Rose! Don't say such a thing! You're not gonna get arrested."

I didn't want to think about it, especially since I was preparing for my first date ever. "I certainly hope not, but it's something I have to consider. There's circumstantial evidence. Deanna Crawfield says it's a possibility."

Violet frowned. "I refuse to consider it. You didn't do it and they'll catch whoever did." She turned her attention to the receipt. "This is an odd list."

"Maybe for you, but it's mine."

"I noticed you checked off *kiss a man*."

"I already told you I had. That should come as no surprise."

"I hoped it was some kind of rebellious exaggeration. But now that you mention it, why are you so eager to go on a date after your wonderful kiss? Does it have anything to do with the woman in Joe's backyard?" She looked a little too smug.

"I told you I don't wanna talk about it."

Violet tried to hide her smile but not soon enough. "Go blow dry your hair and I'll show you how to put on makeup. That is if Aunt Bessie didn't show you already."

Aunt Bessie had, but it was all so foreign to me. I figured I'd need to be shown multiple times before I felt comfortable putting it on. Violet had brought some of her makeup, thinking I might not have any of my own, which I didn't. Yet.

I already felt like I was moving at light speed. Every time I saw myself in the mirror I paused, startled by the stranger looking back at me. This new person still took some getting used to. I'd told Violet that it was just hair, but it was more. It signaled the shedding of my old life. When Momma died, the padlock to my jail cell fell off, making me free. While I burst out running with my freedom, every once in a while I had to stop and figure out where I'd run to.

When Violet finished applying my makeup, which was thankfully very little, she gave me a good look-over and declared me ready. I still had twenty minutes until Steve showed up.

"So what's Steve look like?" I asked, putting away the clothes I had pulled out earlier.

"He's got blond hair and blue eyes and is cute as a button."

Granted, I was new to the whole dating world but *cute as a button* didn't sound like the way a woman wanted her date described.

Violet planted herself in a chair and turned on the television.

"What are you doing?" I asked.

She flipped through channels with the remote. "I'm searching for a show that isn't animated and doesn't involve cars or guns."

"But why are you searching for it *here?*"

She glanced up and smiled, wickedness twinkling in her eyes. "Because I can't watch that at home. If I didn't know better, Rose, I would suspect you're tryin' to get rid of me."

She was right. I wished she'd leave, but technically, it was her house now, a subject we still needed to address. But not right at that moment, minutes before Steve showed up.

"You're not going to embarrass me are you?"

She touched her hand to her chest and her eyes

grew wide with fake innocence. "Of course not."

"I'm warnin' you Violet Mae, you embarrass me when he shows up and I'm not leaving with him."

She held her hands up in surrender. "All right, all right, I won't embarrass you. I just want to make sure you get off okay, since it's your first date and all."

I grumbled and walked into the kitchen to get a glass of water, unable to stop myself from looking out the window into Joe's backyard. The dog wasn't there and when I craned my neck to look out the front, I didn't see his girlfriend's car either.

A loud thumping on the front door broke my concentration and I smacked my head into the window. Steve was early. Rubbing my forehead, I walked to the front door while I shot a look of warning at Violet, who was already getting up. She sat down in the chair, a grin on her face. I grasped the doorknob, took a deep breath, and opened it.

Joe stood in front of me, wearing a sheepish look. I turned back around to see Violet stretching her neck, trying to get a look out the opening.

"It's not him. I'll be back in a second." I slipped out the door and shut it behind me. "What are you doin' here?" I hissed. "Shouldn't you be with your girlfriend?"

"Rose, that's why I'm here . . . to explain." The look on his face told me he was prepared to do a lot of digging to get himself out of his mess.

I had to admit he looked good, really good, but I couldn't let his looks sway me. "I'm not interested in anything you have to say. You tricked me into thinking you liked me." I kept my back to the door and I turned the knob to go inside.

"But I do like you, Rose, if you'll just let me explain."

"I don't have time for your explanation. My date will show up any minute and I don't want you standing here when he does."

"Your *date?*" The expression on his face said that was the last thing he expected to hear.

I walked closer to him. "What? You think I'm incapable of gettin' a date, Joe McAllister? Is that why you thought you could lie to me when you really had a girlfriend?"

His eyes widened in what appeared to be genuine surprise. "No, Rose, of course not, and I didn't lie. I swear."

I opened the door and looked over my shoulder at him. "Go swear somewhere else, Joe. I don't wanna hear it."

I shut the door on him, amazed at myself for standing up to him, even if I was shaking.

"What was that all about?" Violet asked.

"I don't want to talk about it," I said walking away. "Don't you need to be goin' somewhere?" I was irritated that I let Joe get to me. I didn't want to go on my first date in a foul mood. I hid in the bathroom and tried to calm my nerves when I heard another knock a few minutes later.

"I'll get it!" Violet called from the living room.

"No, you *won't!*" I said, hurrying out of the bathroom. "I'll get it." I stopped at the door and took a deep breath before I opened it.

Mildred stood in the doorway. I groaned and instantly regretted it.

"Now listen here, young lady. I knowed you been raised betta than that. And don't think your little show on the front porch the other night escaped my notice."

I doubted I could juggle fruit on the front porch at three a.m. and escape Mildred's notice. "I'm sorry, Miss Mildred. I was expecting someone else."

"Yeah, the playboy that moved in next door to ya, huh? Well, I seen he's already been here too. I'm surprised you two weren't performin' vile acts in broad daylight again."

All I needed was for Steve to show up and hear Mildred talking about me making out with Joe. I turned to Violet in desperation, but she had already gotten out of the chair and walked up behind me.

"Well, hello, Miss Mildred! What do we owe the pleasure of your visit tonight?" Violet's cheerful voice cut the tension in the air.

"I saw your car in the driveway and wanted to come tell you hello."

I sincerely doubted the truthfulness of that

statement. Violet's car had been in the driveway all afternoon.

Violet put her hand on Mildred's arm and pulled her through the front door. "How sweet of you! Why don't you come in and have a glass of tea with me?"

"Don't forget to put your jam away when you get home," I told Mildred, silently cursing my visions while I shut the door.

Mildred grumbled as she moved past me, giving me an evil glare. She had never hid the fact that she shared Momma's belief in my demon possession. Violet gave me a wink as they left the room. I had to admit, I owed her.

There was another knock. My front door had seen more action in one evening than it had in the last two months. I took another deep breath and opened it, half expecting to see Joe again. Instead, I saw the Pillsbury Doughboy, or as close to what I'd ever see in real life. He was missing the chef's hat and the kerchief, but his face was a pasty white and chubby, with big wide eyes like the Doughboy. His button-down shirt barely contained his wide, round gut, and the buttons threatened to pop. I resisted the urge to poke his belly with my finger to hear him giggle.

"Rose?" he asked, his voice shaking from fear. At least I think it was fear, from the look of pure terror on his face.

Nope, no giggling.

"Steve?" I asked, but I already knew it was him from the tie he wore and the Walmart flowers he held in his hand. Either that or he was a really generous Jehovah's Witness. "It's very nice to meet you." I said, trying to sound cheerful.

He stood in silence, staring at me with his big round eyes.

"Do you want to come in?" I raised my eyebrows in a happy, questioning look.

He remained rooted to the porch. It occurred to me perhaps Joe or Mildred had applied Super Glue on the wood slats.

"I'll just grab my purse," I said and he thrust the flowers toward me. "Oh, are those for me? Why, thank you!" I took the flowers, leaving the door open and Steve on the porch.

"Here!" I shoved the flowers at Violet in the kitchen. "Take care of these."

Violet's face lit up like a kid getting cotton candy at the carnival. "He brought you flowers?"

I glared at her.

"Who brought y'all flowers? The devil next door?"

"No, Miss Mildred." Violet said, patting Mildred's arm. "It's Rose's date."

"Date?" Mildred crowed. "After she carried on with that Yankee?"

"Don't worry, Miss Mildred. Steve's a good boy, good Henryetta stock. He's Stan Morris' grandson."

I already regretted agreeing to this date and I hadn't even left yet. I grabbed my purse and headed out the front door before Mildred and Violet decided to start checking Steve's teeth. He stood exactly where I left him, wearing the same terrified expression, except he leaned to the side. I worried he would fall over trying to see something in the living room.

"Looking for something?" I asked, glancing over my shoulder.

If possible, his eyes got even bigger as he violently shook his head.

I shut the door as I realized what he was looking for—evidence of Momma's murder. We started walking across the porch to the steps and I caught the glance he shot my direction, a look of fear. *He thinks I killed Momma.* There was no way I could go out with him. What I couldn't figure out is why he agreed to go out with me in the first place.

I stood next to the passenger door of Steve's car. "Steve, I . . ." My words stopped on my tongue. Joe sat on his front porch, drinking a beer and watching my every move with a suspicious glint in his eye.

Crappy doodles.

Steve waited for me to finish.

I smiled up at him with my sweetest smile, which I hoped would convince him I was incapable of murdering anyone, least of all my own Momma. "I just wanted to tell you how delighted I am that you're taking me out to dinner." I said loud enough for Joe to hear. To finish it off, I raised up on my toes and kissed Steve on his pasty cheek, surprised it didn't taste like biscuit dough. I hoped Joe didn't see Steve cringe at the contact.

I sat in the front seat, waiting for Steve to get in, smiling my fake happy smile. I was almost surprised to see him get in, half expecting him to run screaming down the street. I had to admit he had a nice car, one he probably didn't want to leave behind with a murderer. If I could murder my own Momma, I bet he could only imagine what I would do to his poor Buick.

We drove to the restaurant in silence, me fidgeting with my hands on my lap and Steve gripping the steering wheel with both hands, hanging on for dear life. He occasionally darted looks toward me out of the corner of his eye as if I was gonna attack him at any moment.

Steve pulled into the parking lot of Jaspers, one of Henryetta's nicest restaurants, which wasn't saying much. People in Henryetta weren't that fancy, in spite of all their bloodline talk. But Jaspers was a decent steak house, or so I heard. I'd never been there.

Steve opened my car door and the door to the restaurant, like a good upstanding boy from the South would. Any Southern mother who found out her son didn't hold a door open for a female of any age would get his ears boxed, regardless of the woman's criminal history.

After we were seated, I appraised Steve while he scoured his menu. He wasn't an unattractive man, just plenty soft around the edges and then some. He didn't see much sun either, from the look of his skin. I had suspected electricians were a little rougher. More like Joe, a thought I instantly squashed down.

There was no Joe.

"So Steve, Violet tells me you're an electrician," I said in a voice so sugar-laden that I expected to be attacked by a swarm of honeybees. Someone had to start a conversation or I would choke on the fear oozing out of Steve's pores.

He looked up startled. "Yeah." Then he jerked his head back down again.

I sighed. This was gonna be a long night.

"I've never been here before. Do you recommend anything?"

He mumbled something inaudible.

I debated letting it go but decided I'd make him talk to me whether he wanted to or not. Then I realized how ridiculous the whole situation was and burst out laughing.

Steve's head popped up, wide-eyed, mouth dropping open. He looked like he expected me to start waving a rolling pin around any minute. I wondered again why he asked me out. Then it came to me, as obvious as Suzanne's bleached hair. Mike was Steve's boss. Mike had forced him into it.

I was on a pity date. Only worse.

Just when I was about to excuse myself to the restroom, the waitress showed up to take our drink orders. Steve mumbled his drink to the waitress, who had to ask him to repeat it twice. I ordered water. I almost ordered wine, to knock number nine off my list, but didn't want to waste it on Steve.

"So, Steve, how long have you worked for Mike?"

Still looking down, Steve mumbled something.

"I'm sorry, I couldn't quite hear you. What was that?"

"Four years."

The waitress returned with our drinks and took our orders. Disappointment dampened my hunger, but I decided to get a big dinner and take the leftovers home. I felt a momentary bit of guilt over spending Steve's money frivolously, but decided he could deal with it. Sure, he might be miserable, but so was I.

Rose Gardner was done accepting miserable.

I ordered a big steak with a baked potato and a salad. The waitress walked away and Steve no longer had his menu to hide behind.

We sat in silence, despite my continued attempts at getting him to talk. Finally, I gave up. I checked out the decor and the other patrons. My eyes roamed halfway around the room stopping for a couple of minutes on a big group celebrating someone's birthday. I smiled, wishing I was with them, and then my gaze moved a couple of tables away.

I locked eyes with Daniel Crocker, the man that triggered my vision at the DMV. He sat with four other men. The others were involved in what appeared to be a serious conversation, but he watched me with open curiosity. I looked away, a blush beginning to flush my cheeks. Did he know who I was?

I excused myself to go to the restroom. Steve looked eager for me to go, and I rushed down the hall. Why would Daniel Crocker be looking at me? Was he the one who murdered my mother? I couldn't imagine that he knew it was me. Even if he remembered me from the DMV, I looked completely different now.

Violet had put a compact of powder and tube of lipstick in my purse. I applied both, taking an ample amount of time on each. When I couldn't stall any longer, I went back out to the table only to find Steve's chair empty.

I sat down, wondering if he had gone to the bathroom, too. After a few minutes, the waitress returned with my food. She looked apologetic.

"Your date said he suddenly didn't feel well and had to go. But he paid for your dinner and left money for you to take a taxi home."

I felt like crying although, for the life of me, I couldn't figure out why. I didn't even like him. But if someone like him dumped me, then I really was a pathetic loser.

"Could you just box it up?" I asked. "I think I'll take it to go." I stood up and grabbed my purse. "In fact, I'll just wait out front." I couldn't stand the embarrassment of waiting alone at the table.

She patted my arm. "For what it's worth, sweetie, you can do a whole lot better than that weasel. You go wait in the bar. My name's Bridgette. Tell the bartender I sent you over and he'll take care of you. I'll box this up and bring it over."

The crowded bar roared with conversation, not surprising on a Saturday night. I spotted an open stool at the counter and sat down. The bartender walked over.

"What can I get for ya, darlin'?"

"Um, Bridgette said to tell you she sent me over." I had no idea why, but I couldn't see a reason not to tell him.

"Oh, so *you're* her." He looked me over. "Bridgette told me what happened. I can't figure out why a guy would walk away from you, darlin'. His loss." He shook his head. "Drink's on the house. What's it gonna be?"

"Uh, a glass of wine?"

"Red? White?"

I had no idea. "White?"

"Chardonnay, Pinot Grigio . . ." his list

continued and I was lost. He saw the confusion on my face and laughed. "Not a wine drinker, eh?"

He was a burly looking guy, with tattoos and piercings, but he had a friendly face. His nametag said Sloan. For whatever reason, I trusted him. "Honestly, I'm not really a drinker at all. I only had my first drink a few days ago."

"Ah, a virgin in our midst."

I felt my face burn and only seconds later realized he meant a virgin *drinker*.

"Don't worry, darlin', I'll take good care of you. Be right back."

I waited for Sloan to return with my drink, when I heard a voice in my ear.

"What's a pretty little thing like you doin' alone? Where'd that Great White Whale get off to?"

I turned around, half expecting Joe to be standing behind me. Instead, it was Daniel Crocker. My heart leapt into my throat.

"Uh . . ."

He slid in between my stool and the one next to me, which was occupied by a woman deep in conversation with the man beside her.

He leaned his head close to mine. "I'm Dan. What's your name?"

I froze in panic. I knew I had to say something. "Rose."

"Ah, a fittin' name for a beautiful flower such as yourself. Can I get you a drink?"

"I . . . I already have one. Coming. He's bringin'

it." I was babbling like an idiot. I had to get it together.

He laughed. "Do I make you nervous, Rose?"

I resisted the urge to bolt from the room and run all the way home. I had to find out if he had something to do with Momma's murder, or at the very least if he recognized me. The latter was answered immediately.

"Do I know you from somewhere?" He tilted his head to the side to study me. "You look so familiar."

I shook my head. "No, I don't think so. I'm sure I would remember you." He looked different than he did in the DMV. That Friday afternoon, he had been scruffy and unshaven. Tonight he was cleaned up and I had to admit he looked much better, but he exuded an aura that left me feeling oily.

"I'm usually pretty good with faces and I'm sure I've seen yours, I just can't figure out where. Hmm . . ."

Sloan returned with my wine and glanced at Daniel, then raised his eyebrows. My eyes widened and I hope I conveyed my concern. Sloan's smile fell and he engaged in a stare-off with Daniel. "What can I get for you, Dan?"

I about fell off my stool when I realized Sloan knew him.

"I'll take a draft beer, and if I can work it out, this pretty little thing."

Sloan leaned forward looking into Dan's face, all friendliness gone. If I had walked in and encountered this Sloan, I would have waited in the lobby instead of at the bar. "This here's my little sister. I suggest you go pick up some other 'pretty little thing'."

Daniel Crocker's body jerked, his face turning a bright red that I suspected wasn't from embarrassment. He and Sloan glared at each other a bit longer. Daniel's eyelid twitched. His face lit up with an evil grin. "It's not like she was wearing a fuckin' sign or anything." He left without his beer.

"Thanks," I said, humiliated that I needed saving. I had to admit I wasn't sorry he left even if I hadn't gotten any information out of him.

Sloan watched him walk away then gave me a half-hearted smile. "Well, since you told me you were new to drinkin', that pretty much told me you were new to hanging out in a bar, too. You gotta watch out for guys like him. They'll see you as fresh meat, no offense."

"None taken." I was clueless to the minds of men.

"You look really green. They'll latch on and try to take advantage of you. If you're gonna hang out in bars, you're gonna need to be more assertive."

"Thanks."

"I'll keep an eye on ya. When you're ready to go, just let me know and I'll call a taxi."

"Thanks, Sloan." I took a sip of my wine while

166

I tried to calm my nerves. I welcomed the warm tingly feeling, but decided I would only have one. I couldn't risk acting like I had with Joe. Heavens knew that someone like Dan wouldn't stop because I was drunk, making me appreciate what Joe had done that much more.

Melancholy washed over me thinking about Joe, bringing confusion with it. I thought he liked me until I found out he had a girlfriend. I tried to cheer myself up knowing I had just taken care of two more things, drinking wine and going to a bar. Five items done. Twenty-three to go. But sadness overshadowed my joy.

I asked Sloan to call for a cab.

I gave myself a pep talk during the short taxi ride home. First, Daniel Crocker was some weird coincidence and had nothing to do with Momma's murder. While I had to admit he was slimy, my overactive imagination tied him to her death. Surely, murderers didn't lounge around bars trying to pick up women. Wouldn't they be hiding out?

Second, it was Steve's loss. I wasn't the only woman to have an awful date, even an awful first date. I could do better. There were other fish in the sea. And all those other idioms. I actually felt better when the driver pulled up in front of my house. Until I discovered Joe still sitting on his front porch. I got out and walked to the side door, trying to pretend he didn't exist.

"Where'd your date go?" Joe called out.

Ignore him.

"Did you kill him before he could bring you home?"

I wanted to tell him that murder was nothing to joke about, but had to admit that Steve being so scared of me was a tiny bit funny, especially since I was half his size.

"You're goin' to run out of rolling pins soon."

I jerked my head around and glared at him. *Don't answer him!* I fumbled in my purse, looking for my keys, cursing myself for not digging them out in the cab. I found them and hurried to open the locks—the locks Joe installed for me—before I did something I would regret. My heart was already beginning to soften. That wasn't good.

"Rose, can't we just talk about it? Please?" His tone had changed, the teasing gone. I wanted to talk to him so bad, and do even more with him something fierce, but I couldn't trust him and I didn't trust me. I went inside, shutting the door behind me.

Joe McAllister couldn't be part of my life.

Chapter Ten

The phone rang nonstop for an hour after I came home. I finally answered, deciding I couldn't avoid talking to Violet any longer. She apologized profusely, and although she didn't deny that Mike forced Steve into the date, she didn't admit to it either.

The next afternoon she came back to take care of the rest of Momma's things. While we sorted through boxes and photos in Momma's closet, we discussed what to do with the house. Violet was adamant we split it fifty/fifty. We decided to have a couple of real estate agents come give us an estimate of the value of the house and go from there.

The next morning was Monday. Time for me to go back to work. I set my alarm earlier than usual since it took me a bit longer to get ready than it used to—the only downside to my new hair.

I walked into the DMV, my thermal mug of coffee in my hand, expecting the stares of my coworkers but still not fully prepared either.

"Well look at you, Miss Rose, all purty." Betty crooned. "What happened, did you go and find yourself a man?"

I laughed, feeling a blush creeping its way up

my neck. "No, my aunt came to visit. She's a hairdresser and she cut my hair. It's no big deal."

Suzanne, shot a sneer in my direction. "Somebody got new clothes, too. What happened to the gunny sacks?"

I shrugged.

"Looks like your mother's death agrees with you."

Her smug tone confirmed that she knew I was a suspect. I ignored her.

The morning went by quickly with lots of customers. Thankfully, most were pleasant and easy to please. Working at the DMV was a soul-sucking job. If I was changing the rest of my sad life, why not change my job too? The idea lit a spark of hope and I began to daydream about possible career choices. I called the next number and glanced up to see Daniel Crocker standing in front of me.

My eyes almost popped out of my head.

And from the look of him, his did too.

"You?" he asked.

I took his paperwork off the counter, wondering how he had gotten it back and why he hadn't processed it already. But then I remembered his insurance card had expired. Maybe he had just got it replaced.

He rubbed his chin, then leaned his forearm on the counter, looking down at me in confusion.

"Weren't you the girl who fainted last time I was here?"

I gave him a tiny smile. "I don't know, maybe." I checked his paperwork. Everything seemed to be in order this time.

"How many of y'all faint around here anyway?" he asked in amazement.

"Well . . . I guess I'm the only one," I answered, trying to shrink into my chair.

"Sloan isn't your brother, is he?"

Crap, crap, crap. "Why do you ask that?" I asked, trying to keep my voice cheerful and professional.

"He's a cop, isn't he?"

My head shot up, my eyes wide in shock.

He leaned his head over the counter. "So I guessed right, huh?"

I had no earthly idea what he was talking about. "You really must have us mixed up with someone else. Sloan's just a bartender and I work at the DMV." I grabbed a sticker out of the drawer and stapled it to his registration paperwork. "See? I process license plates," I said with a forced smile. "Everything is in order this time and you're all set." I handed him his forms. "You have a nice day now."

He gave me a snarly glare, then walked away, looking over his shoulder.

"Jeez, I'm glad you processed him," Suzanne said. "He stalked this place all last week. He'd come in and look around and leave, sometimes coming in a couple of times a day. I wanted to call the police but Betty wouldn't let me. Guess he had a thing for you. Go figure." She said the last part with disgust. Almost as if she were jealous.

I tried to figure out what happened. Why did he ask if Sloan was a cop? And even if he was, what did that have to do with me? I didn't have time to dwell on it, because the rest of the day was one big swarm of customers with complicated issues. It didn't help matters that I told one man he would be in a fender bender the next day and a woman that her deep freezer got unplugged.

By the time we closed, I was worn out and couldn't wait to get home to take a bath. I could enjoy one as long as I wanted without Momma pounding on the door, telling me I was taking too long. I tried to find some guilt over the thought, and finally found it, but I had to dig deep. I was sorry she got killed, but I didn't miss her harping on me all the time.

If that wasn't an evil thought, I didn't know what was.

When I pulled in next to the house, I couldn't stop myself from looking for Joe's car. I thanked God for the empty driveway; otherwise I wasn't sure I could be responsible for my actions. I missed him. How that was possible, I didn't know. I hardly knew him. I didn't even know what he did for a living, yet I missed him. I sounded like a hormone-riddled teenager. In a way, I supposed I was.

Dirty plates and glasses filled the sink. Part of me wanted to just leave them for the next day since no one forced me to do them now, but the responsible part of me said to wash them. Perhaps if I dragged the responsible Rose out, I could trust myself not to run across the driveway to talk to Joe.

I told myself I could take a bubble bath when I finished the dishes. A little motivation. I piled the dishes in the sink and started to wash. When I opened the dishtowel drawer, I was surprised to find a Walmart bag. It was the nightie I'd bought and stuffed in the drawer the afternoon Joe came over to help me paint.

I hurried through the dishes, casting glances at the Walmart bag. Maybe I could wear it after I took my bath. That sounded decadent. A bubble bath, *with candles*. Then the nightie. I was turning into a wanton woman. I smiled at the thought. Too bad none of those things marked anything off my list.

I filled the tub with warm water and a lavender bubble bath, an old birthday gift from Violet. I found some candles and lit them before sinking into the water with a book, relaxing in the warm glow of candlelight and the smell of lavender. I could get used to this.

When the water cooled off, I got out and patted

off with a towel, staring at the nightie that lay folded in a heap on the toilet seat. Could I really wear it?

Oh for heaven's sake Rose, it's a nightie you're going to wear in your own home. It's not like you're posing for Playboy.

I slipped my arms through the straps of the gown, letting the silky fabric slide down my body. I reveled in the feel of it and turned to look at myself in the mirror. For the first time, I felt sensuous. I knew I should feel evil, but I didn't.

I felt sexy.

I gasped at the thought. I'd never felt sexy in my life.

As I stood in front of the mirror, watching the silky fabric cling to my curves, I couldn't help but think it was a shame this didn't check anything off my list. Of course, there was the empty number twenty-nine. I could write *wear a nightie* in the spot, or *take a bath by candlelight*. But neither seemed big enough to put in the space. I'd leave it empty for now.

I went through the list from memory. Was there something else on there I could do tonight?

Dance. The conversation I had with Joe jostled its way into my head.

"You've never danced?"

"Nope."

"Now that's a damn shame. Everyone has danced in their living room."

I could dance in my living room.

I blew out the candles and made sure the curtains in the living room were closed. I had a CD player in the hall closet, but the only music I had was Momma's gospel CDs. I wasn't sure it was really possible to dance to gospel music, even if I got around the wrongness of it. Then I remembered Daddy had an old AM/FM radio he would sometimes listen to while working outside. Last time I'd seen it was out in the shed.

Grabbing an oversized sweater from my room, along with a flashlight and the key to the shed, I opened the side door. The coast was clear, so I hurried to the shed, not running but not walking either. A giant magnolia tree shaded the corner of the backyard, making it hard to see the padlock on the metal shed door. But I didn't want to turn on the flashlight until I got inside. What if someone saw me? After a bit of fumbling, I managed to get it unlocked. I slid the door open, trying to minimize the squeaking. During the daytime, it didn't sound so loud when I opened the door to get out the lawnmower, but in the quiet evening, it echoed off the trees.

I slipped through the small opening and cracked the door about six inches behind me, flinching at the screech. The air in the shed was stifling. I hadn't opened it in over a week, obvious from the slightly overgrown yard. The smell of gasoline and mildewed grass permeated the confined space, making me want to gag. I turned on the flashlight and edged my way past the mower toward the rear, stubbing my toe on the gas can. It banged into the metal wall, vibrating the sides with a loud rattle.

Crappy doodles.

I stopped, muttering to myself to be more careful. The radio wasn't going anywhere. I needed to slow down, but the confines of the space tested my rising anxiety, my claustrophobia eating at my nerves. Turning sideways, I slid past the mower and managed not to kick anything else. Daddy's old tools and odds and ends littered the rusted shelves against the back wall. The radio was tucked behind a power tool case on the top shelf. As I stretched to reach it, I heard the squeak of the metal door. I turned in panic and saw the door shut.

I was trapped inside the shed.

Later I thought of a handful of things I should of have done, but I didn't do any of them. Instead, I did the first thing that came to mind. I released a blood-curdling scream loud enough to rouse every neighbor in a two-block radius.

"Rose?" Joe's muffled voice called outside. The door scraped open and he filled the doorway. "What on earth are you doin' in here?"

I still stood on the chest, my arm reaching up, frozen. At least I had stopped screaming. Instead, I bawled like a baby, to my utter embarrassment.

"I was gettin' the radio . . . and the door closed . . . and I thought I was trapped . . ."

Joe pushed his way past the mower to reach me. "I heard noises out here and thought someone was prowling in your shed. I didn't know it was you."

He helped me work my way around the clutter into the night air. I couldn't make myself stop crying.

Joe leaned down and looked into my eyes, smoothing my hair with his hand. "Hey, are you okay?"

I nodded. Physically, I was fine, in spite of my shaking.

He pulled me into a hug and I laid my cheek against his chest, trying to compose myself.

"I didn't mean to scare you. I'm sorry." He rubbed my back.

"It's okay," I said, my tears finally subsiding. "I'm just terrified of being locked up."

"Why?"

"My Momma used to lock me in the closet sometimes." My voice trailed off in embarrassment. What on earth possessed me to confide that?

"Your mother locked you in a closet?" He sounded incredulous. "Why?"

"Punishment." I couldn't admit that she locked me up when I saw things about people. At first, she thought I was spying and she tried to teach me a lesson. Later, it was because I scared her.

"What on earth could you ever do to warrant such a thing?"

I didn't answer. Nothing could justify what I'd endured.

We stood there a moment, me in his arms, his breath in my hair. My fear dissipated, replaced with another reaction.

"What were you looking for in the shed?" Joe finally broke the silence.

"The radio, but I couldn't quite reach it."

Joe dropped his arms and went into the shed. "On the top shelf?"

"Yeah."

He emerged from the shed with the radio in his hand. It was old and encrusted in dirt. "Is this what you were after?" He held it out.

I nodded and took it from him. "Yes, thanks."

"Need anything else?"

I shook my head, still having trouble forming words.

He closed the shed and we walked in silence to my side door. I expected him to say something about the other night, to try to explain himself again. I'd listen this time, but he didn't.

I reached for the doorknob. "Thanks . . . I think." He helped me, but only after he scared the tarnation out of me.

"I'm sorry. I really was trying to help."

I hesitated, not ready for him to leave yet. "Would you like to come in?"

An array of emotions played across his face. First, happiness, from the way his eyes lit up. Then indecision dimmed the gleam. And at last, resignation. "I can't. I'm sorry."

"Oh . . . okay."

"I'm right next door if you need me." It came out as kind of a sigh.

I didn't answer, just went in and shut the door behind me. I took a couple of deep breaths while I tried to slow my racing heart.

I was too late. He'd changed his mind. I set the radio on the table, no longer wanting to dance.

I tossed and turned in bed, shadowy images haunting my sleep. I dreamed I heard glass breaking. And then realized I wasn't dreaming. I sat up in bed, straining to listen. Just when I was about to lay back down, I heard the creak of a window, the wood scraping the frame as it opened.

I jumped out of bed and stood in the doorway, trying to determine where the sound came from. *Momma's room.* I bolted down the hall and into her room, just as a dark figure dressed in black and wearing a stocking cap stuck his leg through the window and I screamed. He jerked his head up, whacking it into the window frame. I grabbed a broom I had left in the room when Violet and I cleaned and started beating the prowler, who hung half in and half out of the opening. My wild swinging broke the glass in the upper window.

The burglar worked himself out the window and fell to the ground, scrambling up and bolting toward Joe's house. It took me a second to realize I was still screaming.

Get a grip, Rose. He's gone.

I tried to turn on the lights, but whoever broke in must have cut the electricity. Again. I heard pounding on the side door, causing my panic to return. What if the intruder was trying to get in the side door?

"Rose!" Joe shouted between the banging. "If you don't open this door, I'm gonna break it down!"

Relieved, I shouted, "I'm coming, give me a second."

I fumbled with the locks and turned the knob just as Joe burst through, half-naked. He stood in front of me wearing nothing but a pair of boxer shorts.

"Are you okay? I heard you screaming and when I got outside, I saw someone running from your house. I tackled him, but he knocked me off and got away."

In the dim light of the streetlamp pouring through the window, I saw multiple scrapes covering his head and back.

"I'm fine," I said, trying to settle down. "I heard someone breaking in and found them halfway in the window, so I beat them with a broom 'til they fell out."

"Why would you *do* that? Why didn't you run away?"

I hadn't stopped long enough to reason it out. Joe was right. I should have run away, or at least called the police. More than likely, the person climbing through my window meant to kill me. I began to shake and collapsed in the kitchen chair next to me. I sucked in gasps of air as everything got fuzzy, now an all too familiar feeling; I was gonna pass out.

Joe figured it out as I did, kneeling beside me as he pushed my head between my knees. "You're all right. I'm not gonna let anything happen to you."

The feeling subsided and I sat up, still shaking with fear.

"Can you call the police now?" Joe asked.

His question caught me off guard. "You didn't call them already?"

The contours of his face hardened. "No, I can't. You have to do it."

"Why?"

"I'll stay here until you call the police and then I'm going back home. Don't tell them I came over and don't tell them I chased off the person who broke in. Just tell them you beat them with the broom and they ran off."

"But why? Maybe you can tell them something about the person."

Joe stood up and reached for the phone. "It's

dead. You're gonna have to use your cell phone. Where it is?"

"In my purse . . ."

Joe grabbed the phone out of my bag, which still lay on the kitchen table. "I can't explain, Rose, just trust me. They can't know I was here. Can you dial 911 or do you want me to do it?"

I snatched the phone out of his hand, suddenly angry. "I can do it. If you're gonna go, just go already. I don't need you, Joe McAllister. I fought the person sneakin' into my house off all on my own. I surely don't need you to press a couple of buttons on the phone."

Joe hesitated, then pulled me into his arms and kissed me, making me forget that I had to make a phone call at all. He leaned back and caressed my cheek. "Thank God, you're all right." He gave me a smile, a wicked gleam in his eyes. "I love your nightgown."

Then he turned around and walked out the door.

Chapter Eleven

I waited for the police to arrive, alternating between anger and fear. What if I hadn't woken up? What was up with Joe? Did Daniel Crocker have anything to do with this? It seemed an incredible coincidence that he saw me in the DMV in the afternoon and that night someone broke in. But when the police took my statement, I knew I couldn't tell them anything about him. What would I say? "You see, officer, it all started when I had a vision of myself dead . . ." They'd just haul me away to the funny farm, although I wondered if it might be the safest place for me at the moment.

The police went out back and did all their investigating, whatever that entailed. I hoped at the very least the incident would take their suspicion off me for Momma's murder, but when I asked they wouldn't tell me anything. They were there for hours while I sat on the chair in the living room, dozing off and on in my exhaustion. When they left around four in the morning, I struggled with what to do. I was too scared to sleep alone in my house. I didn't want to call Violet and wake her just so I could get a couple of hours of sleep. Instead, I went into the kitchen to make a pot of coffee, which I realized I couldn't do without electricity. I looked over at Joe's house.

Why couldn't I tell the police he'd been there?

A niggling of worry slipped into my mind. What if Joe had something to do with it? I really didn't know much about him. Could it be possible? I dismissed the thought, burning with shame. Joe had been there for me when I needed him. He'd never done anything to make me think badly of him. Well, other than tricking me about his girlfriend. But that hardly made him a suspect in Momma's murder and the break-in. Sure, I found it odd he didn't want any involvement with the police, but plenty of people didn't like police. It didn't mean anything.

Yet, I couldn't completely let it go.

I got ready for work and took the fastest shower in my life, peeking around the curtain to see if someone had crept back into the house, waiting to attack. I wondered how I got into this situation in the first place. Why would anyone want to kill me? I wasn't a threat to anyone, and I'd never even seen Daniel Crocker before that Friday at the DMV.

I left for work much earlier than necessary. Joe's car still sat in his driveway, and I hurried in case he decided to come out and talk to me. I didn't feel like seeing Joe McAllister. I was tired and cranky and worried if he confronted me I might actually hit him.

Arriving at work over an hour early, the DMV parking lot looked barren. I laid against the headrest to close my eyes, for just a moment, and dozed off. Loud banging vibrated my side window. Startled, I jerked upright and found Betty standing next to my car. I rolled down the glass.

She peered in. "Girl, what in blazes are ya doin' out here?"

I told her about the break-in and my fear of falling asleep in my house.

"You sure don't need to be workin' today," she said. "Take the day off."

I had already taken a week of vacation time off the week before and going home was the last thing I wanted to do. Home no longer felt safe. For the first time, I considered letting Violet keep the house and moving somewhere else. Somewhere bad people couldn't find me. But leaving the county wasn't an option.

We were busier than usual, which could have kept my mind off my troubles. But the ringing cell phone in my drawer kept reminding me my problems were still waiting. I turned it to silent, but my drawer sounded like a vibrating bed in a cheap motel, which drew more than a few strange looks.

Between customers, I checked my caller ID. I had calls from Violet, my attorney, and the police. I asked Betty if I could return that one. Perhaps if

185

I proved myself agreeable, I would look less suspicious.

I snuck off to the back room and called the detective assigned to the case. He told me they hadn't come up with anything yet, but had more questions and wanted me to come into the station. Next, I called Deanna who admonished me for talking to the police without her there.

"I don't care if it's about a hangnail. If you talk to anyone with a badge, you call me first."

When I told her that my presence had been requested at the police station, she groaned. "Don't go. Just wait for me to set up a time for us to go together and I'll get back to you."

I still needed to call Violet and I needed to have someone come fix my window. And turn back on my electricity and phone. Plus, I could barely keep my eyes open from my lack of sleep. Betty came to check on me and I apologized for taking too long, tears in my eyes.

"Rose, go home. We're fine without you."

I started to protest but stopped. I was tired and needed sleep before I faced my police interview. The first place I thought to go was Violet's.

I called her on the way over and filled her in on the previous night's activities, leaving out all references to Joe. When I knocked on her door, she opened it after the first rap and pulled me into a huge hug. I would have cried if I weren't so tired.

"Can I go lay down and take a nap?" I asked. "I've been up since one this morning."

"Of course!"

But as I walked down to Ashley's room, my phone vibrated. It was Deanna telling me that I needed to be at the police station in thirty minutes.

She met me in front of the station, looking very professional but grim. "Don't you answer a single question unless I tell you to, got it?"

I nodded, wondering why she acted so concerned. Two hours later when we emerged from the police station I understood.

"I'm not gonna lie to you, Rose," she said. "It doesn't look good."

"I don't understand. Why would they still think I killed Momma after the break-in?"

"They think you staged it, because so much broken glass was outside the house versus inside. If the intruder broke the window to get inside, the glass would be on the inside."

"There was glass inside!"

"But most was outside, meaning the window had been broken from inside."

"I broke the window beating him out the window! What about the utilities being turned off?"

"They were cut with hedge trimmers with the name Gardner written on them and neighbors said they heard noise coming from your shed hours before the incident. One said they saw you going out to the shed."

My heart plummeted into despair.

"I'm going to ask you again, Rose, and I need you tell me the God's honest truth. If you answer yes, I can still help you but I have to know, one way or the other. Did you kill your mother?"

"No!" I nearly shouted, horrified she thought it possible.

"Did you stage the break-in to make it look like someone was after you?"

"No," I answered, more resigned. It looked really bad.

"There's a chance they're going to arrest you for your mother's murder and possibly other charges like filing a false police report for the break-in. The real question is if they will charge you with manslaughter or second-degree murder." She focused on something over my shoulder, lost in thought. "I think you'll escape a charge of first-degree murder, although you had the argument in the early afternoon and the murder occurred in the evening. They could very well accuse you of spending the afternoon plotting your mother's death."

I heard her words but they didn't sink in, floating on the surface of my consciousness, bobbing and teasing me with their seriousness. This couldn't be happening. *Me,* Rose Anne Gardner, accused of murder. I began to laugh.

Deanna's eyes widened in astonishment, then she patted me on the shoulder. "You're in shock. It's okay, it's a normal reaction, actually."

My laughter died away just as quickly as it started. "How much longer until they arrest me?"

"You're not a flight risk and they're still trying to piece things together. I suspect possibly a week, week and a half, depending if they find any new evidence. Everything they have is circumstantial. They're hoping to find a solid piece of evidence before they file the charges so they'll wait for results from the crime lab."

I wasn't sure if that made me feel better or worse.

"Go home, hang tight and wait. I'll give you a call when I hear something."

I drove to Violet's, later wondering how I had gotten there. I remembered getting in my car and staring at the steering wheel for what seemed like forever, and then I was in Violet's driveway, still staring at the steering wheel.

This couldn't be happening.

Violet waited for me at the door, having seen me pull into the driveway, actual proof I did drive. I looked into her anxious face, not sure what to say.

"How bad is it?"

I told her everything then asked, "Can I go take a nap? I'm so tired, I'm about to fall over."

She sent me to Ashley's room. I snuggled down into bed in the Pepto-Bismol colored room and fell asleep, so numb I barely felt the tears falling down my cheeks.

Hours later, I heard a rustle of noise. I squinted into the assaulting late afternoon light. Ashley stood next to the bed, watching me.

"Hey, sweetie," I said, still groggy from sleep.

"You look like Sleeping Beauty," she whispered.

"Thanks, Ash. Come snuggle me."

I laid on my side and she climbed in, pressing her back into my stomach. I nuzzled her wispy-fine hair and inhaled the scent of baby shampoo. Wrapping my arms around her waist, I pulled her closer.

"Tell me a story, Aunt Rose." She clasped her hands over mine. The tenderness of the gesture poked my heart, reminding me that if I were convicted of Momma's murder I would spend years in prison. I would never have children.

"A story?" I asked, trying to refocus as fresh tears burned my eyes.

"About a princess and a prince."

I spun an elaborate tale about a prince lost in the woods, but rescued by a princess galloping by on her goat. The princess then helped the prince, who had lost his pet frog, which they found in the company of a rabbit family in a carrot patch. When the frog was found, the prince returned to his castle and the princess left on a quest to find the fabled, yet much coveted, magic red shoes.

"That's not like the princess stories on TV," she said, giggling.

"No, it's not. But don't let other people tell you

190

who you're supposed to be. You just be you, even if you don't do things like everybody else."

She turned, and reached her hand to my cheek. "Like you, Aunt Rose? You're not like everybody else."

Looking into those deep blue eyes, I realized it was time to take my own advice. For better or worse, I was me. I had visions of people, whether they—or I—wanted them. I had to accept them and learn to make the best of it. And just as suddenly, I realized I had lost a lot of living, twenty-four years' worth, squandered in my fear, embarrassment, and self-pity. I didn't want to go from one prison to another without living at least a little. If I was going to jail, I planned to fit in all the living I could first.

I smiled into Ashley's sweet little face and felt a vision coming, as if on cue. This time I accepted it and without my usual resistance, the vision lasted longer than any I'd ever had before. I was in the funeral home. Violet was crying and leaning into Mike. They stood next to a casket with an open lid. I walked slowly toward it, fear gripping my heart. I was short since I was looking through Ashley's eyes and I couldn't see over the side. Mike picked Ashley up and I stared down into the casket.

It was me.

I looked peaceful and serene lying in the casket, like I was taking a nap. Violet stood next to

Mike, openly sobbing now. I felt nothing as I watched, a void of any feeling, as though I was already dead. I glanced around the room and saw a sign on an easel with my picture on top and wording underneath.

Rose Anne Gardner
Born November 8, 1986
Died June 12, 2011

Then I was back on Ashley's bed, looking into her smiling face.

"I'm going to die," I whispered.

"Like Snow White?" Ashley asked in excitement. "Are you going to eat a poisoned apple?"

"I don't know," I said, the corners of my mouth lifting into a sad smile.

"Will your prince come wake you up, Aunt Rose?"

"No, Ashley, that's make believe. Princes don't do that in real life."

"Hmm . . ." she said, lying on her back.

I was grateful she was four years old and didn't comprehend the meaning of my words.

I was gonna die.

Suddenly, prison looked pretty good.

Chapter Twelve

There's something freeing about knowing the date of your death. All your fears of living vanish away. Worried you'll be in a car wreck? Afraid you'll fall off a roof and plummet to your death? Unless it was June twelfth, I had nothing to worry about.

It was also strange, like somewhere a big digital display counted down the moments until I died. I didn't know the time, but I knew the day. I had less than a week left and I was done frittering my life away.

Where did I start? What did I do? The list, of course. All the things I'd always wanted to do but was too afraid to try. Twenty-three tasks left to accomplish in five days. Why was I wasting time in Ashley's bed?

I scrambled up, kissing Ashley on the forehead. "Aunt Rose has to go home, Ashy!"

When I bolted down the hall, Violet looked like I had just announced plans to join the circus. "Where are you *going?*"

"Home," I said, grabbing my purse.

"What? You can't go there! What if someone tries to break in again?" Her voice rose in panic.

I yanked her into a tight hug. "It's okay, Violet.

I'll be all right." I didn't add *for another five days anyway.* No sense worrying her any more than necessary.

"But, Rose . . ."

"I love you, Violet!" I yelled over my shoulder and headed to my car.

I tried to remember my list, hoping to do something on the way home. *Get cable . . .* I picked up my cell phone and found the number for the cable company. They said they'd send someone to install it the next day. I had to ask off work to meet the cable installer, then decided to call in sick for the entire week. I sure wasn't going to waste my last five days at the DMV.

Get my own place . . . Violet said she would sell the house to me, so that made it mine. Two items just like that. Maybe this would be easier than I thought.

As I drove through downtown, I noticed a pickup truck stopped at the edge of the park. The tailgate hung open and a large metal cage sat in the grass. A puppy romped next to it.

Get a dog.

I turned around and drove back to the truck, parking to the side of it. A family with two small children played with the puppy. A bigger dog, but not by much, sulked in the corner of the cage when I walked up.

"Can we get him, Daddy?" the little boy asked the man who appeared torn.

He bent over, rubbing the back of the puppy's neck. "Well . . ."

The boy and his younger brother began a chorus of pleases that would have softened the staunchest of men. The father caved.

I watched it all transpire, taking delight in the children's happiness. The way the puppy's owner kept glancing at me I realized I probably looked like some kind of child predator standing there.

"Is that your last dog?" I asked, looping my hand around the strap of my purse.

"That's my last puppy. I've only got the mother left. She's just a mutt, though. Nobody wants her. I was gonna drop her off at the shelter on my way home."

I looked down at the whimpering dog in the cage. She was small, definitely a mutt and not cute like her offspring. Her gray and black fur was short and wiry. She had short legs, a long body, and pointy ears and snout. She looked like a cross between a terrier and a rat.

"Can I see her?"

The owner looked at me like I'd lost my mind, which I supposed I had. I knelt down. "What's her name?"

"Muffy."

"Come here, Muffy," I beckoned, patting the ground. "Come here, sweet girl."

The dog crept toward me, her head hunkered down and her tail between her legs. She stopped at the opening of the cage. I stroked her neck and behind her ears. She cautiously left the cage and sat next to me while I continued to pet her.

"She's a good dog," the owner said. "She's scared of other dogs, which don't work out so well on my farm. In fact, she's pretty much scared of everything. I'm surprised she came out of the cage to you. She don't normally take to strangers."

Muffy's sad eyes looked up at me. My tummy tightened with empathy. We were a lot alike, Muffy and I, both afraid of the world and what was in it.

"How much is she?" I asked, taking the sides of her face into my hands.

"I ain't gonna charge you nothin', you can just have her. Like I said, I was gonna take her to the pound, although, honestly, I didn't want to do that. She just showed up at my farm one day and had a litter of pups a couple days later. I kept her and the pups until they was ready to go."

"What do you say, Muffy? Wanna come home with me?" I could have sworn she wagged her tail, or she may have moved it to pass gas, which was highly probable from the stench suddenly filling the air. I decided to go with the wag.

I tried coaxing her into the car without much success. Finally, I scooped her up, surprised to find her lighter than she looked, and plopped her into the driver's seat. She peered up at me.

"You gonna drive? That'd be a sight. A driving

dog. What? No? Then scoot over." But she didn't budge, so I sat on the edge of the seat and pushed her over to the passenger side with my hip.

The farmer loaded up the cage, laughing.

"We're puttin' on a show, Muffy. Let's go home and get some dinner."

I drove with the windows halfway down. Muffy stuck her face over the top of the glass, her tongue hanging out. I prayed she didn't get carsick.

When I pulled up, I noticed Joe's car in his driveway. *Why're you even looking?* That man was a confusing mess. I only had five days left. Instinct told me that wasn't nearly enough time to figure out Joe McAllister.

I carried Muffy into the house. After I set her down on the kitchen floor, she began sniffing everything while I rummaged through the refrigerator for dinner. I couldn't remember the last time I went to the grocery store.

"Whatcha want for dinner, Muffy? There's not much here."

Muffy didn't answer. She turned around in circles, then sat in the corner of the kitchen behind the table. She laid her head on her front paws and stared up at me. I'd never seen such a pathetic sight in all my life.

I made scrambled eggs and fed half to Muffy, half to me. Afterward, Muffy got a really strange look on her face. Uncle Earl had made a face like that after eating a batch of bad pickles once and that didn't turn out so well. I ran to my bedroom and found a belt, which I strapped around Muffy's middle section. I was afraid I'd choke her if I put it around her neck.

We barely made it outside before Muffy squatted next to a bush and made the nastiest mess I had ever seen. Talk about false advertising. They forget to mention that part of pet ownership in the dog food commercials.

"Feel better?" I asked Muffy in a baby voice. "I promise to take good care of you in the five days I have left." It was then I realized in five days I wouldn't be around to take care of her. I'd been a pet owner for less than an hour and I was already failing miserably.

"What do you mean you only have five days left?"

I whipped my head around to see Joe a few feet away.

Crappy doodles.

He looked angry. Not just angry, menacing.

"Where you goin' in five days, Rose?"

"Nowhere. Not that it's any of your business, Joe McAllister."

He heaved a sigh and kicked a piece of gravel. "You're right, of course. What you do is none of my business." Then he stood next to me, whispering in my ear. "You seem like a nice girl, Rose, I hate to see you mixed up in something really messy."

His breath sent chills down my back, all the way to my toes. How could this man do this to me? What on earth was he talking about? Then I realized he was looking toward the dog and the huge pile she just made.

"I admit it was kind of impulsive to get into such a commitment, but I think I can handle it."

Joe stepped away, his eyes wide open, like he'd stepped into a pit of rattlesnakes. "So you admit you're involved?"

"Well, yeah. The evidence is right in front of you." I tugged on Muffy's belt. "Come on, Muffy. Let's go in the back." I yanked and pulled and ended up dragging her to the backyard. Unfortunately, Joe followed me.

"What are you thinking, Rose? Do you realize what kind of trouble you've got yourself into?"

"Joe, seriously, it's not that big of a deal. Lots of people do it."

He raised his hands to his head and groaned, spinning around in frustration. He stopped and looked more serious than I had ever seen him, even more than the night Momma was murdered. "I've got to get you out of this. Maybe it's not too late."

I huffed and stamped my foot. "You seriously think I can't handle a dog? Do I appear *that* irresponsible?"

Joe turned as pale as a ghost and I expected him to fold up and float away any minute. "A *dog?*" he choked out. "You're talking about a *dog?*"

"I know dogs are lots of trouble but I've always wanted one and I figured, why not? I'm a grown woman."

Joe looked torn between guilt and relief.

I cocked my head to the side and studied him. "Wait, what were *you* talkin' about?"

An ornery grin lifted one corner of his mouth as he lifted an eyebrow and darted his eyes toward Muffy. "You call that thing a dog? Looks like a ginormous rat to me. And what on earth do you have around that poor creature's gut?"

I took offense to him insulting my dog and put my hand on my hip, glaring. "First of all, she is not a rat; she is a *dog*. Granted she's not some pedigreed foofoo dog, but she's my dog. And second, it all happened so fast, I didn't have time to get her any supplies, so I put a belt around her to bring her out. I was afraid she'd run away."

"Why's it around her stomach and not her neck?"

"I was worried I'd choke her."

Joe snickered. "That is the *ugliest* dog I have ever seen."

"You hush! Muffy can hear you!"

"Muffy?"

"Yes, Muffy. And quit insulting her. She has a very delicate temperament." I lifted my chin to show my distain. At that moment, Muffy squatted and let out the loudest fart I had ever heard, accompanied by the nastiest and worst smelling pile I had ever experienced. The reek of it filled the space around us and I couldn't help fanning in front of my nose. *Traitor.*

Joe started belly laughing, leaning over his legs.

I was getting angrier by the minute. "What's so funny?"

"Your delicate dog." He said in bursts of laughter.

"Come on, Muffy, we don't have to take this." I gave the belt a tug and Muffy farted again.

I thought Joe was going to fall over. I wished he would so I could kick him. Afraid to pull on her again, I gave her a tug anyway and the air filled with stench.

Joe gasped for breath. "You should put her on one of those shows like World's Amazing Pets. Muffy will make you a fortune."

I couldn't help but smile. It was kind of funny. "So Muffy has a flatulence problem. I'll just put her on a high fiber diet."

I started giggling then, and we sat on the lawn, both of us laughing together in my backyard. It felt so good to share something funny with someone. I wanted lots of laughter to fill my last five days, but the thought of it suddenly sobered me.

There was always the chance it wouldn't come true, like the last vision of my death. But I knew that was a fluke. The majority of my visions came true. And since I had no idea how to change it, I had to accept it for what it was.

"Hey," I said, realizing Joe had distracted me. "If you weren't talkin' about Muffy earlier, what were you talkin' about?"

His smile disappeared. He hesitated before he asked, "Who said I wasn't talkin' about Muffy?"

I shot him a nasty look. "I'm not an idiot, Joe."

He leaned toward me and whispered into my ear. "No, but you are beautiful." His head stayed there, his breath warming my cheek and neck. Every nerve of my body jumped to full alert.

"I like your dog. I think she's full of potential." His voice was low and husky in my ear.

I had a hard time concentrating. "Why did you leave last night?" I asked, the words tumbling out in a rush.

"Because I was a fool. What man could leave you?" He put his finger on my chin and turned my face toward his.

"Why do you keep changing the subject?" I whispered.

His eyes watched my mouth. "Why do you keep askin' questions?" His head lowered slowly until his lips were on mine. I forgot about questions. I even forgot about Muffy until she howled.

I jerked away, startled. "What? What's wrong?" I asked her.

Joe laughed. "I don't think she likes me kissing you."

I reached over and rubbed her head. "It's okay, baby. The big bad man isn't kissin' me anymore."

Joe leaned back, his hands braced behind him. "I take back what I said about your dog having potential."

"So what were you talking about earlier?"

"Your dog."

I turned to him and raised my eyebrows. "I'm experiencing déjà vu."

"Why did you tell your dog you'd be leaving in five days?"

We sat in silence for a few moments while I rubbed Muffy behind her ears.

"Where are you going, Rose? I thought you weren't supposed to leave the county."

"Who said I was leaving the county? Last time I checked, county lockup was in Fenton County."

Joe sat up. "What are you talking about?"

"The police think I staged the break-in to take the focus of Momma's murder off of me. My attorney expects them to arrest me by next week." It was all true, even if it wasn't what the five days meant. "But if you went to the police and told them you saw someone, it might get me off the hook." And give me one less thing to worry about.

Joe leaned his elbows on his knees, grasping his head in his hands. Then he let loose a string of obscenities. "I can't." His head still hung between his arms, muffling his words.

It didn't matter, the meaning was clear enough to pierce my heart. I got up and started to walk away, but he grabbed my wrist. I stood there, neither one of us saying anything. I kept waiting for him to say he changed his mind or let me go, but he did neither. He couldn't have it both ways.

"I thought you were my friend, Joe." Tears burned my eyes and made my words scratchy. "You're just going to sit here and let them arrest me."

"Why didn't you tell them about me?" He sounded like he was in pain.

"Because you asked me not to."

He looked up, his eyes full of guilt and anguish. "Why didn't you tell them anyway?"

"Because I'm gonna leave it up to you and hope you pick me over your silly pride." He didn't say anything, his face begging my forgiveness and I knew I lost again. I always lost. Why did I think this would ever turn out differently?

"Stupid me." I jerked my arm away and picked up Muffy's belt.

"Go home, Joe. You just keep hurting me and I keep lettin' you. Please, just go home." I started crying and I didn't care, I had no pride left. I'd left that behind the minute I let him kiss me after finding out about Hilary.

But Joe didn't get up. He sat there in the grass having the nerve to look all tortured and angsty when *I* was the one about to get arrested.

When I settled into bed that night, I told Muffy it was her job to protect me if someone broke in again. It was then, as I drifted off to sleep, that I realized I'd never told Joe I wasn't allowed to leave the county.

Chapter Thirteen

Early the next day, I vowed I was done with Joe McAllister. If I didn't know I was going to die in four days, I might tell the police anyway. But this way I could die and let Joe suffer in his own guilt. He could spend the rest of his life wishing he'd done the right thing.

But I began to wonder if he'd feel guilty at all. How did he know I couldn't leave the county? Why wouldn't he go to the police? The night of Momma's murder, why did he tell me he was "just the neighbor" as though he could actually be something more? What if Joe McAllister, the man who helped me paint my living room, who gave me my first kiss and made me laugh until I cried, played a part in Momma's murder? What if he was the intruder who broke into my house?

It seemed inconceivable. But there was no refuting he had information I hadn't given him and that he wouldn't talk to the police even though he knew my arrest was inevitable. Everything pointed to him being involved.

But why would he do all those nice things for me including putting new locks on my door, if he wanted to kill me? I closed my eyes, and sank into the big chair in the living room, remembering

Joe's breath on my neck and his lips on mine. How could the same man want to hurt me?

Muffy began to whine and set her chin on my knees. I opened my eyes and smiled at her forlorn face. I had no idea dogs could look so sad. I rubbed her head, surprised I'd become so attached to her already. "What's wrong, Muffy?"

She set her paw on my lap, whining.

"Do you need to go outside? I need to get you some dog food. And a leash." Muffy's butt made an odd noise and a stink filled the room. I waved my hand, trying to move the smell. "And perhaps some diapers. Whew!"

The cable man arrived at nine, and left an hour later since I only had him put in one line. When I signed the ticket, I mentioned my surprise that he came out the day after I called.

He chuckled. "I've never seen that happen. It must be your lucky day."

My lucky day. I liked the sound of that.

I'd studied my list while I waited for him to finish. To my amazement, I had checked off nine items already. Of course, there was the empty number twenty-nine to deal with, but I decided not to worry about that one. I'd already had enough new experiences, any of which I could plug in the space.

I needed a plan. I had four days left. To get them all accomplished, I needed to complete five a day. Which five would I do today?

I decided to pick out the items that looked the hardest. Maybe I could do one of those a day. Those were: *the Seven Deadly Sins in one week, ride in a convertible, do more with a man, go to Italy, ride a motorcycle, fly in an airplane, play in the rain.* That was seven and only four days. The sins needed to be spread out anyway. I just needed to make sure I did two a day and I'd be done with time to spare. The two that worried me the most were going to Italy, which seemed out of the question, and play in the rain. What if it didn't rain between now and Sunday?

I decided to worry about those two later. Today, I'd just wing it with the sins. And for the other wishes, it seemed logical to start at the top. Buy some makeup, visit a beauty salon, get a pedicure. The next item: ride in a convertible. How could I do that?

I'd rent one. I got out the phone book and looked up a car rental agency. "I'd like to rent a convertible."

"How long? A day? A week?"

Shoot, why not a week? I told him I'd be there within an hour.

When it came time for me to leave, Muffy followed me around, hanging her head and tucking her tail between her legs. "Don't be doin' that," I said, rubbing her head. "I can't take you with me, but I'll bring you back a surprise when I come home, okay?"

Muffy seemed unconvinced.

With all the farting she'd done, I decided it would be safer to keep her in the bathroom. Definitely an easier clean up if she made a mess.

I started out the door and saw the wooden box on the kitchen table, where I left it days ago, still in the paper bag. As an afterthought, I grabbed the bag and threw it in the car.

I was ready to see what was inside.

The rental agency was the first stop. I'd never rented a car before, but it proved easy enough, and I left with a white Sebring convertible. I climbed into the front seat and studied the buttons until I figured out how to put the top down. The heat had risen to a nearly intolerable level, the high humidity causing steam to rise from the pavement, but the whole point of having a convertible was to put the top down.

I drove toward downtown and realized why I always saw people who drove convertibles wearing sunglasses. The blinding sun made it difficult to see. Necessity instigated my next stop. Walmart had a multitude of sunglasses on display. After trying on multiple pairs, I finally decided on one with black plastic frames and large, dark lenses.

As I walked toward the pharmacy section, the lingerie department caught my eye. I blushed thinking about Joe seeing me in my nightie. Further down my list *wear a lacy bra and panties* lingered. I forced myself to ignore the utilitarian underwear I usually wore, and focused on the lacy, pretty things.

They were beautiful and came in so many colors and styles. Wickedness took hold of me. Why wear lingerie only one day? Why not every day for the next four days? I picked out white, black, lavender and red, the evilest of all. No one would ever see them, so why not? I took them into the fitting room and tried on the black set first, amazed the woman returning my gaze in the mirror was me. I looked like a Victoria's Secret model.

I was buying all four.

I'd just have to make sure to wear the white lingerie on Sunday. When they found my body.

For the first time, the seriousness of it hit me. I was going to die. My breath caught in my chest, and I gasped for air, sitting down on the dressing room bench.

I'm going to die.

I let myself have a good cry, right there in the Walmart fitting room, wearing nothing but my wicked black bra and panties, the price tag poking me in the side. Was this really how I wanted to spend my last four days? Working my way through a list ranging from committing all Seven Deadly Sins to *doing more with a man?* I looked back on the last twenty-four years, all wasted, and stared at my tear-streaked face in the mirror.

Hell, yeah.

I dug through my purse and found a package of tissues, blew my nose, and wiped away my tears. *Enough. You've had your cry, you were owed one. But now you're done.* I still had items on my list to do today.

After I bought makeup and a collar and food for Muffy, I headed to the beauty salon. I talked to a stylist and since Aunt Bessie had already cut my hair, we decided I should get highlights, pretty caramel-colored ones that blended in with my dark brown hair. And a manicure to go with the pedicure.

When I left a few hours later, I wondered why I never did these things before. Why I waited until the last days of my life to feel pampered and beautiful. People tell themselves there's plenty of time to do it all, but most of the time they never see death coming. I sat in the front seat of my rented convertible thinking of all the living I had left to do.

I wasn't ready to go home yet.

I put the top back down, slid on my sunglasses, and headed for the highway, driving seventy miles an hour, the wind blowing through my hair. I never felt so free and alive. This was how I wanted to remember living, if you remembered anything after you were dead. I filed it away in a spot in my mind, a scrapbook of memories to take to the afterlife.

Careful not to cross the county line, I turned around at the exit before I reached the edge. I sure didn't want to spend my last days in jail.

On my way home, I remembered the wooden box in the trunk. I didn't know how to go about opening it, so I took it into the hardware store and asked a clerk. He suggested cutting it with bolt cutters. He set the box on a counter and pulled out the biggest pair of scissors I had ever seen. With a couple of quick snips, he cut both links of the padlock. "Who's Dora?" he asked, pulling the lock free.

"Hopefully, I'm about to find out."

I drove to Violet's house. It seemed fitting we open it together.

"What are you doin' here?" she asked, surprised to see me at three o'clock in the afternoon. My new highlights and flashy convertible must have thrown her off, too. I supposed it looked like I was going through a midlife crisis. An end-of-life crisis was more like it.

"I got the lock cut off the box. I thought you might want to help me open it." I carried it into the kitchen and set it on the island. We both sat on stools staring at it as if we expected the lid to pop open on its own.

"I'm scared to find out what's inside," I finally admitted.

"I know. Me, too."

"But we've got to find out sometime, right?" So

I grabbed the lid in both hands and flipped it open.

At least nothing flew out.

I pulled it closer and Violet and I both looked inside. A diamond engagement ring lay on top of a stack of papers. Lifting it out, I twisted the ring in the light, watching it sparkle.

"Whose is that?" Violet asked in awe. "I never saw Momma wear anything like that."

"I don't know . . ." my voice trailed off as I studied it. It was a big diamond, about a half-carat, with tiny diamonds surrounding it on a white gold band. "It's beautiful." I placed it on my right ring finger. It fit perfectly. The sparkly stone was so mesmerizing, I couldn't take my eyes off it.

Violet shook her head. "I can't believe Momma gave you something like that."

"Neither can I." I couldn't even imagine where she would have gotten it.

"Well, what else is in there?" Violet sounded excited, her giddiness infectious.

I pulled out the next item, what appeared to be an old savings account passbook. I opened the cover and read the inside page. "Dora Middleton." I turned to Violet. "I guess we found out who Dora is."

"Well, not really. We found her savings account book, but I don't remember any Middletons in our family, and look," she pointed to the address below her name. "She lived in Shreveport. I don't recall any family living in Shreveport."

"Shreveport's not very far, Violet. That doesn't mean anything." But she was right. I didn't remember any of our family living in Louisiana, either. I opened the book and checked the balance. I felt like I was snooping in someone else's business, but reminded myself it belonged to me now. "Violet, there's twenty thousand dollars in there."

She took the book out of my hand. "Why on earth did Momma give this to you?" she asked in amazement, then raised her face, wide-eyed. "It has Dora Middleton's name on it. How could it be yours?"

I shrugged and looked inside the book. "The last entry was in 1986."

"The year you were born."

We were silent for a moment, staring at the book. My right hand felt heavy from the unaccustomed weight of the ring.

"There's more in there," Violet said.

I pulled the papers out of the box, attempting to wrap my head around the fact I might own twenty thousand dollars. Unfolding the papers, I read the top line. "The Last Will and Testament of Dora Colleen Middleton." I stopped to see Violet's reaction. "Why is the will of someone neither one of us know in a box left to me?" And by Momma, no less. That part surprised me the most.

"I don't know," Violet said in a gasp. "Read it!"

"Blah, blah, blah . . . and to Rose Anne Gardner, my daughter . . ." My voice trailed off in shock. *"My daughter?"*

Violet jerked the papers out of my hand and scanned down to my name. "How can that be?"

"I dunno . . ."

We looked at the will, trying to make sense of it.

"Aunt Bessie said one day I would want answers and she would tell me what she knew." I looked into Violet's blurry eyes. "Do you think she knows about this?"

She wiped a tear trailing down her cheek. "How could she not? The big question is how did *we* not know? You know people in this town can't keep a secret to save their life."

"Is she your mother too?" I asked. Did this mean we weren't sisters?

Violet bit her trembling lip. "No, I have pictures of Momma holding me in the hospital. I never thought of it before, but I don't recall ever seein' any of you in the hospital when you were born."

I slowly shook my head. "I don't understand. This doesn't make sense. Could I be adopted? Do you remember anything about when I was born?"

"I'm only two years older than you. I don't remember anything about when you were a baby. But I do remember spending a long time at Aunt Bessie and Uncle Earl's farm. I never really thought about it before. During the wintertime and spring, I think. I remember snow . . ." Her words sounded like they were tumbling off a ledge as she fell into her memories.

"I need to call Aunt Bessie." I stood up to grab my cell phone out of my purse.

"Rose, wait!"

The anxiety in Violet's voice stopped me.

"There's a picture in here!"

I spun around to the image Violet held in her hand, an old color photo slightly discolored around the edges. A woman held a tiny baby, her face radiating so much happiness it permeated from the photo. The baby's face was clearly visible, in spite of the blanket wrapped around its body.

"Rose, that looks like you," Violet said in awe.

The baby's cheeks and eyes looked a lot like the pictures of me when I was one and two. I peered closer at the woman's face. The way she smiled, the way one of her eyes squinted a tiny bit more closed than the other, the curve of her chin. Before Violet turned the photo over and read the back and confirmed it, I knew this woman was my mother. I'd seen the same face in the mirror only a few hours earlier.

"Dora and Rose, November 8, 1986 . . ." Violet read. "Then below it says 'My precious girls'." Violet looked up in shock. "Rose, this is written in Daddy's handwriting."

Chapter Fourteen

I leaned over the photo. The handwriting was definitely Daddy's distinguishable chicken scratch.

I pulled it out of Violet's hand, turning it over with trembling fingers to study the woman's happy face, the face of my mother. At that moment, my world stopped spinning and gravity evaporated away. The pieces of my life no longer fit neatly into a perfect picture, albeit an unhappy one, but one I knew. My entire life had been a lie.

While Violet called Aunt Bessie, my eyes remained glued to Dora's face, willing her to float out of the photograph and tell me everything. Instead, she sat frozen in time on a country blue-and-white checkered sofa, holding a tiny me. Who was she smiling at? Daddy?

"Aunt Bessie is cancelling all her clients for the rest of the day and is coming right over, but she has to tie up some loose ends. It's probably going to be another hour and a half."

I suddenly remembered Muffy. *Crappy doodles.* Strike two on responsible pet ownership.

"I have to go home." I stood up and grabbed my purse.

"What?" Violet's mouth fell open. I wondered if Violet would get high blood pressure from

all the surprises I had thrown at her the last week.

"I'll come back, I promise. I just forgot about Muffy."

"Who's Muffy?"

"My dog. I left her alone all day and I need to go let her out." I hated to even think about the possible state of my bathroom.

"Your *dog?*" Violet stumbled backward. I literally pushed her over the edge with that one.

"I'll explain it to you later. I just have to go."

I ran out of the house, temporarily surprised by the convertible in the driveway. My day came rushing back and now it felt so superficial. I drove home, leaving the top up, not finding any joy in the car anymore. It was a tangible item that had no meaning in my life.

I found Muffy in the bathroom, lying on the cold tile, her face on her paws. She looked as sad as I felt. We made a good pair, she and I. *Can you be soul mates with a dog?* I wondered as I put on her new collar and attached the leash. If only I had found her sooner. But before a couple of weeks ago, I hadn't even considered looking.

I watched her sniff the grass and relieve herself all over the backyard. She seemed to be less timid and I wondered if she would be bouncing all over the place in a week. Then I remembered I wouldn't be here in a week. What would happen to Muffy when I was gone?

Tears stung my eyes. *Lucky day, my ass.*

I started to laugh at the absurdity of it all and it was then that I felt Joe's presence. I hadn't heard him, between my laughing and my crying. I turned to face him. He stood at the corner of the house, watching me with brooding eyes. Then he came toward me, as if in slow motion and a million thoughts went through my head. *Why was he home so early? What was he doing back here? Did he really care about me?*

He stopped about a foot in front of me and stared down into my face. The worry in his eyes answered my last question.

"Rose," he said, his voice full of regret and pain. Even in my inexperience I recognized the longing in his smoldering dark-brown eyes.

I studied him, amazed he really did want me, and not like Daniel Crocker had in the bar. This was different.

His eyes widened when I reached up to touch his cheek. Then he closed them, seeking refuge in his despair. I brushed the hair off his forehead, intrigued at how soft it felt between my fingers. I had never touched a man other than Daddy, well, other than the few times I had kissed Joe. But in those moments, I had been lost in myself and hadn't paid attention to him. It occurred to me I might never get another opportunity. I let my fingertips trail down his cheek, feeling the stubble of his five o'clock shadow. My thumb skimmed across his lips, warming with the rush of air from his sharp exhale. The muscles in his shoulders looked like they were melting as his tension fell away.

I did that to him.

I was hungry to know more.

I moved both hands to his waist, dropping Muffy's leash, and lifted up the edge of his T-shirt. His eyes flew open in alarm and he started to say something, searching my face for an explanation. The intensity in my eyes willed him to be still. He seemed to understand and let me lift his shirt up and over his head, pulling it off the rest of the way himself. Then he waited, the pain on his face more profound than before. I wondered what he saw on my own.

We were a pair, he and I, even more so than Muffy and me. Both lost in misery, only his was of his own doing and mine was thrust upon me. But misery is misery, no matter what its cause and we were both drowning in it. I had no idea why he wouldn't go to the police. But in that moment, I knew he would never hurt me, not if he could help it. I had four days left and I didn't want to spend it alone. In the end, it didn't matter what his motives were. I'd be dead. The first twenty-four years of my life had been a lie; would it be so bad if the last four days were too?

I reached my hands back up to his cheeks, marveling at the contrast of his soft skin and the roughness of his beard. I slid my hands down his neck, feeling the bob of his Adam's apple as he swallowed, and down to his chest. The rise and fall of his breath became faster under my palms. I closed my eyes and absorbed the moment, attaching it to the scrapbook of memories.

My hands slid lower, down his sides, stopping at the waistband of his jeans. I ran my fingers up his back, feeling his muscles tense as I stepped closer, reaching higher. I stood pressed against his bare chest, my hands splayed across his upper shoulder blades, feeling the heat of his body seep into mine. I opened my eyes to look up into his questioning ones and smiled, the tiniest of smiles. If I never got more than this, I'd die happy.

My smile was the catalyst that freed Joe from his trance. His arms reached around my back, pulling me even closer as his lips found mine, hot and needing. The kisses on my front porch and the night before where nothing compared to the primal force pulling me to him now. Those had been flirtatious and fun. This was desperate and hungry.

I discovered I'd lied. I wanted more.

Joe's hands seemed to be everywhere at once, on my back, in my hair. One hand moved to my breast and I gasped, surprised at the fire that burst within me at his touch.

That got Joe's attention. He lifted his face and pulled my head to his chest, sucking in a deep breath and releasing it slowly. My heart hammered away, while the rest of me questioned why he stopped.

"We can't do this, Rose," Joe said, his heart racing in my ear.

"What? Why?"

"We need to wait."

I didn't even try to hide my disappointment, proof I truly had become sinful. "But I only have four days. There isn't *time* to wait." The words fell out before I could censor them.

Joe wrapped his hands around my arms and jerked me backward. "That's the second time you said that. What happens in four days?" He looked angry, far angrier than he had a right to be.

"What does it matter to you, Joe? Why do you care?" I asked, defiant. What right did he have to question me?

His face softened and his grip relaxed, but he still held my arms. "I care about you, Rose. I don't want anything to happen to you."

It was my turn to get angry. "Yeah, I can tell by the way you're running off to the police to clear my name." I jerked my arms away from him, searching for Muffy. "It doesn't matter. It will be over soon."

He grabbed my shoulders and spun me around. "Why do you keep sayin' *that?* What aren't you tellin' me?" he asked through gritted teeth.

I stopped to reevaluate the situation. I only had four days left and while Joe's character was currently suspect, I somehow knew he wouldn't hurt me. As long as I ignored the not-clearing-my-name part. I didn't want to fight with him. I liked Joe a lot and it wasn't like I was looking for a long-term commitment here.

That made me laugh.

Joe's eyes widened and he looked like he expected me to start strutting around the yard like a chicken. "This isn't funny, Rose."

"If you only knew what I knew, you'd be laughing." I laughed a few seconds more and stopped. "Or maybe you wouldn't."

He tried a different tactic. He pulled me close and whispered in my ear. "Why don't you tell me and then we'll know whether I think it's funny or not."

A fire spread through my body, an automatic response I couldn't turn off even if I wanted to, which I didn't. Let him play his games. I knew what he was doing. "Are you tryin' to persuade me to tell you?"

His hands worked their way up my back, sending chills in their wake. "Tell me," he whispered, kissing my neck and I shivered.

If he only knew I'd hold out all night as long as he kept doing what he was doing.

He left a trail of kisses across my cheek but avoiding contact with my lips.

I groaned in frustration.

"What happens in four days, Rose?"

If I'd been capable of laughing, I would have. He played into my hands, not the other way around.

His lips moved to my mouth, soft and tantalizing, but still holding back.

"You told me it could be better," I said.

"What?" he whispered as he moved to my ear, biting and sucking on my earlobe.

I gasped. "The night you first kissed me, you told me it could be better. I didn't see how. Show me how."

"Tell me what happens in four days."

"No, you'll stop," I said, my knees getting weak.

Joe paused. I'd showed my hand, as my Daddy used to say. He pulled away from me, mischievousness in his eyes. "You are wicked, aren't you?"

"No, but I'd like to be if you'd just cooperate."

My answer caught him by surprise and he laughed. "How do you do that?" he asked, catching his breath.

"Do what?"

"Make me forget all my problems." As soon as he said the words, he looked sorry he had.

"What troubles do you have, Joe McAllister?" I asked.

He smiled and raised an eyebrow. "I have secrets of my own."

"That's nothin' I didn't already know. Ordinary people go to the police, especially if their friend's in trouble."

His smile disappeared, replaced by guilt. "Rose, about . . ."

"Joe, it's okay. It doesn't matter."

Shock replaced the guilt. "They're going to arrest you."

"I know, but not until next week."

"Is that why you say you only have four days? You think the police are going to arrest you in four days?"

I didn't want to lie but I couldn't tell him the truth either. I decided it was better to let him believe his theory. Lucky for me, I waited so long to answer that he took it as confirmation.

"Rose, if it comes to that I'll tell them everything I know. I swear. I just can't go right now. Will you trust me?"

If I was thinking long-term, I didn't know that I would. I had no guarantee Joe was a safe bet. But four days? What could happen in four days?

"I'll trust you until Monday." I wasn't sure if I had told a lie or not, considering I'd be dead Monday. I reached up to kiss him, to seal our deal. But he leaned back, keeping his mouth out of reach. "No, we can't do this until Monday."

"What?"

"I want to prove that I'm trustworthy. I won't touch you until Monday, then you'll know I really like you and I'm not wanting to take advantage of you."

"Maybe I *want* you to take advantage of me."

Joe laughed and shook his head. "I'll take advantage of you after Monday."

"That doesn't help me at all. It's on my list and I have to do everything on my list by Sunday, preferably Saturday."

He looked confused. "I thought you said Monday."

I groaned in frustration at my slipup.

He forged on. "My guess is they're trying to get evidence to make the charge stick. It's all circumstantial at this point, right?"

I narrowed my eyes. "How do you know that?"

He shrugged. "Common sense. I watch *Law & Order* just like everyone else."

"How'd you know I couldn't leave the county?"

"What?"

"I didn't tell you I couldn't leave the county, but yesterday you knew. How'd you know that?"

He scowled. "I told you, *Law & Order*. In any case, the police are waiting for the DA and he's not going to file the charges on Sunday. It wouldn't happen until Monday at the earliest."

I raised eyebrows. "And you know this from *Law & Order*?"

He grinned and shrugged again. "TV is very educational."

"Yeah, I wouldn't know about that. So are you gonna help me with my list?"

"You mean your Walmart List?" He looked

downright ornery when he said it. "You're working on your list?"

"My *Wish* List; I have thirteen and a half already." I lifted my chin, daring him to mock me.

"How do you get a half?"

"I bought the bra and panties, I just haven't worn them yet."

Joe started choking and his face turned red. "Excuse me?"

"Number nineteen. *Wear a lacy bra and panties.*"

It took him a second to speak. "I suppose you need me to help you with number fifteen?"

"You know what number fifteen is?"

"Of course, how could I forget *do more with a man?* But technically, you did. We got to second base if I remember correctly, and I'm *positive* I remember correctly." He winked.

"Ha, barely! You very well know what I meant. I am not goin' to die a virgin!"

"Who said anything about dying?" His words were sharp enough to cut through ice.

"Figure of speech." I waved my hand, trying to convince him. "Who knows what will happen to me in jail."

He looked like he didn't believe me. "Well, tonight I'm not doing more. I'll eat dinner with you and hang out with you, but I'm not helping you with number fifteen," he finished with a frown.

"If you don't want to help me Joe, you don't have to. I can always find someone else. Why, just the other night I had a man practically offer."

"Your date?" he scoffed.

I turned up my chin. "No, someone else."

His expression changed. "Who?"

"It doesn't matter. I turned him down, but if you don't help me, I'll find someone else who will."

"Don't do anything stupid, Rose."

We stared at each other. "You're tryin' to boss me around again, Joe. I won't stand for it. I let people boss me around the last twenty-four years. I'm sure not gonna be bossed around my last four days." My voice was hard and cold. "I'll give you until Saturday night."

I picked up Muffy's leash. "Come on, Muffy."

"I thought we were eating dinner together," he called after me.

"I never agreed to dinner, you just assumed. I already have plans."

I glanced over my shoulder and saw his stunned face. I kind of felt bad for him.

"Help me with my list," I blurted out.

He grimaced. "I already told . . ."

"No, the rest of them." I'd realized it would be more fun to experience everything with someone I cared about. I had to admit I actually did care for Joe. "Do you work on Saturday?"

"No . . . but you have Sunday too."

"No, Saturday. I want them all done by mid-

228

night." I only knew that I would die on Sunday, I didn't know what time. It could happen at 12:01 a.m. for all I knew, although I hoped it was closer to 11:59 p.m.

"I need to see your list again, to see what you still need."

"I still owe you dinner for the lock. Come over tomorrow night and we'll go over it then."

Joe looked happier. "Okay."

"And if you're lucky, I'll wear my new bra and panties."

He shook his head. "You're not gonna make this easy for me, are you?"

I smiled, but it didn't quite reach my eyes. "Not on your life."

Or more accurately, mine.

Chapter Fifteen

I hated to leave Muffy home alone again, especially after I ignored her so much while I'd thrown myself at Joe. Thank goodness we were behind my house, not that it mattered. Did dead people care if their reputations were besmirched? In the end I brought Muffy with me, hoping it wouldn't upset Violet. My secret hope was Muffy would wiggle her way into Violet and Mike's hearts and they would take her when I died.

The look on Violet's face assured me she had not become immune to the barrage of surprises I kept throwing her way.

"Is this your dog?"

"Her name is Muffy and she is very sensitive."

Muffy tooted her sensitivity on Violet's doorstep.

"Oh, dear Lord. The stench . . ."

"She just needs more roughage in her diet is all, give her a chance. Little Mikey pooped out some nasty stuff, and I still love him."

Violet didn't look convinced. "You seem more cheerful than when you left."

"I've had some time to get used to things." *As well as some other extracurricular activities.*

"Aunt Bessie called and said she'd be here in about ten minutes."

I led Muffy out to the backyard. Ashley ran behind us, excited to have a dog in her home. Thankfully, she seemed oblivious to Muffy's physical inadequacies.

"Thanks a lot," Violet said when I came in, sarcasm dripping off her words like butter slathered on corn on the cob. "You know she wants a dog."

"I'll share Muffy with her. She can visit anytime."

Aunt Bessie gave us both big hugs when she arrived. Mike came home from work early and bounced little Mikey on his knee, keeping him distracted. Violet brought the box to Aunt Bessie in the living room. Violet and I sat on the sofa.

Aunt Bessie perched on a side chair, looking more nervous than I'd ever seen her. She looked down at the lid. "I haven't seen this box for years."

"You've seen it before?" Violet asked.

"Yes, it was Dora's." She stroked the lid, almost as if she touched Dora herself.

"Is Dora my mother?" I asked. I didn't have time to dilly-dally. My giant death clock was ticking down.

Aunt Bessie looked up with a sad smile. "Yes, Dora was your mother."

I knew this already from the evidence piled in

the box on her lap, yet hearing the words spoken out loud felt like a gavel coming down with a final decree. I released a small cry of dismay. Violet reached over, enclosing my hand in hers.

"How can this be, Aunt Bessie?" Violet asked. "Is she my mother too?"

"No, Violet. Your momma is your mother." She smiled at me again. "You both know that your momma was a difficult woman to live with, but years ago, she did try. She loved your father something fierce, but your father was a soft man and her sharp tongue wore him down. After your momma had Violet, she became consumed with her, pushing your daddy to the side. She waited a long time to have Violet, thinking for years she'd never have children. Your father began to work more hours to help buy all the extras your momma wanted. That's when he met Dora, who'd recently moved to Henryetta from Shreveport. Her family was from around here and she'd run off to the city for a little excitement. Dora was sweet and soft, everything your momma was not. nodded in my direction. "With you. Your daddy had to choose who he wanted to be with and he chose Dora."

Violet squeezed my hand and I wondered if I would still be able to use it when she finished.

"Right before you were born, Rose, he left your momma and moved in with Dora. I hate to say it, but he was the happiest I ever saw him." She grimaced toward Violet, "No offense, Violet. He loved you, too."

Violet nodded through her tears. I put my hand on top of hers. She turned to me, her quivering lower lip lifting into a smile. My heart broke seeing her so hurt.

"When you were born, Rose, your daddy said he finally found what he'd been looking for his whole life. He and Dora were very happy, even though they weren't married. He had filed for a divorce, but your momma wouldn't have any part of it and vowed to fight him every step of the way. She made him promise to keep it a secret from everyone, so no one in Henryetta even knew for sure, although lots of people suspected."

"Where's Dora now? Why did Daddy go back to Momma?" I asked.

Aunt Bessie's lips pursed together and she chose her words carefully. She looked at me, tenderness on her face. I knew the answer before she even spoke the words.

"She's dead, darlin'. She died in a car wreck, right before the Christmas after you were born." Aunt Bessie's eyes teared up. "Your momma, she was bound and determined to get your daddy back. So she went to confront Dora after she got off work. They had a terrible fight in the parking lot, and your momma threatened Dora, said she'd see her dead before she'd let your daddy go." Aunt Bessie shook her head. "Dora ran off the road on the way home and crashed into a tree, killed instantly. We were all so thankful you weren't in the car. The police thought it looked like the brake lines had been cut, but honestly, the police in Henryetta have always been known to botch investigations. So in the end there was no proof that your momma had anything to do with it, even though the police suspected she did."

Violet and I clutched each other's hands in stunned silence.

"Well, your daddy, he was devastated. He loved Dora with all his heart, but he had a new baby." Aunt Bessie wiped a tear off her cheek and looked me in the eyes. "He loved you, Rose, but he was too upset to take care of you. Part of him died with Dora that day. So he brought you to Earl and me. Your momma swooped in and convinced your daddy that she forgave him and begged him to come back home. But she couldn't lose face with the town, so she and Violet came to live with us for several months, until enough time elapsed that people would buy Rose as her own.

"I thought it was a terrible idea, but your daddy was too grief-stricken to care. He meant the best for you, Rose, but I could see the hate in your momma's eyes the day she laid eyes on you. As you grew older, she hated you even more. You were the spitting image of Dora, a constant reminder that your daddy wouldn't be with her if Dora hadn't died. Your daddy tried to defend you in the beginning, what little I saw. While he thought he deserved your momma's wrath, he never thought you did. You remember the summer you spent with us when you were seven?"

I nodded through my tears.

"I tried to convince your parents to let you stay with us, your Uncle Earl and I. We never had children and my heart couldn't take how she treated you. But in the end she said no, what would people say? And your daddy had long since stopped trying to stand up to her, even for your sake. Dora would have been so upset to know what became of you. She loved you, child. I know your momma was an awful mother, but for two months you had a mother who loved you enough to make up for all the hate your momma had for you."

We sat in silence, taking it all in. Finally, I held out the ring on my hand. "I found it in the box."

Aunt Bessie nodded. "That's the ring your daddy gave Dora."

I clutched it to my chest. My mother, my real mother who loved me, had worn this ring. I hoped holding it next to my heart would make me feel closer to her, but I only felt empty and cold. And cheated.

"Do you think . . ." Violet stopped to clear her throat before starting again. "Do you think Momma killed Dora?"

Aunt Bessie was quiet. "I don't know, Violet. I would sure hope not. How could someone do such a thing, no matter how upset they are? And even if they did, how could they live with it? If she did, she made her own life hell, as well as the hell she made for you girls."

"What about Daddy?" I asked.

"I loved your father to death, he was my brother, but he made his own hell. He could have done more to protect you girls, should have, but he wallowed in his own misery. He paid for that, too."

Violet spoke up. "There were other things in the box. A savings passbook, Dora's will, and a photo of Dora and Rose."

Aunt Bessie opened the lid and pulled out the passbook first. Violet must have put the papers back in order. I suddenly felt bad abandoning her with the mess of it all. I had the luxury of running away and leaving her to pick up the pieces. I'd done it our entire lives. Violet had always been the stronger of the two of us. I got used to leaning on her and letting her take charge. It seemed unfair that I became upset with her now for telling me what and how to do things when I had encouraged it all along.

Life was a complicated mess.

"The will says the money in the savings account is Rose's."

Aunt Bessie nodded, pulled the will out, and read it. "The savings account, her parents' farm, there's some oil stock as well." She looked up and nodded. "I knew about all of it. Your daddy told me after Dora died. Her family was long gone; your daddy was all she had, but she never put his name on any of it, just Rose's. Earl and I watched after it all, waiting."

"Waiting for what?" Anger rose inside me. I lived in hell for twenty-four years. For what?

"Until it was the right time."

I stood up, my blood boiling with rage. "The right time? And who got to decide that? If Momma hadn't been killed, neither one of us would know right now." I shouted, "Our entire lives are a lie! We had a right to know!"

"You're right, Rose. You had every right, but it wasn't my place to tell you."

"Wasn't your place to tell? So you just watched her abuse me, *us,* and no one says a word because it's not the *right time?* Did you know she used to lock me in a closet? I would pound on the door, screaming and begging her to let me out. Violet would stand outside the door, crying and pleading to Momma to let me out, but Momma would hit her and tell her it had nothin' to do with her. We lived through hell. If that wasn't the right time, when was?" My tirade left me shaky and light-headed, but my outrage remained, simmering in resentment.

"Rose." Violet tugged on my arm, crying. "Sweetie, I know you're upset."

I sat down next to Violet. "Upset? Aren't you

upset? Daddy, Aunt Bessie, Uncle Earl, they all stood by and watched her abuse us. I had money," I pointed to the box on Aunt Bessie's lap, "money we could have used to escape from her, but no one told us. They just left us there."

"I wanted to tell you, Rose, it wasn't that easy. I promised I wouldn't," Aunt Bessie said through her tears.

"Promised who?"

She hesitated. "Your daddy."

Daddy. I couldn't forget his involvement in all of this, him more guilty than Aunt Bessie. Daddy had a front row seat to what Momma had done.

I started to cry.

Violet pulled me into a hug and rubbed my back. "It's okay, Rose. Shh . . . it's okay. It's just gonna take some time."

Time was the one luxury I didn't have. I'd been cheated out of working through all the emotional garbage of our parents' past. And worse, I would be leaving Violet to work through it alone.

"There's something else in here." Aunt Bessie said, lifting a small square of paper out of the box.

"What is it?"

She opened it and froze in shock. When she recovered, her eyes clouded over. "It's from your momma. It's a note to Rose."

I wiped the tears from my cheeks, then shook

my head. "I don't want to hear it, Aunt Bessie. I can't take any more."

"I think you want to hear this, child."

I nodded for her to read.

Dear Rose,

I know I've been a bad mother to you and there were days I tore myself up with guilt over it. At first I tried to love you like I did Violet, but in the end Violet turned against me, too. Your daddy, Violet—they both stopped loving me, all because of Dora. In my heart, I knew it weren't your fault, but you were Dora's, never mine. Your eyes reminded me of it every day, shining with the softness she had in hers, taunting me that your daddy wanted her, not me. Your visions were the last straw, when I finally gave up trying to love you. I'm ashamed to admit, every time I hurt you, in my heart I was hurting her. Later, when you were older, I realized what I had done, and God help me, I tried to stop, but old habits are hard to break.

The irony is that in the end, you were the only one who stayed with me. Your daddy's body may have died last year, but his spirit died years ago, his body just waiting to catch up. Violet, she left to marry Mike as soon as she got a chance and I hardly saw her after that.

But you, Rose, you were there for me, taking

care of me in spite of all my meanness. I watched you sometimes when you weren't looking, amazed at the gentleness of your spirit and even though I beat it down as often as I could, I envied it. You had what I never did.

I should have told you about your mother a long time ago, but I was afraid if I did, I'd lose you, too. You're all I had left.

Believe it or not, I do love you.

Momma

Hearing Aunt Bessie read Momma's letter was the first time I ever heard Momma say she loved me. I began to sob. And didn't stop until well into the night.

Mike slept in Ashley's room and Violet and I clung to each other, crying in her bed. I had no idea what Violet cried for. Did she feel guilty for hurting Momma? For choosing me over her? I cried for never getting the chance to know the Momma who wrote that letter, all the years lost to her pain and pride. And I cried for her. I couldn't imagine the pain she must have endured forced to face me every day, rubbing her nose in the fact she would forever be second choice, Dora's leftovers.

When I finally fell asleep, long after Violet, I cried for me, and all I would miss and all I would lose. It wasn't fair. Life wasn't fair. But then again, I'd learned that lesson a long, long time ago.

Courtesy of Momma.

Chapter Sixteen

Aunt Bessie left after Violet and I went to bed, but not before she told Mike she had all the papers for everything left to me in the will.

And that I was a millionaire.

The next morning I sipped hot coffee trying to clear the fogginess in my head when Mike announced I had more money than God. That's not what he actually said, and technically it wasn't true since I only had $1.5 million, but it might as well have been a trillion. I didn't understand how it could be possible, but Mike said Uncle Earl and Aunt Bessie were the executors of Dora's estate. Daddy didn't want to deal with it, so Uncle Earl took over and had a knack for investing. He had cashed in the oil stock, made some smart investments, and more than quadrupled my worth over the years. That amount didn't even include Dora's parents' farm. And to imagine I'd been worrying I'd be homeless when Momma left everything to Violet. I supposed the right thing to do would be to give half to Violet. She planned to do the same with Momma's possessions. But why waste time on the details of half when I'd leave everything to her anyway?

I hadn't brought dog food for Muffy and eggs

had turned out to be a fiasco the other night. I really didn't want to be alone and it turned out, neither did Violet. We agreed I'd leave Muffy there and run home, shower then come back to spend the day with Violet and the kids.

A few blocks from my house, the convertible sputtered and coughed such thick plumes of black smoke into the air I worried the EPA would swoop in and contain me and the car at any moment. Instead, it died, right there on the curb.

So today wasn't my lucky day, either.

I walked the last few blocks, hot and sweaty by the time I got home. It was only midmorning and already burning up outside. I nearly drained a glass of ice water before calling the rental company to let them know where the car had died. I told them I'd be in later to pick up my old one. I'd had my fun. I didn't need it anymore.

Violet fed Muffy some hotdogs before I left (after I told her the consequenting results were her full responsibility) but it meant I didn't have to hurry back. I had planned on a shower but decided a bath sounded better, especially since I needed some time to mull over the events of the previous night. After I refilled my glass with more ice and water, I set it on the bathroom counter and climbed into the steaming bath. I leaned my head against the porcelain edge, hoping my pain would seep into the warm water. I knew that was too much to expect, so for now, I'd settle for skimming some off the top.

I lay there, dozing off, when I heard a noise in the kitchen. I jerked upright and sloshed the water in the bathtub. The sounds stopped.

Someone was in my house. And heard me.

I climbed out of the tub, shaking with fear, unsure what to do, but trying not to splash any more water. I was naked in my bathroom and my clothes were in the bedroom. Should I lock the door? The doors were thin; it wouldn't take much to break it in. Whatever I decided to do, I needed to do it fast.

I grabbed the towel lying on the toilet seat, wiped the water off the floor, and closed the shower curtain halfway, hoping to hide the water in the tub. The door to the hall stood slightly ajar. Footsteps were moving in my direction.

Fighting my rising hysteria, I opened the linen closet door and slipped in, carefully closing the door. I clutched the wet towel to my chest and over my mouth, trying to stifle my gasps for air. The bathroom door creaked open and footsteps thudded on the tile floor. Then stopped. The person could open the closet door at any moment. I tried to hold my breath, scared of being heard. Then I remember the glass of water. If they saw the ice, they would know I was somewhere in the house.

A million thoughts raced through my head. Whoever it was would find me naked, right before raping and murdering me. Surely, I was safe since my vision told me I wasn't supposed to die until Sunday. That knowledge gave me little consolation, trapped in a closet where old memories spewed into my head, reminding me of the hours spent locked in the dark.

Just when I thought I would give myself away with an outburst of hysterical crying, the person walked out of the bathroom. Chill bumps spread across my skin and water dripped off my body as noises came from my bedroom. Objects crashed and drawers and doors slammed. The sounds moved farther away, and I guessed the person had moved into Momma's room. I wasn't sure how much longer I would last before my claustrophobic frenzy overcame me. Loud swearing and banging moved into the hall adding to my anxiety. It sounded like the intruder hit the other side of the closet wall. The sheetrock vibrated violently, and the wooden shelves jabbed into my back, scraping against my skin. I couldn't contain the cry that escaped from pain, but I hoped the towel muffled the sound.

I discovered the intruder was a man from the vulgarities he spewed—about me and life in general—as he made his way back into the kitchen. I heard items flying in all directions and the ricochet of something metal bouncing off the vinyl floor. More cursing followed. It was obvious the man hadn't found what he was looking for.

I listened to the full-out assault on my kitchen, unable to contain my panic. I covered my face with the towel, wadded up extra-thick and sobbed as quietly as I possibly could.

The noise stopped. Hiccups shook my shoulders, and I bumped into the closet door with a bang.

Footsteps moved back down the hall.

I needed a plan. I wasn't about to let someone kill me, standing naked in the linen closet. But my choice of weapons was sadly lacking. All I had was a wet towel. And my fingernails. I'd gouge his eyes out, then he couldn't see me naked.

I had no idea how one went about gouging a person's eyeballs out but I supposed it had to be done. Too bad I just got a manicure the day before.

I wasn't sure what to do with the towel. Drop it? I needed both hands since he had two eyes. Unless he had an eye patch, which seemed doubtful. But he'd see me naked. Then again, if I was going to blind him maybe I should give him something worth seeing for his last view. I couldn't bring myself to do it though, stand naked in front of a strange man. I bit the towel in my teeth and held my hands out in a claw like stance, somewhat reminding me of a velociraptor ready to attack.

The click of heels on the tile floor alerted me to his entrance into the bathroom. They made a dull thud, the sound Mike's boots made on Violet's kitchen floor. Ordinarily, the sound would have been barely audible, but in the silence and my fear, I heard every foot fall.

I hoped to use the element of surprise, waiting for him to open the door and planning to leap out. My adrenaline surged, ready to pounce. His cell phone rang, making me jump. I caught myself before I banged into the door.

"Yeah," he barked. His voice sounded young, but rough around the edges from too many cigarettes.

I heard muffled words coming from the phone.

"I said I'd be right there. I've got some loose ends to tie up."

Since I didn't have the gouging plan fully coordinated, I hoped he'd just leave.

He cursed again, calling the person on the other end a lot of very ugly names. "I'll be right there." He left the bathroom, giving the wall a good kick on his way out. The kitchen door slammed.

I snuck out of the closet, amazed I'd calmed down so much coming up with a plan. Maybe I was capable of a lot more than I thought.

Wrapping the towel around me, I hunched over and looked out the front windows. The back of a head disappeared into a beat-up looking black pickup truck with the name *Weston's Garage* printed on the side, the letters rubbed off around the edges. The truck looked old and reminded me of a quilt with patches of rust spots and mismatched paint.

The man slammed the door closed and took off down the street. It surprised me he wasn't more subtle. I only hoped Mildred had seen everything then remembered Thursday mornings meant Mildred was busy performing her presidential duties at the Garden Society meeting. Across town.

Discouraged, I turned around to view the damage left behind. Broken dishes and glasses were strewn everywhere. The junk drawer contents had been dumped onto the kitchen table, but when I checked my purse, my wallet appeared intact.

What had he been after?

I moved down to my bedroom, noticing the hole he beat into the wall in the hallway in his frustration. That had to be patched up, as well as the hole he kicked in the bathroom. In my bedroom, clothing had been dumped and thrown all over the room. In Momma's room, boxes of photos were scattered everywhere like new fallen snow.

I sighed with weariness. I really didn't want to deal with this right now. Calling the police crossed my mind, but that could take hours and I doubted they'd believe me anyway. I tiptoed my way through the mess in the kitchen to check the door. I could have sworn that I'd locked it when I came in. But I found it unlocked and the door didn't look busted in. The police definitely wouldn't believe me now.

In the end, what did it matter whether I called or not? It wasn't like they were going to do anything about it.

The phone rang, startling me out of my thoughts. I answered it cautiously. Momma didn't believe in caller ID so I had no way of knowing who waited on the other end.

"Rose?" Joe asked, sounding surprised.

"Joe?"

"What are you doing home? Why aren't you at work?"

"Why are you calling me if you didn't think I was home?"

"I was gonna leave a message." He paused then let his anger loose. "Where were you last night?"

"Excuse me?"

"You left and never came home, where were you all night?"

He was really starting to make me mad. Who did he think he was, anyway? "That's none of your business, Joe McAllister! I don't answer to you."

"I was worried about you, Rose. First your mother, then your break-in and the murder last night. I was scared something happened to you."

"Wait a minute, what murder?"

"A bartender from Jaspers."

The blood rushed out of my head and pooled in the tips of my toes. "What? *Sloan?*"

"You *knew* him?" Joe didn't sound as worried as he did before.

"Well, I wouldn't say I knew him that well. We had a dealing." I sure wasn't going to admit to Joe I needed help fending a man off. "I can't believe it." I sank down in a chair. I didn't know how much more bad news I could take.

We were silent for a moment, while I let the information soak in. "What happened to him?" I finally asked.

"He was shot behind the restaurant after work. Execution-style."

"What does that mean?"

"They shot him at point-blank range, but they probably tried to get information out of him first."

"Oh, my . . . why would someone do that?"

"You tell me."

My heart skipped a beat. "How would I know?" He was so exasperating. "I had one dealing with him and you think I know why someone killed him?"

"For such a quiet town, it's more than a little coincidental that your mother is murdered, someone breaks into your house and a man was murdered last night. Someone you had a *dealing* with."

If he only knew about my break-in minutes earlier. "Do you think the police will figure out I knew him?"

"That depends, Rose. How well did you know him?" Bitterness drenched his words.

"You very well know I didn't know him in the

way you're insinuating. I think I'm done talking to you, Joe."

"Wait!" he called out, pleading, before I could hang up.

"What?"

"I'm sorry. I don't want to fight with you. I was just worried and apparently jealous."

Jealous? Joe jealous over *me?* For some reason I didn't totally believe him. *Three more days* rang through my head. Besides, I had to admit I liked the idea of Joe being jealous. "So where did you think I went last night?"

"I was worried you ran off and did something crazy like sleep with some guy before Monday."

"And why do you care?" I couldn't help asking.

He paused, then answered, soft and sexy: "Because I want it to be me."

I couldn't stop the sharp intake of air from the instantaneous fire igniting in my gut. "Then don't make me wait until Monday," I whispered. "Maybe we can work out some kind of compromise."

He paused again. I had a feeling Joe was doing some conscious-wrestling. He was trying to be honorable and I was trying to drag him down. I really was wicked. I almost felt bad. Almost.

"We can talk about it tonight at dinner. Remember?"

"About that . . ." I glanced around my kitchen with a grimace, unsure I could have everything cleaned up by then, or if I even wanted to. "I'm not sure I can cook."

"We'll figure something out. I'm more interested in the company than the food."

"Maybe we could eat at your place. I could cook there."

He paused again. "No, that's not going to work. My house is a wreck. A total bachelor pad."

I frowned. He didn't have any trouble letting Hilary in there. I rolled my eyes. I didn't want to think about Hilary. "Okay, well we'll figure it out later. See you tonight."

"Wait, Rose, where were you last night?" He didn't sound jealous. He sounded anxious.

"At my sister's house."

I could have sworn I heard him mutter "thank God" under his breath.

We hung up and I pulled out the phone book and called a cleaning company, offering to pay extra if they were there within the hour. Next, I called Violet and told her I had a slight delay. While on the phone, I noticed my Walmart receipt under the junk spread across the table. I pulled it free, looking over the items. I still had things to do today.

"Violet, how about we go to the park for a picnic? We can get food on the way. It'll be fun. We can bring Muffy."

The maid service arrived ahead of schedule and was immediately taken back by the state of the kitchen. An older Hispanic woman shot a look of disapproval in my direction when she noticed the hole in the hallway wall. I shrugged and murmured something about wild parties. I instructed them to throw everything in Momma's room into the now empty boxes. In the kitchen, they could toss anything broken and put everything else away. I handed a set of keys to the woman and told her to hide them under the mat outside the door. A totally obvious place, but it wasn't like locked doors kept people out anyway.

After I got the cleaning service squared away, I called a taxi to take me to the car rental agency. They apologized over the trouble and offered me a new car, but I told them to just give me a refund on the unused days.

When I got to Violet's house, she appeared surprised to see my old car but didn't ask questions. We loaded the kids and Muffy into Violet's minivan and headed to Henryetta's new splash park.

After we spread out a blanket under a tree, we settled in to eat, the kids excited to play in the water. Violet and I convinced them to eat the majority of their lunch before they took off, leaving Violet, Muffy and me behind.

The sun bore down as we stood at the edge of the splash park concrete. Ashley tugged on my wrist, pulling me toward the fountains, looking up at me with pouty eyes. I didn't have a swimming suit, but decided I might never get the chance again. I hadn't seen a weather forecast for the next few days, but today it was hot and sunny, with no clouds in sight. There was a good possibility it wouldn't rain between now and Sunday. Maybe this could count for *play in the rain.*

Violet held Muffy's leash while I ran in, hands over my head, screaming from the shock of the cold water pelting my skin. I shrugged off my inhibitions, tossing them away like an old tattered coat. The chains wrapped around my life slipped off one link at a time with every puddle I stomped. I almost cried from the freedom. Ashley and Mikey laughed as we spun in circles and ran through pools of water. I'd never done this before, completely let go of everything. I felt so light and free I expected to float up into the sky and become lost in the nonexistent clouds above. Violet stood on the edge, eyeing us with a wistful look in her eye and I realized she never had either. I was the chain that tied her down.

I ran to Violet, my clothes soaked and clinging, and saw the wistful expression in her eyes. I stood in front of her and simply reached out my hand. Indecision flickered through her eyes, the fear of letting go. I gave her an encouraging smile, holding my palm face up. She looked into my eyes, tears filling her own and she slowly lifted her hand to mine.

We stood in the Henryetta splash park, me

looking like a drowned rat and Violet in her prim and proper outfit, her hair perfectly in place. Our fingers locked in a tight squeeze and I knew I owed this woman so much. As long as I lived, even if it was only three more days, I would never forget her incredible love for me.

My heart swelled with love and gratitude until it overflowed and filled my eyes with tears, falling and mingling with the sprinkler water that dripped down my face. I smiled, my chin quivering with emotion, then I tugged.

She was reluctant, so I eased her into it. I, of all people, knew how hard it was to give into frivolity. Violet skirted the edge of the concrete, resisting. Ashley ran over and grabbed Violet's other hand. Mikey clapped, excited Mommy was going to play.

Muffy sat off to the side watching all the commotion with disinterest.

When I thought Violet had enough time to adjust, I yelled to Ashley, "Let's get her wet!"

Ashley and I each pulled a hand and Violet screamed and protested in between bursts of laughter. She dug in her heels, leaning her bottom backward as we dragged her toward a huge spray of water spewing from a fire hydrant.

"No! I'll get my hair wet!" she screamed, but this only spurred Ashley on more.

We got her directly under the water, Ashley and I circling our arms around her, holding her under the spray, all three of us squealing. Mikey sat at the edge giggling and clapping. "Momma! Momma!"

Somewhere in the park, someone turned on music. I leaned over to Ashley giving her a mischievous look. "Let's dance!"

And at two o'clock in the afternoon on a hot June day, for the first time in my life, I danced. It wasn't the romantic dance I envisioned when I wrote *dance* on my list, but it was so much better. I looked up into the cloudless sky, flung my arms wide open and spun in circles laughing until I cried. Violet shook her head, a tiny smile lifting the corners of her lips. I grabbed Violet's hand, Ashley pulling the other. We danced in circles, making fools of ourselves and not caring what anyone thought, just being free.

My heart burst right open, right there under the rainbow spray, as I watched Violet let go of her wariness and dance and squeal with her children. Violet had given me hope and love all those years; I had given her so little in return. But that Thursday afternoon, I gave Violet something just as precious. Freedom. I set her free. When I was gone, there would be no regrets for her. Violet turned to me, Mikey on her hip and Ashley twirling around in the sprays. Pure joy radiated from her face and I couldn't contain the happiness billowing like a mushroom cloud. Another memory for my scrapbook.

I wiped the tears streaming down my face and ran into the water, spinning Ashley around to her delight. We played for another half an hour until Mikey looked like he was about to fall over with sleepiness. None of us were ready to go, so we changed the kids out of their wet suits and into dry clothes. We lay on the blanket under the tree, letting the warm breeze dry us. The kids fell asleep within minutes. Violet and I looked up at the leaves of the oak tree hanging over our heads, the soft rustle a soothing lullaby.

"Do you still think of me as your sister?" Violet asked, breaking our silence.

I turned my head toward her. "Of course, Vi. You're the best sister I could have ever asked for."

Her eyes filled with tears, "I wasn't sure, because of Momma . . ." her words trailed off, and uncertainty hung between us.

"Vi, I don't care about blood. It never mattered to me like it did to Momma." Which made total sense now that I thought about it, Momma's preoccupation with blood. "I love you, Violet." My voice tightened as tears stung my eyes again. "You were there for me when you could have walked away and saved yourself. Momma would have loved you more if you hadn't taken my side. You gave up so much for me. What have I ever given you?"

Tears trickled from the corner of her eye, across the bridge of her nose and dripping to the blanket beneath us. Her lip quivered as she struggled to speak. "You gave me you."

The dam of tears broke again and I cried softly, grateful for the love I didn't deserve because the gift of me didn't seem to be enough.

Chapter Seventeen

I took a nap on the blanket, a short one, but long enough to make me feel groggy and slightly muddled. Muffy lay next to me, her face on her paws, soft snores coming from her tiny body. Leave it to me to not only get a farting dog but a snoring one, too. But she was a good dog and I was grateful she was mine. I reached my hand over and scratched the back of her neck.

Lying there with the soft breeze tickling my skin, I realized this is what people meant when they said *it's the little things in life*. I felt the tears returning. Enough tears. There wasn't enough time left to waste on tears.

When the kids woke up, we loaded everyone into the minivan and headed to Violet's house. It didn't take much convincing to get Ashley to jump on her trampoline in her backyard with me, especially considering she had begged me to jump many times before. When we tired of jumping, we played dress up. Ashley gave me a makeover, placed a tiara on my head and we paraded around the house using our princess waves. Afterward, I convinced Violet to teach me the basic elements of knitting.

"Now? Let's do it next week."

"No," I said a little too abruptly.

Violet narrowed her eyes. "What's the rush?"

I'm going to die on Sunday and it's on my list of things I wish to do before I die didn't sound like an appropriate answer. I shrugged then tried Ashley's puppy face. "Please?"

Violet laughed, "I need to get dinner started."

"Just a few steps . . ."

"Stitches."

"Just a few stitches. Please?"

Violet relented and thankfully I was a fast learner.

"What do you want to make?" she asked as I cast a long row of uneven stitches.

"I dunno, a scarf?"

"That's pretty easy. You keep up at that pace and you could be done in a couple of weeks."

I didn't have a couple of weeks, but that didn't matter. I just needed to learn how to knit.

I washed my face before I left. I would have just enough time to make sure my house had been put together before Joe showed up.

When we got home, Muffy sniffed around our yard, reacquainting herself with the territory and marking all the appropriate places. I pulled the keys from under the mat as Joe pulled in.

"Please don't tell me you had those keys under your rug," he said as he got out of the car.

"Okay, then I won't."

He groaned as he walked over. He looked dirty, his hair a scroungy mess. Streaks of grease covered his hands and ran up his arms. He smelled of sweat and gasoline. As crazy as it was, I had never seen him sexier.

"Why would you do such a thing?" he asked, but not in his usual bossy tone.

"It was only this one time. The cleaning ladies left them under the mat since I wasn't home when they finished."

"Cleaning ladies? Why would you need a cleaning lady? Your house is spotless."

I shrugged. I really didn't want to go into the morning's events. "Maybe I should have sent them over to your house instead, since it's so messy and all."

He laughed but sounded a little uneasy. "Yeah . . . what do you want to eat?"

I unlocked the door and turned around to face him. "I really don't have much food to cook." I didn't really see the purpose in making a grocery store run at this point.

He leaned on the side of the house, trapping me against the door. "Who needs food?"

I pushed against his chest, "You're nothin' but a big tease, Joe McAllister. You have no intention of giving me what I want."

He kissed me and I silently cursed his ability to make me forget what I was arguing about.

"I'll give you everything you want and more . . . on Monday."

"Argh!" I growled as I turned around and

opened the door. "That still doesn't solve our dinner dilemma."

"We can order out and have it delivered. What sounds good?"

"Chinese," I said the first thing that popped into my head. I'd never had Chinese food and it was on my list. Momma said she wouldn't eat food made by communists.

He smiled, a real smile, not his usual teasing or taunting smirk. It made him look like a boy, the way his eyes sparkled. I smiled up at him like an idiot, lost in his eyes. They were a dark brown, but I could see little flicks of almost black scattered around his pupils. I realized he had asked me a question.

I cringed, giggling. "Sorry, I was caught up in the view." My boldness amazed me, but at this point, I had nothing to lose.

He actually looked embarrassed and his cheeks turned red.

I laughed. Joe McAllister blushing. That was a sight I never expected to see. "Obviously, I didn't hear your question."

"Do you want to order it? I need to take a shower." He stretched his arms out from his sides to emphasis his point.

The image of Joe in the shower popped into my head, which didn't help anything. I shook my head to clear it. "Yeah, sure. I can order. What do you want?"

A slow smile spread across his face, but he answered, "Kung Pao Chicken."

I repeated it in my head several times so I'd remember. "Go take your shower you big tease, then come back over."

I walked into the kitchen, unsure what I'd find but it looked put together. Then I got out the phone book, which had seen a lot of action in the last couple of days. I had no idea what to order, but the restaurant had a menu printed in the phone book. I knew I liked beef and I liked broccoli, so beef and broccoli seemed like a safe bet. They said they'd deliver the order in thirty minutes.

I was still a bit damp from the afternoon, so I put on another pair of lingerie, the lavender set, and threw on a skirt and blouse. I checked my hair in the bathroom. It looked flat and lifeless, but I didn't see the point of doing anything other than fluffing it a bit. I didn't have on any makeup, not that I usually did, but I wanted to look good for Joe. I carefully put on some mascara, which I was still getting the hang of, and some blush.

Joe still hadn't returned so I checked Momma's room. All the photos and items were deposited back where they belonged. I grabbed a box and sat on the bed and pulled a photo off the top. It was a picture of the four of us at Violet's graduation. Momma and Daddy flanked a beaming Violet, in her blue cap and gown. Momma's stern face overshadowed Daddy's, with his vacant eyes. I stood on Daddy's right, staring off to the side. I remembered that day. I'd watched Uncle Earl, wishing I was with him instead of my own family. Hearing that Aunt Bessie had wanted to raise me was a surprise. I couldn't help but think how differently my life would have turned out if that had happened. But to live with them would have meant leaving Violet. I was glad I stayed, in spite of all the pain.

I pulled out the next photo. They were all out of order now and this one was Violet and me, when we were little, standing in front of a Christmas tree. I didn't remember that Christmas, but we looked to be about five and three, in our flannel pajamas and holding our baby dolls. We looked happy, ear to ear smiles on our faces. Why couldn't I remember that? A happy time?

Tears filled my eyes again, as I pulled out the next photo. Daddy and me, in the backyard. He was kneeling, planting flowers. Six-year-old Rose looked happy but I saw something missing in my eyes. No wonder I didn't have friends when I was little. I looked like a zombie.

I wore a pair of gloves and held a small garden shovel, ready to help Daddy. I studied his face, searching for any signs of regret. It was amazing how using a new filter to view your life could change your perception. I wondered how he could stand by and watch Momma do what she did for all those years. The tears fell down my cheeks. I was so tired of crying. I sniffed and wiped one cheek with the back of my hand, startled to see Joe standing in the doorway.

"Sorry, I didn't mean to scare you." He moved toward me and sat on the bed, wrapping an arm around my back. "I came in the kitchen and you weren't there, so I decided to look for you. Why're you crying?" He looked down at the photo. "Is that you?" He took the picture from my hand, getting a closer look. "And that must be your dad. I see the resemblance."

For some reason that made me cry harder.

"Hey," he said, wiping away my tears. "What's wrong?"

"What would you do if you found out your entire life was a lie?"

His face lost all expression. "What do you mean?"

"It doesn't matter. Not anymore. I don't want to spend any more time thinking about it."

"Are you in some kind of trouble, Rose? Tell me, maybe I can help you."

I shook my head. "I've got more trouble this week than most people have in a lifetime. But it doesn't matter, after Sunday it won't matter."

"What happens Sunday?"

His eyes looked so kind, like he really cared. Maybe I could tell him. I was tired of keeping this secret to myself. My eyes welled up again, to my dismay. "You'd never believe me if I told you. I can't even tell Violet."

"Your sister? Why can't you tell Violet?"

"I don't want to scare or worry her."

He put his hands on my shoulders and turned me to face him. "You won't scare me. I might be worried but I can take it. I'm good at working out problems. Maybe I can help you with yours."

I wanted to believe him. If only I could find a way out of this. I sniffed. "I'm afraid if I tell you, you won't like me anymore." If I told him I had visions, he'd think I was a freak, just like everyone else. Or he'd call me a liar. I didn't like either alternative.

"No, Rose, I swear. There's nothing you can say that will make me not like you."

I wavered, so tempted. What was the worst that could happen? He ran screaming and never looked back. But I liked having him around; I didn't want to lose him.

He stroked my cheek with his hand. "You don't have to do this alone. Let me help you." His last words were soft and soothing, like a caress.

I closed my eyes and leaned my cheek into his hand. It felt so good to be touched. I risked losing this if I told him. I might not get the opportunity again before Sunday.

"I really like you, Rose. This isn't just physical. I like *you* but we can't make this work if you won't be honest with me."

That made me cry harder. He only reminded me of what I would never have.

"Hey, hey. That wasn't supposed to make you cry. I thought you liked me too."

"I do."

"Then trust me."

Trust was a tricky thing. Usually the person asking for the trust had to prove they were worthy to receive it. Had Joe proven himself trustworthy?

The doorbell rang.

Joe groaned his frustration. "Wait here. I'll get it."

I watched him jump up and walk out of the room then followed a few seconds behind. I didn't want to be in this room full of painful memories anymore.

Joe paid for our food. I went into the bathroom, disturbed to see my mascara had smeared beneath my eyes. Maybe that was why I never wore the stuff. I grabbed a washrag out of the linen closet, which reminded me of the intruder that morning. Joe must have been on the same wavelength. He stood in the partially open door and leaned against the frame.

"Why are there holes in your walls?" he asked quietly, but I knew him well enough now to hear the undercurrent of irritation.

I wet the washrag and swiped beneath my eyes. "From the intruder."

"I thought they never got inside. I thought you said they fell out the window."

"You ask too many questions, Joe. How come

you're the one asking all the questions and never answering any?"

"Fine, try asking one."

"Fine." I turned to face him, leaning my hip into the edge of the counter. "I don't even know what you do. What's your job?"

"I never tried to keep that from you. You just never asked."

It was true. I never had. "So what is it?"

"I'm a mechanic."

That made sense, considering how his hands and arms had been covered in grease.

"Why did you move here?"

"I needed a change."

"Why?"

He got a sheepish look on his face. "Girlfriend issues."

"Hilary?"

"Yeah." He didn't say anything else.

I shot him a look of frustration. "Seriously, can't you volunteer anything?"

He groaned, grabbing my hand, and pulled me into the kitchen. "We dated for a couple of years. Okay, we lived together at the end. But it didn't work out so not only did I move out, I moved away." He started pulling the containers out of the bag and setting them on the table.

I got a couple of glasses out of the cabinet. "But why Henryetta? Most people want *out* of Henryetta, not in."

He tilted his head to the side in a half-shrug. "There was a job here and I needed a job."

"So why did Hilary show up?"

He stopped and rested the back of his legs against the table. The kitchen was small enough that he could grab my arm and tug me toward him. He pulled me to his chest and looked into my eyes, brushing the hair off my cheek. "I didn't invite her here. She invited herself. She wasn't my girlfriend at that point, although she hoped to be when she left. But I sent her away, Rose. It made me furious when she told you she was my girlfriend. I would have sent her away that night, but I tried to be courteous and I let her spend the night, in a separate room. She left the next day. You saw that."

"Why didn't you tell me?"

"I tried. You wouldn't listen."

I suddenly felt stupid. "Joe, I'm so sorry. I thought . . ." I looked away in embarrassment.

"Hey," he put his fingers under my chin and turned my face to his. "I don't blame you. It looked bad and you didn't know me very well. That's how I knew you really liked me though. You knew about Hilary, yet you were still interested in me."

"So why can't you go to the police?"

The blinds of honesty closed in his eyes. They looked cold in contrast. "I can't answer that.

Tonight." He stressed. "If you give me until next week, I think I can tell you then."

"And you won't help me with number fifteen until you can tell me?"

He nodded. "I want you to know everything first, so you don't think I tried to trick you."

The *next week, I think* began to sink in. "Wait a minute," I turned my head to the side, scrutinizing him. "You keep telling me *Monday,* but it might actually be later."

"What difference does a few days make? You've waited this long, what's your hurry?"

"Maybe I'm tired of waiting."

"What happens in three days?"

"Why won't you go to the police?"

We reached a stalemate, and Joe wasn't pleased. He just lost his upper hand. But instead of getting angry, he sighed. "Let's eat."

We sat down, the mood heavy around us. It made me sad and depressed. This wasn't how I wanted to spend my time with him. He was hiding things from me, but I didn't want to spend the two days I had left figuring it out. Since he was hung up on my insistence that Sunday was the day everything had to be done, maybe I should just pretend it didn't exist.

"This is good. I've never had Chinese food before."

Joe's mouth fell open in shock. "What? If I had

known, I would have ordered. How did you know what to get?"

He laughed when I told him my reasoning. "You need to go to a Chinese buffet. You can try all kinds of different things on a buffet and then you'll know what you like next time you order."

"Maybe we could go next week," I said, trying my new tactic.

The merriment in his eyes fell away. "I thought the world was going to end on Sunday."

I shrugged. "Maybe you've convinced me it won't. So what do you say? Wanna go with me?"

I couldn't help noticing he wouldn't look me in the eye when he spoke with a chipperness I wasn't used to hearing him use. "Yeah, sure."

That seemed odd. Maybe he and Hilary really weren't over, but it didn't matter if they were or not. I only needed him for two more days. Facing death made me shameless.

Joe tried to restore our lighthearted mood and demonstrated how to use the thin wooden chopsticks in the bag. He showed me how to hold them like a pencil and pinch the ends together, then had me try. We held our chopsticks in the air, pinching at nothing in the air. Joe was pretty adept with chopsticks. I just made a mess.

I laughed. "Maybe if I can master this, I can put this in the number twenty-nine spot."

"Oh, yeah. Get your list and let's go through it."

"Why do you want to help me?" Even though I

vowed not to ask questions, this one made me curious.

"Don't take this the wrong way," he looked at me, cringing a bit, "but I've never met anyone who has had so few life experiences. I like watching you live 'em." He smiled. "Plus, it sounds fun."

I retrieved the list and set it on the table between us. It looked more battered than the last time he'd seen it.

"I see you've checked off more things."

"Yeah, and a few more things today." I picked up a pen off the table. "Today was *dance* . . ." I checked it off.

His eyes twinkled. "You danced?"

"Yeah, in the Henryetta splash park." Last week I would have been embarrassed to admit it. Today I was proud.

He chuckled. "I sure would have liked to have seen that."

"Dress like a princess . . ." *Check.*

"Why am I missing out on all these? Was this while you were dancing in the Henryetta splash park? What were you wearing?"

"No, it was *not*." I laughed. "It was later. My niece Ashley put a tiara on me and enough makeup to help me establish a new career as a prostitute."

"I might like to have a say in your career choice." His voice was low in my ear.

If I had any hope of crossing off fifteen, I would have let him go on. Instead, I gave him a playful shove. "We have work to do. Focus."

"Learn to knit." *Check.* I waited for him to say something. When he didn't I turned to him. "No comment?"

He raised his eyebrow in an apologetic gesture. "Knitting doesn't do anything for me. Sorry."

I laughed. "What if I said I was knitting you a scarf?"

"Are you?" The excitement in his voice surprised me.

"I could be . . ." I gave him a wicked look. "For a price."

"Monday. Moving on."

"Picnic in the park." *Check.*

"You really never went on a picnic in the park before?" He asked softly, sadness creeping into his voice.

"No, but you know, it's okay. I did today."

"How could you not experience all these normal things?"

I knew what he meant, but his words stung. Normal. Just a reminder that I wasn't. "Momma was strict. She didn't believe in having fun; picnics were frivolous things. Gardners did not do frivolous things."

He took my hand in his, slowly stroking his fingers along the back and up to my wrist. "Your mother sounds like she was a hard woman to live with." His other hand moved up to my hair as he looked into my face. "You've had a lot of pain in your life. I'm sorry."

My vision got blurry from tears. I didn't want to cry with Joe. I looked down at the list. "Oh," I said, trying to sound cheerful. "I forgot one."

Joe moved the hand in my hair down to my back, holding me in an embrace like I had seen Mike do with Violet.

"Wear a lacy bra and panties." *Check.*

Joe started to cough and then laugh.

"Why is that funny?" I turned to face him, ready to pounce on him for making fun of me.

His eyes grew dark. "Trust me, there's nothing *funny* about what you just said. You just caught me off guard." His arm around my back pulled me closer to him, so my shoulder fit into his chest, his hand pressed against my arm. "Listen Rose, I know you're very inexperienced, and I know that you're not used to talking about things like this, so I feel I would be remiss if I didn't warn you that you can't just talk about these kinds of things with guys."

"But I'm talkin' to you about it."

"Well . . . I'm different. A lot of guys would take advantage of the situation. You're too trusting. I don't want you to get hurt."

"Why are you different than other guys? Do you not want to, *you know?* with me?" I still couldn't bring myself to say it. "It's okay if you don't want me, just tell me." If he didn't want to, it would hurt, but I'd rather know now.

Joe groaned, long and deep, and his arm tightened around me. "You have no idea how much I want you. But I can't yet, I just can't and you don't know how hard it is. In fact," he turned my head to look at him, his eyes burning with desire. "All I can think about at this moment is the bra and panties you're wearing under your clothes. What do they look like? What color are they? What do you look like in them? I think about how I can take your clothes off so I can see."

"Lavender," I whispered. "They're lavender."

He groaned again and kissed me, smashing my body against his. I was at an odd angle, and felt awkward but he soon made me forget. His lips claimed mine while his hands slid up my back, under my shirt. I wrapped my arms around him, fearful he would stop, but Joe showed no intention of stopping.

He pulled me out of my chair so I sat on his lap, how he managed it, I had no idea. There were only so many things I could concentrate on at a time. I sat across his legs, his arm around my back the other hand working on the buttons of my blouse, his mouth driving me mad. Who said men couldn't multitask? Joe seemed to be very good at it.

He moved his hand from my back and pulled

his lips away from mine. I started to protest but saw him gazing at the front of my shirt which now gaped open, revealing my bra. His hands moved to my shoulders, slowly slipping my blouse down my arms. It fell to the floor behind me.

I knew I should be embarrassed, but I couldn't help feeling empowered, that I was the one who made him gape like that. I felt sexy. And alive.

Joe's hands moved to my waist and slowly up my sides, teasing me with anticipation. Then his eyes searched mine, his full of longing and regret. "I can't stop myself any more, Rose. You're the only one who can stop me now."

His mouth moved to mine, a hand on my breast, slipping inside my bra. I gasped in surprise, amazement and need. I never knew I could feel like this. His mouth followed behind his hand, astounding me even more.

I clung to him, silently pleading for more even though it felt like a greedy request, but he must have understood. The next thing I knew, he carried me to my room.

He dropped my legs to the floor, and we stood next to my bed. I turned to face him, my almost bare chest against his shirt. I wanted to feel the skin of his chest against mine. I reached for the bottom of his shirt. His hands joined mine and we lifted it off together, then he tossed it on the floor. He found the button of my skirt, undoing it and then the zipper. It fell, puddling at my feet. I absently kicked it to the side and looked up at him, wondering what happened next.

"God, you're beautiful," he murmured running his hands up and down my back as he studied my front. His hands stopped at the clasp of my bra on my back. "It's not too late to stop, Rose. You only have to tell me no and I'll stop immediately."

"Why would I want you to stop?"

His mouth was on mine again, my bra soon gone and his mouth moved down to my breasts until I moaned. I was almost embarrassed but an overwhelming need overshadowed shame.

"Oh Joe, please . . ."

"What do you want, Rose? Do you want me to stop?"

"No!" I nearly shouted. "Don't stop!" But I didn't know what I needed either. What I felt was primal and instinctual. I had no idea *what* I needed, I only knew I needed it or I would die.

If all my senses hadn't been thoroughly occupied at the moment, I would have laughed at the irony of it. Maybe that's how I died on Sunday, from lack of sex.

Somewhere in that thought process, Joe moved us to the bed, and shed his jeans. I made a mental note to compliment him later on his multitasking. His skills were quite impressive. He wore a pair of boxers and lay on his side next to me. My view of him was somewhat obscured by his angle, frustrating me. I wanted to see more.

His mouth and hands made me forget.

His hand slid down into my panties and I was sure I was going to die tonight, my vision got the date wrong, but I didn't care. I couldn't think of any better way to go. I even heard bells. Maybe they were the bells on Saint Peter's gate.

I came to my senses the moment Joe's body was gone, like in the *The Time Traveler's Wife.* Maybe that was Joe's big secret. Maybe he time-traveled.

But Joe was still in the room, on the floor, digging his ringing cell phone out of the pocket of his jeans. He looked at the number. "Shit!" he said before he answered. "Yeah." His brows furrowed as he listened. "Yeah," he said again, and then he hung up.

I heard guys weren't big on talking on the phone, but that call was ridiculous.

"I've gotta go." He sat on the edge of the bed and scrambled to put his jeans back on. Then he stuffed his feet into his still-tied shoes.

"What? *Now?*"

He reached over and pulled my head to his, giving me a quick kiss. "You have no idea how badly I want to finish this, but I have to go."

"Will you come back?" I couldn't have gotten this close to stop now.

"I don't know how long this will take. I'll call you tomorrow. We'll work on your list tomorrow night."

He grabbed his shirt off the floor and pulled it over his head as he walked out of the room.

I threw on the first thing I could find, a T-shirt that didn't cover my bottom. My panties, amazingly enough, were still on my body. I ran after him.

"Joe, wait!" I stood in the kitchen doorway, watching him climb into his car. I didn't care who saw me. "Where are you going?"

"Work."

"At nine o'clock at *night?*"

He was already in the car, but got out and stood next to the door. His face changed. He wasn't my Joe anymore. If I had run into this Joe at the bar in Jaspers I would have run home. "Don't ask me questions, Rose. If you're smart, you'll stay out of this. Now go back inside." The last part was a direct order. One he expected me to obey.

I didn't tell him to stop bossing me around because for one thing, his car had already left, and for another, I was too scared. For the first time since I met Joe, I was honest to goodness scared of him.

Chapter Eighteen

Joe didn't come home until around two in the morning. I felt like Mildred, snooping through the window, as I spied on him. But Joe didn't go directly in his house; he went to my shed. He opened the door, slipped inside and came out less than a minute later. What could Joe be up to?

And how did he get in?

Joe went inside his house. As he passed my bedroom window, I noticed his clothes were dirty and grimy, like he'd been rolling in dirt. A million questions ran through my mind, but I was tired of pondering it all. I just wanted to go to sleep and so did Muffy. She lay on my bed and looked irritated that her glares hadn't stopped me from getting up and down. I finally fell asleep, cuddling Muffy, until I couldn't take the smell rolling out of her every ten minutes and covered my head with a pillow.

The next morning, I made a pot of coffee and stared at the television. Here I had gone to the trouble of getting cable and I still hadn't watched it. So I turned it on, flipping through two hundred channels until I found a rerun of *Little House on the Prairie*. I spent most of the morning slumped in the chair, which made me frustrated. I had a day and a half left to live and I was watching reruns.

I made myself shower and dress, and then clean up the mess in the kitchen. There wasn't much to clean but we'd left out Chinese food cartons and the chopsticks were stuck to the table. I threw everything away and found two fortune cookies, still unopened. In twenty-four years, I had never had a fortune cookie, which seemed pitiful. I ripped the cellophane wrapper open and broke the cookie in half, pulling out a rectangular paper.

Your future looks bright and promising.

I almost laughed. I must have really bad karma.

The phone rang, and I jumped. Everything startled me these days, obviously with good reason.

"Rose? What are you doing home? Why are you off work again?" Joe asked.

"Joe, if you don't think I'm home, *why* do you keep calling?" I asked, suddenly weary.

"I wanted to leave you a message." He sounded like a kid caught throwing rocks at the neighbor's window. "I wanted to apologize for last night."

I sat silent, unsure what to say. He took my silence as encouragement.

"I was really harsh with you and I shouldn't have been. I didn't expect to be called into work last night. They called me in for a tense situation and it made me short. I'm sorry."

I still didn't say anything, unsure how I felt. Why did he have to be so complicated? But then, if that wasn't the pot calling the kettle black, I didn't know what was.

"Can I make it up to you tonight? I want to take you out to dinner. We can go to the Italian restaurant, Little Italy. Then you can check off *go to Italy* since you can't actually fly there before Sunday."

My eyes burned. "You remembered *Go to Italy?*" How did he remember?

He heard the crack in my voice. "Oh, Rose, don't cry. I'm so sorry about last night. Of course, I remembered. I remember everything about you, including your list. Please, just give me another chance. I promise to make it up to you."

I wiped the tears off my cheeks. I'd be an idiot to say yes. I wanted to ask him why he was in my shed the night before, but then he'd know I'd been snooping on him. Why did I have to like him so much?

"Please?" He was begging, desperation clinging to his voice.

It was a public place, what could happen? I'd make him answer my questions and if he didn't answer them to my satisfaction then I'd just avoid him all day Saturday.

"Okay," I sighed.

I heard his exhale of relief.

"But I'll meet you there. We'll go separately."

"Why? No, never mind. I don't care. How about seven-thirty? I'll make reservations."

"Okay, I'll see you then."

I hung up, exhausted. There were a million things I needed to do, but I couldn't face a single one. Instead, I went to bed to take a nap, pulling an afghan over me.

Muffy sat on the floor by the bed and whined. I patted the space beside me. "Come on, Muffy."

I woke up hours later, rested but groggy. For someone not used to naps, I seemed to be getting my fair share. I looked over at the clock. It was six o'clock. I had literally slept the day away.

Unsure whether to dress up or go casual, I decided to go fancy since I might never get the chance again. I wore a red sleeveless dress with a deep V in both the front and back. The slim skirt hit above my knee. I almost hadn't bought it, wondering where I would wear such a thing. Now I was glad I did. I decided to wear my red lingerie underneath. Might as well go all the way. I flipped the ends of my hair out and put on makeup. After I put on my strappy black heels, I looked into the mirror and felt pretty. No, beautiful. I felt like a princess.

I pulled up to Little Italy right at seven-thirty but didn't see Joe's car in the parking lot. I ordered a glass of wine to sip while I waited. And waited. At seven-forty-five, Joe still hadn't shown up. I pulled my cell phone out of my purse, surprised to see a text message Joe sent only a minute earlier. I wondered why I hadn't heard it ding, and saw it was still on silent.

Can't make it. Tied up at work. I am so sorry. I'll make up to you tomorrow. Promise.

I shook my head. *Over my dead body.* Then I laughed at the irony. Give him a day and it would be.

I couldn't help but wonder what was wrong with me. Two dates and both guys left me stranded in a restaurant. One thing was sure, I wouldn't go hang out in the bar and get the bartender killed.

The thought made my heart skip. *Oh my goodness, had I gotten Sloan killed?* Joe had a good point. That was a lot of activity for a small city like Henryetta, all of it having something to do with me. The memory of Daniel at the DMV came back.

"Sloan isn't your brother, is he?"

"Why do you ask that?"

"He's a cop, isn't he?"

Daniel Crocker thought Sloan was a cop and I was somehow involved with him.

Oh my God, I got Sloan killed.

Facing my own death was one thing, but causing the death of someone else was completely different. It made being stood up on a date seem pretty insignificant.

I paid for the glass of wine and left, unsure

what to do. I felt drawn to the funeral home. Sloan's visitation might be tonight. I could pay my respects. It was the least I could do if I really got him killed.

I drove past the building, the parking lot filled with cars. It didn't mean it was Sloan's, but I knew one way to check. It was so crowded I had to pull into the gravel overflow parking. Picking my way through the gravel proved a challenge, considering I wasn't used to wearing heels. By the time I made it to the paved lot, teetering on asphalt felt like walking in flip-flops.

A sign propped up inside the front door announced that Sloan Chapman occupied the Magnolia Room. The Magnolia Room was the big room, which explained all the cars in the lot. I walked down the hall, making my way around the mourners milling about.

"It's such a shame," a woman said to her companion in a hushed tone. "He was such a nice guy."

I knew that firsthand.

Overdressed for a wake, I attracted more attention than I wanted. When I entered the Magnolia Room, at least four times the size of the Jasmine, I stood toward the rear, getting my bearings. A throng of people gravitated to the front, where an elderly woman stood next to the casket, weeping. A younger woman stood next to her, looking shell-shocked.

I found it hard to believe that a week ago I had been in the same spot.

"Did you know him very well?" The man next to me wore a suit, but he tugged at the collar like he wasn't used to being dressed up. I guessed him to be around my age.

I shook my head. "No, not really. I only knew him from Jaspers. He was really nice to me."

"That was Sloan, nice to everyone. He took off to Dallas for several years and came back about six months ago sporting his tattoos and his earrings, but still the same sweet guy. A giant teddy bear."

What little I knew of Sloan, I believed that. "Why did he come home?" I asked.

"His mom is sick. That's her up there." He pointed to the woman up front. "She's got breast cancer. Sloan came home to help her out."

A lump formed in my throat, making it difficult to talk. "I'm so sorry."

He turned to look at me with a quizzical expression. "Yeah, everyone is sorry. The world's a sadder place without Sloan."

The casket lid was propped open, but I didn't think I could bring myself to go up and look. I'd seen enough. I was ready to go.

Turning to leave the room, I saw him standing at the door watching me.

Daniel Crocker.

"I wondered if you'd show up," he said, looking

me up and down. "You look nice. I was about to give up on you but patience is what got me where I am today."

"Where? In a funeral home?" My retort was so unlike me, but I found his cocky attitude irritating, especially if he killed Sloan.

"Feisty, huh? We'll see how feisty you really are." He grabbed my arm. It looked innocent enough, a man assisting a woman, but his fingers pinched deep into my arm. "Let's take a walk, shall we?"

My heart wanted to fling itself from my chest. Should I scream? Should I try to run? I couldn't get very far in my three-inch heels and screaming seemed irreverent to Sloan. Getting him killed was bad enough; I didn't want to disrupt his visitation.

"What do you want?" I asked, trying to keep up with him. I willed myself to be brave. I needed to be brave to get out of this.

"You know what I want. Let's not play stupid."

He continued to drag me down the hall toward the back exit, past the offices. I knew from standing outside with Joe at Momma's visitation that the rear of the funeral home was fairly secluded. Going out there alone with Daniel Crocker was a very bad idea.

"You've got the wrong person. I don't know what you're talking about." I tried to pull my arm out of his grasp without making a scene, but his fingers dug deeper. I almost cried out in pain, but swallowed it down.

"Now, now, Rose. You and Sloan were sly, just not sly enough. Come on."

We moved past the crowd in the lobby and started down the empty hall to the exit. I knew it made a right angle at the end of the hall, turning into a three-foot section at the exit. That area would be completely out of view of the mourners in the lobby. My panic rose like a freak desert flash flood; one minute everything is calm, the next, it was raging out of control.

Keep it together, Rose. You can get out of this.

We reached the end of the hall and I dug my heels into the carpet. Daniel Crocker turned to face me with an evil grin. "Wanna do this the hard way, huh?" He gave my arm a vicious jerk and I flew forward into his chest. He made a low guttural sound. "I like you, Rose. I'd like to think we can work something out."

I had trouble holding down my fear. *You can't give into this panic or you won't be able to think.* I pulled away from him, trying to back up in to the hall visible to the people in the lobby, but he grabbed both of my arms and pulled me toward him, out of sight.

"You wanted your anonymity, which was all well and good until you failed to deliver what you were paid for." He growled into my face. His breath smelled of garlic and onions. "And we had reliable information that you worked at the DMV. I just didn't know who you were until that Friday I came in. I was there trying to sniff you out and the look on your face when you saw my name told me everything I needed to know."

I couldn't hold back the sob that pushed its way to the surface. "I swear, I don't know what you're talking about. I didn't even know Sloan." I choked out.

Daniel pinned me to the wall by the back door. He leaned his body into mine. "Now, now, baby. I thought we were past the games." His eyes traveled down to my chest and back to my face. He smiled, but it was more of a leer. "I like how you've spent the money. If it were just me, I'd be willing to forgive and forget, but my partners aren't as understanding as me. They're tired of waiting."

"I don't know what you're talking about. I don't know what you want." My words sounded like a whine. So much for being brave.

We stood a few feet from the door. Daniel Crocker was bigger and stronger than me. If he wanted me to go outside, I was going outside. At least if I stayed in the funeral home, I stood a chance.

"I want lots of things, baby, but right now I want the flash drive." He leaned toward my neck and took a deep breath. "You smell delicious. I bet you taste as good as you look."

I let out a whimper and he pulled back and laughed. "Like I said, I like you, Rose. Maybe we can work out some sort of compromise that will work in both of our favors."

"What kind of compromise?" I was surprised I got the words out at all, considering that I could hardly breathe.

He ran his hand up and down my neck, his fingertips trailing down to my cleavage. "Meet me at The Trading Post, tomorrow night. Ten o'clock. You bring the flash drive and I'll convince my partners this was all a huge misunderstanding. And if you're lucky, I'll make you grateful I did."

"What if I can't make it?"

Rage replaced his smile, his face exuding pure evil. "You don't want to find out. Be a smart girl and come see me." He released me with a shove, then flung open the back door so hard it smacked into the brick wall. The back of my head bounced off the wall just about the same time a vision started coming.

It was night and I lay on my back in the woods, my limbs at odd angles with a vacant expression on my face. The light of the full moon filtered through the trees, casting odd shadow shapes. The moonbeams lit up the small hole centered in my forehead.

"I'm gonna die."

I wasn't dead yet, but apparently, I was scared witless because I just stood there, as if I waited for Daniel Crocker to change his mind and come back and take me with him.

Snap out of it, Rose. Move.

I needed to get it together. I had a little over twenty-four hours to come up with a flash drive.

Chapter Nineteen

I went back to the Magnolia Room and sat in a rickety folding chair in the rear. I'm not ashamed to admit I bawled my eyes out. I got a few stares, but I figured I was at a wake, it felt like an appropriate place to cry. An elderly woman brought me a box of tissues and patted my back.

"There, there child. It's the way of life, from ashes to ashes and dust to dust. It was Sloan's time to go."

It was Sloan's time to go.

Was it my time to go? I didn't have a flash drive to give to Daniel Crocker. I had no idea what was supposed to be on the flash drive. Maybe I should go to the police.

"Let me get this straight, Ms. Gardner. Your mother and a bartender were killed all because of a flash drive a customer who showed up at the DMV asked for. And what is supposed to be on this flash drive?"

The police were out.

I was out of my league here. I had no idea what to do or who to turn to. And then I did. Joe. He'd offered to help me before. Maybe he could help me now.

I pulled my cell phone out of my purse and saw

I had missed five calls and one message from Joe.

Rose, please call me back. Please. I have to talk to you.

I moved to the lobby and dialed Joe's number. He picked up on the first ring.

"Oh, thank God. Where are you?"

"I'm at Sloan's visitation."

"You're what?" His voice was cold. "You told me you hardly knew him."

"I told you we had a *dealing*. I still hardly knew him."

"Then what are you doing there?"

Getting accosted. "I don't know Joe. It seemed like the right thing to do." To my irritation, my tears started flowing again.

"Rose, are you alright?" His voice softened.

It made me cry even harder. "No."

"Stay there. Let me come get you."

I wanted to protest, to insist I was perfectly capable of taking care of myself, but I had been as brave as I could for the moment. I started to sob again.

"I'm coming. Don't leave. Just wait for me there." His words were rushed, like he was already running out the door.

I found a chair in the lobby and wept in fear as I faced the inevitability of my death. Sunday had seemed so far away, but it was right around the corner. Would it hurt when I was shot in the head? I'd been so worried about leaving life, I hadn't given much thought to the dying part. I cried even harder, slumped over in the chair, my face on my knees making the hem of my dress wet with tears and snot.

I felt hands around my arms, pulling me up and I couldn't stop the shriek. I jerked away, wild and desperate. Daniel Crocker had changed his mind and came back to get me.

"Shh, it's okay," Joe said, pulling me up. "You're okay."

I collapsed into his chest, sobbing.

"Come on, let me take you home."

He led me out the front door. He put his arm around my back, supporting me. I got in the front seat of his car and barely remembered the drive home, just his hand pulling my head to his shoulder, his hand on mine.

When we parked in the driveway, he took my purse and dug out my keys then got out and opened the door. I'd gotten out of the car at that point, stumbling in the dark and the gravel. He came over and picked me up with little effort, carrying me through the door. He kicked it closed behind him and placed me on my bed.

He leaned over, stroking my head, then kissed my cheek. "I'm gonna take Muffy out. I'll be right back."

I cried harder. What would happen to Muffy? I still hadn't made arrangements for her.

Before I realized Joe had been gone very long,

he was there, lying on the bed with me, his stomach to my back. When I finally calmed down, he handed me tissues from my nightstand.

I rolled onto my back and looked up at him.

He rubbed my cheek, looking down into my face. "As flattered as I'd be if you were this upset over me not showing up at the restaurant, I suspect this is about something else."

I bit my lower lip looking up into his kind eyes. Could I trust him? "Remember when you asked me if I was in trouble?"

A variety of emotions crossed his face before he answered. "Yeah, but you wouldn't tell me."

I paused, still unsure where to start. Maybe I could start with the DMV and leave out the vision. "The day before Momma died, a man came into the DMV. I'd never seen him before." How did I explain the next part without giving away my freak show? "He thought I recognized him. I didn't feel well and I fainted." All of that was true. I just left the vision part out. "He left, but without his paperwork, which I thought was really weird. The next night Momma was killed."

Joe watched my face intently, a little too intently to suit me. What did he hope to hear?

I paused to regroup. Maybe this wasn't a good idea, after all. But how did I get out of it without looking like I was hiding something?

"You said you had a dealing with Sloan Chapman. What kind of dealing did you have?"

"I went to Jaspers on my date with Steve. Only Steve didn't really want to be there. So I went to the restroom and when I came back, he'd left. He told the waitress he didn't feel well, but he paid for my dinner and for my cab ride home."

"Sounds like a real gentleman," Joe muttered sarcastically.

"Well, I guessed he didn't have to do it, pay for my dinner and the taxi. My brother-in-law forced him into the date. Anyway, I went into the bar and decided to order a glass of wine, since it was on my list. The bartender, Sloan, was really sweet to me and helped me figure out what to order, since I didn't know anything about wine."

I stopped again trying to read Joe's expression. He looked guarded.

"While I waited for Sloan to bring my drink, the guy from the DMV showed up. He saw me in the restaurant and followed me into the bar. He said he was really good with faces but couldn't place me. It happened after Momma's funeral, after Aunt Bessie cut my hair, so I looked totally different. In fact, I still can't believe he recognized me."

Joe's eyes softened and a tiny smile lifted the corners of his mouth. "Sure, your hair's different and your clothes fit you better, but your face is still the same. You were pretty before you changed your hair, Rose."

I blushed. I hadn't realized he'd noticed me before I showed up on his front porch the night

Momma died. "Well, he recognized my face, but couldn't place me, and it really bothered him. He was friendly, a little too friendly, and Sloan told him I was his little sister and to get lost. Then Sloan called the taxi and I came home."

"What happened the next time you saw Sloan?"

"Nothing, I never saw Sloan again."

"What else?"

"What else, what?"

"That can't be the end of your story. What else aren't you telling me? What you told me isn't enough to throw you into hysterical crying."

I sat up, anger rising. "Why are you getting so irritated? I'm telling you what I know."

"No, you're not. You're lying to me." He sat up too, his eyes narrowing.

"There's more to tell, but if you're going to be ugly to me, I'm not telling you anything."

His face softened. He leaned his back against my headboard and pulled me into his arms, my cheek against his chest. "I'm sorry. You're right. I'll be quiet and listen."

What did Joe McAllister have to gain from me? Why did he want to know my secrets so badly?

"Um . . ." My mind scrambled to come up with what to tell him. He knew there was more, I had to tell him something. Joe rubbed my back, making me torn between enjoying his touch and being suspicious. "The Monday I went back to work, he came back. The woman I work with said he'd been in every day the week before, looking for something or someone. But the day I came back, he came to my counter, with his paperwork. He told me he knew Sloan wasn't my brother."

"How did he know that?" Joe continued to rub my back.

"I don't know, he just said he did." Should I tell him that he thought Sloan was a cop? I began to think that the less I told Joe, the better. I'd tell him just enough to make him think he knew everything. "That night was the night someone broke in, and of course the police didn't believe me."

I suddenly pictured Joe standing in my door in only his boxers and scratches and welts on his head and back.

The intruder had on black clothes and a stocking cap. I'd hit him in the back and head with the broom. What if Joe was the intruder and stripped off his clothes and came to my door, telling me he got hurt tackling the guy?

"Go on," Joe said, rubbing my back again.

My heart began to race. "Ummm . . ." I didn't know what else to tell him.

"Why did you go to the visitation tonight?"

"You didn't show up and I thought about the night Steve left and how guys kept standing me up, and it made think about Sloan so I thought since I didn't have anything else to do I'd go and pay my respects." I was rambling and talking too fast. He would figure out he was making me nervous. I forced myself to slow down. "So I did."

"What happened?"

"Excuse me?"

"What happened at the visitation?"

"Nothing," I said, trying to sound innocent.

His arm tensed and he paused before he resumed rubbing my back. "Rose," he cooed into my ear. "You can trust me."

The way he said it made me almost think I *could* trust him. Almost.

"Nothing happened. It just made me think of Momma and I got really upset."

Joe tilted my head back and looked into my eyes. His were guarded and searching as he stroked my cheek. "Are you sure? Are you sure that's all?"

I closed my eyes, dismayed at the response my body had to his touch. His lips were on mine, soft and insistent, my resistance crumpling. *I can't trust him,* I tried to tell it. *I can't tell him anything.*

Muffy whined at the edge of the bed. I lifted my head up to check on her, but Joe pulled me back down, kissing me and making me forget.

"What was his name?" he asked, whispering in my ear.

I couldn't think, only feel, as he drove my body crazy.

Making me forget.

I sat up, bumping my head on his. I reached up to rub my head, while Joe looked confused.

Joe was always coaxing information out of me, using my body against me. My guts clenched. Joe didn't like me at all. He was just like Daniel Crocker. Only he used different tactics. And his were much worse.

I bolted to the bathroom, afraid I'd be sick. I locked the door behind me.

"Rose? What's wrong?" Joe followed and called outside the door.

"I don't feel well. I'll be out in a minute," I said, hanging over the toilet. The linen closet door caught my eye.

Joe called after the person tore apart my house, surprised I was home, expecting me to be at work. The person who came in didn't break the door to get in and might have had a key. Joe could have taken keys when he put the locks in. Why did he put the locks in?

Questions tumbled violently in my head, but they all pointed to the same thing. Joe was not only using me, he wanted something from me. I had to get him out of my house.

I opened the bathroom door.

"Are you okay?" he reached out to touch me and I tried not to recoil.

"It's been a really rough night. I think maybe you should just go home."

"I can stay with you." He actually had the nerve to look hurt.

I made a face, unsure what to say. I didn't want to look too obvious.

"I'm gonna go to the bathroom. You think about it and you can tell me what you decide when I come out. Okay?"

I nodded and went into my bedroom looking for Muffy. She lay on the floor, looking sad.

"Were you trying to warn me?" I whispered to her. I leaned down and rubbed her head. "Good girl."

I heard a rattle and jumped, my heart jolting. I didn't know how many more surprises I could take tonight. Joe's cell phone vibrated on my nightstand.

I tiptoed over, which was ridiculous, sneaking up on a cell phone. I picked it up, seeing a number on the screen with no name attached. What should I do? It was wrong to consider answering, yet I needed answers. I waited too long and the vibration stopped. My heart raced as I quelled my disappointment. It was better that I didn't answer. What would I have said? The phone vibrated again. Joe had a voicemail.

I listened for him, still in the bathroom. The toilet flushed and I knew I had maybe thirty seconds at the most. I pressed the button to listen.

"Everything's going as planned. We have confirmation she was seen with him. Let me know if you find out anything. Otherwise we stick to the schedule."

The message was short and abrupt, but there was no mistaking the identity of the person leaving it.

Hilary.

Chapter Twenty

I set the phone down on the nightstand just as I heard the bathroom door open. I was quivering like a Jell-O salad just shook out of its mold. How was I gonna hide *that?* I lay down, my back to the door. Muffy jumped up on the bed and laid beside me, her head on my legs as if she watched for Joe.

He came into the room and sat on the edge of the bed. He rubbed my arm. "Hey, are you feeling any better?"

Muffy lifted her head and whimpered.

I was scared.

This was Joe. Joe who helped me paint and stood outside the funeral home with me, handing me tissues. Joe who laughed with me until we cried over Muffy and her intestinal issues. Joe who taught me how to use chopsticks and about drinking and kissing. And more. I felt so hurt and betrayed it overshadowed the fear. But I couldn't confront him with any of it. I had no idea what he was capable of. Turned out, I didn't really know him at all.

"Yeah, I'm just tired."

"I can stay and just hold you. It might make you feel better."

Ten minutes ago, I would have killed for that.

"Nah, that's okay. I'm about to drift off to sleep. You go home."

He hesitated, like he wanted to say something and then he stood up. "If you need me, I'm next door." He started for the door, Muffy's head moving as she watched him.

He picked up his phone and looked at it, then leaned over and kissed my cheek. "Sweet dreams."

It took everything within me not to snort. Nightmares were more likely.

"Call me tomorrow, okay? We still have to work on your list."

I'd begun to hate that stupid list. My list got me mixed up with him in the first place, that and my overly aggressive hormones.

I lay on the bed, and about half a minute later the kitchen door opened and closed. I waited a few more minutes, then got up and snuck out into the kitchen, half expecting to find him waiting in a chair, but found an empty room. I went to lock the door and discovered Joe had already locked it. How did Joe lock the deadbolt? I searched my purse and the table for my keys.

A scrap of paper lay on the counter.

Rose,

I took your keys so I could lock up for you and you didn't have to get up. Call me as soon as you're awake so I can return them.

Joe

Crappy doodles. Now, I was trapped and had less than twenty-four hours to figure out what kind of information this mystical flash drive contained, certain Joe was after it, too. Why else would he care about Sloan?

I looked out the front window onto the street. A few houses down, an unfamiliar car parked on the curb. I ran to the hall closet and searched for the binoculars. They were hard to find in the dark, but I had told Joe I was going to sleep. I couldn't very well turn on any lights or he might consider it an invitation to come back.

Once I found them, I crept to the front window and looked at the car. A man sat in the front seat. Looking right at me. Thank goodness he didn't have binoculars or we could have waved to each other.

Crappy doodles.

Who was he? Who was he with? Daniel? Joe? Someone else?

I sure didn't want to be trapped in my house all night and now, more than ever, I needed to get out to my shed and see what Joe had been doing out there the night before. But first I needed to change clothes. I put on a T-shirt and capris, suddenly wishing I'd paid attention to what I was wearing in my vision. I sure didn't want to be caught dead wearing that.

Muffy gave me a dirty look. I had a mind-reading dog.

There were two doors out of my house, the front and the side. Both were in plain sight of the guy in the car. If I left, it had to be out the back window. I found the flashlight and went to one of Momma's bedroom windows. It would be tricky getting in and out with the window almost four feet off the ground. It only proved the intruder had long legs to be able to get his leg in the window in the first place. Like Joe's.

I'd show Joe McAllister what I was really capable of with a rolling pin.

As an afterthought, I unlocked my front door, so if I got caught I could say I went out the front. I opened the bedroom window and pushed out the screen, unsure of the best way to go about climbing out. I'd never done that before, climbed out a window. Maybe I could fill that in spot twenty-nine.

Maybe I wasn't ready to give up my list yet.

I threw the flashlight out the window. I decided to stick my left leg out first, and there I hung, my head still inside, hanging onto the ledge. I was gonna have to fall. So I just pushed myself out and landed on the side of my left leg with a thud. That would hurt tomorrow.

I'm gonna make Joe McAllister pay for this. After I'm finished beating him with my rolling pin, I'm gonna stick it up—

Muffy whimpered in the window.

"No, Muffy, stay there. I'll be back in a minute," I whispered.

Muffy rested her chin on the ledge.

In my haste, I hadn't thought about the fact Joe was probably still up, evidenced by the lights on in windows on the back of his house. I sprinted for the tree line at the far corner of my yard, hoping he wouldn't look outside. I stayed in their shadows until I reached the back corner of the shed. When I reached the edge, I realized I hadn't grabbed the key to the padlock, and was about to beat my head against the metal wall when I saw the padlock wasn't even on the door. Joe must not have put it back on the other night.

I slid the door open, pushing gently to minimize the screeching sounds, only it didn't make its usual creaks and groans. Had Joe oiled it? I slipped inside, turned on the flashlight, and began to look around. Nothing appeared out of place. The beam of light searched the corners, illuminated the shelves, nothing. I shuffled my way around the lawn mower, my foot hitting something hard and I swung the light down. A yellow shop towel lay on the ground, partially shoved under the lawn mower. I squatted to pick it up, surprised to find the towel wrapped around a heavy object. I put the flashlight between my legs and unrolled the cloth, nearly dropping it when I saw what it contained.

A gun. A handgun.

The combination of finding a gun and being in the shed, caused panic to slip in and take hold. I had to get out of the dark, confined space, but what did I do with the gun? I had to get rid of it. I laid the gun, still in the towel, on top of the mower. A plastic bag on the shelf caught my eye. I grabbed it and picked up the gun, wrapping it up in a wad, smart enough to keep my fingerprints off of it. Next I pulled a wrench out of the tool box, wrapped it up in the towel, and put it back underneath the mower.

But what should I do with the gun?

I saw a garden trowel hanging on a hook. I would bury it.

I planted the gun next to my roses, somewhat ironic considering my name and the fact a gun would probably kill me. As I dug the hole, I couldn't shake the fingertips of eerie dread inching its way up my back and nestling in the base of my neck. This was so much like my vision: trees, night, a gun. The only thing missing was the bullet hole.

I gasped. Is that what happened in my vision? Did Joe shoot me with this gun? *Not if I can help it.* I dug even deeper, then placed the gun, still in the bag, in the bottom and covered it with the dirt, smoothing it out so it didn't look so obvious. To finish it off, I spread the remaining mulch around.

I put the trowel back in the shed and closed the door. I'd turned back to the house when Muffy jumped out the window, running over to me. She gave me a defiant look.

"Muffy, I told you to stay inside."

My dog, who believed life was better lived in the slow lane, took off running for the front of the house.

"Muffy!" I whisper-shouted. "Muffy! Come back here!"

Once Muffy started running, she didn't stop. I took off after her, worried who would see us, but more worried she would get away and I'd never find her. She came to an abrupt halt, waiting at the sidewalk, her tongue hanging out the side of her mouth. *Thank goodness.* Surprised how upset I was at the thought of losing her, I knelt down to pet her. But Muffy had other ideas. She took off sprinting down the sidewalk, in the direction of the car down the street. I stood there, torn between catching her and self-preservation.

But really, there was no question. I ran after Muffy. I only hoped I didn't get shot.

I didn't. Instead, I ran into Joe. Literally. I had looked over my shoulder, toward the house to make sure he hadn't seen me, when I ran smack dab into his chest. He grabbed my arms to keep me from falling.

"Rose, why are you running? What's wrong?" His voice rose in alarm.

"Muffy!" I said, looking around him for signs of her. I heard her snort and looked down to see her sitting next to him.

I shot a glare at her. *Traitor!*

"What are you doing out here?" He sounded nervous and grabbed my hand. He began pulling me toward the house.

Muffy trotted along and then stopped and pooped in the neighbor's yard. "Ewww, Muffy! I didn't bring a bag!" But Muffy was a genius. "Muffy had to go out and I barely had time to get her out the door." I'd have to remember to come back in the morning to pick up her mess.

Joe eyed me, tilting his head to look at me. "I see you had time to change into different clothes." He still held my hand in his. My palm began to sweat under his scrutinizing gaze.

"Well, I couldn't come outside in my night-gown, could I?" I answered defensively.

"No, I'm glad you didn't come out in that little purple thing. That might have gotten the neighbor's attention." Joe tried to be subtle, but I saw him turn his head over his shoulder. In the direction of the car.

At least I hadn't gotten shot yet.

"Muffy's done her business. Let's get you inside," Joe said, moving toward the side of the house.

Muffy took off again, to the backyard. I swore if she started digging up the gun, I was gonna bury her in its place. Instead, she ran to the screen still on the grass, and sat down to wait.

"Rose," Joe said, alarm raising the pitch of his voice. "Someone tried to get in your house again!"

Oh, crappy doodles. Play along.

"Oh, my goodness!"

Joe grabbed my arm and took off running, dragging me to the other side of his front porch. His legs were longer than mine and I stumbled a couple of times trying to keep up. He pushed me down between his porch and an azalea bush. Muffy lay on the ground beside me. "Hide down here while I see if they're still inside. Do not come out," he said, his voice lowering into an order.

"Joe! Wait!"

"What?" He turned to face me, worry lines wrinkling his forehead.

The concern on his face stunned me, momentarily making me forget why I called to him. "Go in the front door. The side door is locked." *Thank goodness I unlocked the front door.*

Joe sprinted to the front and disappeared inside. I had to admit I would have been afraid for him if I thought someone was in my house. How could I be frightened for him? More importantly, why did he look so concerned about *me?*

He returned a few minutes later, his stride stiff with tension.

"Did you find anyone?"

"No, and no sign of anyone being inside." He looked up and down the street. "I don't want you sleeping alone tonight. I'm worried they might come back."

The last thing I wanted was to spend the night with Joe. "That's so sweet of you, but I'll be fine. I've got Muffy." I started walking toward the front porch, Muffy trotting next to me.

Joe followed behind.

"Joe, I told you, I'm fine," I said, walking in the front door. I started to close it on him, but he grabbed the edge.

"You've got two choices, Rose. Either I spend the night with you or I call the police to report the break-in. Which is it?"

I usually preferred the none-of-the-above answers, but lately those weren't working out so well. I sighed, irritated. "Fine, you can spend the night."

"Don't sound so enthusiastic."

It was hard to get enthusiastic about sleeping with someone who hid a gun in your shed.

"I'm gonna go lock up my house. I'll be right back."

I peeked out the front window and watched him walk home. When he turned to climb his porch steps, his face looked anxious, not sinister. I began to have second thoughts about his motives.

I put on the ugliest nightgown I could find, which wasn't hard. I had a whole drawer full of them, helping my goal to look as undesirable as possible.

Joe raised his eyebrows when he saw me, but didn't say anything. He led me to my bed and waited while I climbed in. Muffy jumped up and lay down next to me. I expected Joe to get in, but he kissed my forehead instead. "Don't worry Rose. I'm not gonna let anything happen to you." He stood up.

"Where are you going?" I couldn't stop myself from asking.

"I'm gonna sleep in your momma's room. If someone breaks in again I'm going to get the son of a bitch." He left, walking toward the back of the house. He really planned to sleep back there.

I was so confused. Did he want to hurt me or not?

Too wound up to go to sleep, my mind tried to sort everything out. If Joe broke in before, why did he think someone broke in this time? I was no acting coach, but the surprise and worry on his face looked real. And if Joe didn't really like me and care about me, why did he act so worried? If I hadn't heard the message from Hilary, I would chalk all my fears up to an overactive imagination, but I couldn't deny the message.

Everything's going as planned. We have confirmation she was seen with him. Let me know if you find out anything. Otherwise we stick to the schedule.

I couldn't trust Joe.

Chapter Twenty-One

I thought about running away, but all my escape routes were blocked. The man in the car watched the front of the house. Joe slept in the bedroom impeding my escape out the back.

Maybe that's why he wanted to sleep there, to keep me from leaving. But my gut instinct didn't think so. He really thought someone might break in.

Finally, my turbulent thoughts exhausted me and I fell asleep.

When I woke the next morning I thought I was still dreaming. I smelled the delicious aromas of coffee and bacon, only when I sat up and rubbed my eyes, I still smelled it.

Muffy lay on the bed with me, watching the door. Maybe she took her new guard dog role more seriously, although she hadn't done me any favors running into Joe the night before.

I found Joe in front of the stove. He turned and smiled.

"Good morning. Sleep well?"

"Yeah, what are you doing?"

"Cooking you breakfast."

"Why?" I blurted out.

He poured a cup of coffee and brought it to

me, but he looked like my question didn't bother him. "Why not? I was hungry and I figured you would be."

I took the cup and opened the fridge to get creamer. "Where'd you get bacon? I *know* I didn't have any bacon."

"I had some. I went home and got it and pancake mix, too."

"Pancakes?"

"Have a seat. They're almost ready. I noticed your kitchen's pretty bare. Haven't been to the store in a while, huh?"

I sat down. Joe already had plates and silverware on the table. "Well, you know, I've been busy. Plus it's just me."

"It's just me at my house and I'm better stocked than you. Planning on taking a trip?"

"No," I murmured, sipping my coffee.

Joe brought over the pancakes and bacon then sat down next to me. "So, we need a plan."

I choked on my hot coffee, which hurt like the dickens. "A plan?"

Joe stabbed a couple of pancakes on the stack and dumped them on his plate. He looked up and grinned, like a kid excited about to spend his allowance at the toy store, full of anticipation and glee. "A plan for your list. I checked it over this morning and you still have several things to do."

I shrugged. "I don't know. I've kind of given up on my list."

Joe stopped, his fork in midair. "Why?"

"It's stupid," I said with a sigh. "Twenty-four year olds don't go around doin' stupid things on lists."

"Why not?"

I shrugged again.

"Well, I've been looking forward to it. I hate that I got stuck at work and stood you up last night. I'm really sorry, Rose." He reached over and picked up my hand, stroking the back with his thumb. When I didn't respond, he set it back on my lap. "If you like, I can take you there for lunch."

"Nah, that's okay."

"I already have ideas for today but I know how much you hate me telling you what to do, so we can do whatever you want."

I sighed again, and looked at him. "I think I'd rather just spend the day here. Alone. Thanks, anyway." I tried to keep the hurt from leaking into my eyes, but the joy dropped out of his as he studied me.

He was quiet for a moment then took my hand again. "Rose, you have no idea how sorry I am I had to cancel last night. I really wanted to be with you, but we have the entire day today. Let me make it up to you."

If I stayed home, I wouldn't be surprised if Joe watched my every move. But if we went out, I had a chance of getting away from him. I pulled my hand away. "Okay."

He looked relieved. "Do you want to hear my plan or do you want to come up with your own?"

"Yours is fine." I swirled a piece of pancake on my plate, no longer hungry. Being with Joe hurt more than I thought possible, every word out of his mouth a reminder of his betrayal.

"You don't even want to hear it first?" He sounded incredulous. And hurt.

I grimaced and shook my head, putting my fork down. "I'm not hungry. I'm going to take Muffy out and take a shower."

"I already took Muffy out."

"What? She was sleeping with me when I woke up."

"When I got up she must have heard me. We went out, she did her business and then she went back to your bed."

So much for my guard dog.

"Then I'll just take a shower and get dressed. I'll clean up the kitchen when I get done," I said and left Joe in the kitchen.

I took a long time in the shower and when I came out there was no sign of Joe. He must have gone home to get dressed, but the kitchen was clean and a laptop sat in the chair in the living room.

For the first time that morning, my spirits lifted.

I sank to my knees on the floor, turning the open computer to face me. My stomach fluttered, tossing around the bacon and pancakes I'd choked down. The black screen lit up to a bright blue when I pushed the illuminated power button.

I'd never used a laptop, just my dinosaur computer at work and the one at the library. I moved my index finger on the touchpad, getting used to the feel of it. The screen asked for Joe's password. I racked my brain, trying to figure out what password Joe would use, which felt like looking for a leprechaun on Thanksgiving Day. In a spirit of hatefulness, I typed in *Hilary,* stabbing the keys with my fingers. Not it.

I was so intent on my task I didn't notice Joe until he asked dryly, "Do you need help?"

I screamed.

He leaned against the doorway, his face expressionless. "Did I surprise you?"

I jumped to my feet and instantly regretted it. Talk about looking guilty.

"I wanted to check the weather forecast. For today."

Joe walked over, picked up the television remote and pushed a button. "You have cable now. You can find out on the Weather Channel." He flipped the stations until a weather map appeared on the screen. "Why were you using my computer? Where's yours?"

"I don't have one."

His eyes widened and the hard look turned to confusion. "You don't have a computer?"

"No, I mean, yeah. Momma said they were the

gateway to hell. She took the brand name Gateway a little too seriously."

"So where do you check email, write Word
documents, use the Internet?"

"I go to the library, every Saturday. I spend the
afternoon there to get away."

"And that's the only computer you have?"

"Other than the one at work."

He got a strange look which reminded me of
Muffy's face the night I fed her eggs. "I've got
to use the restroom. I'll be back in a minute." He
practically sprinted down the hall.

Guess I pegged that one right.

When he returned, he was more serious than he
was at breakfast. "Okay, let's go." He sounded
like I was marching him to his execution rather
than the other way around.

"Nobody's forcing you into this, Joe McAllister."

"I said we were gonna have a fun day and
we're gonna do it," he said, his voice riddled with
irritation. If I hadn't been so aggravated at him I
would have laughed.

"We still have to get my car," I said, while he
locked my side door.

"Yeah, we will. Later." He handed me my keys
but refused to look at me.

We got in Joe's car and took off down the street.
"Where are we goin'?"

"It's a surprise," he said, his voice gruff and
no-nonsense. He reminded me of the night he left

me to go to work. Fear percolated in my chest. What if Joe was taking me somewhere to kill me?

I started to hyperventilate.

Joe swerved the car to the side of the road. He turned toward me, resting his hand on my head rest. "Are you okay?" He sounded kinder, but it wasn't enough to settle my fears.

I sucked in air like a fish on dry land, but my head just got fuzzier. Both of my hands fumbled for the door handle and I struggled to pull the lever. I got the door open and practically fell onto the side of the road.

"Rose!"

I scrambled to my feet and stood up, gasping for air, trying to figure out what to do. Joe had already gotten out of the car, walking in my direction.

I can't let him get me. I took off running down the sidewalk, away from my house.

It was a stupid plan, in fact, not a plan at all, just instinct. *Run away.* Joe had longer legs and was in better shape and he caught me in seconds. I'd like to say it was because my blood was poorly oxygenated from the hyperventilating, but I'd be lying. He grabbed my shoulders and spun me around to face him.

"Where are you going?" Then he saw my face, the terror and panic. His eyes widened. "Oh, my God, you're *scared* of me. Why?"

I took deep breaths trying to get my wits about

me because obviously my reactions so far hadn't worked out so well.

Joe started to pull me into a hug, but I stiffened and he let me go, dropping his hands to his sides. "Don't run off, okay?"

I nodded, but silently added *until I need to.*

"Why are you scared of me? What did I do?"

I couldn't very well tell him the truth. "You were upset that I used your computer." I mentally congratulated myself for thinking so quickly. Maybe my brain worked better with more oxygen.

Joe heaved a deep breath and put his hands on his hips. "Rose, I just wondered why you were using mine. I didn't realize you didn't have one. I have some work stuff on there that I'm kind of private about."

"Mechanic stuff?" The disbelief was undeniable. *So much for thinking.*

His face started to harden, but he caught himself. "You'd be surprised. Most people don't realize new cars are run by computers."

I had to admit he was good. I almost believed him.

"Rose, we've fought before and you've never been afraid of me. Why are you scared of me now?"

I didn't know what to say. My eyes filled with tears, only maybe I could use it to my advantage. "I'm sorry. First Momma was killed, then Sloan and the break-ins. It's all too much. I'm sorry."

"Do you think I'd hurt you?"

I thought for a millisecond before I answered, "No, of course not."

But it was a millisecond too long. He looked more hurt than he had a right to. "We can go home if you want."

"No! I'm okay. Just tell me where we're goin'." I still hoped to get away and it would be easier to lose him if we were around other people. "I can't take any more surprises right now."

"The park first, to fly a kite."

"Really?" His response surprised me.

"Yeah, I bought one a few days ago. I also planned to dance with you but you already did that one."

I gave him a hesitant smile.

"I was gonna offer to help you with number thirteen but after what just happened, I'm not sure that's such a good idea."

"Number thirteen?"

"Get a boyfriend." He sounded embarrassed.

Regret and sadness for what my life could have been washed through me as I faced the reality of what it was. People died all the time, every day. What did one more insignificant person matter?

What was the point of this stupid list?

When we got to the park, Joe told me he'd hold the kite and I was supposed to run with it. It took several attempts until the kite became sky bound. Joe ran over to me and fed line until it flew higher and higher. He stood next to me but our magic had disappeared, replaced with fear and wariness. Joe sensed it too and asked me if I was ready to go.

We walked to the car, side by side but a million miles apart, and I saw a family setting up a picnic. A mother and father with two small children. The father tossed a baseball to his son and the daughter sat on a blanket playing with a doll. I watched with sadness and envy.

"Why does that make you so sad?" Joe asked after he put the kite in the trunk.

"Because it's what I've always wanted, but I'll never have."

"Why do you say that?"

I looked at him, my face reflecting my emotions. Empty. "Let's not pretend anymore, okay?" I moved to open the passenger door.

Joe shut the door and backed me up to the car. "You're right, let's not pretend anymore." He put both arms on either side of me, blocking me in, but his face was soft and sad. "Come on, Rose. Why are you afraid of me? I keep telling you that I only want to help you. Please, let me help you. Tell me about Sloan."

"I told you everything there is to know about Sloan."

He looked up at the sky in frustration then leveled his gaze with mine. "You're not telling me everything. Why?"

"I need to go to Walmart."

"What?"

I knew it was out of the blue but I needed a flash drive. I didn't have one to give Daniel Crocker.

"Okay, but not yet. We still have to work on your list."

"I don't care about my stupid list anymore!" I shouted.

Joe sighed and dropped his arms. "Well, I do."

He drove to the Henryetta airport, which was nothing more than a couple of metal buildings and an airstrip. But I couldn't help the tiny bit of excitement that lit up my face. Joe noticed but didn't say a word. He'd made an arrangement with a crop duster to take us up, making it clear we couldn't cross over the county line. We sat in the rear seat while the pilot prepared for takeoff in the single engine plane. I was nervous. I really wanted to fly, but I wasn't prepared for the confined space and my claustrophobia threatened to break loose at any minute.

The pilot taxied to the runway and revved the engine, the wind rushing in the open windows from the spinning propeller. I looked at Joe, whose entire focus was on me, gauging my reaction. I turned away embarrassed, but he sensed my hesitancy and gently placed his hand over mine in my lap. When I didn't shake it off, he rested more weight on it.

The plane hurtled down the runway, the engine so loud I couldn't hear myself think. It lifted, ever so slightly and we were off the ground. The wind picked up the wings and we flew higher, over the edge of the runway and the fields. At the end, the plane made a sharp turn, causing Joe to lean into me. The move caught me off guard and my eyes widened, afraid we were going to crash.

Joe leaned into my ear. "It's okay. This is normal."

I nodded, trying to swallow my fear as the plane straightened and climbed higher, making the cars and houses below look smaller. But the fear had already taken hold and the claustrophobic fright I held at bay was nearly ready to explode.

Joe squeezed my hand in reassurance. I knew I shouldn't trust him, but he was all I had at the moment. I squeezed back, trying to slow my breath and calm down, the panic building. Joe put his arm around my shoulders and whispered in my ear. "It's okay, Rose. I've got you." I turned to look at him. His eyes were so sweet and gentle I couldn't believe he would ever hurt me. Why would he go to all this trouble if he wanted to kill me?

He took my stare as encouragement and kissed me. The plane, the fear, the stupid flash drive were all gone and the only thing left was Joe. He pulled away and smiled a smile that looked so genuine I'd bet my life on it, in fact I knew I had. I was literally betting my life on Joe McAllister.

I was either incredibly smart or incredibly stupid. Either way tomorrow would tell.

Chapter Twenty-Two

After Joe helped me calm down, I loved the rest of the flight. When we landed, we went back into town to get lunch at Little Italy. Joe didn't ask any more questions about Sloan or hint at a flash drive. We acted like normal people on a normal date.

I tried to forget about Hilary's phone call. I kept telling myself there was more evidence that I could trust Joe than against.

I had no proof that Joe broke into my house. In fact, the way he acted last night seemed to prove otherwise. I had no proof he broke in the second time either. I didn't even know if he had a set of keys. But what about the gun? And the phone message?

After lunch, we sat in Joe's car and he pulled a piece of paper out of his pocket. "The only things left are ride a motorcycle, play in the rain and number thirteen."

"And fifteen."

"I think you have fifteen covered. Of course, we need to review the Seven Deadly Sins, to see if you've covered them."

I'd forgotten about the Seven Deadly Sins and fifteen wasn't covered.

Joe's cell phone rang and his smile disappeared when he looked at the number. "I've got to take this," he said then got out of the car.

I watched his two-minute phone call unfold, wondering who he could be talking to and what could produce such an animated conversation. Joe was clearly upset when he got into the car. "Do you still have to go to Walmart?" he asked, jamming the keys in the ignition.

"Yeah," I answered, confused by his abrupt change of attitude.

"We need to go there now."

"Okay."

We drove in silence and dread crept back in, a now semi-constant companion. If Joe really wanted the flash drive, he would find it odd when he saw me buying one. I needed to tell him I didn't have it.

"Joe, about Sloan and . . ."

"Rose, stop." He cut me off, his voice harsh. "Don't say another word."

"But you . . ."

"Not another word." He said through gritted teeth, gripping the steering wheel so tight I thought it would bend under the pressure.

Joe pulled into a space near the back of the parking lot. "I'll wait here." He looked straight ahead, his mouth in a tight line.

I started to protest, but changed my mind. It was probably better this way.

I bought the flash drive in the electronics section and headed out of the store, suddenly uncertain I made the right decision about Joe. I stood outside the entrance doors, people streaming past me on either side. If I wanted to ditch Joe, it was now or never. I had my keys in my purse and I could easily walk the mile to my car at the funeral home. I'd hide somewhere until it was time to meet Daniel. The more I thought about it, the more it seemed like a win/win situation. If Joe was bad, I needed to ditch him when he least expected it. If he wasn't, I'd apologize later.

I walked down the sidewalk in front of the store, away from Joe's car. I stopped at the corner of the building, preparing to cross the parking lot.

"Going somewhere?" Joe asked, leaning against the side of the building. He sounded bored, but I knew he was anything but.

My heart stopped and I twisted the bag in my hands. "Uh . . . I was looking for you."

"You must have really gotten turned around. The car's back that way." He looked casual, standing with his back against the brick wall, pointing in the opposite direction with his thumb. But he clenched his jaw and his eyes were cold.

"What are you doing over here?" I asked, keeping my tone light, as though we had just run into each other by accident.

"Making sure you don't get lost." He pushed away from the wall and took my hand in his, but it wasn't a friendly hold. He meant it when he said he was making sure I didn't get lost.

We walked to the car and drove home, both of us on edge. Joe's anger simmered under the surface and my anxiety choked all conscious thought. We were almost home when Joe finally spoke up. "Where were you going, Rose?"

"I told you. . . ."

"Where were you going?" he growled.

"My car."

He let out a long breath. "Why didn't you just ask me to take you there?"

"I didn't want to bother you."

Joe pulled into the driveway, looking toward my house. "I wish I could ask you what you're up to, but I don't want to know, not now." He turned to face me, his eyes serious. "But I'm begging you to stay home and wait this out."

"Wait what out?" Did he know about my meeting with Daniel?

Joe sighed and closed his eyes. He opened them and the anger was gone, replaced with worry. "You're gonna do it, aren't you?"

I didn't answer, just stared at him, wondering what he knew. He got out and went into his house, leaving me in his car.

I sat there for a moment, wondering what had just happened. I got out and brought Muffy outside, watching her sniff around the yard. Maybe Joe was right. Maybe I should just stay home. I didn't have the flash drive. If I showed up without it, Daniel Crocker would kill me. If I didn't go, Daniel Crocker would kill me. I decided I'd rather be dead in the comfort of my own home. I'd just hide my rolling pins.

Relieved to have made a decision, I went inside and found an envelope on my kitchen floor. My name was handwritten on the front, a photo inside. A photo of Violet. Written on the back of the picture, in carefully printed block letters:

See you tonight.

I squashed the paralyzing terror that wanted to take me over. I had to think this through and panic wouldn't help anything. I sat down and took several deep breaths trying to clear my head. What was supposed to be on the flash drive? I decided to call the other employees at the DMV. While I doubted they would tell me anything, I figured I had nothing to lose. But I needed to hear Violet's voice first.

"What's up, Rose?" The children's voices were in the background.

"Nothing, I just wanted to call and check on you."

"Why? Is everything okay?"

"Yeah, everything's fine. I just wanted to call and say I love you."

"I love you, too, Rose. Hey, I think we're throwin' together a cookout tomorrow, want to come?"

"Sounds fun," I said, forcing the cheerfulness in my voice.

"Great! See you at four."

I'd just have to figure out how to live until tomorrow afternoon.

I'd started looking up employees' phone numbers in the phone book when I heard the sirens in the distance, coming closer to the house.

My cell phone rang in my purse. I picked it up, surprised to see Joe's number.

"I'm sorry," was all he said.

The sirens stopped out front. *What did he do?*

The police pounded on the door and shouted for me to come out with my hands up. Muffy whimpered next to my leg. "It's okay, girl," I said as I rubbed her head, positive it wasn't. I opened the kitchen door.

Five of Henryetta's finest greeted me at the door. Apparently, it was a slow crime day.

"Keep your hands up where we can see them," one of them shouted.

I walked out with my hands in the air, fuming. I could wring Joe McAllister's neck with my bare hands. Then the Henryetta police department would *really* have a reason to arrest me.

"Ms. Gardner, we have reason to believe you murdered Sloan Cooper on Wednesday night and the murder weapon is on your premises. Do you give us permission to search your property?"

My heart skipped a beat and my head got fuzzy. Joe had planted the gun on Thursday night. He set me up all along. I was too angry to be hurt. I could be hurt later. "Where exactly do you want to search?"

"Your shed."

I knew I should call Deanna, but I didn't have time to waste. It was already five o'clock and I had to be at The Trading Post at ten. It could take Deanna an hour to get here. Besides, I knew the gun wasn't there. "Sure."

Joe stood on his front porch, gawking like all the other neighbors. The look on his face when he heard me give approval was priceless. I gave him a cold hard stare.

Muffy whimpered in the doorway.

"It's okay, girl," I said. She was unconvinced and paced back and forth at my feet. I addressed the closest officer. "Can I put my hands down now? You're making my dog nervous."

He turned me around and patted me down. "Yeah."

Several police officers had already opened the shed and were removing items, tossing them into the yard.

Muffy came out of the house and stood by me, whining. I leaned down and petted her head.

"May I ask why you think I did this?"

"An anonymous tip."

"Yeah, I bet it was anonymous," I muttered

under my breath. "I have an alibi for that night. I stayed the night at my sister's."

"Are you making a statement?" the officer asked, surprised.

"Take it for what you will."

The crowd on the sidewalk grew quickly. You would have thought it was the second coming of Jesus from the rapt attention the people were giving my shed. By that point, the shed was at least halfway empty, the lawn mower one of the items in the yard. I looked over at Joe to see his reaction. The disbelief and confusion on his face gave me momentary satisfaction. I gave him a smile so sweet it would have killed a diabetic.

"I think I'd like to call my lawyer now," I said. The policeman went inside with me to watch me use my phone. Muffy tagged along.

Deanna was furious with me for allowing the police access to the shed and said she'd be right over. The only reason I called her was because I saw the kind of damage they were doing to my yard, and I doubted they would restore it to its previous state.

I went outside to wait for Deanna. Muffy kept whining and followed close behind.

The contents of the almost empty shed lay tossed in the yard. Even the metal shelves lay on their side. It looked like a redneck yard sale.

A car tried to drive down the street, a difficult task considering all the people crowded on the pavement. It was an older muscle car owned by the high school boy who lived on the corner. Any other person would have driven around the block, but curiosity got the better of him and he pushed his way through the crowd.

When the car reached Joe's house, it backfired twice in rapid succession, sending the crowd into screams and bedlam that rivaled Armageddon.

The officers in the shed began to shout, "Get down! Take cover!" To my amazement, the stout policeman standing at my side dove on top of me, throwing us both to the ground. The crowd panicked even more, running into each other and diving under bushes and cars.

Muffy lost it.

She began to howl and run in circles, nudging me with her nose and whimpering. The policeman swatted at her. She took off running down the street past Joe's house and into the screaming mob.

"Muffy!" I yelled with what little breath I could get into my lungs, while trying to push the officer off my back.

It took some effort to move the policeman, especially considering his girth. I supposed I should have thanked him for putting himself on the line to protect a rolling-pin-wielding, gun-hiding murder suspect, but I was more worried about my dog.

"*Muffy!*" I screamed again, starting to run after her when I finally broke free.

One of the officers grabbed my arm and dragged me back, pulling out a pair of handcuffs and cinching my hands behind my back.

"What are you doing?" I cried out in disbelief.

"You were fleeing the scene of a crime investigation."

"I was running after my *dog!*" I screamed and turned to the street. *"MUFFY!"* And then I began to cry. I'd been fine up to that point, but I was afraid I'd never see Muffy again and I broke out into wails of anguish. Just when I thought I'd seen it all, Joe ran off his front porch in the direction Muffy had gone.

The crowd reassembled. It wasn't every day they saw someone handcuffed. I sat down on the grass by my driveway, not an easy task when you can't use your hands to help yourself down. People took out cell phones and snapped pictures. I was big news for Henryetta, especially with tears and snot dripping down my face that I couldn't wipe away, seeing how my hands were preoccupied.

The police got the crowd settled down, and they confirmed the noise to be the car's backfire. Everything back under control, the officers returned to the task at hand, cleaning out my shed.

Deanna showed up, furious when she discovered me sitting in the grass wearing handcuffs. She asked for a search warrant, just in time for the police to announce they had emptied everything out of the shed and found nothing. The anonymous tip said the gun would be wrapped in a yellow towel under the lawn mower, but all they found was a wrench wrapped in the towel. Deanna told them my sister and aunt would confirm my whereabouts Wednesday night.

One of the officers lifted me none too gently off the ground and uncuffed my numb hands. They began to clear out the crowd and returned to their police cars.

"Hey!" I called, thoroughly irritated. "Are you going to clean up that mess?"

They looked at me as though I'd just asked them to scrub my toilet.

Deanna took me inside the kitchen and reamed me up and down. She told me if I ever again dealt with the police without her present, she would drop me in an instant.

She left, the police left, then finally the straggling crowd left. But Joe still hadn't returned. And neither had Muffy.

It was now eight o'clock and I still didn't know what was supposed to be on the flash drive. And even if I could fudge it, I didn't have access to a computer. Could I go and convince them to leave Violet alone if I showed up with nothing? I had no doubt I'd be dead, but that would be okay if they left Violet alone.

I heard a knock on the kitchen door and it

swung open before I could answer. Joe entered without Muffy, looking devastated. All the fury and fear came roaring out and I attacked him, pounding his chest with my fists.

"I hate you! I hate you, Joe McAllister! You set me up to be arrested and because of you, Muffy's lost and I'll never see her again. *You used me!* You and Hilary must have had fun laughing at poor, *stupid* Rose. You never even liked me! You just used me to get that stupid flash drive and *I don't even know what's on it!* Now because of you, I'm gonna die and I don't have time to save Violet. *I hate you!*"

He let me hit him at first, but he grabbed my fists and held them to his chest when I mentioned dying. I'd said too much.

"Whoa, slow down. What do you mean you don't know what's on the flash drive? Where is it?"

"It's there in that Walmart bag."

He let go of me to tear into the Walmart bag next to my purse. "Rose," he said, his voice rising in panic. "This hasn't even been opened!"

"I know!"

"If you don't have a computer, how are you going to put the information on it? Where's the real flash drive?" He tossed the package onto the table.

"I don't know!" I screamed.

"Did someone steal it in one of the break-ins?"

"I never had it! I didn't even know anything about a stupid flash drive until the night of Sloan's visitation when Daniel Crocker found me and dragged me down the hall, telling me if I didn't deliver it tonight at ten, I was gonna be sorry."

Joe sat in the kitchen chair, his face white. "Oh, my God."

"Get out!"

He looked up, startled.

"Get out of my house!" I screamed, hysterical. "Get out!"

He stood up and I pushed him toward the door. He may have been bigger than me, but I was lucky to have caught him in a moment of shock. He stumbled backward.

"Rose, I can help you."

"Help me? *HELP ME?*" I screamed like a banshee and I had no doubt the neighbors could hear me, but I didn't care. "You mean help me like *planting a gun in my shed?* And callin' the police with an anonymous tip so I'd get arrested for murdering Sloan? Then getting my dog lost! You mean that kind of help? Because no freaking thanks! I don't need your help!" I shoved and beat him with my fists. "Get out! *GET OUT!* Get out of my life!"

He stumbled out the door but recovered before he fell. "Rose, let me explain."

"Explain to this!" I slammed the door shut so hard the wall shook. I locked both locks. Joe

pounded on the door shouting my name, but I went into the bathroom and washed my face. I had less than an hour to come up with some kind of plan to save my life.

Chapter Twenty-Three

I made myself get a grip. I couldn't show up to meet Daniel with a red nose and bloodshot, puffy eyes. Plus, I suspected sex was a way to communicate with Daniel Crocker and I was desperate enough to pull that out of my limited arsenal and use it to save Violet. Nevertheless, I had to look the part to play it.

Clothing proved an issue. If Daniel hadn't seen me in the red dress, and if I hadn't got snot and tears all over the front, I would have worn it. Instead I found a pair of jeans and a silky sleeveless shirt and wore my black bra, which peeked out over the top of the low-cut shirt. I decided this would work better in The Trading Post, which was a bar with a rough reputation just outside the city limits.

Torn between heels and sensible shoes, I chose heels. I had little chance of outrunning anyone, but perhaps looking sexy could help me. Heavens knew I needed all the help I could get.

I opened the flash drive package with shaky fingers and tucked it in my jeans pocket. I was fairly certain they were going to check it and I hadn't figured out how to explain why it was empty.

I gave myself on last look in the mirror, surprised by the image. Maybe I could pull this off.

I went out into the kitchen to call a cab. I'd take a taxi to my car, which was still parked at the funeral home, but it required extra time. While I waited for it to show up, I went outside to look for Muffy, walking up and down the sidewalk and calling her name. I worried Joe would hear me and come out but, he didn't, even though I saw him watching out his living room window. I checked the time on my cell phone—nine thirty-five. I still had time but my nervousness threatened to swallow me whole. I locked the door and waited for the taxi in the driveway, pacing.

Five minutes later, Joe came outside, easing his way over to me as though I was a wild animal and might bolt if he got too close. "Rose?"

"Leave me alone," I growled, looking down the street with my side to him.

"Do you need a ride to your car?"

"I called a taxi."

We waited a few more minutes. I was so anxious I thought I would puke.

"Don't go, Rose." His voice was so quiet I could barely hear him.

I turned to face him and shook my head. "Do you have any idea what you are asking?"

"Do you know what's going to happen if you go with an empty flash drive?"

"What do you care, Joe? Leave me alone!" I started down the sidewalk. Wearing heels wasn't such a good idea if I had to walk two miles.

Joe jogged up to me. "Let me drive you."

"Drive me where?"

"To your car."

I stopped and glared at him. "Why are you doin' this?"

"Rose, I care about you."

That made me livid. "Don't. You. Dare," I spit out through gritted teeth. I started walking again.

"Okay, I feel guilty. I'm trying to make it up to you."

I stopped. That sounded like a more honest answer and my cab still hadn't shown up. Being late wouldn't work in my favor. "All right." I turned around and walked to Joe's car and got in.

We drove in silence for a couple of blocks.

"Do you have a plan?"

I remained silent.

"Rose, do you know what these people are *capable* of?"

"I have a pretty good idea, Joe, which is exactly why I'm going."

Joe stopped at a stop sign. "I can't let you do this."

"You don't have a say. Now drive."

He drove several more blocks. "You at least need a plan. Tell me you have a plan."

"I have a somewhat plan."

"Does your plan have anything to do with the way you're dressed?" When I didn't answer, he continued. "That won't work with him, Rose. He's been put in a very awkward situation by trusting his source and paying already. His partners are breathing down his neck for this information. If you don't have it, nothing will save you."

"I already know I'm gonna die. I'm doing this to save Violet."

He stopped next to my car thankfully still parked in the deserted funeral home parking lot. He shut off the engine and turned to me. "Rose, I'm begging you."

"You have no right to beg me for anything, Joe McAllister. You lost that right the moment you betrayed me. When was that exactly? The night you met me?"

"Rose," he moaned.

"Fine, so you're worried about me?" I said in a sneer. "Come with me, be my bodyguard."

"I can't." He hung his head.

"Yeah, that's what I thought." I started to get out of the car.

Joe pulled me back and grabbed my shoulders. "I'm about to do something that could get me killed, but I can't sit here and let it happen to you first."

"Let go of me!" I tried to jerk away.

"Rose! I'm trying to save you! Shelf your pride for a minute and listen to me!"

I was willing to listen if he was going to help save my life.

"As much as I hate to admit it, you were smart to dress like this. Crocker likes good-looking women. He'll be more lenient with you because of your looks, which is probably why you're still alive. But if he finds out you haven't brought what he wants, he'll kill you."

I tried to remain calm in spite of facing my certain death. "Will he know tonight?" I whispered.

He looked out the front window. "Yes."

I let that soak in. "Will I at least be able to save Violet?"

"I don't know."

I gasped. I had to save Violet.

Joe turned back to me. "So will you change your mind?"

"Not if there's even a slight chance I can save her." I reached for the handle on the door.

"Wait!" Joe sounded desperate.

"What?"

"Give me your flash drive." I didn't move so he grabbed my purse and started digging through it.

"What are you doing? Give that back!" I tried to pull it away from him.

He looked panicked. "Where is it?"

I dug it out of my pocket, unsure I should give it to him. He pulled a flash drive out of his pocket and handed it to me.

"Is this the real one? You had it all the *time?*" I asked.

"No! It's fake. It'll save you tonight, but not past tomorrow. They'll figure out it's a forgery by noon."

"Why are you doin' this?" I wasn't sure I could trust him, but whatever he had on his flash drive had to be better than my empty one.

"You want the truth or the version you prefer?"

"Neither." I turned to the door.

"Wait!"

This was getting old. "I'm gonna be late."

He looked uncomfortable. "Try not to let him get you into bed."

"Excuse me?" I hadn't expected that.

"He's gonna try, which is why you're still alive, but avoid it if you can. You're gonna have to use your head. Rumor has it he's rough in the bedroom. Just be careful."

While I was grateful for that bit of information, it scared the bejiggers out of me. "Thanks," I whispered.

"Rose." His voice broke. "Be careful."

I didn't say anything. I knew I should be grateful, but I was still mad. I got out of the car and walked over to mine. Joe stayed in the parking lot while I pulled away.

The Trading Post was on Highway 82 just outside of town. Henryetta being so small, it didn't take long to pull into the pea gravel parking lot, already half-full of pickup trucks and motorcycles. My stomach tied itself up in knots as I got out of the car. It was one minute after ten. One minute late.

I took a deep breath as I went in and let my eyes adjust to the dim, smoky haze. Daniel sat across the room, at a table with two other men.

Show time.

I walked over to his table, but I tried to saunter, like I'd seen models do on television. I had no idea if I pulled it off or looked like a fool. In either case, Daniel Crocker looked like he appreciated what he saw.

I realized I might get out of the dying part, but I highly doubted I'd get out of the sleeping-with-him part. I hoped I could go through with it.

Daniel leaned his arms on the backs of the chairs next to him and looked me up and down. "Well, there you are, baby. I was just talkin' about ya."

"Oh?" I sat down in the empty chair across from him and tried to look interested. I'd prefer to dump the flash drive in his lap and turn around and leave, but the person with the real flash drive had stood him up for a while. Common sense told me I was gonna have to work my way out of being punished.

"Let me get you a drink. I believe you drank wine when I saw you with Sloan."

I ignored the Sloan comment. "Wine would be great, thanks."

Daniel motioned to a guy next to him with a quick wave of his hand. "White." The guy walked over to the bar. "I was worried you weren't goin' to show, baby. You have no idea how happy I am to see you."

"I disappointed you long enough." I smiled and lifted my eyebrows. I wasn't sure how it actually looked, sexy or stupid, but he still looked interested. I felt like I was walking a tightrope without a net.

The guy returned with a glass of white wine. It creeped me out that Daniel remembered what I had that night. I took a sip and smiled my approval.

My hand rested on the table. Daniel stretched his hand over and covered mine. It felt clammy and oppressive. I resisted the urge to snatch mine away.

"They say business before pleasure, Rose. Seems particularly apropos tonight."

I stood up, carefully pulling my hand out from under his so I didn't offend him. I reached into my pocket, arching my back and thrusting out my chest. I needed to worry about surviving tonight and not the fact I was digging myself into a hole of sleeping with him. His eyes told me he appreciated the view. I put the flash drive on the table and slowly slid it toward him.

He picked it up and handed it to the guy who brought my wine. He waved to the other man, who got up and left. Daniel patted the chair next to him. "I'm feeling mighty lonely all by myself. Come sit with me."

I moved to the chair, trying not to stiffen when he draped his arm around my shoulders and sniffed my neck.

Oh, Lord, I don't think I can go through with this.

"You smell so good, baby. I can't wait to get a taste." He leaned over and kissed me, a wet sloppy mess that tasted like beer and onions. Daniel Crocker had a love of onions. I tried to show him a little enthusiasm, but he noticed the lack of effort on my part.

"Nervous, baby? You got something to be nervous about? I know you're good in bed. McAllister says so anyway."

I couldn't stop my show of surprise.

His hand moved to my leg, skimming the inside of my thigh. "Don't be hurt. I had McAllister keep an eye on you, once I knew it was you. I didn't expect him to watch you so closely though." His hand moved farther up my thigh. "Although he did provide exceptional information." He pinched the inside of my leg. Even through my jeans it was hard enough to bring tears to my eyes. "But you're mine now."

I grabbed my glass of wine and took a good-sized gulp.

The man came and whispered in Crocker's ear. Daniel grinned. "Bring over some tequila shots to celebrate." He turned to me, beaming. "You have no idea how happy I am that you didn't disappoint me."

The man brought six shot glasses, a bowl full of lime wedges, and a shaker full of salt.

"You ever done tequila shots, Rose?" Daniel asked, lining up the shot glasses, three in front of him and three in front of me. They were much smaller than a glass of wine or beer, but I knew they were much more potent.

"No," I said, scared. If a couple of bottles of beer made me jump Joe, what would a glass of wine and three tequila shots have me do with Daniel? Then again, if I was gonna have to do it, I might as well have a little help.

His eyes lit up, but with a scary excitement, not the excitement I saw on Joe's face. "Let me teach you," he said in a leer. "But first finish your wine."

I gulped my wine down. I was going to be incapable of driving. How would I get home?

He laughed when I set down the empty glass. "You *are* gonna be fun. Okay, time for your lesson. I'm gonna demonstrate and then you try it, okay?"

I nodded, my head getting fuzzy.

He picked up my left hand, and licked the back of it, I couldn't help the automatic response to jerk away. But he must have been prepared, because he held on tight and laughed. He picked up the salt shaker and poured salt onto my hand. Licking it off, he rolled his eyes an evil smile widening on his face. Still holding onto my hand, he picked up a shot glass with his other hand and downed it in a second. He slammed it on the table and picked up a lime wedge and sucked on it.

He narrowed his eyes, in what I suspected he meant to be a come-hither look. I just wanted to run. "I knew you'd taste good." He gave the back of my hand another lick. "You're turn."

I would have been nervous trying shots anyway, but doing this with Daniel Crocker released a slow trickle of terror that pooled and rose, threatening to swallow all reason. Daniel still had my hand and stuck his in front of my face. I closed my eyes and licked it.

"Now salt," he insisted with a growl.

I shook the salt shaker on the back of his hand and licked. He actually moaned.

"Now the shot." He held the glass up to my mouth and pushed my head back, dumping it in. Unprepared, I gagged. Daniel held a lime wedge up to my mouth. "Suck on it, baby."

It took everything in me not to vomit there at the table. By the time I got through the remaining two shots, the room was definitely spinning. Between not being used to the alcohol, my vertigo, and fear, I knew I would lose my stomach contents soon. I grabbed my purse and stood, nearly falling over with the sudden movement.

"I've gotta throw up." Apparently tequila worked like beer on my internal censor.

Daniel burst out laughing. "The restroom's back that way." He waved toward the hall. "Don't keep me waiting, baby." I wobbled in that direction as I heard Daniel ordering more shots. I was going to die of alcohol poisoning.

I made it down the hall, to the bathroom and barely made it to the toilet before I threw up. I didn't know how I was going to go out there and drink more. I leaned over the sink and rinsed my mouth out with water. When I raised up, I saw Joe's reflection in the mirror behind me. Before I could scream, Joe covered my mouth with his hand.

"Shhh."

I tried to ask him a question but his hand muffled my words. He removed his hand. "What are you doin' here?" I whispered loudly.

"Shh," he said, "You're a funny drunk at home, but right now I need you to focus."

"You said to use my head, and I'm trying but it ain't so easy. He wants me to go back out there and do it again."

"Do what again?"

"Tequila shots."

"How much have you had to drink?"

"A glass of wine and three shots."

"Shit, why are you drinkin' so much?"

"He's makin' me do it." I felt myself weaving and bobbing around.

Joe grabbed his head in his hands, like his head hurt and he was trying to squeeze the pain out. "Okay," he finally said.

I concentrated on watching him, so his words startled me and I jumped. "Okay, go back?" I started for the door, feeling even fuzzier than when I came in. I turned to Joe and waved a finger at him. "Oh yeah, he ain't followin' the rules."

"What rules?"

"The rules of drinkin'."

"Yeah, Crocker isn't one to follow rules. I'm trying to figure out how to get you out of here."

"Can I go home now?"

"No, not yet. I hate to do this to you, but I need you to go back out there. You've been here too long. He's gonna come looking for you and we need more of a head start. Go back out, do one or two more shots and say you have to throw up again, and I'll be waiting for you here. But leave your purse at the table and don't slip up and use my name. It's a secret, okay?"

I nodded.

"Okay, do what I say and I'm gonna get you out of this." Then he shoved me out the door. I grabbed hold of the wall to hold myself up.

Daniel was excited to see me appear and didn't waste any time getting to the shots.

We did the first round, with some sloppy kissing

after. I wondered if anyone had told him that his technique needed some work. I considered telling him he should take some lessons from Joe, but remembered I wasn't supposed to say Joe's name.

As I started licking the salt off his hand, I felt a vision coming. I saw Joe, in what looked like a mechanic's garage, carrying a package. I heard Daniel's voice say, "Where is she, McAllister?"

When it finished and I was about to say "You're looking for me," Daniel stuck a wedge of lime in my mouth. I had no problem excusing myself from the table this time, and I honestly forgot my purse, barely making it to the toilet. Joe waited for me, hiding in a stall.

"How many did you have this time?" he asked as I rinsed out my mouth again.

"Two."

"We're gonna have to hurry, we don't have much time." He walked over to a window and opened it.

"I get to climb out a window again?" I asked in a whisper. "That'd be the second time in . . ." I tried to think how long ago it was. "Only a few days."

Joe looked outside the window and then climbed out, one leg at a time. He made it look so easy.

"When did you climb out a window?" He pulled me closer and lifted one of my legs through.

"The night after you hid the gun in my shed."

He pushed my head down and out and pulled the other leg through. We stood outside next to a motorcycle and I remembered. *Joe hid the gun in my shed.* He strapped a helmet to my head.

"How can I trust you?" I asked, searching his face for something to convince me.

He put on the other helmet. "Rose, you either trust me or Crocker, which one do you pick?"

It didn't seem like a none-of-the-above moment. "You."

"Good girl." Joe climbed onto the bike and pulled my arm. "Now climb on behind me."

I did with a bit of difficulty.

"Shit, I hadn't planned on you being so drunk. Hold on really tight, okay? Don't let go."

Before I had a chance to answer, Joe started the motorcycle and tore out of the parking lot.

Chapter Twenty-Four

Joe drove like he was trying to ride into yesterday. I felt my grip slip a couple of times and Joe would jerk on my arm and remind me to hang on. But I was drowsy, the vibration of the bike lulling me to sleep.

I recognized our neighborhood, but Joe didn't drive home. Instead, he pulled up to an old detached garage on the street behind our houses and shut off the bike.

"Where are we?" I asked, falling off the bike onto the grass. The garage hadn't been used to store a car in years and the gravel driveway had long since been invaded by the lawn.

Joe knelt down and took the helmet off my head. "I rent this, to store things."

"Like a motorcycle? I didn't know you had a motorcycle." I lay on my back in the grass. The stars in the sky were spinning around me. I felt like the center of the universe.

"That's me, a man of mystery." He lifted the garage door, an old-fashioned kind, a panel that tilted out and back.

"Tell me about it . . ." I mumbled, closing my eyes. The spinning stars were making me dizzy.

I heard him roll the motorcycle into the garage,

then shut the door and padlock it. He pulled me up. "Come on."

I had trouble standing and wearing heels in the grass wasn't going to work, especially in my state. Joe realized this before I did and knelt down to slip them off. He held my shoes in one hand and pulled my wrist with the other. "We have to hurry. We don't have much time." He pulled me to the trees that lined the rear property line and ran between them. Well, I tried to run. It wasn't working out so well.

Joe hunched down. "Climb on my back."

"Why?"

"They're gonna come looking for you. We have to hurry and get home."

I didn't really want to hurry so they could come find me, but Joe seemed to have a plan so I climbed on. He ran through to the trees behind his house, then slid me off. As he tried to help me over the fence, I saw my shed out of the corner of my eye.

"Hey! Why'd you put a gun in my shed?" My words sounded more indignant than I intended.

"I'll explain it all to you in a little bit. We just have to get through the next hour first." He led me to the back of his house, pried open a screen, then lifted the window. "Sorry, I don't have time to be gentle."

He shoved my head and body in through the window. When my top part was in, he pushed the back part of me through and I landed in a heap on the floor. I looked around to orient myself, realizing I was in Joe's bedroom.

He climbed in, replaced the screen, and shut the window. "Okay, time to hide you."

"I'm not so good at hide-and-go-seek."

"Lucky for you, I already picked out a place for you to hide. Your job is to *stay quiet.*"

Joe took me into the hallway and pulled down the attic steps. When he started to push me up, I froze. Joe was making me hide in the attic. "Are there any windows up there?"

"No."

I shook my head so violently I almost fell off the ladder. "No, I can't."

He climbed higher, so that we stood on the ladder side by side. "Rose, I know you're scared and this is gonna be hard. But you can do this. You *have* to do this. Your life depends on it. Now go." He pushed me up, and I scrambled up the steps, trying to stave off the fear.

The attic was unfinished, and the floor joists were filled with insulation. Joe pulled a cord and a single light bulb lit up the space. There were several boxes in the corner to the left, toward the front of the house.

"You're going to hide behind those boxes. It's gonna be tricky since there's no floor and you're drunk as a skunk. But try to keep alert and you can do it," he said, guiding me toward the boxes.

I told myself hiding in a dark attic was better than being dead. Joe got me situated the way he wanted me, my butt on one beam, my feet on another and hidden behind the boxes. He tossed my shoes in the insulation then knelt down, his face in front of mine.

"No matter what happens, you do not come out. Got it?"

"What's gonna happen?" I asked in a whisper, my voice quivering.

"They're gonna do whatever they can to find you. But you stay here. Do not come out, no matter what they say. Okay?"

I nodded, tears blurring my vision.

Joe smiled, but his eyes looked sad. He kissed my forehead. "It's gonna be okay. Just sit tight and be quiet." He scrambled to the attic door and clicked off the light, throwing me into darkness. The door shut and I found myself trapped, alone in the dark. I told myself I wasn't trapped. I was hiding. There was a difference, only I couldn't find it at the moment.

It wasn't long before I heard pounding on the front door. My stomach tightened and my heart took off like a racehorse.

"McAllister! Open the door!"

"Hold on!" Joe shouted.

It sounded like the door crashed into the wall, followed by shouting and a lot of scuffling. The muscles in my back and shoulders locked.

357

"Where is she?" I barely made out the words.

I heard more voices, too soft to understand, followed by more sounds of household objects thrown about.

"I hope you're not that stupid, McAllister. Where are you, bitch?" a man yelled.

My stomach rolled and the drinks from earlier churned in protest. The walls below me shook, causing the wood beams to vibrate. I gripped the wood to keep from falling over.

"Where is she?" The voice echoed into the rafters.

My breath came in shallow pants.

"How the hell would I know?" Joe sneered. They were in the hall, directly under the attic door.

I choked back a sob, covering my mouth to muffle the sound. I could only imagine what they'd do to Joe if they found me.

"It ain't no secret you had a thing for her. Where is she?"

The wall shook with a bang. A groan followed behind it.

"I told you. I'm not stupid." Joe's words sounded strained, as though he was in pain. "I sent her to Crocker, told her to be smart, and give 'em what he wanted. Didn't she show?"

My breath stuck in my throat. Joe was getting beat up because of me. My consciousness became fuzzy and I forced myself to suck in air. I couldn't afford to pass out.

"Yeah, she showed, then she disappeared into thin air."

"What? Is she a magician?" Joe said.

Another slam into the wall and another grunt, long and low. "Look here, Mr. Smart Ass. We know she's here."

"I don't know where she is and you obviously haven't found her here. Is her car in her driveway? Have you checked her house?"

"Her car's not here and we've already searched her house. Crocker thinks you took her."

"I've been here all night. If you don't believe me, go check the engine of my car. I haven't driven it since I dropped Rose off at her car, right before ten o'clock. It would be hot if I went to get her, like I'd be stupid enough to cross Crocker. I'm not a fucking idiot."

"Check," the guy said and someone opened the door and ran onto the porch. Seconds later they were back.

"He's tellin' the truth."

A heavy thud rattled the floor joists.

"Where is she?" he growled.

"I told you I don't know," Joe growled back, but he sounded out of breath.

The wood beams beneath me vibrated after a loud bang and Joe grunted. I bit my lip and tears spilled down my cheeks.

"If Crocker finds out you had anything to do with this, you're a dead man." A few seconds later, the door slammed and the sound of a car faded off into the distance.

I was safe, for the moment, but terrified for Violet. If Crocker's guys came looking for me at Joe's, they were sure to go to Violet's next. I needed to get out. Hysteria bubbled up, tightening my throat. I took a slow breath and held it in my chest before releasing it. I needed to save her, but Joe said to stay here no matter what.

Finally, the silhouette of Joe's head appeared in the opening. "I think it's safe now. You can come out."

"Joe! I have to go save Violet!" I cried out, struggling to crawl along the floor joists. When I got close enough, Joe reached his hand out to me and helped me maneuver to the steps.

"It's okay. I've already taken care of Violet. I'm sorry. I should have told you when I stuck you up here, but I was too scared they were gonna get here before I got you hidden."

"But how? When?"

"I'll explain it all, but I promise you. Violet and her family are safe at your aunt's house."

We reached the bottom and my legs gave out. I sagged into him. Joe wrapped his arms around my back and pulled me in a tight embrace.

"Thank you." I burrowed into his chest and he grunted from the force. I pulled back to look at him, remembering his sounds of pain earlier. Joe's face was bruised, his eye swollen, his lower lip split open. "Oh!" I said, reaching up and lightly touching his cheek. "They hurt you. I'm sorry."

He pulled me into an embrace and cupped the back of my head. "It's okay. I couldn't let him kill you." Joe held me tighter and let out a heavy sigh into my hair.

"Would he have killed me, even though I brought him the flash drive?"

Joe took a ragged breath before he answered, his voice shaky. "Yeah."

I started to shake, and Joe led me into his bedroom. We sat on the edge of his bed, our bodies pressed together. I leaned my head into the crook of his arm. But I didn't cry, I guessed I was past crying.

"How did you save Violet?"

"I called her after you left to meet Crocker. I told her to leave as soon as possible and made her call me when she got to your aunt's house. They'll be safe there until this is all over."

"When will this be all over?"

"Tomorrow, well, today. It's Sunday now."

"What's gonna happen?" I asked even though I wasn't sure I wanted to know.

"Crocker and his little empire are going down."

"How?"

"I'll tell you later. When it's done."

I could accept that. "Crocker said you worked for him and were watchin' me. He said you told him I was good in bed." Indignation simmered below the surface, but the fact Joe saved Violet and me and got beat up to do it trumped my pride.

Joe sighed and pulled me tighter. "Yeah, I did, but it's complicated. I told him I was watching you to hold him off from killing you. He suspected you had the flash drive so I told him I lived next to you and I could find out where it was. If you were dead, he'd never get it. I held him off as long as I could, but like I told you earlier, he was desperate. The person who has it made him look bad, and he had to have the information on that drive before his big meeting today."

"Which is why he would have killed me anyway."

"Yeah."

"But I never had it. Why did he think I did?"

"Because of your reaction to him at the DMV. He knew the person who had it was associated with the DMV. You changed your hair and got new clothes. Then you started spending money, you got a new car and a big diamond ring . . . he thought you were spending the money he paid you. Or rather the person with the real flash drive."

"Did you think I had it?"

He hesitated before he admitted. "I wasn't sure."

"How could you think that?" I pulled away, offended.

"Lots of reasons." He felt me stiffen but pulled me back. "I'm so sorry, Rose, but I've been dealing with a lot of bad people and I've become jaded enough to consider everyone suspect until proven innocent.

"The first time I suspected anything was the night of your mother's murder. You told your sister it should have been you, which I considered a very strange thing to say. You were so insistent you were the one who should have been dead. At that point, I knew you worked at the DMV. It looked suspicious. Why did you say that?"

"You wouldn't believe me if I told you."

"Try me."

"You tell me why else you suspected me first. Did you think I killed Momma?"

"I admit, I wondered at first, but it didn't take long to figure out you weren't capable of murdering someone. But you kept dropping hints that you might be involved with Crocker, like telling Muffy you only had four more days, which just happened to coincide with Crocker's big meeting. So I tried to stay close to you, looking for information."

I had a hard time wrapping my head around the fact that Joe worked for Daniel Crocker. The enormity of it seemed too heavy to hold up. "So it was all a lie. I was right. You were just using me."

Joe turned my chin. "No! I really like you. Yes, I tried to get information but only to save you. Besides, I suspected if you had the flash drive it was because someone was using you or forcing you to do it, especially the night we ate Chinese and you were so upset looking at old pictures. I hoped you would tell me so I could help you."

"Why didn't you tell *me?*"

"Rose, how could I? Tell you I worked for Crocker and that he would kill you if you didn't give me the drive? I knew you wouldn't tell me anything and maybe even run. I didn't want to risk losing you." He paused. "Now tell me why you said you were supposed to be dead instead of your mother."

I hesitated. Could I really tell him? He needed to know the truth about me. "You asked why Daniel thought I knew him the first time I saw him, and I told you I fainted. I fainted because I saw a vision." I paused to gauge his reaction. When he didn't recoil, I continued. "I have visions. I see things about other people, usually stupid things. It's why I don't have many friends. People think I'm weird. I know too much and they think I know it because I'm nosy or snoopin'. That's how I knew about Hilary's dog before I even knew about Hilary. I had a vision of the dog getting out of the fence."

Joe looked like I told him I was the tooth fairy.

"Believe me or not, it's true. When Daniel Crocker came in that day, I saw a vision of me dead, on Momma's sofa. Only it turned out not to be me, it was Momma. Because I didn't come home when I was supposed to."

"This sounds crazy, you know that?"

"Why do you think I didn't want to tell you?"

"Have you had any more? You obviously didn't die."

"I had one Monday. I didn't fight that one, I usually do but I gave into it and it lasted longer than any I've ever had. I looked through my niece Ashley's eyes and she was at a visitation at the funeral home, my visitation. I was dead. I saw a sign that said I died on June twelfth. Today."

"Any others?"

"I saw another one with Daniel, in the funeral home at Sloan's visitation. In my vision, I was in the woods and I had a bullet hole in my head. Dead." I paused, realizing Joe really had saved me. "That's what would have happened to me if you hadn't come to get me."

"Yeah, probably. Why did you go?" Joe asked. "Why not try to change it? You changed the first one."

"I didn't purposely change the one when Momma died. And this second time, I had two visions telling me the same thing, but I had no idea how to change it. The only reason I went was to save Violet."

"Why didn't you tell me? I could have helped you."

"Because I didn't trust you. I saw you hide the gun in the shed and I knew you were tryin' to get information from me about Sloan. Then I heard

Hilary's voicemail Friday night and I knew . . ."

His arm tightened around me. "That's why you were scared of me yesterday morning."

"Yeah."

We sat in silence, both unsure what to say.

Then I remembered the gun in the shed. "Joe, did you kill Sloan?"

"No, Rose. I did *not* kill Sloan."

"Then how did you get the gun that killed him in my shed?"

"That wasn't the gun used to kill Sloan. But it's the same caliber."

"Why did you put it in my shed?"

"To set you up."

"Why would you do that?" I tried to jerk away, but he had a firm grip.

"To save you. Thursday night after I left you, I found out Crocker had given up on me getting the information from you. He said he was going to find you Friday and give you the Saturday night deadline. I knew I needed a backup plan, so I hid the gun in your shed. When I realized you were still going to meet Crocker, especially after you tried to run away at Walmart, I called the police anonymously. I told them the gun that shot Sloan was hidden in your shed. I figured they'd lock you up for a few days until they figured out it wasn't the right gun. I didn't want you to be arrested, but it was better than letting Crocker kill you."

I was mad at him, but I understood. "Did Muffy ever come home?"

"Not that I've seen, Rose, but I was gone most of the night, too. She might have come back and we weren't here to let her in."

"She's gone," I said, my voice breaking as tears flooded my eyes.

"She might come home. That little dog loves you. She just got scared with all the confusion. I'm really sorry. I never even thought about her running off. I tried to find her."

"I know, I saw. Thanks," I said with a sniff. "So why did we come back here if you knew Crocker would send guys looking for me? Why not just run away?"

"Because I have to be part of his big meeting today."

"Why?"

"I just do."

"So you really are a criminal. Maybe a criminal with a conscience, but a criminal."

Joe narrowed his eyes, staring at me. "Do you really believe that, Rose?"

"I don't want to think so, but you work for Crocker. Doesn't that make you a criminal?"

"Maybe I have other reasons for working for Crocker. After his big meeting with his partners today, I won't have to anymore."

"You promise?" I asked, unable to stop the hopeful tone I used. I was having a hard time adjusting to the fact that my boyfriend was a criminal, but he did save my life and he said he planned to give it up.

Boyfriend. Where did that come from? I remembered my list and smiled. "I checked another item off my list. Ride a motorcycle."

"So what does that leave left? Get a boyfriend and play in the rain."

"And do more with a man."

"I told you, you've got that one covered."

"Not quite."

"And when did you play in the rain? It hasn't rained in almost two weeks."

"At the splash park, with Violet and her kids."

He shook his head. "Nope, doesn't count. It has to be real rain." Joe kissed me, his kiss that made me forget things. "So I think the only one you have left is play in the rain because I'd like to take care of the boyfriend wish for you."

"You kiss a whole lot better than Daniel Crocker," I murmured when he pulled away.

The look in his eyes told me he didn't appreciate the comparison.

"When do you have to go to work tomorrow?" I asked, standing up and pulling off my jeans.

"Eleven-thirty." He watched me, his eyes widening as I stripped off my shirt.

I looked over at the clock. "It's three in the morning. I think you need some sleep so you've got your wits about you."

"Sleeping with you will prove a challenge," he murmured, pulling me down on the bed.

"Why's that?"

"Because I won't be thinking about sleeping."

I reached my arms around his neck and pulled his mouth to mine. "Then let's do something to make you sleepy."

And that was how I finally took care of number fifteen.

Chapter Twenty-Five

We woke up around eight and Joe was antsy. I had no idea what he had planned for Crocker's big meeting, and he refused to tell me.

I made French toast for breakfast, just to prove myself capable of cooking, but Joe was too pre-occupied to eat. He excused himself several times to make phone calls in his room. He told me to make myself at home, but to stay inside and away from the windows. He worried I'd go out anyway. Muffy still hadn't come home.

Around ten-thirty, he sat beside me on the sofa, pretending to watch a documentary about prairie dogs on the Discovery Channel.

"I've been thinking about your visions," he said, holding my hand. "Can you *make* your visions happen?"

"No, they just come. I always fought them, but the one I had with Ashley, I didn't fight and it had more details."

"Have you ever tried to have one? To make it happen?"

"No, Momma said they were a sign of my demon possession."

Joe snorted. "It's a good thing I didn't know your momma. You are *not* demon-possessed."

After the last night in bed with Joe, I wasn't so sure about that.

"Why don't you try it," he coaxed, "on me?"

I was torn. Nothing good had ever come from a vision. Why would I *will* one to happen?

"Come on, give it a try. What do you have to do? Touch me?"

"No, they don't work like that. They just happen. I don't see visions for me, though. I see visions for other people, through their eyes. The one with Daniel Crocker was the first time I'd ever seen myself in a vision, and the first time I'd ever seen something really bad. Usually it's things like where someone misplaced their keys."

"Sounds useful."

"It's a nuisance because whatever I see just blurts out of my mouth."

"Like when you told me about Hilary's dog."

I nodded. I didn't want to think about Hilary but I had to know. "Is Hilary your girlfriend?"

"No, we have a working relationship."

I wondered what that meant, but said nothing.

"So what do you say?" Joe said. "Let's try it."

"What?" I asked confused. "A vision? I don't know . . . I wouldn't even know how to begin."

"Since you see visions for other people, maybe you could concentrate on me."

"All right," I agreed with great reluctance. I turned to face Joe on the sofa, sitting cross-legged and held his hands in mine. I closed my eyes and thought about Joe working for Crocker and the big meeting. I concentrated really hard and tried to picture Joe's face in my mind. A little flicker appeared in my head. And then I felt a vision coming. I squeezed his hands and kept concentrating.

I saw a warehouse. It looked like a mechanic's garage. A couple of men carried small bundles and loaded them into a delivery truck. Crocker and some other men came into view and I felt myself being slammed against the wall, Crocker's face in front of mine.

"This is your last chance, McAllister. Tell me where she is or I'm gonna kill you." Crocker held a gun up to my forehead.

"I don't know," I heard Joe's voice say.

There was a gunshot and then nothing.

"He's gonna kill you," I whispered. "Because of me."

My eyes flew open to look into Joe's surprised ones. Then his expression changed, becoming grim before he said, "I figured he might try."

"You knew?" I asked in disbelief.

"I suspected."

"Then why are you doing it? Don't go!"

"Because I think I can stay alive long enough for something important to happen. If I don't go, all of these past months work and Sloan's death will have been for nothing."

"But he's gonna kill you because of me. Crocker

wants me and thinks you know where I am. Maybe I should turn myself into him."

"Absolutely not."

"I'll tell him I ran away, that you had nothing to do with it."

"Absolutely *not*."

"If I do it before you show up, maybe I can stay alive long enough for what you need to happen."

"This is not up for discussion, Rose. He will probably hurt you the moment he sees you, if not shoot you dead first. You've embarrassed him twice."

"But he's gonna kill you. Because of me."

"No, he won't."

"I *saw* it!"

"You're living proof that what you see doesn't always happen. Rose, I can't not go because you saw something happen in your head."

"You're the one who made me try it," I said, hurt by his reaction.

Joe pulled me into his arms and gave me a kiss. "I don't want to leave with us fighting."

"Then don't go."

Joe sighed and got up. "Do not look out the windows. Do not go outside until I come back. If something happens to me, Hilary knows you're here and will come and get you herself. Do not open the door for anyone."

"You make it sound like I'm in jail."

"As far as I'm concerned, you are. Come here." He grabbed my hands and pulled me off the sofa. "How about a kiss for good luck?"

I gave him a good one, trying to make him forget about going. But it didn't work. He walked to the front door.

"Please be careful, Joe," I choked out through the lump in my throat.

He turned to look at me. His face looked like it belonged on Mount Rushmore, his profile hard with determination. "You still have to play in the rain," he said, breaking out into a mischievous smile. "I want to do that one with you. Don't do it without me, okay?"

I nodded, afraid I'd burst out into tears if I said anything.

And then he was gone.

I must have paced a furrow in his living room floor. I glanced at the clock. Only ten minutes had passed. I had no idea how long Joe would be gone. It could be an hour. Or ten. I threw myself on his sofa in frustration, sure I was gonna go crazy before he came back.

Then I heard barking.

I scrambled up. The sound came from the backyard. I ran into Joe's bedroom and looked out the window. Over by my shed, at the edge of all the contents that still littered the yard, stood Muffy. Barking.

Muffy never barked. Why was she by the shed?

She moved next to the rose bushes and howled, a chilling, haunting whine.

My stomach tumbled with nervousness and indecision. That dog meant everything to me. What if she ran away again? I couldn't just leave her out there.

I ran to the front and peeked through the cracks of the curtains. No cars on the street, nothing suspicious-looking. Should I risk it? If I got caught, Crocker would know Joe helped me.

I returned to the bedroom window. Muffy had stopped howling and lay down on the mulch by the roses, waiting for me. She'd turned her body so I could see her back hip and the red splotch on her fur. She was bleeding. I knew I had to go to her. The question was how I could get her and not give myself away.

I'd climb out the back window.

I'd learned a lot about climbing out of windows the last few days, so I was much quicker than the first time I tried it. I even landed on my feet and plastered my body to the rear of the house. Dark rain clouds were rolling in and Joe's yard was more shaded than mine. I could run through his backyard and most likely stay hidden. Then I'd skirt through the trees, make my way to the back of my yard and get Muffy.

The first part worked perfectly. I sprinted to the rear of Joe's lawn and practically vaulted his three-foot fence. It helped that I hadn't put on my shoes. While I was wearing my clothes from the night before, I figured heels were impractical running through wildlife.

I made it through the trees, directly behind the rose garden. It was a good twenty feet from the tree line. "Muffy!" I called. She turned her head to look at me, but kept her head lowered and whined.

"Muffy!"

She continued to ignore me and started digging in the dirt where I buried the gun. Did Muffy want me to dig up the gun?

As crazy as it was, it seemed like a good idea.

I bolted to Muffy and checked her backside first. Dried blood covered the wiry hair on her back left hip, but it looked old. When I tried to look more closely, she dug with her back legs, kicking dirt in my face. I let her go and started scooping dirt with my hands, thankful Muffy had a head start on me. In less than thirty seconds, I had the bag uncovered.

"Now what, Muffy?" I asked, thinking I needed to go back the way I'd come. I guessed I could push Muffy up into Joe's bedroom window.

Muffy whined and ran into the trees. I tried to coax her toward Joe's house, but she sat down in the shadows and whined again.

I kneeled beside her, rubbing her head. "What is it, Muffy?"

That's when I heard the pounding on Joe's

doors. I dropped to the dirt, hidden by the shade of the trees. Two men beat at the door on the side of Joe's house, one of them busting it in with a good kick. I clung to Muffy, shaking. I would have been in the house if she hadn't come back and barked. After several minutes, they came back out, along with two other men. One of them held the shoes I wore the night before. They got in two cars and drove way.

What did that mean for Joe?

I sat in the dirt, stroking Muffy's head. "You saved me, Muffy. Now I think we've got to save Joe." The only problem I saw with this plan was I didn't know anything about saving anybody. I didn't even know where to go, let alone have a car to get there. But I did have a gun, even if I'd never shot one before.

I unwrapped it, careful to point it away from me. I couldn't find the round spinny thing for bullets, then I remembered those were the kind of guns they used in prehistoric times. That covered most of the television shows I'd watched pre-cable. I was looking for the thing at the bottom of the gun. After a lot of fumbling and, I hate to admit, a little bit of cussing, I got it open. It appeared loaded.

Now to get to Joe. I remembered the truck parked outside of my house, the one driven by the guy who broke into my house. Weston's Garage. It seemed like a good place to start.

Weston's Garage was an old battered warehouse

out past The Trading Post, off Highway 82 and a half-mile down a country road. I'd been there once with Daddy, back when I was about thirteen. They worked on service vehicles and tractors. Uncle Earl had asked Daddy to see if they had a part for his old combine. Back then it had been a scary place, with old farm equipment scattered around the warehouse yard like mutant lawn ornaments. Given the circumstances, I supposed it would be even scarier now.

First I had to figure out how to get there. I had no keys, no car, no driver's license and no money. This could be a problem.

I stood up and walked toward my house. I needed shoes and I could think about my transportation issue while I got them. Lucky for me, Daniel Crocker's friends had already opened the door.

His boys could learn a thing or two about being polite houseguests. My house was torn to bits. The intruder on Thursday had been looking for something; this time they did it just to be mean. I was gonna have to pay a cleaning service again and that made me plenty mad.

I found a pair of tennis shoes and slipped them on and I ran outside, still unsure how to get to Joe. Mildred's old Cadillac sat parked in her driveway and an idea sprang to mind. I ran across the street, Muffy following behind, and beat on her door. I was just about to give up when Opal, the elderly neighbor next door to Mildred, poked her head out.

"Mildred's at church, honey. She'll be back after lunch."

"But her car's in the driveway."

"Her son picked her up." Opal came out onto the porch, leaning on her metal walker with florescent green tennis balls on the feet.

I stared longingly at the 1974 white Cadillac. It was a tank. I knew Mildred kept the keys in the ignition. I had an evil idea.

"My car's in the shop and Mildred told me I could use hers. I plum forgot she had church this morning and just wanted to thank her again for lettin' me use it. So I'll just take off and thank her later." I was already moving to the driver's door.

"Are you sure?" Opal asked, sounding confused. "Mildred don't let nobody drive her car."

"I know! That's the amazin' part, huh?" I opened the door and Muffy hopped in. She'd gotten me this far; it didn't seem right to leave her out now.

Opal pointed to Muffy. "I know for a fact Mildred don't let no animals in her car."

I had turned the key, the engine roaring to life. "Thanks, Miss Opal. You have a good day, too!"

She shouted as I pulled away. I turned to Muffy. "I've shot right on past the Seven Deadly Sins and moved onto breakin' the Ten Commandments. We're surely going to hell now."

Muffy answered by lifting her chin and turning her head. I was sure she told me she had nothing to do with the car stealing; she was letting me take all the blame for this one.

In about ten minutes I reached the country road where Weston's Garage was located. I passed The Trading Post, my Nova still in the parking lot. If I had my keys, I would have switched cars. I wasn't used to driving an ocean liner between driving lanes.

I didn't have a plan, but I was smart enough to realize I needed the element of surprise. I couldn't just drive the Titanic up to their front door; then again, maybe I could knock the building down with it. Last time I'd seen the old metal building, it looked pretty rickety. It would probably only take two, maybe three, good rams to knock it down. But Joe was inside, and I couldn't risk it.

I parked the car about two hundred yards down the country road, after I turned the car around to face the highway. Common sense told me we needed a getaway plan. So far, this was it.

I expected to see guys with machine guns or at least shotguns outside guarding the place. But the only thing I found were the tractor parts, even rustier than the last time I saw them and more dangerous since I was old enough to recognize the tetanus risk.

I grabbed the gun out of the car. Woods sur-rounded the building on two sides. A giant parking lot lay between the back of the building and the woods, scattered with delivery trucks like sprinkles dropped on a cupcake. Several luxury cars sat in the lot in front of the entrance. Crocker's business partners, I guessed.

The woods had worked well for me the last twenty-four hours, so I returned to what I knew. Muffy insisted on joining me, jumping out of the car when I opened the door. I told her she could come, but she had to be quiet. It seemed like a stupid thing to say, but I felt the need to tell her something. We couldn't very well synchronize watches. I stopped wearing mine when I got my cell phone.

We crept through the brush, between the trees, and I prayed I didn't crawl through poison ivy. I still wasn't sure it was the right place, until I saw Joe's car was parked in back. The lack of guards outside concerned me.

A metal chain-link fence surrounded the property. I considered scaling it but Muffy would never make it. Besides, I had just mastered climbing out windows, fences were still on my to-do list. I walked along the perimeter looking for any gaps. Muffy found one toward the rear, big enough at the bottom for both of us to crawl under. I knelt down to face her.

"I'm not sure it's a good idea for you come with me, Muffy. Maybe you should wait for me here." But I secretly hoped she would come.

I lifted the fence and Muffy scooted through first. I crawled through but scraped my side on the metal wire. If that was the least of my injuries today, I'd consider myself lucky. We emerged next to a delivery truck and hid behind it while I figured out what to do next. Since I couldn't go waltzing through the front door, sneaking around to the back seemed like the best option.

We dashed across the lot and walked the length of the building to the back corner. Open doors gaped in the middle of the back wall, big enough to drive a truck through. Next to me was a metal door, propped open with a brick. I inched toward it and peeked in. Metal shelves lined the room, stocked with plastic bins. I didn't see anyone so I took a deep breath and opened the door wide enough to slip through. Muffy followed.

Edging along the shelves, I made my way toward the center of the room. It looked like a parts room with a door on the opposite wall. I knelt by the door and opened it just a crack, peeking through the one-inch gap. It was a large room, like the warehouse I'd seen in Joe's vision. Two delivery trucks were parked in the center and men moved stacks of small packages. Joe stood to the side, watching. I didn't see any sign of Daniel Crocker, which was fine by me.

I wanted to tell Muffy we were just going to wait, but she sensed it and sat down beside me. I sat with my back to the wall and Muffy laid her head on my lap. I scratched her neck while I listened to the voices echoing in the warehouse.

Probably a good ten minutes went by without anything happening. I was beginning to think that we'd make it out of the warehouse without any trouble. I wasn't sure why I believed that. I had yet to have anything happen without any trouble.

It started with shouting in the distance, echoing throughout the warehouse. I jerked at the noise and looked through the crack. The stack of bundles in the warehouse was nearly gone, now inside the delivery trucks. Joe was carrying a package. Daniel Crocker descended metal steps with two other men. It looked like they came from an office above the warehouse floor.

"McAllister!" Crocker shouted.

My blood turned to ice. My vision was coming true.

Joe swung his head in Crocker's direction. Rage engulfed Crocker's face and he literally growled as he reached Joe and slammed him against the wall.

"Where is she?" Crocker screamed. His eyes were wild and even from my location, I saw the veins and tendons bulge on his neck.

"How the hell would I know?" Joe asked, looking disgusted. "I'm done with her."

"I don't believe you. The information was fake! *I want the fucking flash drive!"* Crocker slammed Joe against the wall again to emphasize his point.

Two men stood behind Crocker. I guessed they were important from the suits they wore, their stiff postures, and the bored expressions on their faces. They had to be Crocker's business partners.

Crocker pulled a gun out of the back of his pants and held it up to Joe's head. I had already jumped to my feet and stuffed my gun under my shirt, into the waistband of my jeans. I hoped to high heaven I didn't shoot my toes off.

"Where is she?" Crocker growled.

"Lookin' for me?" I shouted, walking through the door. I tried to not look nervous, like I knew what I was doing.

Crocker turned in disbelief. Joe's eyes widened in horror. I hoped to God he didn't try anything stupid.

I walked toward them, hands at my sides instead of up in surrender, even though I was scared out of my wits. I didn't see me surviving this.

"Lookin' for me?" I shot Joe a condescending glare. I wanted Crocker to think Joe had nothing to do with me getting away. I stopped a few feet in front of the group, their mouths all dropped open in shock. Even the men in the suits looked a bit surprised, although their Botox-injected, wrinkle-free foreheads had a hard time expressing it.

Crocker slapped me across the face. I should have seen it coming, but it caught me by surprise. I almost fell over from the force of the blow, but didn't want to give him the satisfaction.

I rose back up, lifting my chin to face him. "Where the hell did you go, bitch?" he shouted, turning the gun toward me.

My cheek hurt and my eyes burned, but I refused to cry. I stood up straight and stared into his menacing eyes. "I was lookin' for a real man. One who knows how to kiss better than you."

I saw the look of pure fear in Joe's eyes before Crocker slapped me again, harder this time. I started to fall to the floor, but Crocker grabbed my arm and jerked me back up before wrapping his hand around my throat. His eyes, wild and feral, reminded me of a rabid raccoon I had seen on Uncle Earl's farm when I was little.

"Why'd you come back?" he growled.

Inside sanity desperately clawed for control, but on the outside I tried to look indignant. "I decided to give you another chance to impress me, although I don't hold out much hope."

The men behind him laughed. The fury in Crocker's eyes turned murderous and the grip on my throat tightened, cutting off my air. I started to feel lightheaded as I gasped for air.

"Give me one good reason why I shouldn't kill you right now," he said through gritted teeth, spittle shooting through a gap in his top teeth.

"I'll give you two," I choked out. "One, you'll never get the real flash drive, and two, you'll never be able to prove you're really a man."

The men laughed again. Crocker growled and

gave me a hard shove to the ground and pointed the gun at my head. I stared at him defiantly, waiting for him to shoot, not daring to look at Joe and give him away.

"Crocker," one of the men said. "She's right."

"You mean provin' he's a real man?" the other laughed.

Crocker leaned over and grabbed my hair in a tight grasp. I couldn't help the yelp of pain I let out when he jerked me off the floor.

"That hurt, bitch? 'Cause I haven't even started yet." He pulled me toward the stairs. I looked toward Joe. He looked torn. I shot him a look that I hoped read *don't you dare*.

We stumbled up the stairs, and I was sure I would have a giant bald spot on the side of my head, not that I would care if I was dead. They could always put a hat on my head although I never looked good in hats.

I was grateful the other two men hadn't followed us. They stood watching the trucks being loaded, glancing up the stairs, and laughing. Joe had come out of his stupor and had begun moving toward the truck. I really needed him to not come upstairs.

Crocker opened the door and shoved me into the office with such force I ran into a desk.

"Where's the flash drive?" He stood in the doorway and I had to admit, he was terrifying. It took everything in me to go through with this.

"Why should I tell you? You'll kill me anyway."
I leaned against the edge of the desk, facing
him. My cheek throbbed and my throat still felt
tight. My heart galloped fast enough to win the
Kentucky Derby.

"Damn straight I will, but I'll make it hurt a
hell of a lot more if you don't tell me."

"Why don't you prove you're a man first?" I
taunted and put my shaking hands on my hips.

He shut the door and slunk closer, stalking his
prey. Crocker stopped a foot in front of me and
grabbed the hair on the back of my head, his
eyes glaring into mine. I still leaned against the
edge of the desk, trying not to stand flush
against him. If I did, he'd feel the gun in my
waistband.

"I like it rough, baby. Think you can handle
that?" His breath smelled of onions again. I was
beginning to believe Crocker brushed his teeth
with them.

"I like it rough, too. Why don't you put that gun
down and show me what kind of man you really
are."

It was sick the way that excited him, but he
slammed the gun down on the desk and pulled
me up. I placed my hand between the gun in my
waistband and his body. He kissed me, his
technique not much better than the night before.
It reminded me of a slobbery Saint Bernard.

I had to get the gun out, and I couldn't do it

smashed up against him. I shifted my butt back just a bit. Just enough to grab the gun.

At that moment, Crocker pulled away and ripped my shirt open down the middle.

Crappy doodles. I hadn't planned on that.

But the side of my shirt still covered the handle of the gun. I narrowed my eyes and lifted the corners of my mouth into a tiny grin. I hoped it looked like I couldn't wait to see what he would do next, when really I couldn't wait to see what *I* was going to do next.

Fear slunk around inside my head, bursting into my consciousness in spasms. He was going to find my gun any minute and when he did, I'd be dead.

He grabbed my hair and kissed me again. Apparently, he was a hair guy. As I fought the urge to gag, I heard a commotion below and decided to use it to my advantage. My teeth clamped down on Crocker's lower lip. I tasted his blood and gagged, releasing my hold. He shoved me away, furious. I pulled the gun out of my pants and pointed it at him.

"I thought you liked it rough," I said, hands shaking. He'd backed up when he shoved me away. He stood in front of the door, about three feet from me. Sounds of the apocalypse rose from below, but Crocker didn't seem to notice. He hunched over, his arms ready to pounce. His eyes bugged out and blood covered his lower lip.

Daniel Crocker was the scariest predator I had ever faced.

"You're not gonna shoot me," he sneered, moving a foot toward me.

"Wanna bet?" I lowered the gun and shot into his leg, nearly dropping the gun from the shock of what I had just done.

"Son of a bitch!" he screamed and lunged for me. I backed out of the way and he fell to the floor, grasping for my feet. He grabbed my legs, and pulled me down. I landed hard on my side. Crocker pulled himself along the length of my body, none too gently, reaching for the gun. I couldn't figure out how to keep it out of his reach and shoot him at the same time. I tossed it into the corner of the room.

Crocker tried to get up to get it, but I clawed his face. Falling on top of me, he reached back to punch me in the face when the door flung open.

"I swear to God, Crocker, you hit her, and I'll kill you," Joe shouted from the doorway.

We both turned to look, but Joe didn't have a gun to back up his statement. Crocker turned back to hit me. Muffy bolted past Joe's legs and jumped on Crocker, biting the arm he held up.

Crocker rolled off me, batting at Muffy, who refused to let go and made wild snarling noises.

Joe rushed over and pulled me up, then grabbed the gun off the desk. He pointed it toward Crocker.

"Muffy, come here," I said calmly, in spite of the shock of what just happened.

Muffy stopped and came to sit beside me.

"It's over, Crocker," Joe said.

Crocker threw a floor lamp at Joe. Joe stumbled backward as Crocker rolled over onto his stomach. He reached for my gun and flipped over. "Not yet," he grunted.

I heard a gunshot and screamed.

Chapter Twenty-Six

I'd heard of time standing still, but until that moment, I always thought it was a figure of speech. When Crocker turned over with the gun, a million things happened at once, yet I was aware of every single one of them. Shouting and crashing downstairs. Crocker pointing the gun. Joe throwing me to the floor. Muffy rushing for Crocker's arm. The sound of the gunshot. My scream. Even with all that knowledge in the moment, I didn't know what I'd find on the other side.

When I looked up, Joe still stood where I last saw him, so I took that as a good sign. Muffy was growling and Crocker shouted and cursed, the gun still in his hand, pointed to the ceiling. Another shot. I jumped up to my feet, trying to get out of the way of any stray bullets.

Muffy had a death grip on Crocker's arm, shaking as she snarled. Joe kept his gun pointed at the man rolling on the floor but couldn't get a good shot with Muffy in the way. I looked on the desk for something to use as a weapon and found a crystal geode bookend. I picked it up, surprised to find it so heavy.

Crocker tried to shake Muffy off but when that

didn't work he started hitting her with his free hand. Muffy held on.

Seeing him hit Muffy pissed me off. And once I let that feeling wash through my head, fury followed right behind it. *How dare he hit my dog? And tear up my house, not to mention my new blouse? Who did he think he was, beating people up and killing them?* He'd messed with the wrong woman.

"Get your grimy hands off my dog!" I flung the rock at Crocker's head.

The geode hit him square in the temple, and his arms crumpled into a heap on his chest, the gun tumbling to the floor with a clatter. Joe ran over and picked up the gun as Muffy hopped off Crocker's body. Joe turned to me, disbelief on his face and just a hint of anger.

"He was messin' with my dog," I said in my defense.

Joe rolled Crocker onto his stomach and pulled his hands behind his back.

"Did I kill him?" I asked, scared I'd broken another of the Ten Commandments. I was really on a roll.

"No, but he'll have one hell of a headache when he wakes up." Joe jerked the electrical cord of a floor lamp out of the wall. He pulled a pocket-knife out of his pocket and cut the cord from the base, then wrapped it around Crocker's wrists.

He walked over to me and tugged me into his

arms. I let myself relax into his chest. "Is it over?" I asked.

"Yeah, it's over." He sighed with relief, blowing hairs on top of my head.

We clung to each other for a minute, thankful we could, then Joe grabbed my arms and pulled me away to face him, anger burning in his eyes.

"What the hell did you think you were doing coming here? You could have gotten yourself *killed!*"

"I was savin' *you,* thank you very much!"

"I told you to stay in the house. I gave you a direct order." He gritted his teeth, making his words muffled.

"You are not the boss of me, Joe McAllister! And besides, Muffy came back and was whining and barking at the back of my house. I couldn't just leave her out there!"

"I told you to stay in the house!"

"If I had, they would have found me! Right after I got to Muffy, four men showed up and busted into your house lookin' for me and found my shoes. So there!"

That caught him by surprise.

"Then I went to get another pair of shoes out of my house and found it trashed by them again . . ."

"Again?" His voice rose. "There was a first time I didn't know about?"

I ignored his question. "Well, it just pissed me

off, having to get another cleaning crew to come and clean up *his* mess again."

"So what? You came here to make him write you a *check?*"

"No, I came here to save you."

"I didn't need you to save me."

"Yeah, I could see that, what with the gun pointed to your head and all."

His face softened and he reached his hand up to touch my bruised cheek. "I almost lost it when he hit you."

"Well, I'm glad you didn't. It would have ruined everything."

"What? You had a plan?"

"No, I just kind of winged it."

"Why in God's name did you taunt him into bringing you up here? When I heard that gunshot, I almost had a heart attack. I had to push my way through the DEA agents that showed up to bust the place. I nearly got myself shot trying to get up here to you."

"I had a gun. The gun you hid in my shed. I thought if I got Crocker alone, I could keep him from you until what you needed to happen, happened."

"So you knew how to turn off the safety?"

"Safety?"

Joe's eyes got as big as the pancakes they serve at The Waffle House.

I shrugged. "I figured out it was loaded, not an

easy task, and I stuck it in the waistband of my jeans. And then when all the noise started happening downstairs, I bit him on the lip."

I could have sworn Joe's face paled and then reddened.

"You realize there were so many problems with that *plan* that you are lucky to be standing here."

"It was all I had."

"No," he growled. "You could have stayed away."

I groaned in frustration. "That again? I had to do it, Joe. Could you have sat at home, watchin' a show about prairie dogs, knowing I was probably gonna be killed?"

He didn't answer.

"Yeah, you proved that you couldn't last night. Why is what I did any different?"

"Because I'm a cop!" he shouted. "That's what I've been trained to do!"

I stepped backward in disbelief. "What?"

"I was undercover, investigating this mess. I'm with the state police."

"So you're *not* a criminal?" I wasn't sure whether to be relieved or angry. I let myself have both. "You *lied* to me?"

"Yes, no." Joe shook his head, looking frustrated.

"You really were just using me?"

He didn't answer right away, and I had all the answers I needed. I headed for the open door.

Joe stepped in front of me. "Rose! Wait! I was investigating Crocker's stolen-parts ring. I was a mechanic and worked on the delivery trucks that came in for their bogus maintenance runs. Instead, they were leaving with stolen parts and the pot Crocker grew in his warehouse. I wasn't even involved in the drug trafficking part until Sloan got into trouble with Crocker over the missing flash drive."

"And me," I reminded him, my voice cold. "Until you thought I had the flash drive. You really wanted it for the police, but it got you into Crocker's good graces."

The look on his face confirmed it. I tried to step around him again.

"So what's on this precious flash drive everyone wants? It must be something special to kill people and waste time foolin' stupid me." I glared up at him.

"Rose, I swear it wasn't like that!"

"You just saved me last night because it was gonna look bad that an innocent taxpaying citizen got killed by mistake."

His face hardened. "You're wrong there. They offered you immunity up until Saturday afternoon, the phone call I got after lunch. Then they said they wanted you to go through with meeting Crocker. They were worried if you didn't show, the big meeting today wouldn't happen."

My heart dropped into my toes. "I see," I said,

letting it sink in. "So how did you save me then? Why?"

"By disobeying direct orders. When my superiors find out what I did, I'm liable to lose my job. But I wouldn't have been able to live with the guilt."

"Am I supposed to feel grateful or sorry for that?" I shouted, about to burst into tears. "I saved you because I care about you Joe McAllister! Not because I felt guilty! Okay, a little because I felt guilty, since I thought you were gonna die because of me. But I saved you because I couldn't bear for something to happen to you. I *like* you. Or I thought I did." I stepped to my left to get around him.

Joe moved in front of me again. "Rose, that came out wrong, that's not what I meant!"

"You were gonna arrest me, weren't you?"

He didn't answer, guilt in his eyes.

"Get out of my way, Joe McAllister."

Hilary stood in the doorway. "Joe, we need you downstairs."

I stared at her, then back at Joe. "So is she your girlfriend or not?"

"Was. What I told you the night we ate Chinese was true."

I studied the man I thought I knew, my heart shattering into pieces. "Thanks for tellin' me the truth about *something*." I walked around him and Hilary backed out of the doorway onto the stairs.

"Rose! Wait!" Joe shouted, running after me.

Hilary blocked his path. "She just needs some time to think this through and you have work to do."

I walked down the stairs, realizing my shirt still hung open, my black bra hanging out for the world to see. Even though it seemed the least of my worries, I grabbed the torn edges with my hand to hold it shut.

"Rose, you can't leave yet," Hilary called out. "We still need a statement from you."

"I don't care. I'm going home. You know where to find me." I walked through the handcuffed men and DEA agents in bulletproof vests, then headed for the wide open doors in the center. Muffy appeared next to me.

"Come on, Muffy. Let's go home."

I parked Mildred's car in her driveway, like nothing had ever happened. I would have filled up the gas tank, but I didn't have any money. Heavens knew where my purse was.

As soon as I got in the house, I called Violet at Aunt Bessie's. I assured her I was fine and that it was all over. When she asked about Joe, I told her he was fine, too. I didn't feel like explaining anything else. Turned out he'd told her the night before that he was with the state police. I guessed I was the last to know.

I took a long shower, my body aching from all the beating it had received. I was thankful I didn't have to worry about someone coming in and surprising me. I also felt a sense of relief, knowing that Muffy stood guard next to the tub if they did. I'd never doubt her guard-dog capabilities again.

I spent the rest of the afternoon sorting through my house, the events of the last couple weeks playing in my mind, exhausted but too riled up to sleep. Around seven, I heard the whine of a small motor in the kitchen.

The side door stood partially open and Joe had a drill, removing my locks.

"What are you doin'?" I asked, irritated at the little skip in my heart at the sight of him. I stopped in front of the opening.

He stood up and reached out his right hand to me, wanting to shake my hand.

I tilted my head and looked at him like he'd just escaped from the funny farm.

"I'm Joe." He shook my hand and gave me a hesitant smile. "I'm your next door neighbor. I saw you had some broken locks and thought I'd do the neighborly thing and fix 'em for you."

"You don't have to . . ."

He picked up the drill again, working on the screws. "I'm a mechanic. And a cop, although I'm not sure I'll be one for much longer. I grew up in El Dorado. My parents still live there. My little sister lives in Little Rock." He looked up, his eyes pleading with me to listen. "That's where I live, too, in Little Rock. I have an apartment there."

"Joe."

He put the drill down, stood up and took my hand in his. "Here's the thing. I met this girl, this beautiful woman who's unlike anyone I've ever met. She's funny, and brave and has packed more into her life in the last few weeks than most people do in their entire lives."

My eyes started to burn.

"I find myself thinking about her all the time. But I hurt her. I didn't mean to hurt her. I'd do anything to take back the pain I caused, but I don't think she'll listen to me. So the only thing I know to do is start over, then maybe she'll give me another chance." When I didn't say anything, he pulled me into his arms, looking into my eyes for a sign that I forgave him. "Do you think there's any way she can give me another chance?"

I'd wrestled with myself all afternoon. I knew Joe was doing his job, that it wasn't personal. I had to look past my own feelings and look at the bigger picture. But how did I know what was real and what wasn't, especially in regard to his feelings for me.

I cleared my throat, trying to dislodge the lump that had formed. "This woman, perhaps she doesn't know what to believe. Maybe she forgives you for doing your job but feels like everything else was a lie."

The soft pitter-patter of raindrops beginning to hit the leaves and the cars caught me by surprise.

The dark clouds that had shrouded the sky all day finally let loose.

Joe cupped my cheek carefully with his hand. His thumb ran under the bruise on my cheekbone. "My feelings for you weren't a lie. But that's why I wanted to wait to sleep together, so there wouldn't be any doubt in your mind." He paused, searching my eyes. "I would do anything to prove it to you."

The corners of my mouth lifted into a small smile. "I'm Rose. I've not done much living in my life, but I met this guy who makes me want to live it. He doesn't even think it's strange that I have visions, but he wasn't who I thought he was."

Joe's eyes clouded.

"I hope to get to know the real him. And besides, he promised to help me fulfill my last wish, play in the rain."

Joe's face lit up right before he kissed me, almost making me forget about the rain. He was always making me forget things. He didn't forget anything though. He grabbed my hand and pulled me outside. He kissed me again as the gentle rain seeped into our hair and clothes.

"Joe McAllister, I thought we were supposed to be playing in the rain."

"I am playing." He laughed before kissing me again, happiness radiating from him. "And I'm only getting started."

Chapter Twenty-Seven

I didn't want to go to work the next day, but I'd already taken two weeks off and couldn't afford to take off any more days. I was out of vacation time. I had all of Dora's money, but I hadn't figured out what to do with it. So, for the moment, I pretended it didn't exist.

I almost called in sick anyway. I looked like a domestic-violence victim with the bruises on my cheek and slightly swollen eye, making me wish I had gotten concealer when I bought my other makeup. It didn't help that I was sleep-deprived. Between giving my statement to Hilary, who showed up around nine, and Joe keeping me up half the night, I was beyond tired.

But happy. For the first time, I felt like I actually had a life worth living.

I still hadn't gotten my car back, so Joe drove me to work. I suspected he would hold off getting it as long as possible. He was trying to find a way to spend every minute he could with me before he went back to Little Rock in a few days. Neither one of us wanted to talk about it, but we also knew our relationship was too new to promise each other anything other than the vow to see each other as often as possible. It hung over our heads like a big cloud of loneliness.

At work, I settled into my desk and turned on the computer, making sure the drawers were stocked with forms, the printer full of paper. Suzanne sat down next to me a few minutes later and was surprisingly quiet. I expected her to mock my bruises or be hateful that I had just taken off another week, but she sat at her desk, subdued.

Just then, it occurred to me the DEA had never figured out who had the real flash drive.

I spent the morning trying to figure out how to get her to confess, like she'd tell me she had a flash drive wanted by law enforcement officials and crime lords. She wouldn't even tell me what she had for dinner the night before. But she seemed sad, so I tried being nice.

"Is everything okay?" I asked in a moment when neither of us had clients.

"What do you care?" she asked with a sneer, but I heard the tears in her voice.

"Look, Suzanne, I know we've had our differences, but I can see you're upset and I just want you to know if you need someone to talk to, I'll be happy to listen."

"Why would you do that? I've been nothin' but mean to you."

"Because you look like you're hurtin'." I surprised myself when I realized it was true. I wasn't just trying to get information from her.

Customers appeared at both of our counters and

we were busy for another half an hour before we had a rare lapse close to noon.

Suzanne looked my direction, her eyes shimmering with tears. "My boyfriend left me last night. With my best friend. I never saw it comin'." She bit her lip as her chin quivered.

I handed her a tissue. "I'm so sorry, Suzanne."

"I thought he was different." She blew her nose and looked at me, narrowing her eyes. "Honey, don't let no man do that to you." She pointed to my face. "They say they love you and they're sorry, but they're just mean, selfish sons of bitches. You can do a whole lot better than that."

My mouth fell open in shock. If someone had told me two weeks ago that Suzanne would be nice to me, I would have suggested they try to sell me some snake oil, because I would have been far more likely to buy that. But I'd changed, and I realized sometimes people acted mean because they were hurting. Suzanne had obviously been hurting for a long time.

I thought about telling her I didn't get my bruises from my boyfriend. The Weston Garage bust had been big news. Daniel Crocker had been locked up in the hospital while he recovered from dog bites and a gunshot wound to his leg. He would soon face multiple charges that included murdering Sloan and my Momma, but that hadn't been released yet. Amazingly enough, my name had been kept out of it. But I had to wonder how Suzanne knew about my boyfriend. I hadn't told anyone. The person with the flash drive would probably know a lot about me since I took the fall for him. Or her.

We got busier and I didn't have time to think about it. Two o'clock rolled around, when I usually took my lunch break. I'd brought my lunch since Joe would be tied up with official state police stuff. He was still waiting to hear what his punishment would be. Joe said he didn't care. Let them fire him, he'd said. But the look in his eyes told me it would hurt him a whole lot more than he'd admit.

I sat at the table in the tiny break room, looking at the bulletin board. One of the other employees had posted pictures of her teenage son from his high school graduation. Betty had posted pictures of her grandkids, right next to the invitation to her retirement party. She only had a few weeks left.

I pulled my turkey sandwich out of a brown paper bag, courtesy of Joe. He was appalled at the lack of food in my house and insisted on packing my lunch. When I pulled out an apple, a note fell out onto the table, written on the back of a short grocery store receipt.

I'm counting the hours until I see you tonight.

Joe

I wondered again how I got so lucky. I had a smile on my face when Betty walked in.

"How're ya doin'?" she asked, sitting down in chair next to me.

"Pretty good."

"You look like your doin' really well after all you've been through. I didn't expect you to be in today."

In the middle of taking a bite of my apple, I nearly froze. Was she talking about Momma or the weekend?

"You know, if you need more time off, you can take it without pay. I know it's against the rules, but considerin' all ya been through . . ." She patted my hand, giving me a look of motherly compassion.

My heart raced. "So Betty, you must be excited about your retirement. Do you have any big trips planned?"

"Nope, not unless you count movin' as a trip. We're movin' to Dallas, to be close to my kids and grandbabies."

I suddenly remembered Betty had a son who moved to Dallas before I started at the DMV. He had been arrested for drug possession and trafficking right about the time I started, five years ago. It wasn't any secret he'd been involved in a gang. I racked my brain, trying to remember his name. Bobby Joe.

"I bet you're excited about spending more time

with those grandbabies," I said, taking a nibble of my sandwich, trying to choke it down along with my anxiety.

Betty's face lit up. "Oh, they're getting so big without me. I'm movin' down the street from 'em. I'll get to see 'em every day."

My heart in my throat, I asked, "How's Bobby Joe? He still at Hutchins Prison?"

Betty's mouth and eyes froze in her smile but the sparkle vanished. She looked like a wax replica of the smiling Betty who was there a moment ago.

"He's doin' just fine. Why'd you ask, Rose?" She still appeared friendly, but her left eyelid began to twitch.

A tight smile hardened on my face. "I dunno. I was just thinkin' about him."

She continued watching me with her plastered-on smile, and I lost my appetite. "Well, I need to get back to work," I said, getting up and throwing my bag in the trash. I had forgotten Joe's note on the table and reached over to pick it up.

"Is that from your new boyfriend?" she asked, her words like imitation maple syrup. They sounded sweet, but left an artificial aftertaste. "You waited so long for him. It'd be a shame if you lost him so soon."

I turned around and hurried to my desk, scared witless. What did she mean by that? I reached into my drawer, to get my cell phone out of my purse and send Joe a text message, but as soon as I opened the drawer I remembered I didn't have my cell phone. For all I knew, it was still at The Trading Post, stuffed under a counter. I couldn't call him on the DMV phone. For one thing, personal calls were strictly forbidden. For another, if I got on the phone, Betty would surely come over and investigate.

I just had to wait for Joe to pick me up at five o'clock. It was two-thirty now; I could surely last a few more hours.

We were slammed with customers at the end. It was a good thing because it kept me busy, but I couldn't concentrate. Suzanne gave me weird looks and Betty looked at me with a knowing expression that looked more and more grim the closer it got to five.

When the last customer left, Betty locked the front doors and she walked over to my counter. "Rose, could you stay a little late so we can discuss your vacation situation?"

It was such a reasonable request, how could I refuse? "Um," my tongue stumbled, searching for words, "Joe's pickin' me up. I don't wanna keep him waiting."

Betty smiled, the corners of her mouth lifting up, but her eyes cold and hard. No one but me seemed to notice. "That's okay, honey. It won't take but a minute."

Everyone packed up their belongings and headed for the back door. I started out the door, too.

"Rose," Betty called. "It's only gonna take a minute." Her words were thick and sweet like honey off a comb, yet I heard the threat that hid beneath.

I was already out the door, my heart beating frantically while I searched the parking lot for Joe's car. "I was just lookin' for Joe. I wanted to tell him I'd be another minute."

"Come on, darlin'." Her grip told me she wouldn't take no for an answer. Before she pulled me in, I dropped my purse to the ground, propping the door open.

"Now, let's just go to my office, shall we? I have some paperwork you need to fill out."

"But Joe . . ."

"Didn't I tell you? Joe called and said he was gonna be a few minutes late. But I told him that I needed to keep you for a bit, and I'd bring you home."

My heart fell into a pit of fear in my stomach. I pulled harder, knowing full well I'd look like an idiot if I was wrong about Betty. Who would believe it? This was Betty, everybody's mother, yet self-preservation overrode idiocy as I struggled against her grasp. In the end, it was pointless to struggle. Betty was taller than me and outweighed me by a good seventy pounds.

"Rose, if you just cooperate, this'll all be done in a minute and you'll be free to go."

She dragged me into her office and shoved me into her chair. A piece of paper and a pen sat on the desk. I looked up confused.

"I need you to write me a note. Then you're free to go. That sounds okay, right?"

I nodded, my chin trembling, to my disgust. When was I ever going to be strong?

"You can thank your boyfriend and his love note for this idea."

I picked the pen up in my hand and tried to calm my panic. She wanted me to write a note, how bad could that be?

"Okay, now start writin'. *I, Rose Gardner, confess to possession of the flash drive.*"

"What?"

"Write." It was the first time I had ever heard Betty sound really mean.

"Why would I do that?" I asked. She had lost her mind.

"I know how much you love that sister of yours and her kids. It'd be shame if something happened to 'em. Now write."

I had pinned my hopes on Joe showing up, but that dream was gone. I had to go along with her until I could figure out how to get away. I wrote, my handwriting looking like scribbles from my shaking hand.

"That's good, makes you look upset," Betty said

looking over my shoulder. She made me write a confession admitting to owning the flash drive, destroying it, and duping Daniel Crocker. "Now, they'll think you did it and they'll stop lookin'."

"You didn't really destroy it, did you, Betty? Where is it?"

"It's in my safe deposit box. After I made my deal with Sloan, I realized I could get more money for it in a bigger city."

"I don't even know what's on it!" I cried out in frustration. "If I'm gonna die for a stupid piece of plastic I should at least know what's on it."

"Information about several gangs in Dallas and Houston, their weak spots, their business activities and partners. Interestin' stuff."

I realized she didn't deny I was going to die. I felt nauseated. "And you got it from Bobby Joe?"

"Yeah, stuff he knew from the gang he was in, other information he stumbled upon in prison. He finally came through for his momma. Are ya done?"

I handed her the paper and she read it over. "Okay, looks good, let's go."

I got up and she grabbed my arm again, leading me out of the office to the back door. "Where are we going?" I asked as we walked through the darkened back room.

"We're goin' to set up your suicide."

I thought about digging in my heels and trying to fight her, but figured I had a better shot at getting away outside. Fear made my stomach churn. Maybe I could throw up on Betty and work it into an escape plan.

The cracked back door made Betty stop.

"How'd that door get propped open?"

She swiveled her head around, then stuck her foot forward to kick my purse out of the way. She was promptly tackled by none other than Joe. I barely got my arm out of Betty's grasp before she tumbled to the ground.

You would think it would have been an easy match for Joe, but Betty was scrappier than she looked. It took Joe a good minute to get her handcuffed.

"Are you okay?" he asked me when he finished, panting from his exertion.

I nodded. "What are you doing here? I thought Betty said she'd bring me home."

"She did, but I didn't want to wait, so I came by anyway and found your purse in the door." He helped me outside and around Betty, who lay rolling around on the ground. "You know, you lose more purses than any other woman I've ever met. What's this, three in one week?"

I glared at him.

He pulled me into a hug. "I didn't think you'd just leave your purse in the door, in spite of your track record, so I snuck in and listened."

"You left me in there with her, Joe McAllister?" I pulled back in dismay, looking up at his face.

"Sorry." He looked sheepish. "But it seemed safer than coming in. I was ready to act if I needed to." He leaned over and gave me a quick kiss. "Surely, you've figured out I wouldn't let anything happen to you if I could help it."

He was right. I knew he'd risk his life to save me. He already had and his job, too. I heard sirens in the distance.

"Henryetta's finest on their way," Joe snorted. "I called them once I knew what was going on, even though I told them no sirens. They sure love their sirens. I'd dare to say they've seen more action in the last couple of weeks than they've had in the past ten years."

I laughed. "I know I sure have."

Joe laughed too then gave me a serious look. "Rose, it's only just begun, you know."

I didn't know if he meant the action with criminals or the action between the two of us. I was just about to ask, but then he kissed me . . . and I just plain forgot.

Joe broke our kiss, leaving me breathless. "Oh, I forgot to mention one more thing." He lifted his head with a grin. "My name's not Joe McAllister."

Acknowledgments

First, I want to thank my children, especially my younger ones—Julia, Jenna, Ryan and Emma—for their patience, or at least their tolerance of all the time Mommy spends in front the computer working. I'm sorry for the literally countless times you've called my name and I didn't hear you because I had my headphones in. Mommy loves you.

Second, many thanks to my alpha readers for *Twenty-Eight and a Half Wishes*: Brandy Underwood, who's read every novel I've written, God love her, and isn't afraid to tell me when something doesn't work. And Kristi Eggleston who beta read a previous book, *Chosen*, and loved it so much that she eagerly volunteered to read again. My goal was to make her love this book as much as *Chosen*.

Third, *Twenty-Eight and a Half Wishes* wouldn't be the book it is today without the invaluable help of my critique partners—Trisha Leigh, Eisley Jacobs and Kathy Collins. They loved this book and believed in it as much as I did, so much so they weren't afraid help me make it better. A special thanks to Trisha for not only being a crit partner but a friend, who's watched me laugh and cry (literally) over this book and offered me wine and encouragement. She always believed it was "the one."

And lastly, thank you to my family, friends and blog readers of my family blog, There's Always Room for One More, who didn't call me crazy when I announced I was going to write a novel for NaNoWriMo in November of 2009. Three books later I had *Twenty-Eight and a Half Wishes*. Your encouragement and love for all the stories I write keep me going.

That and the voices in my head.

Center Point Large Print
600 Brooks Road / PO Box 1
Thorndike, ME 04986-0001 USA

(207) 568-3717

US & Canada:
1 800 929-9108
www.centerpointlargeprint.com